BLOOMS OF DARKNESS

THE BROKEN PROPHECY BOOK I

ANNA APPLEGATE

HELEN·DOMICO

CONTENT NOTES

This book contains content that some readers may find triggering such as:

On-Page Violence
Threats of Violence
Torture
Kidnapping
Grief
Death
Mental Health Struggles (Anxiety, Panic Attacks)
Profanity
Open-Door Intimate Scenes

Read with Care <3

To our fellow morally grey, fantasy romance book lovers ... we too have a shadow daddy addiction. We hope that you have room for one more.

*And to **Henry Cavill**.*
Not that this needs an explanation, but thank you for being the most exquisite, flawless inspiration for all book boyfriends. Ever.

PROLOGUE
22 YEARS AGO

Blood spatter marred the walls of a quaint cottage in the dead of night.

The Fates demanded blood be spilled for a sacrifice yet to be discovered.

Agonizing screams of grief echoed off the stone walls and lingered, even after the vision faded.

This vision, *this* vivid nightmare, promised to haunt Vivienne for the rest of her long Fae life.

She witnessed many dark occurrences, both in the past, and in futures still yet to come to this broken land.

As a Royal Seer it was expected.

Tonight, however, the vision shattered through her sleep and drew her from her bed, urging her outside of the palace walls. She grabbed her trusted mare from the stalls and raced toward the small village of Valeford, only a few hours away.

Lightning crashed across the sky with a fury Vivienne hadn't witnessed in nearly a century. Something fated was turning, shifting. She prayed nature's turmoil meant fate was falling into place and *not* falling out of alignment. Nature's erratic response made it difficult to discern whether it supported Fate's calling.

Thunder boomed seconds later, followed by another flash of lightning above, and her black spotted horse kicked onto its hind legs.

"Easy, girl," Vivienne murmured. "Easy."

Time wasn't on her side. If the wind and storm's ferociousness indicated nature's feelings, she had to get to the cottage now. Any further delay could mean not arriving at all.

Her horse raced with speed and grace, toward the quiet town the king's sister had fled to only half a year ago to protect the babe.

The baby Vivienne had immediately sensed held no magic.

Regardless of her lack of magic, she was royalty. Something about tonight mattered to the Fates enough to jolt Vivienne from her sleep. The atrocity occurring around this baby riled nature.

Blood. Vivienne's premonition, red with fury and blood, provided no clear picture of whose lifeblood spilled in the night. She prayed it wasn't Illiana's. Not the babe's.

The small cottage finally appeared as Vivienne crested the hill to Valeford. Fae, filled with unnatural darkness, lurked at every corner. Each flash of lightning brightened their faces and illuminated their erratic movements. It appeared as if they were high on some sort of magic, an unnatural magic.

Lightning struck again and she heard screaming. The closer she drew to the cottage, the louder the screams sounded, breaking through the crash of thunder.

No, Vivienne thought.

She jumped off the horse, straight into a puddle beside a small garden. A coppery-scented wave struck her.

Blood. Lots of it.

She barreled through the door and found Elisabeth rocking the babe in her arms. The horrific sight of blood spatter along the walls led into the next room and drew Vivienne away from the crying healer and baby.

There on the floor lay the king's sister and her husband, butchered. Vivienne's hand flew to her mouth, but she steeled her heart, willing her body to remain in control so she wouldn't heave the contents from her stomach.

They must flee this place.

And fast.

Despite the move from the palace, the safest place for the future heir required returning straightaway.

"Elisabeth," Vivienne said, kneeling in front of the castle healer. Elisabeth was strong. She would help get them all home safely. Vivienne only needed to get through to her.

"Elisabeth, can you hear me?"

Shaking, Elisabeth still rocked baby Illiana in her arms as she slowly met Vivienne's gaze and nodded.

"We must go. Right now. We have to get the babe to the king," Vivienne said. "Elisabeth, they could return."

Her words seemed to snap the healer from her shock, and she rose from the ground with Vivienne's hand to guide her.

"Can you ride with the babe?" Vivienne asked.

Elisabeth nodded once more. "I'll protect her with my life." A faint glow surrounded the baby and burned slightly brighter at the healer's words. Although she spoke in a mere whisper, the determination in Elisabeth's eyes gave Vivienne no concern as they fled from the cottage.

Vivienne rushed to the small stable at the back of the home, as quickly as her feet would take her, praying to find an additional horse. Noticing one had remained, she cried in relief, sending a prayer of thanks up to the Fates for the gift. By the time she rounded the cottage, Elisabeth and the baby sat perched upon the mare, ready and waiting.

A shriek sounded from behind them.

From the rear of the barn, one of the Fae from earlier came into view.

"Here!" he shouted, pulling his fingers to his mouth, whistling shrilly.

"We don't stop," Vivienne commanded, clicking her tongue at her horse.

Into the night they fled for the safety of the palace walls. The safety only the king could provide. The safety of never having to relive a night of blood and terror again.

They rode hard, Vivienne glancing behind them as Fae ran and followed on horseback.

"Faster, my friend," she shouted.

They pressed on, galloping over hills through the muddy terrain the storm created. Eventually, those following gave way, but it didn't stop their desperate escape.

When the city walls came into view, only a few miles from the palace, the storm subsided. Nature, it seemed, had been soothed. Vivienne now knew for certain nature's vengeful response revealed its anger at the horrors around the babe.

She was important.

The kingdom needed her, even if they didn't understand exactly what the Fates had in store.

Vivienne helped Elisabeth dismount. "You need rest, my old friend," she said. "I'll take her to the king and queen. Rest, and then I'll bring her back to you."

Elisabeth hesitated, but eventually conceded, handing Vivienne the beautiful baby girl. The glow extinguished as Elisabeth carefully relinquished her to Vivienne.

Vivienne moved quickly from the courtyard toward the king and queen's chambers.

The babe didn't shed a tear. No, instead when Vivienne gazed upon her face, she gave her a smile and cooed.

Danger hadn't dampened this little one's spirits.

Before Vivienne and the babe reached the doors to the royal chambers, they flew open. The queen let out a cry, and the king, with tears in his eyes, looked at Vivienne. "They're gone."

It wasn't a question. Vivienne pulled the blanket from the baby girl's face and handed her to the king.

As soon as Illiana rested solely in the king's arms, Vivienne tensed. The flow of ancient magic crawled through her veins, taking over her body.

When she spoke, an eerie white clouded her vision as a prophecy came into existence.

Void of magic, a heroine born,
Destiny calls, though faint and torn.
Many will come from across the land,
Yet only the strongest will win her hand.
With lover's touch, she shall ignite,
Without it, perish from the kingdom's blight.

CHAPTER I

The night's shadowy darkness brushed against my sweat-slicked skin like an old friend.

Perhaps it was, seeing as there weren't many Fae who could claim its title. At the rate I trusted others, perhaps the shadows of night could have an oh-so-honored spot on the short list of those I called friends.

I tilted my head back, rolling my neck. The thatched roofed homes on the outskirts of the city were a reminder I neared the crowded edge of town. I leaned against the alleyway wall while trying not to choke on the scent of stale beer permeating the air. The stench only increased the closer I drew to my destination.

Murmuring voices sounded, and a young couple strolled by my hiding place, none the wiser of my presence. I continued toward the end of the city limits, my soft-soled shoes silent against the cobblestone streets.

The stone wall protecting the city loomed ahead of me. Once there, I could move faster, not having to worry about slinking around guards to get to the meeting point. Guards were everywhere in this city, even outside the palace. Supposedly, they were throughout Ellevail for my benefit, but kept me caged instead, since I was prohibited from leaving the palace grounds without an escort.

My stomach churned, acid creeping up my throat, and I paused to quash down the unease. Sneaking out wasn't something new. Wandering the streets in the dark while I moved unknown in the night, brought me comfort and a sense of freedom. But tonight seemed different.

The message I'd received for this meeting varied from those I generally entertained. Likely because it arrived from outside my normal channels and the network I'd so carefully built.

Somewhere behind me, a whisper of fluttering wings beat twice and the hairs on the back of my neck rose. I waited, stilling my entire body, except for my rapid heartbeat, which wouldn't cooperate. This time when I paused, I grasped the hilt of my dagger. Inching closer to the wall and pulling my hood farther forward to hide my too-fair skin and recognizable, unique rose gold-tinged hair, I waited.

Two breaths.

Three breaths.

With a heavy step, the shadow following me made itself known, as a pebble skittered across the cobblestone path. I twisted, grabbing the arm of my stalker, my dagger leant gently on his throat.

"I told you I didn't want you coming tonight," I hissed against the man's ear, his coarse stubble bristling against my skin.

Ian Stronholm's laugh quieted as I held my blade against his neck. "Lana, you do know that's a real dagger. While I'd love a scar to show off to the ladies, I don't want to deal with blood on my shirt, or telling Lucinda I soiled it again when she only just cleaned it."

Despite being a few inches shorter than Ian's six-foot-tall frame, I held my ground. Lowering my blade, I shoved him forward. I didn't care if he'd been my friend for over twenty years, I hated my request being ignored. *Loathed* it. "I said I didn't need you this time."

"And if you think I'd let you meet with a stranger, who knew how to contact us outside of Corbin and Leif, you don't know me at all." Ian brushed the collar of his black tunic back into place and cocked an eyebrow at me. "Besides, you're the damn crown princess, Lana, who is forbidden from leaving the palace grounds. Sneaking out alone at night is a poor choice and one I care not to explain to the king." A teasing smirk pulled at his lips.

The wind playfully swirled a few loose strands of blond hair, which escaped the band he used to pull it back. He studied me, knowing he had struck a nerve and daring me to bite back with another retort.

I crossed my arms, furious at him for putting himself in danger alongside me, but also glad for his company despite its dangers. I wanted—no, needed, to take this meeting alone to prove to myself that I could. A way to prove to myself I was capable of accomplishing something on my own. Capable of more than simply wearing a tiara and being the princess in our world of gifted Fae. But perhaps the desperation to feel anything other than stifled and kept in a cage made me a bit short-sighted.

"The message was addressed to the Hidden Henchman, not Princess Dresden," I huffed as a bit of my rage dissipated.

Ian leaned in closer, backing me against the wall, as he attempted to rein in the anger in his voice. "There are two people who we thought knew how to get messages to the Hidden Henchman—Corbin and Leif. Knowing a mystery message appeared outside of our network, and to the castle no less, is worrisome. Even if they don't know you're the princess, they know the Hidden Henchman can be found inside its walls."

I stepped around his large body, but not before shoving my

9

shoulder into his stupidly hard chest. He was right. Damn him, he usually was.

"Fine. However, they learned of the Hidden Henchman, their letter said they needed aid for their village. It doesn't seem nefarious. Yet."

"Yet," he agreed. A knowing silence passed between us before we pressed on.

Side by side, we slipped into a familiar pattern. As we trekked forward, Ian motioned when to move, slow down, or halt with various hand signals we'd developed over the years. After skirting through the last few cobblestone streets, we finally approached the ancient stone wall built to protect the city of Ellevail. A wall reinforced not only with magic, but with layers of rock and sand over the past two decades, as rumors of evil and darkness spread from our border towns.

Almost by second nature, Ian and I clung to the shadows, as we observed two armed guards march past. Right on time, as always. Neither of us moved immediately, waiting a few beats after the sound of their boots receded from the cobblestones before we continued toward our exit.

"Here we go." Ian winked and ran across the back alleyway. Carefully, he lifted the grate, leading to a small tunnel outside the palace walls. We'd discovered the loosened grate years ago and never said a word about it to the guards or groundskeepers. He signaled to me as soon as he deemed it safe to move.

One quick slip through the narrow entryway and along the damp tunnel, and suddenly, I stood in another world.

Being on this side of the wall never ceased to amaze me. The starry expanse of the open sky, no longer strangled by the too-close-together stone buildings and walls of the city, stole my breath with its beauty. The earth-rich scent of the air, and the whispering sound of wind through the trees and grasses, complemented by noises of insects and animals, were nature's serenade. Although the city and palace of Ellevail were beautiful in their own right, the surrounding stone walls meant to protect its citizens left me claustrophobic and suffocated. I so rarely had an opportunity to leave, so I savored these quick moments of freedom.

Out here, all of nature's magic freely roamed and played. Out here, nature displayed its gifts, reminding us of the source where Fae power originated.

As I tilted my head back to breathe in the fresh air and freedom, Ian carefully replaced the grate, cautious of making any noise capable of alerting others to our location. While I appreciated his keen eye for detail and surreptitious skills, he took too long. I strode on ahead, determined to be on time for the meeting with the strangers who requested the Hidden Henchman's services.

"You do know you're going the wrong way," Ian whispered loudly.

We may be on the other side of the wall, but eyes and ears were everywhere.

I jerked my head behind me, noting his playful smile as he tilted his in the opposite direction.

"I knew that…I'm not a total idiot," I grumbled more to myself than to him. I spun around and darted through the last few remaining spruce trees, growing just on the outside of the city's wall.

"I never said you were." Ian threw his perfectly toned arm around my shoulder. "This isn't one of the usual drop spots, just in case something wasn't right," Ian added after a few paces in silence.

"Well, I clearly would have been at the wrong meeting place and never learned what they wanted at all," I said. "Guess you can accompany me after all, *Captain*."

"Your Highness, what an honor you bestow upon me." Ian withdrew his arm and held his hand out toward me.

I hated conceding almost as much as I hated being ignored. Regardless, I took his peace offering as we hopped from a dead log, before standing in front of an open clearing, overlooking a beautiful wildflower field.

Tonight's crescent moon cast little light on us, but I could see enough. The wildflower field stretched far off into the night but had a small walking trail used for harvesting along the left side. It would be nearly a mile's walk before we entered Eomer Forest, the vast tree line appearing small in the distance.

Ian took the first steps into the field, and I followed along. We traveled in companionable silence, so accustomed to one another, we didn't speak until we'd breached the first row of trees in the forest.

"You're awfully quiet," I said. "No fun tonight at the pub?"

Ian flashed me his signature grin, one which always earned him such beautiful company. "I'll have you know I had to turn down a breathtaking barmaid for you this evening."

"Well, maybe if we hurry, you can make it up to her."

Ian held his hand up, halting our progress. "We're close." He slipped on his black eye mask. Then, he stood in front of me, checking the black hood of my cloak, along with the same kind of black mask he wore, only mine hid the upper part of my face as well. Only my mouth remained uncovered. The hood came so far forward it also concealed my hair.

The disguise I donned, regardless of the discomfort and stifling heat in the warmer months, had worked so far. No one who'd heard rumblings of the mysterious Hidden Henchman had yet to even fathom a connection to their only Princess.

I swatted at his arms when he went for a second pass. "You know, you're more mother hen than Captain of the Guard."

"Yes, well, I do have a duty here," he said gruffly.

I tensed. "We're providing goods to the people of this kingdom who need them. We're not doing anything illegal."

Ian chuckled. "I know what we're doing isn't illegal, Lan.

It's me letting the sole heir to the throne sneak past city limits to be part of these meetings with Fae we don't know that worries me."

Before I could make a move to shoo him away, he smacked my hands down and tested the mask himself with one final tug. "Add in the fact your father, my *King*, has specifically told you not to get involved in the rumors of dark magic at the borders, and yes, I'm going to *mother hen* you about your concealment."

"Fair point," I grumbled.

Ian's comment about my father not wanting me involved in the darkness in our land stirred the same questions they always did. But now wasn't the time to let my mind wander. I pushed my issues aside, instead refocusing on the wooded forest around us.

"Ready?" I asked.

Ian rolled his wrists, cracking his knuckles, and shifting on his feet a few times, loosening up to prepare for any potential trouble. Then again, he always seemed ready for a skirmish. While lanky growing up, he'd packed on weight in the form of muscle as he trained all day, nearly every day, as a Royal Guard. Last year, he became the youngest captain in recent history, and just a few short months ago, named my personal guard as well.

Pride burst inside of me at his dedication to moving up the ranks and earning the spot. Of course I'd take Ian a thousand times over Ruppert, the miserable bastard who recently retired. Although, in reality, Ian had been single-handedly doing the job of protecting me since we were children. A part of me hated he had been ordered to protect me, no matter what. I didn't like thinking about what it entailed, even if he claimed he would do it with or without the king's will.

"What are friends for?" he'd always said.

We continued into the forest, moving silently through the trees. Although I may have lacked the magical abilities I should have as a Fae princess, I'd learned plenty during my own extensive training about blending in with nature.

Ian held up a fist, signaling to stop. I followed his gaze to two figures ahead of us in a small clearing of trees.

Our meet.

"The man standing must be Storm. He said he would be wearing a red broach on his cloak," Ian murmured close to my ear as he stood at my back, his eyesight infinitely better than my own, especially at night.

Storm stood stoically, unmasked, like most of the other Fae we aided. He scanned the woods as we hung back, concealed by a thicket of brush. He dressed entirely in black, with a leather-looking tunic covering his chest, and a sword strapped to his side. On his right shoulder lay a red broach, resembling a small flame, pinned to a black cloak so dark it could blend with the darkest of nights. The wind whipped around us and wove through his hair. He wore half of it pulled back in a ponytail, while the remaining light-brown strands rested just below his shoulders.

The other Fae sharpened his blade as he leaned casually against a tree. His black cloak, woven with an intricate, subtly swirling grey gave the illusion the man wore shadows. From this angle, I couldn't detect any discernible features, aside from ridiculously broad shoulders and massive height. Even leaning, the unknown Fae appeared taller than his counterpart.

Ian squeezed my arm and moved beside me. When I met his gaze, I noted apprehension etched into his brows. I understood his hesitation. These strangers exuded power and presence to which we weren't accustomed. Even cloaked in shadows, Storm's companion's magic practically sang around him.

Only a small number of Fae in our kingdom wielded magic that could be sensed by others from any sort of distance. This stranger just so happened to be one of them.

I broke Ian's stare, turning to study the outsiders a few moments longer, the cloaked man in particular.

As if my focus stirred his attention, the hood of his cloak shifted and now faced me. A tingling sensation crept along my arms, despite the long sleeves of the black fighting tunic staving off the cool night air. A buzz hummed through my veins, and I didn't dare move with the stranger looking in my direction.

Ever so slightly, black wisps of hair extended from the very top of his hood. The cloak concealed his features just as well as mine, yet, somehow, it seemed as though he stared straight into my eyes, into my very soul.

I knew my reasons for hiding, but what motives did he have to not be seen?

"Are you going to stare at us like prey all night, or finally grace us with your presence?" His deep voice rumbled with authority throughout the space between us.

The comment caused Storm to jerk his gaze in our direction. Aware we could no longer quietly observe, Ian and I emerged slowly from the brush and strolled toward our potential allies.

"You must be Storm," I said, extending a hand as I approached. "It's nice to meet you."

"You're a woman?" The stranger's scoff had me instantly hating him, especially when combined with the smart-ass remark seconds before. Mister Shadow Cloak's attitude grated on me already.

Men and their domineering bullshit. I had to deal with it at Court, but most of the time, the people of Brookmere who needed help in the past, wouldn't have cared if I ran the streets as a bloody mythical dragon if it meant they would get the aid they required.

"Is there a problem?" I asked.

"No problem." Storm's gruff voice didn't falter as he shot a glare at his partner.

A dark chuckle escaped the stranger. "At least the ridiculous nickname makes more sense."

Storm stiffened as his associate flipped his sword, spinning it in a circle before straightening from his tree. "With a name like the Hidden Henchman, surely you must drive utter fear into the hearts of all the royals so blatantly ignoring their kingdom's problems."

I crossed my arms, tapping my fingers against my forearm. "I didn't create the moniker, it just stuck."

I wanted to argue that the royal who mattered stood right here, but I would never give away my identity so easily. A princess—no, *the crown* princess—wandering around commoners and thieves at night would bring more of a scandal than I wanted. Far too much attention and trouble than it was worth.

The shadow-cloaked man tossed his blade up to hold the hilt in his hand. Ian shifted, instantly sensing the change in weapon position. Casually, as though he couldn't be bothered with the conversation, he situated himself in front of me, touching his blade. "Put the weapon down or we're gone."

The stranger's hood slipped back slightly, revealing a glistening set of white teeth, a stark contrast to the blackness surrounding him.

"Enough," Storm said, firmly outstretching his arm in front of his companion, who obediently backed away a few paces. "We need provisions and want to know if you can assist. That's all this is. Don't mind my incorrigible companion. He doesn't get out much."

"Maybe you shouldn't bring him to future meetings when there's something important on the line for you," I said sharply, pausing for a moment. "Regardless, we are here to help. Next time use the system in place instead of thinking you're above the other Fae who request our aid."

"Other Fae? So, you are aware of how many are in need, yet you do this alone instead of petitioning the Crown for assistance?" The obnoxious sidekick's sarcastic mouth made me want to throw a dagger at him to shut him up.

Breathe. They were people in need.

I'd survived far greater hells than an arrogant Fae thinking too highly of himself. Besides, I charmed an entire Court—without an ounce of magic in my bones. I could handle a bitter man who prattled on about things he knew nothing of.

"Unrest is growing. We're working on it," Ian jumped in. "Now tell us what you need so we can all be on our way. One wouldn't want to stay in the woods too long at night."

"Unrest" was certainly one way to describe it. The king had made me swear to stay away from gossip at Court, specifically, discussions and whispers of events happening at the border towns.

"It's a minor threat, being handled by the guards," he'd told me.

The way our people continued reaching out to the Hidden Henchman for aid with food, clothing, and more, exposed something more going on than just a minor threat. Something important eluded us because everything pointed to this being more than a "minor" threat.

Or worse, the threat, minor or not, had gone ignored by my father. Not handled well enough, if at all.

My determination only grew to get to the bottom of this blight, with or without my father's assistance. When I ruled this kingdom one day, I would need to understand the threat. And fast.

A snap of a twig had knives drawn, but as the doe who caused the disturbance looked up at us, it hastily retreated into the woods. As if the animal knew trouble brewed and it shouldn't linger. A sense of urgency to get back to the castle crawled through me. We could not get caught.

I pivoted back to the men. "What aid are you looking for?"

Storm's gaze shifted to his partner before he proceeded.

17

"Five hundred silver pieces, three hundred pounds of meat, and a few barrels of mead should hold people over enough."

Ian coughed. "Would you like a Pegasus as well?"

"You promise aid, but really plan to give mere scraps?" Storm's friend snorted his apparent disgust.

Although I refused to give our company my back, I shifted to stand closer to Ian, positioning myself so I could partly conceal what I said. I knew full well if the other men attempted any sort of trickery or backhanded maneuvers, Ian would end them. "I don't want to haggle with men trying to help our people," I whispered.

Ian's gaze shifted between our guests. "We still don't know what village they're from, or if they can be trusted. This whole thing is off, I just don't know how yet."

"I agree," I said, sensing his wariness along with my own. "But I will not barter when we know we could get the supplies easily. I think we should do it."

"It's your show, Hidden Henchman. I'm just here praying I get to draw my blade." A glimmer of excitement danced in his eyes.

I rolled my own at the comment he punctuated with a wink, before facing the men ahead of us once more. "Done. You'll find a piece of parchment with the date and time of the meet waiting for you at Dukes Pub inside the city in eight days. The drop point will be along the western edge of this forest, near the end of the riverbed. You must bring an empty carriage. You'll say the phrase of these lands and knock twice upon your seat. You will bring no one else."

Although quick to criticize me the entire meeting, neither of the men revealed if they were surprised at how easily I'd agreed to their request.

It didn't matter. I would have agreed to nearly anything, because ultimately, what they were requesting helped my people.

A people who seemed to be growing more and more

unwell over the last three years. The thought brought a sour taste to my mouth as my stomach churned.

The wind suddenly picked up and viciously blew through the clearing, almost whipping strands of my easily recognizable hair from beneath my hood. I peered up at the sky. A warning—if nature sent the signs I believed.

Ian gripped my shoulder just as Storm drew his sword. I didn't fear the movement this time, because Storm's attention focused elsewhere. He stared straight ahead into the night where the doe had disappeared only minutes before.

"Something's here," Ian growled.

Silently, I reached down, drawing my short dagger from its sheath on my thigh. The long pause amongst our small group allowed dread to creep into my body as though it slithered from the soil itself.

Slowly, Storm took three steps forward, gliding along the forest floor without snapping a single twig.

A hiss from the darkness served as the only warning before a ragged battle cry roared from behind the trees.

One Fae emerged, wielding an axe wildly. His eyes darted between the four of us, before making his way straight for Storm. His movements were jerky and disjointed, as though he had little control of himself. His face twitched sporadically.

He appeared like a normal Fae, except for the jerky sway to his step. That and the hunger sparkling in his eye, like that of a man gone mad.

Insane.

I flinched as the newcomer's axe connected with Storm's sword. The man moved fast, faster than many of the Fae in our Royal Guard. His body practically blurred with his movements. A strange hum of magic radiated from him, almost as if electrically charging the air. One I'd never encountered before, despite being around some of the most powerful Fae in our lands.

Sword in hand, Storm's companion darted in front of his

friend, battling alongside him, and the two engaged in a dance, which had me mesmerized. Mouth agape, I simply stared, frozen.

They'd fought together before. Many times, if I had to guess.

"La—" Ian almost shouted my name, and the slip had me adjusting my dagger, twisting in his direction.

I shifted too slowly. A blade came out of nowhere, slicing my leathers, but failing to penetrate my skin.

I tripped sideways, caught off guard and startled at the force of the blow.

Although Ian's weapon had stopped this surprise second assailant, it hadn't been enough to prevent the attack completely.

With a sharp inhale, I flipped my dagger, prepared to fight, just like we had trained.

Ian battled another Fae possessing the same erratic movements, as though there were too many things he wanted to destroy, and not enough time.

The wind whipped through the clearing inside the forest again, and this time, the warning didn't arrive in advance of the threat.

No, this time, the wind carried three more wild-looking Fae out from the trees.

Each of them hummed with the same strange dark magic. The static in the air around us made it seem as if nature itself recoiled, shaken at their presence.

Surveying the additional Fae creeping toward us, I stared. Except there weren't only three. There were *more* strange sets of eyes appearing in the darkness beyond. Additional Fae approached, and Ian still fought, battling the man who had tried to attack me.

I gripped the steel in my hand. Because suddenly, it wasn't four on three. Instead, we were utterly outnumbered.

CHAPTER 2

"Ahhh," a terrifyingly deep, blood-curdling scream swept through the dark woods as nearly ten assailants rushed forward.

Ian's focus remained undeterred, even as the strangers charged. The clang of weapons snapped me into action. For the first time, I fought for my life, no longer in the safety of the training pits.

Ian brought his sword down, atop the man who had attacked me, finally defeating him. But two more men wielded their swords as they challenged him. I gripped my own weapon hard, preparing to strike at the first opportunity. The attackers were nearly animalistic. They dodged Ian's blows with ease. It was so rare for a civilian to be able to fight with such stamina.

As Captain of the Royal Guard, Ian didn't surprise anyone by being the best fighter in the kingdom. Even without his Fae magic, his skill set made him an intimidating opponent for anyone to take on. Add in the abilities he had as a shapeshifter Fae, and he proved to be deadly. He maintained a keen sense of awareness and the ability to predict where someone might move next. These attributes, combined with his brute strength, made him a formidable adversary.

Yet, his skills weren't enough to quickly stop our current attackers.

As the two Fae engaged Ian, Storm and his companion raced past us, directly into the onslaught of their newest targets.

My shoulder connected with Storm's friend as he ran by, and a jolt burst through my entire body. The same warmth I'd felt earlier, as we hid in the brush, seemed to magnify tenfold at the short contact. To refrain from falling, I had to quickly catch myself, thankful my legs were in a ready stance.

The stranger's hood flung back at our touch, and I caught a quick glimpse of his sharp jawline and the black strands of hair hanging slightly around his eyes. Before I could observe anymore of him, he sprinted so far ahead of me, I wondered if his magic gave him multiple abilities, another rare trait.

"Hidden Henchman, now would be a good time to help," Ian quipped.

The sparring I'd done in the training ring never seemed this bloodthirsty. I knew if I didn't move and join this fight, Ian would be hurt. Frozen only a second longer, I steeled my nerves.

Ian spent years training me. Now I would put that training to the test. I refused to be a powerless princess sitting idly on a throne as her kingdom suffered.

As Ian held the man's attention and swung, landing blow after blow, I knew I'd have the element of surprise the moment I joined the fray.

Ian moved with the precision of a warrior, executing blocks and blows against the crazed men time and time again. The attackers were unable to gain a foothold, despite their attempts to put Ian into a defensive position.

In the foray, Ian's next two sword maneuvers would have one of the men leaning away from me and should trap his sword against Ian's, long enough for me to launch my own attack.

I leapt as Ian swung his sword over his head and brought it crashing down. A move he had me practice repeatedly in the past year. In a breath, the man became distracted and unable to lift his sword from beneath Ian's, exactly as planned. I lunged toward him, refusing to hesitate as I plunged my dagger into the side of his throat.

Ian grunted in my ear as his blade slid from beneath the bizarre Fae and blocked a strike from the other assailant. Although Ian barely had time to breathe, I froze.

My hand shook, trembling at the blood staining my skin, but I didn't let go.

I shivered as I yanked the dagger from the side of the man's neck, his eyes wide in his final moments before he sank to the ground.

I had killed a man.

A hissing to my right alerted me to danger as the hilt of a sword hit me across the face.

"Agh," I cried.

Our fight remained far from over.

I could hear the swords of the others, each of us now engaged with our surprise attackers. I ducked at the assailant's swing coming for my head again, attempting to move to the ground with my leg to drop him. I underestimated his strength, and instead, fell too far forward.

Rolling as quickly as possible, I righted myself, facing him before he could swing at me again.

The man I fought grinned as another joined him, faster than I could react. The pair circled me, forcing me backward. The movement pushed me farther away from Ian and closer to where Storm and his friend were battling four men themselves.

Storm grunted and barked, "Not sure I want to do this without using—"

"Only if it's dire," his friend growled back, slamming his sword into the gut of one of the attackers.

Ian's fight grew worse. There were now four men descending upon him.

Again, I stopped mid-fight, unable to move. A flash of a distant memory played across my mind, and my hands loosened at my sides.

A cold, dark stone room, sweat dripping down my back. Shaking from concentrating as hard as I could, struggling to will a blade of grass to peek its head through the cracks in the ground. The angry shouting echoing in the stone room over and over again, screaming at me to produce some sort of magic. Any magic.

"If you cannot produce magic, your loved ones will perish. Their blood will be on your hands, Illiana."

"You are a disgrace to the royal line. Pathetic."

Ian coughed up blood, hurt. The soldiers kept beating him. I lifted my hand toward him, but my body refused to move, refused to access any magic to save Ian. I needed to get to him, but my feet were like lead on the ground.

"It's real!" A voice broke through my mind. "This is real! You have to move. Now!"

Ian.

The forest came into focus. Ian still fought the Fae around us. And he'd pulled me out of my frozen stupor, as he always had on too many occasions.

This is real.

A fist collided with my face, sending me to the ground immediately.

Definitely real.

The assailant stepped on my wrist, kicking my dagger from my hand, disarming me faster than any of the guards I'd trained with ever could. A *crack* sounded as his hand shot out, pulling roots from beneath the earth as they wrapped around my wrist like a rope.

Earth Fae.

He tugged me by the wrist—away from the fight and deeper into the woods.

With one arm still free, I grunted in frustration, reaching toward my boot where I stored a spare dagger.

Across the clearing, Ian still battled his four attackers, while Storm and his friend moved in sync, dominating their own assailants. Damn it all, they weren't in a position to help.

"Get off of me," I shouted, twisting to reach my blade once more.

My cry caught the attention of both Storm and his friend, and within a second, the hooded figure turned, staring straight at me. In the blink of an eye, he disappeared amongst the trees, and instead of waiting for help, I resumed my struggle to obtain my last dagger. My fingertips brushed the laces of my boot.

Just a little further. My fingers wrapped around the hilt, and I jerked it out.

Before I could use the blade, my head slammed forward against the cold dirt, and my vision blurred. The attacker's blade sliced my forearm open as I tried to catch myself. Blood oozed from the wound, while my head swam from the blunt force of my fall.

This is not where I die.

The weight on my back let up. Twisting around, I plunged the dagger into the side of the man gripping my arm. Simultaneously, Storm's friend stood behind me, slicing at the other attacker's neck before gutting the man despite my lodged dagger.

My attacker gagged on his own blood, falling forward, spattering red onto my cloak as he fell to the ground.

My arms were yanked once again, this time by the cloaked stranger. His firm grasp, surprisingly comforting, as my back slammed into his chest with the sudden movement I made to stand. I trembled at the closeness, but he didn't let go. Instead,

25

he held me from behind a moment longer, until I had my feet firmly beneath me.

"You're welcome," he said haughtily, already rushing back to where Storm still fought.

"Thank you," I whispered, trying to catch my breath. He fled before he'd heard it. I wobbled once, before regaining my balance.

Storm's laugh echoed around us as he yelled, stretching his arms out to his side. Fire flickered at his hands, and from his palms, he threw the glowing orbs toward two assailants.

My jaw dropped as I watched them flee, bodies wrapping in flames. A fire completely generated by one Fae. The smell of smoke hit me and burnt my nostrils.

Storm had downed two of the attackers with his fire power. *Fire.* The magical ability to wield an element existed in myths and legends. Nothing more. The idea of it seemed impossible. Yet, Storm used the power effortlessly.

Exactly who *were* these Fae?

I ran toward Ian, wanting to help him any way I could. As I approached, he dove forward, but before he could reach the last attacker, the man turned and fled, escaping to the safety of the woods beyond.

Storm's arrogant, far-too-powerful-looking companion bolted after the fleeing man, but only for a moment before Storm shouted, "Kade! You can't."

Kade.

The mystery Fae had a name now.

He halted at his friend's warning, shoulders tensing. I noticed his chest heaving, even from where I stood yards away, the effort it took to contain himself visible. He jerked his hood over his head, composing himself once more before pivoting and stalking back toward us. Slowly, panting quietly, trying to catch his breath, he turned to Storm, their gazes boring into each other in what appeared to be a silent standoff. The air returned to its sweet scent, the charge of electricity gone as quickly as it came.

"Tits and daggers," I cursed, earning an eye roll from Ian. "Why did they look——" I paused, unsure of the word to use. "Cursed?"

"Because they *are* cursed," Kade muttered to himself, stepping over one of the slain bodies toward his associate. "We call them dark ones."

As Ian approached closer, I scanned his body from top to bottom for any injuries. He moved rigidly, standing tall as he gave me a small shake of his head. "I'm okay."

With my body now stationary, the wound on my arm throbbed and stole my attention. Blood dripped down my hand to my fingertips, and a sliver of white peeked through the skin. The bastard had cut through to the bone. I had forgotten about the injury during the heat of the battle, but the pain slowly returned now that my adrenaline waned.

The sound of a blade moving through the air came from behind us, followed by a *thud*.

Kade ripped the shirt from one of the dead Fae at his feet and crouched beside him, inspecting something on the body, looking for something. But what?

Despite the pain, my wound would have to wait, because right now, all my focus centered on Storm and Kade.

My gaze sharpened, and while my arm had dropped, I kept my knife still, and readily available. From the tip of my blade, a single drop of blood splattered to the ground. "What village did you say you were from again?"

Details be damned, we had to figure out who these men were. If Kade had powers as unique as Storm's, we would need to know. Who were they really? I couldn't stop the barrage of questions coursing through my mind.

Storm rose, standing straighter, visibly pressing his shoulder's back. "We didn't——"

"Everywhere and nowhere, Hidden Henchman," Kade jumped in, cutting off Storm. He drew his blade across the dirt-stained tunic of one of the dead men, cleaning off the blood. A small smile shadowed his face from beneath his hood.

Kade's vague answer did nothing to ease my worries and left me with more questions than when I arrived. I held Storm's stare, ignoring his companion. "From now on, if you require something, go through the proper channels. This will be the last time we accommodate any request sent to me directly."

Storm's jaw ticked once but he nodded in agreement.

"I saved your life, and you treat us suspiciously?" Kade snorted.

Storm shoved his companion, who tsked but turned, bowing with a mocking flourish of his hand. "As you wish."

Ian's entire body tensed at the same time mine did—I could feel it.

He didn't know. *This* Fae couldn't ever know my secret. He was just being an ass. He hadn't a clue he currently spoke to royalty, and his bow didn't contain any sort of true reverence.

I hoped.

Meeting his gaze, I narrowed my eyes at him. Oh, what a mistake. A *big* mistake—because those eyes were as unique as Storm's fire power. They appeared as though clouds of a thunderstorm itself had settled in them. The grey coloring stood out even more due to his tanned skin and midnight-black hair.

I swallowed, praying it wasn't as audible as it felt. This particular Fae—*Kade*—may use his strikingly good looks to get what he wanted in any other situation, but I would not be swayed.

Turning away from the two men, I moved toward Ian, but my step faltered due to the pain in my arm.

Ian reached for me. "May I?" he asked.

Nodding my agreement, he immediately took in my injury,

inspecting as much as he dared before we returned home. His gaze met mine and I realized he worried, likely thinking the same thing as me. "We're leaving before anything else decides it's out for blood tonight," he said.

I stumbled over a rock, displaced from the fight. I attempted to right myself as fast as I could, while Ian clutched onto my good arm to lead me away. He'd observed the depth of the wound and knew I needed to see a healer, much to my dismay.

Besides, Ian had a point. If additional attackers returned, my assistance would be limited in my current state. Even if Storm and Kade's magic outmatched any I'd witnessed, neither Ian nor I were prepared for another ambush tonight.

As subtle as possible, I looked at the two men once more. I refused to think about my lack of magic, my *weaknesses*, in front of strangers. Not wanting them to scent the fear I held so close to my heart.

"May nature guide you," I said, imparting the line of luck all of Brookmere bestowed on friends.

Storm inclined his head, but Kade acted as if he didn't hear. *Asshole.*

Ian didn't wait to see if our companions walked away, instead quickly guiding us back toward the city walls. "At least Storm had his friend on a tight leash," he huffed. Stopping in our tracks, he spun around to look me straight in the eye. "They're dangerous."

"It's likely they can hear you," I said. I didn't look over my shoulder to perceive how far the two men were. Hurriedly, we moved toward the wildflower field once more. Clouds drifted freely through the sky, obscuring our moonlit path.

A soft caress touched my skin before we cleared the woods, likely my imagination as adrenaline from the battle faded.

A tremor coursed through me, and I tugged my arm from Ian. It quickly turned to all-out shaking, which took a few breaths to get under control.

His perceptive gaze studied my every movement as we continued. Clearly, he had concerns about what had happened tonight.

"You're going into shock." His eyebrows furrowed. "Come on, the quicker we're inside the palace the sooner we can come down from the fight properly. And get this arm healed."

My silence spurred Ian to intertwine his fingers in mine. "You did everything right. You were fantastic, Lan."

I nodded, keeping up with him until we were practically jogging toward the safety of the palace walls.

Twenty minutes later, we married up with the shadows of the gates, slipping back inside the city through the grate, unnoticed, and moving along the cobblestone streets once more.

It should have been concerning how easily we could escape from the palace and city, but together, we'd done it enough times, it had become second nature. The consequences of getting caught were not ones we were willing to consider.

At the foot of the north end of the castle, Ian shifted his weight into the side of a large, loosened slab, revealing the tunnel we utilized to get in and out of the palace. Known only to a select few, it provided the perfect route into the palace, avoiding most of the guard stations.

Gingerly, I placed my uninjured arm against the cool rock, steadying the hammering of my heart. I stabbed someone. I helped *kill* someone. The blood coating my hand hadn't come merely from my own injury, the "dark ones" blood mixed with it as well. The one man I'd killed, in particular.

A cursed man if Storm and Kade were to be believed.

What kind of curse plagued our lands so much so that it caused such feral aggression?

The meeting had promised to be strange, finding the letter requesting aid had reached Corbin directly at the castle, instead of being left at the forest drop spot he checked weekly.

Add in the attack, and there were suddenly far more questions than answers.

As we moved through the tunnel, my wound throbbed, and an ache settled deep in my bones. The blood continued flowing. *Damn it.* I'd definitely need the healer. The deep injury would likely become infected if not cleaned properly. A wound like this would draw too many questions from the king and queen.

It should have been an injury I could handle on my own.

Ian looked back, his hand slick from sweat, mixing with blood from my arm. Ripping his mask off, he stuffed it into his pocket, steadying his hand on me.

"We need to get you to Elisabeth, quickly, before your arm becomes any worse." Ian read my mind more often than I cared to admit. After knowing someone for twenty-two years, it was to be expected.

My breathing hitched, growing shallower as I panted harder with each step. The adrenaline rush depleted completely, and my body rebelled by reverting to a sluggish pace. I had to pause and place my head on the cool tunnel wall to steady myself. Ian pulled a small cloth from his pocket and wrapped it around the wound to avoid blood dripping on the palace floors.

Just a few more minutes. I could do this.

"Elisabeth said she would be in her room tonight," I wheezed. "Just get me inside and then return to the barracks, before anyone asks any questions."

"I will make sure you are safe before I take my leave," Ian whispered, releasing my arm and reaching for my hand instead. "I will take the punishment if caught."

I squeezed his hand. "Then let's hurry."

Soon, the narrowing tunnel opened to the castle grounds, just outside the northern gardens. We sprinted through the gardens and grabbed the servants' doors, leading to the kitchen. Ian creaked them open and peered in both directions.

It may be the middle of the night, but our path still took us through a common area where anyone in the castle could linger.

I sucked in a breath. A shadow danced along the stone walls in the moonlight. Ian gripped my arm, noticing it, too. A figure approached.

Tension immediately dissipated as a spiky tail came into view, followed by the furry paws and body of the palace pugron. Despite its cute, smooshed nose, short stubby legs, soft fur, and friendly appearance, one wrong move, and the beast would light you on fire with its breath.

"Lucien," I hissed as the playful stray wagged its dangerous tail in a flurry.

Ian knelt and the pugron rubbed along his calf as he petted the creature, careful to avoid the spikes on the beast's back as well. "Shh, good boy. Run along and make sure Lana's scent is covered."

Ian swore to the Fates themselves, to anyone who'd listen really, that the beast understood him. As the pugron retreated and retraced our steps, I believed him.

There weren't any other sounds now that Lucien strode away. Nature provided once again tonight, guiding us, undeterred.

We entered the castle itself, silently shutting the door.

Through the open glass windows, a shadow cast our path from the moonlight's glow. We found a figure hunched over near one of the far counters, muttering and mumbling.

My body stiffened at the sight.

Ian clasped my hand, each of us recognizing the lone figure the moment their back straightened, before they had even turned upon sensing us.

"Andras?" I hissed, recognizing my father's Royal Adviser in the middle of the night.

His back straightened fully as he whipped around.

"Princess Illiana." His tongue ran over his teeth as his mouth curved in a gruesome grin.

A grin that haunted too many nightmares.

Daggers above.

Of all the assholes to run into, it had to be this monster.

"What, pray tell, are you doing out of your chambers at this time of night?"

I shifted, subtly pulling my arm from Ian's grasp and placing it behind me. "Andras, I could be asking you the same thing."

"Your father woke with a fever and I'm gathering a cup of tea for His Royal Highness. Common in my role. What's not common is a princess out with the help"—He looked Ian up and down with disdain—"in secret."

"I couldn't sleep, so I asked Ian to accompany me for a walk in the gardens. A bit of fresh air has helped to clear my head. I am on my way back to my room now," I said, hoping my voice sounded bored and not as on edge as I felt.

Andras narrowed his eyes, unquestionably debating informing the king he'd found me with Ian when he returned to my father's chambers. Sometimes I'd swear he could see right through me. "Captain Stronholm, return to the barracks immediately after Princess Illiana is in her room. We wouldn't want any further rumors flying around about the princess, now, would we?"

People were far from subtle when speaking of the two of us. It felt like a slap in the face some days, the absolute disrespect for him, and me. Andras never cared of the way in which he spoke to me, out of line or not. "Good night to the both of you."

He grabbed the teacup and saucer and strode forward, his long, curly onyx hair stiff beneath the golden circular cap he always wore as he exited the kitchen.

I released a heavy breath. "Bleeding hell. We need to move fast—I am starting to get dizzy." The wound pulsed in my arm. I *needed* to get to Elisabeth now, or Ian would be carrying me the rest of the way.

Without additional interruptions, we made it to Elisabeth's chambers. My partner in crime didn't even bother knocking on her door, dragging me into the maiden's chamber.

Elisabeth gasped as she realized who had barged into her room. "Lana! Ian! What happened?" She took me from Ian, ushering me into a tattered burgundy chair near her workstation.

Elisabeth's small yet cozy room instantly made me feel safe. A four-person table sat by a stone hearth, and her bed rested underneath the window, overlooking the gardens below.

I winced as I unwrapped the cloth and showed Elisabeth my arm. Elisabeth muttered under her breath as she looked me over. "What have you gotten yourself into now, child?"

I tried to laugh, but it came out more as a choke, "Oh you know, a little bit of this, and a little bit of that. What haven't you healed on me these past twenty years?"

Elisabeth clicked her tongue in reprimand. "I've been healing you since birth, don't shorten me those two years, child. You need to be more careful."

"Can you heal it?" I pressed. "Andras saw us in the kitchens. I can't have the king asking any questions."

She eyed me. Although old enough to be my grandmother and could demand I spill my secrets, she'd never pushed for answers when I arrived injured at her door. Some days I wondered if she had put together more than I gave her credit for.

"Well, it will be painful to press your body's ability, but yes, we can heal this tonight. Ian, grab the brown woven basket on the table and we can begin."

"My body has no abilities, Elisabeth," I huffed. My frustration increased as I thought about how I couldn't take care of this myself, unlike everyone else in our kingdom.

No abilities indeed. With my lack of power, I always had to rely on the strength of other's magic in my times of need.

I held the title for not only being the first royal princess born without magic—*ever*—but also the first *Fae* born without any magic. Our kingdom could not find out about my lack of magical abilities, or there would be an uprising. The royal bloodline prided itself on being the strongest and mightiest of the lands, but even the peasants and lesser Fae on the streets held more magic than I did.

This dark secret had been kept by the king and queen, told only to Andras, Elisabeth, and my two friends I held close. If anyone else learned of this, I would never be allowed to take the throne.

I'd spent years in a cold room, experimented and tested on, as a way to coax magic from me, but nothing succeeded. After years of failing, I instead worked on hiding in plain sight to ensure no one questioned me, or my lack of demonstrating the kingdom's magic, which should be prominently on display. I killed myself finding ways to charm the Court, fitting in with the mundane ways of royal life, all in an effort never to stand out. Blending in meant my secret remained safe, regardless of how painful it may be to constantly wear a mask to cover what I truly felt and who I truly was.

Which didn't at all fit in with my running about as the Hidden Henchman. But the Hidden Henchman provided me with an escape, a way to do what I wanted, to be free from the confines of the palace. To be free to move throughout the land and do what I thought best for my people.

Ian returned with two chairs for both Elisabeth and himself, but as I attempted to stand to help him, my body swayed. Once, twice.

"She's coming down from an intense evening, Elisabeth. She had another episode. I think she might—"

One second, Elisabeth prodded the wound through Ian's

warning as the fire heated my body, and the next, my vision darkened, whisking me away to oblivion.

CHAPTER 3

"You're an idiot is what you are, Ian Stronholm."

The fury lacing Kalliah's normally dainty voice told me if my eyes were actually open, I'd spot spit flying from her mouth.

Ian growled right back at her. They would keep this up for days without any intervention.

I laughed, slowly opening my eyes to the sunshine streaming through my window. My bedroom window.

Safe. We were safe in the confines of my chambers.

I stretched my arms, deliciously more rested than I should have been, given what happened last night, thanks to Elisabeth's healing magic.

"I don't know what you're laughing at." Kalliah directed her attention to me. "You two are going to be caught. Or worse, you're going to be killed, kidnapped—*something*."

The final piece to our trio, Kalliah Brennan, had her hands on her narrow hips at the end of my bed. Her green eyes angrily met mine. The true sign of her anger, a few beads of sweat forming on her golden skin, showed just how frustrating she found this conversation.

Kalliah had been with me for ten years, originally as my

attendant. While our first few years together had been difficult, navigating our teenage years together as Princess and attendant, we bonded once we decided the rules surrounding the formalities of Court were meant to be broken. With both of our guards down, we grew inseparable. Besides Ian, she became my only other true friend, something nearly impossible to find as a princess.

When I became of age, I elevated her to lady-in-waiting despite her having limited magical abilities, only able to conjure light breezes of air. The role should have been reserved for someone of a higher standing of magic. Status meant nothing to me, though.

No one questioned me, partly because I never asked for *anything*, and partly because I held the title of "Princess." Kalliah kept to herself, and my mother, Queen Roxana, adored her as much as I did for her fierce loyalty throughout the years.

"Kalliah, it's fine. There's not even a mark anymore… hardly a thing to get a crown in a twist, you know," I joked. I brought my hands behind my head, tugging my pillow forward and chucking it at her as she stood criticizing me from the end of the bed.

Ian howled out a laugh, even though Kalliah batted the pillow away.

I giggled until I saw the deep red color on my hands. A stain.

Blood.

My smile disappeared as I stared at the reddish tinge and the crust around my nails.

To my right, the mattress sank. Ian's strong, calloused hand took mine in his own. "We would have died if we hadn't fought."

"I killed him," I whispered, still staring at my bloodied hands. "Is it real?"

Ian brushed his thumb over my knuckles. "Real as roses," he said softly, using a phrase we'd established long ago.

Kalliah joined us on the bed, taking a seat at the foot. She remained quiet, observing in silent support.

"Technically, I did all of the work, so don't take all the credit." Ian lightened his tone, attempting to alleviate the mood, but the heaviness in his words let me know this was hard for him, too.

"It feels wrong," I whispered.

Ian gently tugged my shoulder toward him, and I fell into a hug. "I'd be more concerned if it felt right after your first kill." He paused. "You will get through this pain. And, if you are faced with a fight again, you know you're able to defend yourself, as long as you can keep yourself focused."

"He's right," Kalliah said. "And with the way you've been taking chances lately, I have a feeling you'll be getting into plenty more confrontations."

Ian nodded in agreement. "I think we should probably increase training, given what happened. I'd ask you to not go to any more Henchman meetings, but I know how that'll go over." He rolled his eyes at his last comment. Our arguments over the supply drops never ended.

"I'm not letting one little scuffle deter me from going on future drops."

I refused to concede. I needed this bit of freedom, or I'd go mad inside the palace walls. I needed to know something I did mattered to the people of my future kingdom.

"I still think it's careless," Kalliah chimed in as she fiddled with her apron. She met my gaze with an earnest look in her eyes. "You came up with the idea, which is more than anyone else did. Now you should leave Ian and his tagalongs to handle Henchman activities."

Kalliah rose from the bed and crossed the room, her chestnut-brown hair swaying as she flicked it over her shoulder. "Especially since you almost got yourself killed. I don't understand how you can continue to take such risks," she huffed, her friendly concern morphing into what seemed to be fearful anger.

"Kalliah, deep breaths. We made it out alive."

In our trio, Kalliah was the only one of us who behaved like they belonged in a Royal Court. Her political acumen and level-headedness helped keep Ian and I in line.

Most of the time.

I glanced at my hands once again. Ian rose and squeezed my shoulder. "Take a minute to wash up. We're right here."

He followed Kalliah out of my bedroom, through the door leading to the main sitting area. I didn't want to be alone anymore, so I quickly jumped out of my gloriously large four-poster bed and left the confines of my bedroom. Jogging across my chamber entrance, I bypassed the sitting area, and into the washroom, closing the door behind me.

I grabbed the lavender scrub and scoured my hands. The grit on the soap removed the particles of blood from my skin, even if it did make my hands raw. As I scrubbed, I tried not to think. Water ran red beneath my hands until I finally scraped the last bits from underneath my fingernails. The reminder I'd killed someone would stay with me forever. The pain it took to clean the blood seemed a small price to pay for a life.

I killed a man.

Inhaling deeply and exhaling four times to gather myself, I glanced in the mirror, expecting something to appear different. But the reflection still showed the same Lana. Blue eyes. Rose gold hair. Magicless. All me.

Now, I was a killer as well as a liar to my kingdom.

I am Illiana Dresden. I am stronger than the darkness within me.

I didn't look in the mirror again, but I did stand straighter and exit the washroom.

Kalliah and Ian were still taunting each other.

"Speaking of Ian's tagalongs," I began, searching for a moment of normalcy. "Last I checked, one of those tagalongs, with the bright-blue eyes, and hunky arms, convinced you to train with us a few months ago."

"What's this now?" Ian asked, his curiosity clearly piqued.

Kalliah frowned, her eyes narrowing. You could practically see the steam about to come out of her ears. "You are mistaken, I don't even know their names."

I waggled my eyebrows at her.

"I thought you wanted to train with me because I'm your best friend," Ian said, crossing his arms over his chest. "I'm hurt." A playful pout started to sprout across his face. He coughed to hold in a laugh.

"Why don't the two of you stop whatever this is you think you're doing. I don't have time to gossip like you. Now focus and tell me what you learned at this oh-so-important meeting?"

Kalliah flopped onto my window seat, overlooking the gardens, her favorite spot in my chambers. Honestly, the entire main sitting area served as my favorite place to relax. I had selected two beautiful hunter-green chaises and a lighter green couch with gold trimmings on the edges and pillows. The table placed in the center had intricate designs in the woodwork, carved by one of the locals in the city. All of the pieces formed a semicircle in front of a white and gold fireplace. The staff helped me pick roses constantly, and this summer, they were blooming so beautifully, I couldn't help adding more and more vases to the mantle and table.

Out of patience, Kalliah waved her hands at me exasperatedly, as if to say "Proceed."

Ian stood, placing his gloves on the table before taking a seat comfortably with his hands on his knees, swiveling his gaze between myself and Kalliah, waiting for the grand reveal.

I gave in, unwilling to push her too far this morning. I moved to sit next to her, when a knock on my door stopped me.

Ian stood quickly, moving to his formal guard position by the front of the room, facing the entryway. Kalliah grabbed a deep red robe from my wardrobe to cover the thin fabric of my black nightgown and tossed it at me.

Answering my door with my guard *inside* my room while wearing my nightgown, likely started the rumors of Ian sleeping with me to get his promotions in the Royal Guard.

Kalliah stood at the door, her hands pressing the nonexistent wrinkles from her beige apron, giving me another moment to tie the robe quickly around my waist.

The three of us had been scolded enough about our casual demeanor, and we didn't want to deal with it again. Seamlessly, we shifted into more appropriate positions for a guard, lady-in-waiting, and princess.

I cracked my neck and steeled my nerves as I donned my perfect courtly princess mask before giving the go-ahead nod.

Kalliah opened the door—anyone on the other side would enter and find us each playing our expected role.

I waited to hear who Kalliah addressed. "Good morning, Counselor Braumlyn. What can I do for you?"

Of course. I knew he wouldn't be able to resist taunting us after last night.

Andras sauntered in, with his typical arrogant swagger, and scrutinized the room. Undeniably taking notes to report back to the king, on how I might be slacking as a princess, yet again. My bedroom door hung open, making it easy to notice the bed a mess, pillows on the floor, clothes strewn about the room. He strode toward the balcony door, still not mentioning why he decided to grace us with his unwanted presence. Surveying the grounds below, for some reason, he made a small noise of disapproval before shifting to face us.

"The king would like to see you in the private dining room as soon as you are dressed." I shivered as his attention lingered on me and tugged my robe closer.

He directed his attention to Ian. "Captain Stronholm, be

certain all your duties are accounted for today. You claimed you are capable of handling both the role as Princess Illiana's personal guard and Captain. I would hate to see you demoted after earning such accolades so quickly." A smirk played across his face as he prowled toward the door to leave. He *so* clearly enjoyed these displays of dominance.

The first thing I would do as Queen one day would be to banish him from Ellevail. Well, if Ian didn't kill him first.

Ian, standing at attention, quickly bowed to Counselor Braumlyn as he exited the room. Andras would likely be in the dining room later, watching me squirm. I would bet my favorite sitting area he'd told the king he saw me last night.

The door closed, and we released a collective breath, tension leaving our tightened shoulders.

"Could that guy be any more of an asshole?" Ian asked as he moved back to the sitting area to pick up his sword.

"Seriously," Kalliah muttered.

I swiveled my gaze between my friends and sighed. "I guess it's time to learn what my father has in store for me today. We'll continue this conversation later. There are things we should discuss."

Ian tilted his head in acknowledgment. "I'll see you both later," he said, his jaw ticking as he grabbed his gloves and exited my chambers.

I lifted my chin, believing it may help prepare me further for whatever discussion merited the private dining room. Heading toward the door, Kalliah grabbed my arm and yanked me back. "I think showing up in your nightgown to breakfast with the king isn't the smartest choice," she said. "Father or not."

The laughter spilling from my mouth felt good compared to the heaviness of guilt I had woken with this morning. "Andras pisses me off so much, I forgot I wasn't dressed."

As soon as I returned to my room, Kalliah helped me dress in my brown training pants and a white tunic, since my regular training was scheduled in the pits later this morning. As long as my father didn't derail my plans like he so often did.

"Ian," I said, "he's upset."

Kalliah's hands paused before she continued lacing up the leathers I wore over my white tunic. "Besides Andras hounding him at every possible moment"—Her eyebrows rose —"the rumors some people have spread are nasty. Though they're doing it to discredit Ian, they also cast you in a poor light. Ian loathes the rumors. You know it, and I know it."

"It's not his fault, though. I'm shocked the rumors aren't of the three of us being together." I snorted, my chest tightening when I thought of how critical and demeaning others were of Ian only because of his status as the youngest captain. And my friend.

"There are rumors of the three of us now," Kalliah said bluntly.

I arched an eyebrow in surprise, sensually turning my body toward her, my hand cupping her face, whispering, "I had no idea I was your type."

She spun me around and resumed knotting the leather on my back. "You aren't," she said, snickering, while playfully slapping my shoulder.

This time, my laughter couldn't be stopped as Kalliah filled me in on some of the spicier rumors I'd missed recently. My cheeks ached as I finished preparing myself for breakfast.

When I stood before the dining room door fifteen minutes later, my stomach had dropped like a sinking pit. Perhaps it could pull me under in some way so I could avoid this. I knew Andras would have said something and having a talk in the king's private dining room instead of the main one, meant he didn't want to risk being overheard.

Great.

The king's private dining room, located on the main floor of the castle, may not be a central location, but there were simple routes to get to the throne room and the larger dining and dance hall from here. This more personal space boasted a sizable rectangular table surrounded by empty chairs. A room only used by my father for three reasons— when he wanted alone time with my mother, to make a point, or to maintain some sort of secrecy, even if rumors spread through this castle at an ungodly rate.

The strong scent of smoked meat filled my nose, as I entered. I opened the door so quietly, even the guard standing at attention did a double take. The skills I gained over time sneaking throughout the realm, allowed me to enter silently enough so I could study my father sitting at the head of the table, eating his breakfast alone for a few moments.

Two more Royal Guards stood a few paces behind him— silent, straight-faced, and seemingly unbothered by the power filling the room, both from his Fae abilities, and his commanding presence. My mother had yet to join him.

The king held the most power of all Fae in the land, as had all the royals who previously led Brookmere. The Fae were able to manipulate anything occurring in nature. A small gust of wind could be formed into a tornado. A few drops of rain could become a downpour in moments. The earth, when respected, answered the magic in our veins.

Well, the magic in *most* of our veins—my own seemingly forgotten.

I flexed my fingers, shifting my attention instead to how long I could stand by the door before the king noticed me.

*Nine... ten...*I counted in my head, not only for the game my father and I played but hoping to also calm my escalating nerves about the upcoming discussion.

His icy-grey hair lay swept to the side. The purple and gold robe seemed large on his slimming body. The king never let anyone know his true age, and acted as young as ever, but in the past few months it seemed time caught up to him. Even if we Fae had immortal lives, something strange was happening to my father, for he had aged drastically. Most Fae aged naturally, slowly. With a smile, I thought of Elisabeth and wondered how old she might be.

The man before me, though, refused to admit to anything revealing his weakness, including his ailing health. Nearly as adamantly as he refused to acknowledge how severe the crisis had become at our border towns. My brows furrowed as I shivered, trying not to think of whether his mysterious illness and the issues throughout our land were connected.

Fifteen... sixteen...

A soft wind closed the door behind me. "All right, I can't let you think you've bested me this long, now." The aging king looked up from his meal and winked as he ushered me over to the open seat near him.

"You knew I was at the door, didn't you?" I asked. "I made it to sixteen this time."

He touched the side of his nose. "Oh, sixteen? You are getting better. I believe you only made it to ten the last time we played. If I hadn't been expecting you, you may have claimed an even higher record." A smile spread across his face. A smile reserved only for his family outside of Court.

I laughed, aware I'd never be as powerful as him, even if he did act as though I could be at times. A plate of bread, soft cheese, and fruit waited for me, along with a cup of hot dandelion tea.

I dipped into a quick curtsy before I moved to the open seat. "Good morning, Father."

I looked at my father, waiting for him to tell me why he'd called me here. The dandelion tea was a trick to butter me up, usually reserved for when he wanted something. Although my favorite, it had grown scarce over the recent years due to whatever blight troubled our lands.

After all, Earth-wielding Fae could hardly be expected to focus on dandelions when they were needed for things like vegetables, fruits, and grains.

"Well, Illiana, my dear, how are you this morning?" My father using my given name set me on edge even further. He *really* wanted something. "I heard you had trouble sleeping last night."

Ah, okay, I could play this game, too. My lip curled. Andras *had* gone gossiping to the king after our run-in last night. Typical of the "esteemed" Counselor Andras Braumlyn to try to stay in the king's good graces by revealing my every move. Andras believed secrets and gossip were the key to the king's heart. The man was noticeably missing from this morning's conversation, thank Fates.

"Oh, yes, nothing to worry about, Father, just a bad dream. I needed to clear my head. A stroll through the gardens and some fresh air beneath the stars did the trick, though. You know it has always been my favorite."

"And what of your bleeding arm?" His eyes narrowed, waiting to hear what response I could come up with, believing he had bested me. The game continued. A game I lost on too many occasions, but perhaps not today.

I answered without even skipping a beat. "I tripped near the rose bushes. You know, the spot where the moon doesn't shine? Behind the *enormous* statue of you... Silly me. I stumbled straight into the bramble and cut it." I speared a strawberry from my plate, popping it in my mouth and not bothering to finish chewing it all before I continued. "It's already healed, would you like to inspect it?" I smiled coyly, playing with the fruit and cheese on my plate as if I had no care in the world.

"Ah, yes. Lucky for you, Elisabeth is the best healer." My father's gaze lingered so intensely I could feel it on the side of my face as I picked up a slice of cheese. "And how about your walk outside the gate? With Ian?"

I coughed, choking as I reached for my water. Shit, he really *had* bested me this time. "I'm sure I have no idea what walk you're referring to." *Father - 65, Lana - 3.* How did he

47

always win? I guessed they didn't call him the king for nothing.

"Lana," he said sternly, his icy-blue eyes narrowing, "I have cared for you your entire life and know when you're lying to me. That wound originated from a blade according to Andras. Which means you were training with Ian, *again*. Since no one corroborated your training in the castle, and no reports of sword fighting on the streets in the middle of the night could be found either, you did it outside the palace walls."

My shoulders slumped forward with relief at his assumption. I kept my head hanging low, desperately trying to pass as being caught red-handed. When, really, for a moment, I feared my father might know all about the Hidden Henchman and my secret mission.

"Sorry, Father." I set my fork down, staring at my hands. "I wanted something outside of the stagnant training pit. I wanted to be in the field."

"You could have been killed," he snapped. "You are *forbidden* from leaving Ellevail's gates. How many times do we have to go through this? Does my word as King mean nothing to you?"

Instantly, I sat up straighter. The king raised his voice so rarely, especially at me. He had my full attention now. His face harsh, as if daggers were bolting straight from his eyes. My heart pounded. I was *really* in trouble this time.

"You could have been killed," he said again, only quieter. "Do you understand what that would mean?" When I didn't answer, he continued. "It means the end of our royal line, Illiana. The kingdom would have no heir to the throne. It means we would lose you." His voice returned to its normal tenor as he continued. "You are this Kingdom's hope. And with the prophecy—"

I winced at the mention of the ridiculous prophecy. The prophecy ruled every decision made about me. About my future. "We don't even know if Vivienne's prophecy is legitimate. I could be destined for nothing and——"

My father's eyes flared, heating instantly. "Do not tempt the Fates with such talk."

I stared at my hands again, willing my heart to stop racing, even as my anger grew. The Royal Seer had one true prophecy when I was a baby and nothing but mere ramblings since. Yet my father took her word as definitive, never second-guessing it for one moment.

He sighed, grumbling, as he reached for an apple from the bowl on the table. "I am happy you are strong and want to train. I gave Ian my blessing to provide you with lessons occasionally, when it did not interfere with his duties as Captain. I gave him my blessing for you to train on the grounds of this palace and it is what I expect. I will not tolerate my wishes being ignored again. Do I make myself clear?"

I nodded. "Yes, Father. I'm sorry." Genuine fear coursed through my veins. If he reacted this strongly to a simple training session—*Fates*—imagine how he would react to my work as the Hidden Henchman. He could *never* find out.

"Now that's settled." The king took a bite of the crimson apple, the spray of its juices hit my face as he chewed.

His eyes widened, and we laughed together as I patted away the juice. The worst was clearly over. We were still giggling when the queen walked in, tension easing from the blow-out moments before.

I pushed away from the table, starting to rise when she shooed me down, planting a kiss on my head instead. "Don't be ridiculous, Illiana. Sit and eat."

She kissed the king, and a pang of loneliness swept through me as it always did, observing the beauty of their simple acts of love for one another. Most days, I wasn't a pining-for-love fool, but it didn't stop me from dreaming of a partnership and love like theirs.

I chewed my cheese and bread for a few more moments, before I wiped my hands on the napkin and started to rise. Escaping while I still could without the round-two lecture from my mother might be the smartest move to make.

"If you'll excuse me, I'm sure I've got some sort of princessely duties to attend to," I joked.

I'd barely made it halfway across the room, when my father began one of his coughing fits. My mother rushed to his side, rubbing his back, trying to get him to drink some water from the nearby glass.

Nothing helped.

"Guard!" she cried, pointing to the Fae in uniform closest to her. "Fetch Elisabeth at once! As fast as you can!"

He didn't even bother bowing before running out of the room.

"Lana." My mother's voice came out calmer, not as commanding as she'd been when she spoke to the guard. "You may leave, darling. All will be fine. Elisabeth will be here in a moment and all will be well."

I hesitated, but my mother continued to shoo her hands at me to leave. I watched my father doubled over a few more moments, before obeying the queen and exiting the dining room.

Gently, I closed the door, hoping Elisabeth would be there soon to heal my father. Or try to. What started as a slight cough had progressed into these uncontrollable fits.

I didn't know what it meant. I brought a trembling hand to my chest, inhaling and exhaling slowly.

All will be well, I repeated my mother's words in my head and hurried away from the doors.

It had to be well. Because becoming Queen right now wasn't at all something I was prepared for.

CHAPTER 4

The sounds of my father coughing chased me farther away as I moved throughout the castle, toward the escape the open air promised.

I needed a moment to breathe. A space to clear my head after everything from the last twelve hours.

Exiting out of one of the side garden doors, I immediately ran into Ian. And by ran into, I mean, slammed into him. I bounced off his chest and gasped, as he chuckled at my clumsiness, gently grabbing my arms to steady me.

"Just the person I hoped to find. It's time." The sparkle in his eyes meant this morning would be hard.

It had become a regular occurrence for Ian to coerce me into going on those damned awful runs with him. Not only had he focused on my strength, but he insisted I needed to be able to run far without fail if something were to ever happen to him.

The first time he had taken me on a run, I retched my breakfast in the center of the city market. We'd only made it half a mile. Now, nearly a year later, I could run miles and miles without needing to empty the contents of my stomach.

"I'll give you fifteen minutes to change and meet me at the

front entrance." Ian's grin, normally contagious, wreaked of threats.

I pursed my lips. "I'll have to run to my room and to the front to make it."

"I know. Fourteen minutes."

My legs seemed to obey before my head, and I shouted back at him as I ran toward my room, "I hate you as a trainer."

"Thirteen."

I shouted in frustration but didn't stop. His ruthless methods were to thank for who I had become, and while I hated the pain of training, I loved him for it.

I stripped myself of the confines of the leathers Kalliah had dressed me in earlier, opting for the tight, all-black training gear I loved so much. I couldn't help but admire the way it clung to some of the muscles I'd developed. I buttoned the top, pausing once at the jagged scar along my ribs. It had been tingling lately, aching like a reminder I couldn't be rid of. I didn't have time to despise the mark right now. I was up against the clock.

I ran out of my door with one shoe on as I hopped into the other, jumping the last few steps of the marble staircase and sprinting toward the front entrance of the castle.

Ian bounced back and forth on his feet when I made it back to him. "A minute to spare," I said, punctuating my declaration with a little victory dance.

He hummed his approval.

Rolling my neck, and quickly stretching my arms, I nodded, ready to begin. We started off slow, jogging around to the front of the palace, and down the long carriageway, leading to the main road, running toward the heart of the city.

The palace took up the entire back half of the city, surrounded by floral hedges, which looked like anything but the gate they were. The gardens behind the palace were open to everyone year-round, allowing Fae from all over Brookmere to come and explore the beauty Ellevail had been graced with by nature.

Many believed the soil at the palace also held magic. The most luscious and abundant crops were grown here, then shared with as much of Brookmere as we could feed.

Ian increased our pace slightly just like he always did every few minutes.

The first buildings scattered near the palace belonged to the wealthier members of society. Their perfectly trimmed gardens drew in the eyes and appreciation of most, but none rivaled the palace's.

The charm on the outside masked many more vile things within. Vile might be a stretch, but the actions of some of the wealthier Fae were usually ugly, despite the exquisiteness they surrounded themselves with.

Never trust something is as it appears at first glance.

I'd never forget the first lesson my father taught me after being old enough to bow hunt with him. We stumbled upon a razorven drinking from a stream. The white, four-legged beast's eyes were closed as it drank deeply with its long, slit tongue. It looked peaceful.

My father held a finger to his lips, silencing me before slowly stepping back, retreating with me. The beast turned its head, opening red orbs for eyes as thick black hairs rose along the spine of its back, and I screamed. My father used his magic to create a wall of vines, completely blocking the creature from us as we ran.

I never would have guessed its hairs were poisoned and flexible, capable of slicing and paralyzing its victims in moments, before devouring them.

The animal haunted my dreams for a week before my father finally convinced me razorvens were rare outside of the Southern Forests, the hunting grounds that all manner of nightmarish beasts called home. The Southern Forests were avoided by nearly all Fae of Brookmere. I let myself breathe again, safe knowing there was plenty of distance between me and more razorven.

Never trust something is as it appears at first glance.

And damn if the sentiment didn't ring true for Fae as well.

A group of children gathered around one of the fountains in the middle-class area of Ellevail as we passed. A boy gathered water in his hands, shaping it like a flower and handing it to one of the girls, much to the delight of her friends.

I nudged Ian's shoulder to get him to look.

"Don't embarrass him by having the princess watching him flirt," he scolded.

"I would think the princess being impressed would only improve his standings."

Ian snorted. "You know nothing about boys."

Shoving Ian playfully, I sprinted ahead of him as we rounded some of the shops that always had the most beautiful displays.

While Fae didn't use their magic for everything they did, many clearly presented it proudly. Liam Dorian, the local butcher, unmistakably fed his animals crops enhanced by his exceptional earth magic. His meats were enormous and tasted divine. While Matricia Maygan's dresses flew off the shelves because of the incredibly soft, fine silks she created and strung together better than anyone else.

I attempted not to feel as though I didn't contribute anything, but it hurt some days, witnessing Ellevail thriving with their magic intertwined throughout everyday life.

"Race you to the gates," Ian shouted, sprinting ahead.

"Cheater!" I yelled, my sides aching, even if my strength had improved greatly after all these months.

The clear distinction between the societal castes of Fae in our world were evident everywhere, but especially in Ellevail. The moment one passed the imaginary line separating the middle from the lower, it seemed like a different city altogether. The bustling bright streets were dimmer, the colors muted. The magic here weaker and harder to see as readily, and most of the lesser Fae performed jobs for the middle and upper classes. Jobs they couldn't accomplish solely with magic.

Ian tagged the gate before I'd even rounded the last corner of the street.

"Now, back to the palace." He ran by before I could protest.

I groaned. Ian knew I hated the run back. Ellevail's city cascaded slightly downhill from the palace, the city stretched out in front of it, requiring us to return *uphill*.

We took another street back to the palace, this one busier, and people shouted and waved at me and Ian as we ran past them.

I watched my people with a genuine smile on my face, and even the ragged breaths I had trouble getting in couldn't stop me from enjoying it.

Besides, I didn't want to appear weak in front of them, so regardless how winded I became, I still ran.

Ian slowed to a stop once we entered the official palace grounds around the side entrance.

A stitch in my ribs had me gasping. Almost immediately, my vision blurred.

I swallowed, lifting my arms over my head to help air flow into my lungs just as Ian taught me, but the stabbing pain in my ribs hit too close to the already irritated scar. The lack of breath took me back to dark places. Dark dreams.

What can you see? What can you feel? What can you hear? Elisabeth's voice sounded in my head.

I can see the leaves on the trees, swaying in the breeze. I can feel my tunic tight around my body, skintight, but supporting me for ease of motion. I can feel my toes inside my shoes, and the dull ache in my calves.

I breathed, my vision clearing, bringing me back.

I couldn't often fight off panic attacks when they came,

and a tear pooled in my eye as I gratefully grounded myself more firmly in the here and now.

The sound of a throat clearing came from the shadows near the edge of the training pit, and Corbin emerged. A scar ran down the length of his face, adding to his already intimidating stature. Working in the stables certainly helped his natural physique. He raised his head toward Ian, the sunlight gleaming off the strip of copper hair pulled back over the shaved sides of his scalp. Next to him, Kalliah rose from a wooden bench along the wall.

I knew, given the large request from Storm and Kade, the men had a lot of work to do. "No rest for the Hidden Henchman, huh?" I whispered, pinching Ian's side.

He ran toward Corbin, while I remained behind, entering the pit to cool down and work on my flexibility with a bit of stretching. I grew stronger every session, every week. I'd started scared and wobbly, and I developed and grew, strengthening my muscles to make up for the fact I couldn't strengthen my magic.

Kalliah approached.

"Want to join me?" I grinned, still recovering my breath.

She kicked out a foot, showing the brown flats she wore when she strode around the palace grounds or with me in my chambers. "Sadly, I'm not prepared. By sadly I mean, thankfully."

I snorted in response, and she stood leaning over the railing of the pit and let me finish my series of stretches.

Ian returned after only a few minutes, his face tight.

I arched an eyebrow at him, moving toward the edge of the pit near Kalliah. "Are we good?"

He nodded once. Although he didn't say more right away, Ian surveyed our surroundings and then walked toward us until we were close enough to whisper. "I had Leif and Corbin looking into Storm and Kade, trying to find anything they could."

My eyes widened, waiting to hear what had been discovered.

Ian rubbed the back of his neck, then sighed. "They can't find anything on them. At all."

"That's not necessarily strange. There aren't reliable records in all the towns," I said, trying to convince myself it wasn't weird. "It's not like we have their full names, either."

Ian pursed his lips. "Magic like theirs should be rumored to exist somewhere, though."

"We will just have to be vigilant and careful when we do the drop this time," I calmly stated, examining my nails, as if we hadn't just fought for our lives the night before.

"If the drops are going to be like last night, you are not going anymore," Ian commanded, using his "Captain of the Guard" voice.

His tone left no room for argument, but it never stopped me before. "I can handle myself, I proved so at the meeting."

This time he spoke to me through gritted teeth. "You just want to know more about their magic. It is not safe for you to be there."

Before I could continue the argument, a sharp whistle sounded behind us. "Lady Kalliah," our head housekeeper shouted. "The princess is expected at lunch today."

Kalliah grumbled at the summons. "Guess playtime's over. Shall we, Your Highness?" She grabbed my arm before I could respond, leaving Ian behind.

He and Corbin had last-minute details for a drop this week, in addition to preparing for the new supplies we had to provide Storm and Kade.

I had duties to attend to as Princess.

Closing my eyes, I left the Hidden Henchman part of me in the training ring and pulled Princess Lana Dresden from deep inside of me.

Just another one of my many necessary masks.

CHAPTER 5

My body shook uncontrollably.

Despite the commands, I kept my eyes closed tightly. I couldn't see anymore. I couldn't watch my failures again today.

"Your father deserves better than you," the man hissed. "Who could ever bow to a princess who adds nothing of value to her people?"

"No," I screamed as I heard the swift sound of a dagger unsheathing. "No more."

"Lana."

I flung my arm forward, slapping at the hand touching my shoulder.

"Lana, it's me." I looked up into Ian's face.

It was only a dream.

Rubbing my hand over my face, I leaned my head back and took a long, slow breath. "Sorry, I must have fallen asleep. Is it time?"

Ian knelt in front of the chair in my sitting area. I'd been preparing for the drop, so I couldn't have been asleep too long.

"Are you okay to do this?" Ian asked softly.

I glared at him, clenching my teeth. "I'm not weak."

"I've never said you were. Not ever." Ian's voice cracked.

My mind constantly told me people saw me as weak. But Ian never did. Mostly because he lived through years of taking care of me as he dragged me from the darkness in my head. Through it all, he never once made me feel less than or weak. He worried then, as he worried now.

"I'm sorry," I said, pinching the bridge of my nose. Finding my confidence again, I added, "I'm okay. I just didn't mean to fall asleep."

He nodded, holding out his hand to help me rise. "Everything is ready. Let's help your people, Lan."

Down our usual pathways, we snuck through the city. Once we slipped through the grate in the city walls, we only had a half a mile to walk before we met up with Corbin and Leif. They snuck out the carriage of supplies earlier, along with a horse for me and Ian.

"Your Highness." Leif jumped down from the carriage and bowed his head. His brown curls fell slightly into his face at the motion.

"How many times will I have to tell you that the bowing isn't necessary, Leif?" I asked. "Especially on drops where we're co-conspirators?"

He grinned and the dimple Ian swore let him get away with anything appeared.

"No trouble, I hope?" I directed my question to Corbin, who approached with one of the two available horses.

For all the drops we coordinated together, it still seemed like he kept his distance. His emerald eyes met mine as he shook his head slightly, handing over the reins. "None at all."

The two Fae, Georgina and Harold, who had made this request a few weeks ago, were from a fairly small border village. Even taking the small size into consideration, their request hadn't included much, so we added extra coin and grain to it. Sometimes people requested so little it made this feel even worse. They weren't willing to ask for more than the bare minimum.

After a few short miles, Ian inclined his head. He tugged the reins on his beautiful black stallion, flinging out his arm, signaling us to halt.

The horse scuffed his hoof on the ground twice, agitated by something only Ian and the horses could sense.

"Stay here," he said. Ian jumped off his horse, tossing me the reins. He ran three steps before leaping, shifting instantly into his hawk form. He soared away toward our drop location.

"Surprised he doesn't shift into a damn cat with his agility," Corbin muttered behind me.

Leif stayed with the carriage, his gaze trained on the sky beyond.

Corbin rubbed at his stubble. "Go slowly, Hidden Henchman. We'll maintain our distance but keep moving in case anything is amiss."

Slipping on my hood and mask, I clicked my tongue at my horse, not needing to tug on Ian's. He remained by my side just as Ian would have. We continued ahead, at a much slower pace than before.

A minute later, Ian reappeared in hawk form, plummeting to the ground, and shifting, landing on a knee. His clothes materialized around him as he rose.

"We've got trouble. They've been ambushed. Let's go."

He slung his leg over the side of his horse and grabbed my arm. "Stay here with the goods and—"

"Don't you dare," I snarled as I yanked my arm from his grasp. "Leif, jump on," I shouted over my shoulder. "You don't get to tell me to stay behind," I said to Ian, my glare hopefully communicating the finality of my decision.

He sighed but relented. Leif jumped onto the back of my horse, and in moments, Corbin had somehow unbridled the carriage horse.

We rode hard toward the drop spot, galloping to help the Fae who awaited us.

The metallic scent of blood hit my nostrils before I could discern the scene playing out in the clearing.

The assailants were exactly like the ones who had attacked in the forest earlier in the week.

They possessed that same unnatural jerky movement to their gazes, shifting and jumping from place to place like they had more energy than they knew what to do with. The air instantly turned hot as an electric current charged around the dark ones.

"No!" I screamed as one of their swords gutted Georgina in one quick movement. She fell to the ground in a heap and the four of us launched into an attack.

Ian went straight to assist Harold, fighting all who stood in his way.

Leif and Corbin engaged their own marks, and two of them set their sights on me.

"Come and get me," I growled through gritted teeth.

I would not falter this time. I'd remain in the present. Whoever these cursed Fae were, they were terrorizing my people, and I refused to let it stand.

There may not be much I could help with yet, but I would be Queen of Brookmere. These dark ones would not ruin my kingdom.

The blade of my sword clashed forcefully against one of the dark ones. I threw all the weight of my training behind me. He sliced at me like a perfectly trained killer, twirling to meet every one of my offensive strikes. He moved so fast, I could scarcely keep up. He eventually caught me in a fraction of a mistake and advanced, putting me at even more of a disadvantage with my lack of magic.

His offensive attack continued our fight, slowly moving away from the others as he directed me toward the woods. Exactly like the last time.

This would not be the end of me, though. I dug deep into my mind—into the training pit and skills I'd been perfecting with Ian. I may not have perfected many, but I had a handful of techniques, which were flawless if I remained in the right headspace.

The fight had transformed into a dance, a brilliant, bloody dance. Although outside of my norm, I savored it. Ian's teachings flowed through my veins as though I'd been born to battle. I spun to my left and struck my opponents, the world around me quieting to a dull buzz.

"On your right," a familiar voice shouted, snapping me from my calm state as a current of warmth tingled down the length of my spine.

"What are *you* doing here?" I hissed as Kade's sword stopped a dark one I hadn't noticed.

"You're welcome," he shouted back, our eyes locking for a mere second. A flash of confusion whispered across his face, gone before I could even blink.

More of the dark ones arrived in a never-ending stream, not giving me a moment to distinguish where they were coming from. The smell of blood and the pounding of metal overwhelmed my senses.

"Any day now, Storm. I can't pull much right now," Kade growled, fighting off two men.

"Sure, leave the hard work to me," Storm bit back, slamming his sword into the gut of an attacker, leaving Kade to deal with one. "No problem."

The pair joined the fight, like avenging angels, destroying the dark ones with ease as they crossed their paths.

"This would be much less severe if the king didn't have his head in the sand and actually looked out for his people," Kade grumbled, slicing a dark one across the throat.

Blood spattered, soaking his blade, and fitted black pants, but he didn't stop.

A sword above my head rattled my blade, but I fought it,

grunting through my teeth. "The king is doing everything he can."

Kade chuckled. "You are a naïve one, aren't you?"

My sword connected with the attacker's, locking us together in a power of wills. I feigned to the right, just slightly, enough to kick dirt in his face. Clawing at his eyes, it distracted him enough to make the kill. My blade slid straight into the man's stomach, his blood spilling upon the dry ground.

Guilt threatened to consume me as the light went out from his eyes, but I would have to mourn the death and my innocence later. Not now. Not with this battle far from over.

Having a moment of respite, I directed my attention to Kade. "It's certainly bold of you to speak such treasonous words. You are a stranger to the palace. You know nothing of what goes on within its walls. The king tries to learn how to defeat the darkness, not send men aimlessly out to fight it."

My words sounded far truer than I believed. A deep-seated part of me hoped my father remained unaware or misinformed of what occurred across our kingdom. He loved our people, and if he knew those beings were so close to Ellevail, he'd take action against the dark ones who plagued us.

Kade defeated his assailant swiftly. "I didn't think the Hidden Henchman would be so loyal to the man who gives her a purpose, Little Rebel."

"Little?" I seethed. "How incredibly predictable you are, attempting to knock a woman down by calling her small."

Another one rushed upon me, taking me away from my brief moment of rest.

"Everyone is little compared to me." He chuckled, leaving me to my fight.

Perfect. I didn't need the distraction. Except when I stopped, I realized the attackers were gone, piles of them strewn about the grass near Kade and I. Surveying the others, I realized only a few remained. Ian fought one last Fae. Storm dealt the killing blow to his assailant, while Corbin and Leif ran toward the fallen Fae from the village who requested our aid.

Storm brought a dark one to his knees, holding him by the shoulders and bringing a ball of flames near his face.

Kade grunted a few feet from me, caught between two assailants.

"I'll never break," the dark one hissed at Storm, and my attention jerked to their position. "You know nothing of our plans."

Storm whipped a blade across the collarbone of the Fae, and as the shirt fell away, I noticed a thick black circle, surrounding a thinner, tapered shape. It appeared similar to an eye. Black ink stood out on the sunken, pale skin of this particular dark one, marked clearly beneath the center of his collarbone. A low-button shirt would have revealed it, as well as Storm's slash job.

A hiss at my right and a stinging sensation on my leg distracted me.

A dark one who escaped Kade had nicked my calf with his blade. The arrogant bastard still fought, though. I was mid-spin when I glanced his way, noticing him lost in his own fight.

The dark one twirled his blade in his hand. "He will keep coming for you. You can't stop us." His head twitched, jolting like a pulsating vein before he charged, running in more of a zigzag pattern than straight at me. His movement allowed me to use the latest set Ian taught me and I sliced across his stomach, his scream dying as another blade ripped through his neck.

I whirled around, only to come face-to-face with Kade, his bloody sword at my throat.

The cold steel pricked my skin, but I held steady. A darkness shadowed his eyes, but they grew even darker as he looked me over, his body tense and his breathing choppy.

Prepared to push him away, I put my hand to his chest. "Kade," I said. I had meant to shout, but it came out softer.

He blinked, his sword remaining at my neck, but his eyes cleared the longer he stared at me, until he looked down to my lips, and they immediately shifted back to grey.

His cocky grin returned.

"Get your blade away from her, *now*." Ian seethed.

As soon as Ian spoke, Kade's grin faded.

I didn't need Ian to run interference with this man, though. Not as I previously needed him all the years before.

"I vowed to destroy the last Fae who threatened me with a blade." I didn't step away, didn't back down, and Kade's lips twitched into a small smile.

"Careful, Little Rebel," he said. "Violent words tend to lure me closer, not push me away."

He lowered his weapon at the same time Storm tugged him backward, putting space between us. He clasped Kade's shoulder, and I didn't miss the way he stared at his eyes, looking for something.

Maybe Kade only had outbursts when his eyes darkened.

"You all right, brother?" Storm asked. I turned from the pair, not ready to believe Kade was anything but an asshole.

"How are you here? How did you find us?" Ian's fury mingled with his power, rolling off of him in a display of dominance.

Kade didn't appear the least bit intimidated. "With our superior magic and senses," he said, "we smelled a fight."

Storm crossed his arms. "We'd been following a group of dark ones."

"I think you mean to say, 'thank you.'" Kade glared at Ian. "Be happy we were here, and let's all move on, shall we?"

Corbin cleared his throat to get our attention. "Georgina and Harold both fell," he said. "We didn't plan to be away and would be missed from—" He hesitated, glancing at Storm, then Kade. "We don't have time to do the drop ourselves." Corbin watched his words carefully, his message unwavering.

The drop had failed.

My heart tightened. Georgina and Harold had only been trying to help their village. They'd done so willingly, aware of the danger, and their lives had been sacrificed.

"We'll take the supplies to the town. Where were they from?"

I whipped my head toward Kade. He'd go out of his way to help strangers?

"Winershire," Ian said, scratching his stubble, looking at me. "Hidden Henchman, it's your call."

I shifted my gaze between Storm and Kade. They had fought with us twice now, likely saving our lives in the process. Conceding, I nodded once in confirmation.

"We have ways of knowing if the supplies got to their destination," Ian said. "If you are stealing from us, we'll know."

"Yes, sir, *Little* Sidekick." Kade winked at me at the nickname he had given Ian.

Rolling my eyes, I signaled to my own companions. "Corbin, obtain the goods and hand them off to Kade and Storm. Gentlemen." I faced the two of them. "Let's hope after your own drop, I never have to see your smug faces again."

CHAPTER 6

Wrapping my arms around myself, I attempted to stave off the rising goose bumps on my flesh as I stared out of my open balcony doors.

The chill in the air wasn't merely from the cool spring breeze, but from the thoughts consuming my mind. I searched the sky for Ian's hawk form as I replayed the infuriating, obnoxious comments from Kade.

My emotions had been wavering since leaving Corbin, Leif, and Ian last night after they coordinated the return of the unused goods, and the empty carriage.

The way Kade spoke so callously of my father had completely gotten underneath my skin. Although I was furious at my father for withholding secrets about the kingdom, the likelihood of him ignoring the problem seemed unlikely.

I knew my father. He loved our people. He loved Brookmere. He'd never knowingly ignore such a terrible plight, but the way Kade spoke about him worried me. If Kade felt this way, were there others who felt similarly?

Were the people in the border towns feeling abandoned? I created the Hidden Henchman after overhearing reports of our people struggling for food and basic necessities in many of our towns. Crops were withering in places previously abundant for centuries. The thought had scared me into doing something. Not for myself or my father, but for my people. We lived in Ellevail, protected from the atrocities happening outside the city walls. The startling contrast of learning such horrifying reports of crops going bad, and unrest spreading, broke my heart. I wanted for nothing, and no one would miss those goods within the palace walls. But my people would benefit greatly. They deserved a life as beautiful as we had here in Ellevail.

The Hidden Henchman was only created to supplement the aid I thought my father already provided. What if I was wrong? What if the people's unrest came from feeling abandoned completely by its Crown?

A short cry from a hawk sounded overhead. Ian's call. His hawk form appeared in the sky, sweeping over the balcony, before he flew down beneath it.

Time to talk about what in the Fates actually happened at yesterday's drop.

A short staircase led straight into the heart of my immaculate garden. While smaller than the grand gardens visitors frequented around our palace, mine was still exquisite. Small hedges of roses of all colors, clustered together between marble pillars, and white stone seats dotted the space. Butterflies and bumble bees buzzed about the other flowers, feeding on the bounty of nature's gifts.

The serene peace made it one of my favorite places to be. The sweet floral notes calmed the rising panic in my chest and imbued a strength, as if nature itself would always be there to rise within me. Even without magic.

I hurried down the stairs and toward the back of the garden where we normally met.

This place existed as a sanctuary for another reason as well—it provided a private space to discuss all things Hidden Henchman with Ian, Leif, and Corbin.

From behind a white marble pillar to my left, Ian appeared.

"Leif and Corbin are almost here," he said.

"We are here," Leif countered from behind us.

Pivoting, I observed Leif and Corbin enter from some of the more concealed brush.

I had to hand it to our little group —we had this system worked out well. The ease with which we'd fallen into our areas of expertise seemed as if Fate itself played a part in our schemes. We made a great team. Pride swelled within my chest at the trust built between us, the secrets we all held together.

Leif and Corbin may not know every part of me like Ian and Kalliah did, but over the course of the Hidden Henchman's existence, I'd dropped more and more of the "princess" persona around them. Some days I could fully be myself. Almost.

"So," I began. "Last night was—"

Ian rubbed his temples. "Deadly? Horrific? A disaster?"

Corbin snorted.

"We survived, though." Leif shrugged, flashing me a grin.

Corbin crossed his arms and leaned against one of the pillars. He ran a finger over his leather-bound arm. "Storm and Kade were…" He paused. "Helpful."

"Helpful. It's one way to describe it," Leif added. "They are also powerful. Powerful in a way I haven't felt before."

Ian brushed a dirt-streaked hand through his blond hair. It always hung loosely in waves at his shoulders after shifting. "If Fae with that magnitude of power are seeking assistance, then who knows what is going on out there. It's curious they'd need our help at all, quite frankly. If they can't stop what's happening in their own village—" He didn't finish his thought. "And that's before we even discuss how it's possible they knew we were doing a drop or where we were last night."

71

"They could have truly been following some of the dark ones like they said," Leif offered, cracking his knuckles.

"Rumors are spreading every time a carriage returns to the stables from long journeys," Corbin said gruffly. "Issues at the borders are getting worse, and we know the trouble isn't contained to just the outskirts of Brookmere now," he continued. "Besides seeing these dark ones with our own eyes from the meeting in Eomer Forest and the drop, the villages requesting help are getting closer to Ellevail. We've already received another letter requesting aid since Storm's came to us."

Closing my eyes, I attempted to regain the inner peace gleaned from my garden before my cadre arrived.

Leif cleared his throat. "Kade had you more riled than I've ever seen, Your Highness."

I glared, daring him to say anything further. When he held his hands up, conceding, I settled with a shrug. "He disrespected my father the entire fight. You know how I feel about cocky men in general."

"It's not safe to let your emotions get to you in a fight," Ian remarked. "Especially during a battle where we could easily be overpowered."

A lecture brewed in his eyes. We stared at each other until one of the others coughed, deliberately in a blatant attempt to distract us.

"We'll need to be careful in the coming weeks, make sure we aren't being followed, be more cautious when we're together," Ian said. "For the time being, since we had two outsiders learn so much about us, vigilance is key."

He was right. The fact Kade and Storm found us at all should be concerning. The number of times they'd done it now—even worse.

"What about the other request that came in?" I asked Corbin.

"The request is simple," Corbin began. "Leif and I could

handle it by ourselves with no issue. No need for multiple meetings. Just need a few bales of hay and starter plants their Earth Fae can enhance and grow."

"Well, that's a bit of good news," I said, relieved.

"You two take care of the new request. Quietly," Ian commanded, sighing deeply. "About Storm and Kade's drop next week…" He trailed off, seemingly to halt this discussion altogether.

Silence fell amongst us. I shifted my gaze between my three companions. "Is there something wrong with the plan?" I asked. Each of the men seemed fidgety, rocking back and forth, and refusing to make eye contact. It set my nerves on edge.

"You have come so far in your training, Your Highness," Corbin lauded. "You wield your weapon well, and during the fight yesterday, you were focused and powerful."

Corbin, who barely paid anyone notice, had me suspicious, complimenting me out of nowhere. Something twitched inside of me, a deep-rooted discomfort about myself and my abilities.

"Because of you," Leif added, "our people are finding aid, when before, they felt unheard."

"Stop it," I said. "What is this about?"

"You can't come on anymore drops." The words tumbled out of Ian's mouth, as if he couldn't hold it in any longer.

A sinister inner voice, which had been with me throughout my life, hissed in glee, giving itself a sense of validation.

"Excuse me?"

Unworthy. Weak. Nothing.

"This has nothing to do with what you're capable of," Ian continued. "And everything to do with a threat we don't know enough about."

"A threat I've helped with twice now, just like you."

"Lana…" Leif took a step forward.

I hated knowing a part of me understood this decision.

73

"Stop," I said. "I am the princess. My word is the one you will obey. There is nothing I should demand of you without facing it myself."

Ian's gaze filled with a sort of remorse I hadn't seen in years.

In a whisper, he said, "As your personal guard, I forbid it."

My jaw clenched.

"There is one heir to the entire kingdom, Lan. One," he continued, his voice firmer the longer he scolded me. "Until we understand what this infection, or insanity, or dark magic is, I will not risk the heir to the throne's life."

I lifted my chin, keeping my teeth solidly together to save my lip from quivering.

"I will not risk my best friend," he murmured.

A rustle in the gardens beyond had us pausing our conversation, immediately putting us all on alert. On instinct, I reached for the dagger hidden on my thigh. The slit of my velvet aubergine dress allowed for easy access.

After waiting in silence for a few moments, I directed my attention to Ian. "We'll come back to this later," I whispered. "This conversation is far from finished."

Corbin and Leif nodded one after the other before disappearing amongst the thick brush of the roses. Secret pathways carved between the hedges led to a small hidden exit, allowing for easy escapes such as this.

Ian shifted into his hawk form as soon as I strode into my room, his gaze heavy while I tiptoed up the garden stairs.

Despite it being petty, I slammed the doors, not bothering to glance back, even when I heard his caw of farewell.

CHAPTER 7

"How long will the moping last? Kalliah said from my chamber doors, her hands on her hips. "Because after four days, I'm sick of it."

Staring at the empty fireplace, I wondered how long it would be before Ian and I talked about the upcoming drop for Storm and Kade. I knew I had been petty. The past few days of silence between us made *everyone* uncomfortable. We hadn't had an argument like this in years. In fact, we had only ever had an argument like this one other time, but we vowed never to speak of that day ever again.

"He didn't mean to imply you weren't capable, Lan," Kalliah said gently.

The difficult part about opening yourself up to people and letting them see beneath your mask is they start to see you all too well. It becomes impossible to hide, even when you wish you could.

"I'm sick of the tone," I snapped. "Don't coddle me. I don't need to be babied. If you have something to say, just say it."

"Fine, you're being absolutely snobbish and let's add in selfish as well. Ian's job is to protect you, and you know that

75

better than anyone." Kalliah slammed my chamber door shut, locking it behind her before moving to stand in front of me. "You aren't able to heal yourself. It's not an insult, it's the truth. You don't have magic to do so. So, should you suffer a wound Ian can't heal, while you are both fighting this unknown enemy, and you can't return to the castle in time to be treated by a healer, you die. Brookmere is left without an heir and your family's line ceases."

"You are an abomination of all Fae kind. A void," the man's voice sneered.

Water dripped in rhythm to my slow heartbeat. He'd won again today. I let his words sink into my heart.

I wasn't worthy of the crown. The throne. A magicless Queen would be a disgrace to Brookmere.

"Lana?" She clicked her fingers, the noise snapping me back to the present. Kalliah hadn't said any of those things. It was *him*. His vitriol made me believe in my weakness.

Kalliah and Ian's words were logical. They were always *so* logical. Everything they said held true. Yet, I couldn't let go of wanting to be a part of this. I couldn't lose this one thing, reminding me I had the power to change our kingdom for the better, even without magic.

"You're right." I sighed, completely defeated. "But I do not want to be a princess in a glass cage."

Kalliah groaned. "I know you don't. This is unfamiliar territory for all of us and ignoring each other isn't the way to handle things productively."

"Okay, okay... I will talk to him, civilly this time." I nodded, resigned with the knowledge Ian had tried to not only be a good friend, but fulfill his duties as my personal guard. "Now, what do I owe the pleasure of your company, besides coming in to kick my ass about being a snobbish royal?"

She grinned. "You have lunch with the king and queen today. Andras reminded me, while I tried to enjoy the tea I had *privately* in the Royal Gardens. That man is forever trying to ruin any quiet moment anyone has to themselves."

Unquestionably, lunch would be another boring afternoon, listening to Andras drone on and on about utter nonsense, just to hear his own voice, as he updated the king and queen on all the happenings in the kingdom. The other royal advisers seemed to have glazed eyes and somewhere to be when Andras got into a mood, ensuring he had the king's full attention.

"And you're here to make sure I don't look like"—I gestured to myself, crinkling my nose at the sight of my wrinkled training ensemble— "this."

"Obviously," she said with a devious grin.

I rose from the chaise and immediately moaned. I'd run on my own throughout the back gardens, well inside the hedged enclosures so I wouldn't need Ian alongside me. I'd thought perhaps it would keep me from sinking further within my mind. Now, the ache in my legs screamed too loud to ignore after such a grueling run. I reached toward the side table where I kept the gift Elisabeth had given me—a salve to rub into my muscles when I first started training. But it had disappeared.

I knelt on the floor, searching around the table to find if I had knocked it over. Kalliah had walked to the wardrobe in my bedroom to choose my dress for the rest of the day.

Scanning under the chaises lined in the sitting area, I caught sight of it. Inching my fingers forward, I latched onto it.

"Get off the floor!" Kalliah chastised. "We don't need you getting any dirtier than you already are. We are cutting it close as it is."

"You act like I'm filthy," I argued, slowly pulling myself off the ground and wiping the dust off of my knees.

I sat before the mirror, reaching down to apply the salve to my calves and thighs. Kalliah tugged my hair while laughing at my grimace before quickly braiding it.

While she worked on my hair I could never style quite right, I applied rouge to my cheeks.

The next few minutes were a blur as I finished changing from my training clothes I'd been lazily lying around in, into a teal-green chiffon dress. The pockets were my favorite part of this dress, along with the lace sleeves. It hugged my curves, making me feel like an adult, not a kid playing dress-up.

Another benefit of training had been my body changing from loose skin and more rounded features to toned and tightened muscle, creating curves, which barely existed before. Even my ass finally rounded out perfectly.

Behind us, my door handles jiggled, along with the sound of a key, and we jumped. Ian flew into the room like a fire had been lit beneath him.

"Andras is coming around the corner. I haven't had time to change," he panted, his cheeks reddening as soon as he finished the comment.

I scanned his attire, stained with blood.

"What happened?" I jumped from the settee in front of the mirror and ran to him, inspecting his stained, darkened tunic. "Are you hurt? Where is the blood coming from?"

"Elisabeth took care of me already." He moved away from me, nearing the door and holding his ear to it.

"Where were you? That's not an explanation of what happened."

Kalliah took a few steps backward, trying to sneak away. Frowning at the distraction, I caught the guilty expression she leveled at Ian.

"One of you, out with it," I demanded.

"We were attacked at Kade and Storm's drop."

My heart sank. I hadn't seen Ian because he knew he wouldn't be able to lie to my face.

"I thought the drop hadn't been scheduled yet," I said.

Clenching my fists at my side, I tried to maintain a bit of my composure. "I thought we were going to continue our conversation?"

"The conversation was over," Ian said. "You wanted to continue, not me. If you still want to have a discussion, we certainly can later. The drop is done, and just like we feared, another attack happened."

I brought my hands to my mouth, steepling them in front of my face. "So, you just ran an entire drop without me."

"If you knew about it, you wouldn't have stayed behind. We simply cannot risk you getting hurt during these attacks. I made the executive decision to not include you, for your own protection." His face steeled with determination, his gaze not leaving mine as he finished speaking.

I stared at him, not recognizing this man in front of me. Ian had never been one to make me feel like I couldn't make my own decisions, and now, he dared make such a big choice for me. Was this fear? Arrogance? Neither seemed like him.

"So, you've taken the position of being a man who thinks he knows what's best for me, have you? Want to lock me up in my dungeon cell next time since I'm such a flight risk?" I sneered.

The reminder of what I endured as a child flashed across his face, and his shoulders slumped as he reached toward me. "Lan, don't act like that. I'm not him."

"No, you just agree I'm unable to provide anything other than being the heir to the throne. A figurehead."

"If you would stop taking everything as an insult directed at you and think about this, it would be better." Ian rubbed his forehead, clearly exasperated. "Please." He reached for me, grasping my hands in his.

My hands trembled, but this time not in fear. In absolute anger.

"I know everyone else thinks I'm weak and broken, Ian, but you've never made me feel that way before. Until now."

Kalliah quietly slipped out the door, and her avoidance meant she had something to hide. Although she'd merely withheld information, she'd behaved as though I'd have a chance to speak to Ian, knowing full well he'd gone ahead with these plans without me.

Ian didn't let go of my hands, despite my attempts to tug away for space. "It's for the best, and it's only temporary."

"You betrayed me. How dare you decide how I live my life?"

With a final tug, he let go.

The walls of the palace felt like they were closing in. Another freedom, which right now seemed like the only freedom left, had been taken from me.

I couldn't do anything to stop it.

Despite knowing we needed more information about our enemy, the choice for me to be a part of the solution remained made for me.

I fled my bedroom, and the pity on Ian's face. I couldn't bear it.

Couldn't bear the truth I'd run from for so long.

In a world where power was currency, what good would a queen be who had none?

CHAPTER 8

Clutching my arms around my middle, holding myself together, I moved with purpose toward the only other place inside the castle walls providing solace.

Elisabeth's room.

She'd know what to say, as always. She would pour me a cup of tea, listen, and then turn everything around.

Rounding a corner, I squealed as I ran into someone moving quickly in the opposite direction.

"Elisabeth." I embraced her the moment I recognized her. "I was just coming to see you." Despite being two inches taller than her, any hug from Elisabeth made me feel cocooned and safe.

Wherever she had been running to in a hurry, she didn't push me away to get back to it. Instead, she rubbed my back. "What's all this now? What's on your mind?"

We never formally informed Elisabeth about the Hidden Henchman, but something told me she knew, nonetheless. She never pressed or asked about it, though. I refused to confide specific details to her in fear someone would learn of what we'd been doing and punish her.

"Ian and I aren't seeing eye to eye right now," I said.

She cupped my cheek. "Everyone argues. I'm surprised the two most stubborn children I know haven't argued more to be perfectly honest." Her smile shone bright, but after taking a closer look, I noticed the puffy, dark bags under her eyes.

"Are you all right?" I asked, linking my arm with hers as we continued down the hall.

"I'm just tired, child. I'm not quite as young as I used to be, and I haven't been getting much sleep recently while tending to your father at all hours of the day and night." Elisabeth patted my hand gently.

"You look more than tired," I said, offering Elisabeth a bit of space to elaborate.

After all these years with her, I knew if I pressed a little and remained quiet, she'd offer more.

Sure enough, a few paces down the hall, Elisabeth sighed, pausing, and pulling her arm from mine to face me. "I'm worried, Illiana. I've never witnessed anything like this before. In all my training and years of experience, I've never encountered a sickness which doesn't respond to my treatments. I'm trying everything I can think of, and nothing is working. I'm unsure what else to do. It's why I've missed our last few weekly tea sessions. I'm so sorry."

I threw my arms around Elisabeth in another hug, engulfing myself in her calming lavender scent. "I know you will figure it out. You are the smartest person I have ever met. You fix everything." I drew away, searching for any sign of reassurance.

But there was none.

Instead, I noticed wrinkles I hadn't observed before, lining her eyes and face.

I leaned my forehead down, resting it against hers. "And regardless of what happens, I know you give all those you heal more than anyone else could." My lip quivered at the thought.

Her failing meant my father would die. I refused to confront that reality.

Elisabeth offered a grim smile, and in a few strides, began rifling through the pockets of her apron. "Enough mushy talk now. Ah, here you go." She handed me a small vial, one I recognized instantly.

A special concoction, a sleeping potion for when my nightmares grew to be too much.

"I meant to give this to you yesterday, but I ran out of time. Let me know when you are running low. Now, I'm off for a bit of a rest before the next time I am summoned." She left me with a quick squeeze of my hand as she made her way down the hall toward her room.

An all-too-familiar pattern of heavy footsteps behind me caused the hairs on the back of my neck to stand on end.

He has no power over you now, I told myself, aware of what I'd see when I turned.

Still, I pressed my shoulders back, lifting my chin as I slowly swiveled to face the arrogant man who enjoyed telling me what to do.

"Princess Illiana." The sound of my name oozing from his tongue made me think vile thoughts. Like how I'd like to cut it out. "You are needed in the king's private dining room." Andras's eyes glimmered. "Immediately."

———

The king straightened in his chair and cleared his throat, his gaze darting between me and my mother. The three of us sat in uncomfortable silence, much more properly than we usually did, in the sitting area to the right of the formal dining room.

At this rate, the tea would grow cold on the table before anyone spoke.

"Illiana, your mother and I have some concerns we need to discuss. Originally, I'd thought things could wait a bit longer, but it seems prudent to move forward sooner." He coughed, reaching for a napkin and holding it to his mouth for a moment before continuing. "As you are aware, you'll soon be twenty-three years of age."

Warning bells sounded in my mind. The tension didn't make sense for a birthday party discussion.

"I'm sure you have noticed I have not been feeling myself recently. According to the laws of Brookmere, if you do not have a husband, then you cannot ascend the throne should something happen to me." My father lifted his chin, preparing to issue one of his decrees.

"Which means, we cannot delay any longer, Illiana. The time has come. You must secure a husband."

Dread coiled in my gut, crawling along my skin, as my heart plunged to the ground. Marriage had never been discussed, and I certainly had no prospects making themselves known.

I opened my mouth to speak, but my father held up his hand to stop me. "I know what you will say, and although it breaks my heart, for the good of the kingdom, I cannot allow you to wait for a love match who may never appear. We have all dreamt you'd find love," he said, "of course we have, but we must focus instead on guaranteeing the kingdom's security. To ensure you are safe and prepared to rule, come what may. You will find a husband, and you will find him now."

I glanced at my mother hoping to find support, but she only stared at me. Her eyes glistened with pain, but she rested her hand atop the king's, demonstrating her agreement with this ridiculous idea I marry immediately. Sympathy, pity, or pain, it didn't matter what she felt. Clearly, I had no ally in her.

"And how am I to find a husband? Shall I skip down the street, for which I am forbidden to walk alone and inquire of volunteers? Any man who may have had an interest had most certainly been scared off with dearest Ruppert by my side.

And now with Ian? I am more likely to attract all the eligible women of Ellevail, before any eligible bachelor." I knew my attitude would get me nowhere, but it seemed like the only thing keeping me grounded while I drowned.

"Nonsense." He scoffed. "We have long thought the prophecy surrounding you referenced an old tradition of our people. With the circumstances as they are, it seems even more obvious."

I blinked rapidly, attempting to process the words he said as he spoke. The prophecy. Of course this had something to do with Fate's dreadful prophecy.

"It has been many, many centuries since the games were held," he continued. "It will not only aid us in finding a worthy suitor but will be a joyous event to offer our people. I've made the announcement across the kingdom as of this morning. The marriage trials have been enacted. The announcement of suitors will begin at a ball next week."

My heart sank farther than I could ever imagine.

"Marriage trials?" I gaped, open-mouthed, at my father. "A competition? For my hand?"

My father nodded. "We thought it might be better than an arranged marriage so we could find someone with strong magic, someone who is loyal and fair. A Fae who has the strength necessary to protect our kingdom."

"Because you believe my strength is so *lacking*," I said, sarcasm dripping from my already-raised voice. I swallowed, realizing I had not come to terms with what my parents had allowed to happen to me when they so desperately agreed to the horrific methods of drawing out my magic. The fury for my younger self collided with the anger at being forced into an unwanted marriage. My jaw hurt from how hard I clenched as I snarled through my teeth. "And what happens when the winner of these games realizes he's married a queen with no magic?"

"His magic will have to be enough for both of you," my

father said. My mother gave him a knowing look, which he tried his best to ignore.

His decision had been made, thought out, and put into motion before he told me, planned so I couldn't do a damn thing about it.

"It's safe for people to travel here, even though it's unsafe for me to leave the city walls. Don't think I'm unaware something is happening to our kingdom, and you refuse to tell me. I shall rule this land one day, and yet I am left in the dark about the troubles we face," I hissed.

"Illiana," my father said, his voice hard, unyielding. I'd reached the point where his tolerance ended. Even my mother sat a little straighter. "This is for our kingdom. This is worth the risk as it will guarantee we have a King and Queen in place for whatever may come."

"I know you dream of love, darling," my mother said from across the table. She successfully spun the conversation from the discussion of what plagued our kingdom. "But your father and I had an arranged marriage and look how incredible it turned out to be. It took several years, but we have fallen into a deep, understanding love we both treasure."

I swallowed the scream trying to burst free from my throat. Slowly, I rose from the chair. "If you'll excuse me," I said, unwilling to meet my father's eyes.

"Illiana." The king's voice stopped me as I reached the door. "Take heart, my love. This will draw in all kinds of men, and we will be able to discern if they are honorable ahead of time. You will have the choice from the top three contenders after the last trial. This ensures you will not be left with the dregs of this kingdom."

"The dregs? I *am* the dregs, Father. The Fates decided I am unworthy of magic, or even a love of my choosing." I scoffed, pivoting to face my parents. "It matters little what I say in response. The decision has been made for me."

"The trials begin in a week!" the king shouted as I shut the doors behind me, not even bothering to bow or offer my goodbyes.

A fierce coughing fit sounded from behind the doors as soon as I closed them.

The queen shouted orders to those nearest her. "Get Elisabeth at once. Between last night and this day, the potions are not working," she said. "Move!"

I rubbed my tightened chest, trying to relieve the pain from the thought of losing him.

He would heal from whatever ailed him. He had always been the strongest in our land, and alongside Elisabeth's healing abilities, not much could bring down Fae in the castle. Nothing anyone knew of at least. He'd be okay.

He'd be okay.

As I repeated the sentiment, blindly moving through the halls, my mind wandered back to the two of them. They were a source of power for each other, and not the magical kind. The kind of power where one could step in when the other felt weaker. The kind of power stemming from respect and true love.

I'd never experienced anything at all remotely close to such a fierce, protective love, at least not in the romantic sense. I hadn't even been in love before. Being stuck inside the palace grounds made having a dating life difficult.

There were plenty of awkward kisses with boys, but given my position, and who I pretended to be in the shadows, I could count on one hand how many had ventured past groping me atop my clothing and getting more of me.

But *love?* Love was a concept I couldn't explore as freely as I wished. Too many people wanted to use me for my title. Use me for my parents' riches. Use me for the glory of living in the castle, or worse, simply to say they bedded the princess.

Love wouldn't matter anymore now, no matter how desperately I craved it one day. My marriage would simply be to the victor of the trials. It would be forced, likely to a brute, who cared nothing of my wishes or desires.

I paused at one of the beautiful gold-framed glass windows. The knowledge of losing this choice left me aching for a life unconfined by walls and guards and the pageantry of the Royal Court.

My mind filled with all the desires I had never voiced as I continued down the endless halls and out of the side entrance, near the kitchen. Down the steep hill, I headed toward the training grounds, not even realizing where my feet lead me. Perhaps my soul knew a bit of swordplay would help clear my mind.

With all the freedoms taken from me, I needed to be somewhere which reminded me my lack of magic didn't leave me without options to protect myself.

CHAPTER 9

Kalliah and Ian were in the heat of their duel, flawlessly using wooden training swords.

She blocked every move Ian made. His smile grew wider each time she accomplished another.

Leif sat on the edge of the pit, his arms crossed as he studied the pair. Kalliah had learned quickly these past few months. She already perfected nearly everything Ian had taught me in my first year.

I sat next to Leif, nudging him with my shoulder. "Don't think I don't see that look," I teased.

He arched an eyebrow. When I wiggled mine, he scoffed. "If I wanted to bed a tiger, yes, I'd go after your lady. But I like my bits intact, thank you very much."

My laughter caught Kalliah's attention, and she and Ian looked our way. "Shouldn't you be off brooding or are we finally going to put everything behind us?" she asked.

I responded with a tight smile. "Nothing like going round for round in the sparring ring to settle the score," I insisted.

Despite wearing a dress, I bunched it up in my hands and jumped into the pit. Misjudging slightly, I stumbled, stubbing my toe on a rock. "Tits and daggers!" I hissed.

"Bleeding hell, Lan, you're a damn princess. You can't run your mouth like a drunk in a tavern." Ian's expression contorted with disgust while Leif choked back laughter.

Ian pointed at Leif. "Don't encourage her," he said. "Go on, you two." He motioned between me and Kalliah. "Show me I've at least taught you something."

"You two are the ones who have stuff to work out," Kalliah said, leaning on her training sword.

Ian shook his head, stepping out of the ring. "She looks like she'd kill me at any moment. You can wear her down a bit first."

I stuck my tongue out before I curtsied to him, obnoxiously low, before assuming my position in front of Kalliah. I retrieved the extra wooden sword from the dirt floor as Leif returned to his duties in the palace.

Kalliah and I circled each other before she dove into a relentless barrage of attacks. I barely had time to block half of her blows, and she managed to get in a few hits right off the bat.

"You're sloppy today, Lana," Ian chastised.

"I'm doing *fine*," I snipped. Anger welled inside of me, waiting to explode like a volcano.

"You're not fine. You've missed the last three parries we've been practicing for weeks. It's unlike you."

I slashed my wooden sword against Kalliah's harder than I meant to. "I'm *fine*," I screeched as Kalliah retaliated and knocked the practice weapon from my hand. "Agh!"

Ian strode toward me as my head hung in defeat. Neither of my friends spoke, but the longer silence grew, the more fury raged inside of me. My body shook, trembling at the unfairness of everything, my breath coming harder and faster than I could manage.

I'd be bartered away through a trial, as though my life were unworthy of choosing who I spent it with, forcing me to choose between men I did not know nor care for.

Bartered away to a stranger who would put more restrictions on me than Ian already did. Depending on his character, my being magicless could be a prison sentence. I would be hidden away from embarrassment alone.

This new "King" could mean losing what little I had left of my own voice.

Ian stood in front of me, placing a hand on my shoulder. He said nothing, but the manner in which he purposefully slowed his breathing, as he'd done beside me so many times before, had me matching his breaths to regain control. As always, his gentle aid, even when I didn't ask for it, helped.

"What's going on in that head of yours? Talk to us." The gentleness of his tone allowed me to take another deep breath and pause, forgetting the words still needing to be exchanged from our earlier fight.

I slowly lifted my head, meeting his worried gaze before shifting to Kalliah, who held the same expression.

Although out of my control, I didn't want to explain this to them. To admit what lay ahead of us. I'd be peddled as a prize for some egotistical prick in a competition.

Depending upon who won, the man serving as the new king could change everything. Kalliah, born with limited magic and a lesser Fae, could be deemed unworthy to interact with Fae royalty at all, and certainly not to the status she was now.

And Ian. *Ian*, who had grown up alongside me. Ian, who held me if my nightmares were too much. Our relationship would be forever changed after this.

No husband would allow a Royal Guard into his wife's bed chambers with or without their presence. No King would allow their wife, their Queen, to go off to the training grounds to practice swordplay and archery with guards, staff, and a lesser Fae.

And then the worst of it dawned on me.

No husband would allow their wife to sneak off into the

91

night and be the Hidden Henchman. Would whomever became King demand I stand to the side? Kept naïve of the darkness troubling our lands, as my father hid from me.

Even knowing my father wouldn't allow me to be the Hidden Henchman should he ever discover it was me either, I could keep it secret from him. How would I keep my comings and goings from a husband if he didn't approve of making the changes I desired? My ability to enact such changes could be stifled by a man who didn't believe in ruling the kingdom the way *I* wished to.

What would happen to the villagers in need if I could not keep providing aid? Would they starve? If I could not provide medical supplies, would someone die? More than one death had already bloodied my hands, and I did not wish to add more.

I stared at Ian's face, his brows furrowed, clearly attempting to discern what could be so troublesome. "My father requested a meeting this morning about my future."

"Let me guess—the prophecy, *again?*" he questioned.

I sighed. "Worse."

"Worse? What could be worse than that ridiculous prophecy Vivienne prattled off eons ago?" Ian stepped back a few paces, flourishing his hands by his temple as though he could see the future, as he always did when mocking Vivienne.

Normally, this would make me laugh, but my face remained neutral, and I mustered all the strength I had left in me. "The king has enacted the marriage trials."

"The marriage trials?" Kalliah gasped. "Why? How? They're practically legend."

Ian ran his hands through his sweat-leaden hair, tousling the slight waves out of place. "There haven't been marriage trials in, what, half a millennium?"

I nodded in confirmation. "They believe the prophecy references holding the marriage trials."

"Well, it's fucking stupid," Ian said.

"Tell me something I don't already know." I wiped the sweat from my forehead.

"When?" Kalliah asked in a hushed tone. Her hands still hung by her side, the sword dangling from her fingertips.

I wondered briefly if either of them was making the connections I had earlier. A new King could mean all new rules, and we'd be expected to be separated even further.

Ian stared, just like Kalliah did, awaiting my response as hurt crept into his eyes.

"One week," I said, choking on fresh tears. Air, I needed air. I gasped again, clutching at my chest as the all-too-familiar tightening spread, zinging down my arms.

Ian quickly wrapped me in an embrace as my knees buckled and I fell to the ground. He held me tight and ran his hands through my half-braided hair, not caring about the sweat clinging to me from our training session, or if we were out in the open. Anyone could see the embrace. Anyone could devise a new round of rumors to circulate.

Kalliah knelt on the other side of me, her hand moving around my waist.

"It'll be okay, Lana," Kalliah assured me.

Ian's grip tightened. "We'll get through this together, like we always do."

I peered up at Ian, quietly asking, "What am I going to do? Everyone will find out I'm magicless."

We remained sitting together until my legs started to cramp from the position. When I shifted, Ian rose first, holding out his hands to me and Kalliah.

He pushed a strand of loose hair behind my ear. "We'll find a solution."

"Even if I'm being stupid with how mad I am at you?" I asked.

Ian smiled at me, kissing my forehead. "Your anger at me is deserved, but it will not make me change my mind. We'll work through it. And this, too."

Tears streamed down my face, and I buried my head in the warmth of Ian's chest, while Kalliah rubbed my back.

They let me cry, out in the open, without rushing me.

When I leaned back, lifting my chin, I looked at each of them. "We'll get through it together," I repeated Ian's words.

"This calls for one more round," Kalliah said.

Kalliah's uncanny intuition made me believe she had a higher level of magical abilities, lesser Fae or not. She always succeeded in distracting me when the pressure of Court, or the fear of my lack of magic, overwhelmed me.

"I let you win before." I grinned, willing a bit of strength back into my body.

We picked up the swords, practicing each position Ian had taught us. The movements were almost soothing as we circled each other, sparring and smiling.

While I may not have control over my future, one thing I knew for certain—I wouldn't be going down without a fight.

CHAPTER 10

I schooled my features, presenting the happy princess everyone had come to know and love while I stood on display for the Court. This mask portrayed my reserved and complacent demeanor, always worn with the hint of a smile upon my face.

My mind protested the act we were portraying to the world as anxious energy crackled inside of me. A delicate smile, and a small wave of my hands to the subjects of our kingdom was all they would see. While inside, I so desperately craved to be anywhere but here.

It had been five days since my father told me the marriage trials would be taking place.

Five days.

It was all the time it took for Fae to gather from across our entire kingdom to attend this evening's ball to witness which men came forth to try to win my hand.

From where I stood on the royal dais, I studied those gathered, chatting, and mingling together. To them, it would appear as though I enjoyed seeing the crowd tonight.

Inhaling, I bit back a sob at how happy everyone seemed to be. At my expense. Any tear escaping would be mistaken for one of eternal gratitude and joy at the offering the king made in my honor. All it would take was a hand on my heart to make the act complete.

Kalliah had outdone herself preparing me this evening. My tiara glistened, a solid purple sapphire, surrounded by diamonds and other purple and violet gems. She had twisted my hair up in a braided crown, aware I hated my long hair flowing down my back when I had to dance the night away.

I caught her attention across the room as she motioned how perfect she thought she did.

The only way to keep from laughing aloud was to avert my gaze and try not to glance her way again.

I knew I looked beautiful. Like a trophy on display. Her intent hadn't been to make anyone else awestruck, but for me to feel battle ready in a different kind of armor. For me to know my power may be lacking in magic, but I could command a room with, not only my title, but my poise and grace.

The doors swung open with a breeze as the king and queen glided into the room, every Fae bowing, including myself. They strode slowly down the gold and purple velvet runner lining the middle of the white marble throne room, their subjects staring at the pair with admiration.

I kept my gaze cast downward, focused on the way my navy-blue dress pooled around my feet. The small, clear crystals along the top layer of tulle shimmered in the soft lights. The lights were a show of power, cast using the king's magic throughout the massive throne room.

The glass-domed ceiling made it appear as if we were not inside a stuffy throne room, but outdoors beneath the twinkling stars. The soft magical lights made it seem as if the stars themselves had descended from the sky. Beautiful vines cascaded over the pillars at the edges of the room, the sprouting wildflowers of our kingdom interwoven throughout.

The throne room, with flowers and illuminations,

reminded me of my personal garden at night, a nod from the king to ensure I would feel comfortable tonight, regardless of my disdain for the event.

Despite wanting to be anywhere but here, surrounded by the overindulgent, powerful Fae of our world, the events were always magnificent, capturing the beauty of the land like our own tribute of thanks to nature.

A breeze across my bare neck signaled the king and queen's arrival in front of me. My father offered me his hand and I rose, placing my own in his.

His gaze searched mine briefly, as though he sought forgiveness despite our fight. Noting the love reflecting in his eyes, made it hard to remain angry. In his own way, he believed these trials protected me. He'd always do what he thought would be best for me, and more importantly, our kingdom.

They trusted in a prophecy of love somehow protecting me, even when I had long since decided our Seer, Vivienne, could only be described as "crazy," but in an eccentric sort of way. I wondered, not for the first time, if perhaps her visions could provide answers about the trouble spreading throughout the lands if she put a bit of effort into it.

Nevertheless, tying myself to a man when I worked so hard to be strong on my own ignited *rage*, not love as the prophecy claimed.

I offered Mother and Father a smile and rose to join them at the front of the dais.

The weight of the stares from across the room were heavy. Quickly scanning the area, I searched for Ian. I hadn't seen him beforehand, in fact, I hadn't set eyes upon him except for a few moments this morning. Surveying the festivities, I noticed him at the back. He avoided my gaze, unlike others in the audience. I couldn't help but feel just a small pang of disappointment. Perhaps I relied too heavily on Ian and Kalliah to get me through moments like this.

I tried not to frown as I focused my attention on the king, who had just signaled for one of the staff to get the crowd's attention. Hardly a job, given everyone waited with bated breath for his announcement, anyway. A small tinkle of bells chimed as a prelude, before the king spoke.

"Friends, from far and wide, welcome to the palace at Ellevail." His voice boomed. The way the room curved allowed his voice to be heard without amplification. "When Queen Roxana and I sent our messengers all over our beloved kingdom, we hardly expected this truly joyous level of excitement. We may be biased about how wonderful Princess Illianna is." He laughed, joined immediately by the guests. "But it is clear the people of Brookmere feel the same."

What a show. The whole thing. People desired his approval, his goodwill. I kept my perfect princess façade in place, staring at him as though I agreed with his every word, exactly as I had always been instructed.

"Tonight's ball is a unique occasion. As you are aware by now, we are enacting the marriage trials. This ancient tradition brings Fae from all over the Kingdom of Brookmere together as we strive to join the people of our land by finding, not the most royal or richest bloodline, but the strongest. The bloodline who will prove themselves in trials, testing strength, loyalty, intelligence, understanding, and justice."

He reached for my hand, and I stepped forward to stand beside him. "It is the winner of the trials who will be deemed worthy of Princess Illiana's hand in marriage, and who will become the future King of Brookmere."

Murmurs spread throughout the crowd.

"Tonight," he continued proudly, "is when those believing themselves deserving enough of my Illiana and our kingdom make their intentions known. Those who come forth will supply your sealed letters of approval and recommendation to my Royal Adviser."

I wondered what such letters would contain. At least it

ensured someone vouched for whomever stepped forward to become King.

My father offered me one last loving look before facing the crowd, dropping my hand, and sealing this fate with one sentence.

"May any who wish to be a contender in the marriage trials, come forward and make your bid," he said.

I held my breath, wondering who might be brave enough to step up first. Perhaps no one would want to compete, and it would save me this entire ridiculous display. I tried not to snicker at my thoughts.

A shuffle went through the crowd, and the first person approached.

My mouth grew dry, and I had to catch myself as it attempted to drop open.

"Captain Ian Stronholm," the king said, his voice seeming amused as he smiled down upon my friend.

My gaze shifted to Kalliah in the back, who only gave me a shrug, as if she had no idea what Ian had planned.

"Your Majesty." Ian knelt before my father, placing his hat in his hands. He donned his finest Royal Guard uniform, the one meant for special occasions, not a wrinkle in the stiff, black- and purple-lined fabric. His medals gleamed on his chest. "I'd be honored to compete for the hand of Princess Illiana, if you'd be inclined to allow it," Ian said, his gaze cast to the floor, unmoving, until the king answered.

"Captain Stronholm, please rise." Ian gathered himself and stood at attention. "You are our fiercest warrior and a loyal friend to not only myself, but to Illiana as well. As the first official contender, you will have the first dance."

Andras moved immediately, scowling as he escorted Ian off to the right of me, beginning the line of contenders yet to come. I nearly missed the subtle roll of his eyes in Ian's direction as he shuffled him along.

I attempted to keep my expression neutral, but inside, my anger flared. I could scarcely keep my trembling hands at bay.

Murder seemed like a suitable consequence. How could he throw his life away for this? My hand clenched into a fist before I reminded myself of my placement in the hall. Here, my reactions would be analyzed by an entire kingdom.

Ian entering the trials without speaking to me first had me reeling. No wonder he'd avoided me today.

The next two Fae were Lords from houses to the north and west of Ellevail. They were announced one by one.

"Lord Levi Thatcher." An average-looking man stood before my father, with no discernible features. His short black hair lay slicked back and his pale skin seemed to glow against the darkness of his suit.

"Lord Casimir West." His short red hair and green eyes complemented each other. Not so bad to look at, his body clearly toned under his clothing. He stood with his chin held high, slightly looking down upon those around him. He clearly thought himself superior to the others already standing in line.

I bowed my head at each contender as they approached, keeping my smile as relaxed as I possibly could.

"Hale Bardot, Your Majesty." My smile became genuine as I met the familiar pair of deep brown eyes, immediately recognizing him. I didn't dare look at Ian, already aware how he felt about Hale.

We had both known Hale for the past decade. He bored Ian to tears, but for me, whenever there were formal functions, we often used one another's company as an escape from our parents. Sometimes through a dance in a ball, others with a walk around the gardens, but there were a few occasions where it had been more.

While the kissing and exploring each other had hardly left me pining for more, it at least meant a friendly face amongst the crowd of strangers.

Hale brushed my hand ever so slightly as he walked by, moving on toward the back of the line.

"Frederich Hansley." A stout-looking, middle-aged man approached. His mustache was as large as his head. *Fates, no.* Perhaps I could issue a royal decree about body hair as my first act as Queen.

Two more names were announced as official candidates, but I lost track of who they were or what they looked like. Ryland Lockbane and Edmund Fairweather. How much longer would this take, and how many more would be allowed to participate in these ridiculous trials? *Fates,* I wanted to be anywhere but here.

"A fine group," the king announced proudly. I looked up, thankful the end drew nearer. "I call for one final chance to enter before the trials officially commence. Are there any other contenders brave enough to vie for my daughter's hand in marriage?"

"Here, Your Majesty." A deep voice thundered throughout the ballroom, reverberating in my chest.

Pushing forward through the crowd from the back of the room, a hulking man, taller than most by a head, pressed toward the front where we stood. My breath lodged in my throat as I tried to force it out. Power radiated throughout the room.

Thick strands of black hair fell loosely across his tanned face as he strode forward, knowing exactly how he commanded the room. All eyes were on him, and the half-smile he wore as he approached the dais. My face warmed at the sight of him, and if I could have pinched myself right there to pull myself together, I would have.

I refused to acknowledge the familiarity of the sensations taking over my body when this prick was nearby. But he appeared before me. The damned mysterious, cocky, rude Fae himself.

Kade.

After speaking about the king so horridly, he wanted to marry his daughter?

I'd only observed him without his hood for incredibly brief periods of time. But the gleam in his damned eyes couldn't be forgotten. *He's not that attractive,* I tried to persuade myself. The number of muscular men with broad shoulders storming around the palace were adequate, a few standing in the contender's line before me. What was one more?

I didn't even bother hiding my eyes narrowing on him.

He bowed at the waist, not kneeling like the others, and rose before being acknowledged. "Blackthorn, Your Highness. Kade Blackthorn."

I noticed more than one of the women in the sea of faces pushing their way toward the front of the room, attempting to catch a glimpse. Men, too, seemed unable to look away, their stares likely from the power radiating from Kade.

My father stiffened, narrowing his eyes in response to that very power filling the space before him. "And where exactly are you from, Lord——"

"Just Kade, Your Grace." He'd interrupted my father, *the king*, something no one generally dared to do.

The king inhaled sharply, clearly taken aback by Kade's lack of manners. He regained his composure before proceeding. "Where are you from, Kade?"

"I've lived in many villages here in Brookmere," he answered. "I'd be remiss to call any of them home at the risk of claiming any one village holds more of my heart over another."

I studied him carefully, *not* only because I couldn't look away. His storm-grey eyes were so uniquely full of arrogance as his gaze held the king's. I scowled, not bothering to hide my reaction. His sexiness infuriated me.

I wish he wore his stupid hood, so I didn't have to notice more about him.

"Kade Blackthorn."

The king announced Kade as an official contender and waved his hand for him to get into line. He strode past me, meeting my gaze and immediately winking. A whisper of warmth slithered over my body as he passed. He smelled of a summer storm. The kind of peaceful, saturated heaven nature left behind once thunder and rain moved on.

His scent drew me closer. Everything about him read like a trap, unless you knew better. Like I did.

There had been no hint of recognition in his gaze. The wink he'd offered me, merely a mastered act, one he surely used on everyone and anyone.

I should be grateful he didn't recognize me. If he learned my true identity, we'd be in trouble. He would have an edge in the trials from knowing my secrets.

Arrogant man.

He'd be trouble. I smoothed my dress, lifting my chin and observing the crowd in an attempt to pretend I didn't notice him as he strode to the end of the line of the contenders.

He wore all black, with grey embellishments swirling along the lapels of his jacket. The only hint of color located on a strip of dark blue outlining his tunic. When he pivoted to take his place in line, he caught me watching, and the devilish grin he sent my way had me snapping my head immediately back toward the king. *Damn it.*

Arrogant indeed, I told myself. I shook thoughts of *that* cocky Fae from my mind. Even if the giggling reverberating from quite a few women in the crowd made him hard to ignore. He almost garnered as much of a reaction from the Fae of Brookmere as Ian did.

They could have Kade Blackthorn for all I cared.

"There you have it. Eight of our kingdom's finest will compete, beginning in two days' time, during the first trial for Princess Illiana's hand." The king started clapping, followed by the queen and the others in the room joining together.

"Now, let the dancing begin. Celebrate! May nature guide you!" The king chuckled as he took my mother's hand and placed it on his arm, returning them to their thrones. They shared a warm look of affection, which made my heart sink further.

"Your Highness." Ian's husky voice at my side quickly reminded me of my anger toward him. I took his hand and planted a fake smile on my face as he led me to the dance floor.

As his hand settled on my waist, I attempted to calm my voice. Instead, it came out as a hiss. "What were you thinking? You cannot compete. This is insane!"

To his credit, he didn't falter in his steps, or stiffen. He *knew* I'd put up a fight. He kept the pace of the waltz played by the quartet.

"I *can* compete, Lana. And I am."

I gripped his arm. "You're throwing away your entire life, Ian. Everything. For what?"

He stared down at me as if my anger was surprising. "Do you think it would be better for a power-hungry nobody to have your hand? Some arrogant prick who would believe you should be kept away from friendships with lesser Fae, from your extra activities? From me?"

I swallowed in an attempt to stop my lips from trembling.

"Or, even better, someone who would exploit the fact you have no magical abilities?"

He led us, dancing all around the room, as though we didn't have a care at all.

"You do this, and you lose your chance at finding your own happiness. You're handsome, and wonderful, and eligible. Every woman in the entire kingdom vies for your affections daily. You could find love," I whispered. "Please don't throw all of it away for me. I can't live with it."

He spun me outward before pulling me in, closer this time

so his lips were at my ear. His breath, hot and needy, caught me by surprise. "I can think of much worse fates than being tethered to you forever, Lan."

We moved the next few paces of the dance, my mind reeling as my heart broke at his words.

"Besides," he said, chuckling, "we already spend all our time together, anyway. A ring and a title will not change us. Now put a smile on your beautiful face. The kingdom is watching."

"Adding fuel to the fire of the rumors already swirling around us," I grumbled.

"Perhaps we shall make the rumors true then. Our children would be absolutely breathtaking." He winked, before spinning me out once more.

He bowed as the song drew to a close, placing a delicate kiss on my cheek before turning away. He knew this conversation would continue, but not here, not now. Even if I could reluctantly admit he had a point. There were worse men than him to marry. Frederich being one of them.

We weren't in love, and our relationship had never been intimate. I refused to let him give up his freedom for me.

As soon as Ian left my side, Lord Levi Thatcher stepped forward. His brash kiss on my hand had me wanting to wipe it on the skirt of my dress.

"Aren't you a delight, Princess?" he murmured, aggressively yanking my body toward him.

Pressed against a stranger like this couldn't be any more inappropriate, marriage trials or not. I drew back a step, locking my arms, so he couldn't draw me close again. "How charming."

With less of a smile and more of a lip curl, I remained focused, nodding and adding a short "mmhmm" here and there. His rambling made it impossible to know if Lord Thatcher even cared that I heard his prattling.

And on it went.

One by one, the contenders took their time, showering me with insincere compliments. Hale stammered a few times, telling me he'd never beheld such beauty. It was difficult to reconcile the grown Fae before me with the teenage boy, who kissed me behind the rose bushes in my parents' garden.

Before the next contender approached, I scanned the room, hoping to spot Kade. He didn't seem to be in the ballroom anymore, at least I couldn't find him with my sweeping gaze each time I turned. Off with one of his admirers, no doubt. I shuddered.

Was I jealous?

No, simply disgusted at the nerve of him sneaking off somewhere instead of dancing as a contender should.

Ryland gracefully bowed, and as we moved across the floor, he tried to make me laugh during the quick pleasantries. He succeeded a few times, too, and made casual, but pleasant, conversation. He kissed my hand before flitting off after his turn, seeming perfectly content to give me time with the other contenders, as if it mattered little to him.

Edmund stepped in next, and the way he confidently took me in his arms, and with his hands in appropriate places, I almost thought it wouldn't be so bad. But that's where all hope ended. He answered questions with one word, not inquiring anything about me.

The mediocre dance with Edmund seemed longer than it should have. An average-looking man, with average dancing abilities, and average conversational skills, Edmund was the least likely person I assumed would care to be King. Let alone enter a competition for my hand. If he won, the most boring life known to Fae kind flashed before my eyes.

I scanned the crowd, looking for something to save me from the boredom when I noticed Kalliah no longer stood alone in the corner.

Leif propped his arm against the wall, leaning in to

say something to her. How on earth did he get away from the kitchen already? I wanted Kalliah to look this way so I could try to get a better glimpse at the expression on her face as Leif smiled and laughed next to her.

She pressed a hand to his chest, and I gasped, Edmund stammering an apology, asking if he stepped on my toes.

"No, I'm so sorry," I said. "Only overtaken with excitement from dancing." He bowed and offered me a reprieve, the Fates finally in my favor.

By the time I turned to look back at Kalliah, she stood alone again. I grasped the hem of my dress, about to make my way toward her, when Lord Casimir West stopped me in my tracks.

Damn it all. This night would *never* end.

Lord West remained quiet as he spun me around, leaving me to play courtier and lead the conversation. I'd take this over listening to another man droning on about his wealth and knowledge, or expertise of some kind, though.

"Have you been to Ellevail before, Lord West?" I asked.

His eyes raked over me, glancing low at my bodice. I wanted to throw a hand over my chest. It wasn't the most modest dress. The corset backing made my chest full and put my assets on display. The short dip hadn't seemed so bad before, but with this man's gaze lingering, I suddenly felt extremely exposed.

"I haven't. But I intend on exploring all it has to offer, my future wife."

A chill crawled up my back as his hand slid lower. I could knee him in the balls right this instant and feign an accident. Perhaps it would teach him to keep his hands, and eyes, to himself. However, an accidental step on his toes would have to do.

"My apologies, my lord," I attempted to say with a straight face.

Kalliah's giggling in the corner indicated she witnessed my "supposed" mishap.

I quickly curtsied and turned to try and find something to drink. However, the large body of a man blocked my path.

I swallowed, tilting my head back to look at the face the muscular figure belonged to. Last time we were close, he had his sword against my neck. My heart betrayed me and skipped a beat. A small gasp escaped, as a delicious chill skittered across my arms. He smiled as if he expected women to be so affected in his presence.

The defiant part of me won, shifting out of the way, but Kade Blackthorn softly grasped my arm. "The next song is about to begin, Princess. I'm sure you weren't leaving before giving all the contenders fair time with you," he said. "Besides, you have saved the best for last." A smirk splayed on his face.

He turned me back to the dance floor and led me toward my final waltz, bowing low as he offered me his hand.

I bowed my head and accepted his hand. "Lord…"

"As I said earlier, not lord. Kade. Just Kade." His grey eyes swirled with mystery as he held my gaze.

I ran my tongue over my teeth, biting back sharp responses as best I could. "It's nice to meet you, *just Kade*. I am Princess Illiana."

His hand wrapped around my body as he held me in a relaxed, yet sturdy posture. He had clearly done this before, and his unwavering composure, even as the crowds of Fae watched his every move, unnerved me.

The king paid especially close attention to this dance. His gaze followed us around the dance floor.

"It's nice to meet you, Princess Illiana," he said, spinning me once. "So, tell me—are all of your wildest dreams coming true? So many strong, capable, men competing for your hand. Hard to imagine there could be anything more enticing for you," Kade teased.

"Oh, yes," I said, fighting the urge to roll my eyes. I steeled my smile as I added, "Being auctioned off to the man with the most strength, while I have no say in the matter is definitely every woman's *wildest* dream. After all, what more to life could there possibly be beyond being desired by a *strong* man?"

Without saying a word, Kade stared at me long enough that I averted my gaze, idly surveying the room instead.

I could not do this. It only served to ignite my nerves further, knowing everyone stared. Even those dancing were looking away from their partners and shifting their gazes our way.

Kade commanded the whole damn room, even while dancing with me.

Danger lurked in his immense power. A danger that meant he'd surely cast a woman aside once he had the crown.

"Eyes on me, Princess," he purred, "They'll disappear into the background, and you can calm your fluttering heart." This time, when he led me in the steps away and back together, he pulled me closer. My chest pressed against his, the lack of space between us distracting me from everything else. He angled his head toward my ear. "Unless your heartbeat is because of me, in which case, I can hardly help it."

"Arrogance isn't charming, Kade." Even with the candid words, goose bumps rose along my skin. My shiver had nothing to do with the temperature, and everything to do with him.

I inhaled slowly through my nose, desperate to calm my racing heart. Stupid Fae hearing and senses noticing my body. The inhale scarcely helped as the scent of rainstorms washed over me. Damn it all, he smelled incredible.

"Have we met somewhere before?" he asked, his voice so low I nearly thought I'd misheard.

My gaze snapped to meet his. He couldn't recognize me. We were far too careful with my disguise, and it had never slipped in his presence. "Does that line often work with your numerous admirers?"

Kade chuckled softly.

I pulled myself together, needing to change the direction of this conversation. "Anything interesting I should know about you, Kade? With your heart spread across the kingdom, shall I expect a rush of angry women at our gates soon?"

His mischievous smile grew as he licked his bottom lip.

Fates help me.

"Thinking about me in compromising positions already, Princess? How forward."

"It's not what I—"

He brought a finger to my lips. "No sense in denying it."

My eyes flared as I attempted to yank myself away from his stupidly intoxicating touch. He didn't release me. Instead, he forced our bodies closer, so I pressed against his strong frame. He twirled us, spinning and gliding across the dance floor as if we'd been dancing together for years instead of only just meeting.

His fingers brushed against my exposed back, and I tensed, heat flooding between my legs. I needed to take the edge off, before these trials began. Somehow. I'd never been able to rely on any of the men in this Court to handle those needs.

If he weren't so cocky and I didn't have so many questions about his intentions, I may have enjoyed myself, the freedom of spinning around the dance floor with him. My chest heaved, my breathing faster and heavier than I wanted it to be in front of him. As we stood chest-to-chest, Kade's gaze flicked to my lips. Something under my skin built, rumbling through my body. I'd officially gone mad. My lips parted as I stared at him, meeting his grey gaze.

His brow furrowed, only for a moment, before he blinked a few times.

The spell broke, and only then did I notice the music had stopped.

Everyone stared.

The trance Kade held me in during our dance left every single Fae surrounding us riveted.

A spectacle.

And the man before me dazzled them all by shaking off the electricity between us, ignoring their stares and flashing me a heart-clenching, blinding grin.

CHAPTER 11

I dropped my hand from Kade's shoulder as though fire ignited within me, burning from the inside out.

Every protocol flew from my mind as I walked away from him without even curtsying. Fleeing to the safety of Kalliah's side along the far-right wall, she grasped my hand, her eyes wide in wonder. The music began again, and people returned to their conversations and merriment. Kade, who had stood silently observing me walk away, had disappeared.

I caught a few murmurs through the crowd at the obvious way we'd stayed together after the music stopped. What on earth had I been thinking?

"Need a cold shower?" Kalliah snorted before she burst into laughter.

My head snapped toward her. "It's not funny. More like awful, I thought I would never have to see his arrogant ass again."

"Oh, Lana, 'awful' is not the word I think anyone would use," Kalliah countered. "He's even sexier than I imagined from when you described him."

"I did not describe him as sexy," I hissed.

She always saw right through me. She handed me a cup of

lemon-infused water, and I tilted it back, finishing in one gulp, wishing for something much stronger.

"More importantly than Kade, what did Leif have to say?" I asked.

Kalliah frowned. "Nothing of importance."

It was my turn to laugh, as I set my cup down on the round serving tray passing by. "Liar." I stood next to her at the wall. "I saw you. If I hadn't been trapped on the dance floor, I would have been able to see what happened when you put your hand on our dear, innocent Leif's chest."

"Does it matter?" Kalliah scoffed.

"I'm just wondering." I tugged at her arm. "Are you all right?"

"I don't know anything about him. Nor do I care to. He said something about a message for Ian. I can't recall." She turned her head away from me.

Kalliah was more reserved with her emotions more than Ian and I. I knew when to tease her and when she wanted space, and right now for some reason, she wanted space.

Valuing someone meant honoring their boundaries, and while she had many, they were worth recognizing.

I changed the subject, desperate to appear busy enough with her so I wouldn't be stolen away again. "Did you know what Ian was planning?"

She sucked in a breath. "No," she said. "Not at all. But are you surprised? He'd die for you. What's a marriage?"

"Kalliah, he's like my brother. You do know what married people are expected to *do*, right?" I stared straight into her green eyes, hoping she understood my hesitancy.

She laughed again. "Well, you certainly are entertaining this evening. If you think you'll convince him otherwise, you've lost it."

"I have to try." I rubbed my arms, cooler now since I wasn't on the dance floor, spinning and surrounded by bodies.

Or perhaps it had more to do with coming down from the high of dancing with my *last* partner, specifically.

"You wouldn't be you if you didn't say that," Kalliah said softly. "He left toward the barracks. I'm sure you can catch him."

I squeezed her arm. "Thank you."

Regardless of what happened in the coming months, one of us had to live a life of freedom. Since it sure as hell couldn't be me, I refused to give up until I convinced Ian it would be him.

Even if I hadn't planned to hunt down Ian, I endured enough revelry and attention for one night. I had done my duty. Danced and smiled, and with the amount of wine and drink flowing freely, at this point I'd hardly be missed.

I quickly scanned the throne room. For once this evening, not one Fae paid any attention to me. If I wanted to escape unnoticed, I had to do it now.

Moving along the outer walls, I continued toward one of the doors, walking slowly without any sudden movements so I wouldn't bring any attention to myself. An exit to one of the smaller, lesser-used, staff hallways, lay just within reach. It would be an escape allowing me to move unseen through the palace.

I slipped through the large, wood-framed door and closed it quietly behind me. The short corridor ahead would pop me out into one of the main passages in the palace. One with vast windows and ledges to sit on every few steps. The design of the palace, and everything inside of it, allowed us to view the beauty of nature.

Footsteps clopped behind me before I could leave the servants' corridor. Bleeding hell, it better not be one of the contenders.

Unfortunately, it was worse.

The Royal Seer, Vivienne Nazar, stood with her head tilted to the side, staring at me while appearing lost and confused. Although the same age as my mother, her body revealed more signs of wear.

Her wiry grey hair could never be tamed with all the random kinks and curls throughout. She often wore robes, only found centuries ago, always declining the new styles and fabrics the king offered.

"Going, going, gone, so soon, are we, Lana?" she questioned.

"Yes, I needed some air," I said. "It was starting to feel stuffy."

"The umbra isn't always a blight. No, no." She shook her head and then smiled. "Not with the right blaze."

I stared back, placating her with the kindest smile I could muster. We had all learned over the years the best way to deal with Vivienne is just to let her talk and prattle. Apparently, ever since she made the prophecy ruling my entire life, nothing she said made much sense, with everything coming out in riddles. Every once in a while, she would have moments of clarity, but they were rare.

"I will be sure to keep it in mind, Vivienne. Have a good night." I backed up a few paces and veered down the hall before she could say anything else and trap me there even longer with her nonsense. I couldn't even be sure if she noticed I left as she toyed with the fraying ties of her robes.

Ian hadn't made it too far from the throne room. As soon as the small hallway door dumped me out into the main corridor, I found him, staring out the largest window in the hall, his foot perched on the bench beneath it, hands resting on his hips. He appeared stoic in the moment, still in a way he usually wasn't.

He noticed me and I caught his shoulders sag slightly.

Lifting my hands in surrender, I offered a small smile. "I don't want to fight."

His lips twitched and he returned his focus to the window, shaking his head. "After everything we've been through, I find

I'm frustrated you don't understand I take protecting this kingdom, and you, very seriously."

"I know you do——"

"Lana," Ian said, facing me. "What is so hard for you to grasp? I promised you I'd never leave." Loyalty and stubbornness swirled in his eyes. "I swore it as a boy, and I have worked hard to never break your trust or falter in my promise. Don't you remember?"

I did remember. I remembered being a lonely child. Lonely and scared I had no magic while everyone around me did. Fearful adults who should have been trustworthy had instead thought my lack of magic needed to be fixed by any means necessary.

Ian had been with me throughout the aftermath of all my "training sessions" growing up, picking up the pieces from the torture I endured for years. Holding me in the dark while I cried in his arms. Making sure Elisabeth remained close if I needed a sleeping potion for the nightmares plaguing me.

When the potions didn't chase away all the fears, Ian never left, holding onto me and promising me he'd never leave.

He stayed. He soothed. Despite the years of respite after the torture in the cells beneath the castle ended, he never made me feel as if I were a burden.

Because of his unwavering support, I couldn't take this away from him. He'd given enough of himself, enough of his life, to me already.

"You've already sacrificed your childhood protecting me, Ian. I don't want to watch you give up your future, too."

He frowned, turning as he cupped my cheek, brushing his thumb along my face. "We were both lonely children and needed each other. Caring for my best friend wasn't a sacrifice. It never will be."

What could I say to make him hear me? Panic gripped me. He was so damn stubborn.

"The rumors are bad enough, you were handed your position because you're 'sleeping' with me, Ian. They'll doubt even more how hard you've worked, and I hate it," I said, touching his arm when he dropped his hands from my face.

Ian smiled down at me, shaking his head. "I don't care what any of them think. My duty to protect you extends to this as well, and unless there's someone worthy in the trials who captures your attention, then I'll win and that will be that."

I wrinkled my nose, growing agitated. "What about someone worthy of you?" I asked. "What if a few years into this you meet your mate?"

"My mate?" Ian burst into laughter. "You're the only person I know who even believes in mates anymore."

I glared at him, defensiveness welling inside me on top of the already-rising tide of desperation.

His gaze softened. "Mates haven't existed in thousands of years. Only a few Fae have ever come close to feeling that inexplicable pull of true love. Even the king and queen had an arranged marriage. Waiting for a mate would be a lonely existence."

Arguing with him would get me nowhere, so I had to go back to something more tangible.

"And what about not being unable to be Captain of the Guard and— "

Ian shoved off the ledge and walked away from me. "It's done, Lana. I've officially entered the trials. The conversation is over."

We rounded a corner to a split staircase, one leading down to the barracks, one up to the guest wing. I had to jog to catch up.

"You can't walk away from me, please don't do this," I shouted, perhaps a tad too loud.

Ian held up his hand and flung it back down, instantly looking defeated. "Let this go. There's nothing you can say to change it, and I won't keep arguing with you. We've fought enough."

He jogged down the steps, leaving me behind as I let out a defeated cry.

I grabbed the skirt of my dress, frustrated at how the layers slowed me down and jerked them to the side. Whirling around, I ran into a hardened chest, which seemingly materialized out of nowhere.

"Tits and daggers!" My hand flew to my mouth in fright, my heart pounding.

A deep chuckle vibrated through me as I stepped back.

"Hello, Little Rebel," Kade murmured, a devastatingly beautiful smile tugging at his lips.

My gaze met his, but I kept the shock of Kade using my pet name as the Hidden Henchman from my face. I refused to let on that he was right and somehow managed to maintain a straight face. "I'm sorry, you must have mistaken me for one of those other women you have conquered in your tours of Brookmere. If you'll excuse me, sir, I will be going."

I went to move around him, and he softly placed his hand on my shoulder.

"I didn't think you were one to lie," he said. "Although, your interest in my conquests is intriguing."

"In your dreams."

Kade moved closer to me, removing the space I'd created moments before. "I think after our dance, it's in *your* dreams." He stretched, making a big show of his height. "I was merely enjoying the view before retiring for the evening. It's been a busy night."

He strode past me and leaned against the windowpane, acting as if he had been doing it all along.

I should have walked away. Instead, I wanted to use the moment alone to learn why the hell he showed up tonight. After all, why would he willingly attempt to marry into the royal family, when he clearly despised us?

119

"Why did you enter the trials, Kade? Surely you can't be so desperate to find a woman. There were plenty who looked like they'd give you anything you wanted in the ballroom tonight for a mere dance. They'd do even more to be your wife."

His lips twitched as he studied me, eyes sparking with interest. "You noticed other women watching me? That almost sounds jealous."

"If you can get your arrogant head out of your ass, maybe you can answer the question," I retorted, undeterred.

He ran a hand over his jaw. "I think I'd look good in a crown," he said and shrugged. "Or maybe it's something else." A tingle down my arms kept me on edge. My eyes narrowed on the power exuding from him as I stood in his presence. The night seemed to adore him as much as the women in the ballroom. I'd have sworn the edges of darkness in the hall caressed his body.

"My reasons are my own, but probably somewhat similar to everyone else. Power, wealth"—He looked me up and down with a needy sort of desire—"all those benefits."

My cheeks heated, this time not only with my own desire as I struggled to maintain my composure. "Ah, yes, focused on power, even though it's my name which would grant it to you. Me, the daughter of the king you so vocally despised the last time we were together, claimed by you as a damn trophy." The absolute arrogance and his presumptuous nature of claiming me and this kingdom, akin to a piece of meat at the slaughterhouse, drove me mad.

"Claiming what's mine would be, in fact, one of the rewards, yes." He inched closer to me, and the tingling spread even further, enveloping me almost completely.

I swear, beating my body into submission to rid myself of the ridiculous way it responded to him needed to happen sooner rather than later.

I shifted, attempting to still the warmth coursing through

me at his presence. "I'd have to be willing, and you're far from getting *that* benefit," I spat back.

"And yet you're still here, talking to me." He shifted himself to block my escape down the hall toward my chambers.

I straightened. "I've had enough revelry for one evening and am retiring to my own room. As you recall, you had nothing to do with me coming out here."

"Yes, your little sidekick may have drawn you out here," he said. "But you're still standing here now because you're intrigued by me. I have that effect on people."

Kade grinned again, unable to wipe the smile fully from his face the entire time we talked, or fought, or whatever it was we were doing. He moved from the window, taking a step toward me, and reached out, gripping my chin, tilting it up to have a full view of my face.

My breathing grew sharp at his touch. "Men always think cockiness is sexy," I stated, pulling my chin from his grasp, but I didn't back down. I looked straight into his eyes, unyielding. "How wrong they are."

His gaze went to my lips, his mouth partly opened, and he stared momentarily before meeting my eyes again. "I'll enjoy taking my time making you fall to your knees before me, Little Rebel."

I shuddered, and not with disgust like I wanted to. He couldn't win this verbal spar. I brought my hands to his chest, letting them linger while trying to ignore the strength I felt beneath my touch.

"Don't you worry about my knees, Kade," I said. I stood on my tiptoes then, running my hand over his chest before wrapping it around the back of his neck. I pressed my body against his, trying to keep my wits about me. I'd have the last say here. My lips lightly brushed against his ear as I whispered, "The only thing falling will be you, onto my sword."

I took three paces back, confidently twirling my body before I threw him a wink over my shoulder. Then, I strutted up the stairs to get as far away from Kade Blackthorn as possible before I did something stupid.

Something like lingering in the dark corridor to see more of his damn sexy grin on his face as I left.

CHAPTER 12

My head jerked back with a firm tug.

"I swear your hair had animals burrowing in them." Kalliah sighed. "What did you do?"

She yanked the brush as I watched her attacking my normally straight, fine hair. I grinned at how her face contorted as she stared down a knot I hadn't been able to get out myself.

"Who's overreacting now?" I teased, wincing as Kalliah grew aggressive with the brush.

When she finally got the tangle free, she refused to let me do anything else to my own hair, slapping my hands away any time I moved them close to my head. I laughed because I knew this would annoy her and she knew I was doing it on purpose to make her mad.

"So, thoughts after the other night?" Kalliah asked, as she braided my hair with a small plait on each side, leaving the remainder down, meeting in a ponytail.

I sighed, looking at her through the mirror. "Well, I was surprised to find Hale come forward. It's been a year since I've seen him last. Perhaps at the celestial ball?"

"Ah, yes, the infamous celestial ball. He almost fell onto his face, tripping over himself after Andras caught the two of you making out in the rose gardens." Kalliah giggled.

"Do you *have* to remind me?" My cheeks heated, and I pouted, worse than a petulant child. "We were just getting started, too. Andras ruins all my fun."

Kalliah laughed a bit more. "Andras is a weasel, and a monster, but not the topic of *this* conversation. Hale wouldn't be too bad. Not great by any means, but not terrible. Who else?"

"Lord West is only interested in my chest, and Lord Thatcher seems overly attentive there, too. Those two need to go." Kalliah appeared as if she were ready to burst. I stared at her even harder. "What is that face for?"

"Frederich!" She snorted and cackled so much, the green ribbon she attempted to tie into my braids fell to the floor. "How is he *not* the first person we're talking about? His *mustache*! I've never seen anything like it."

"I thought if I didn't bring it up, perhaps it wouldn't be real? Awful doesn't even begin to describe it!" I tossed my hands in the air.

"Well, I wouldn't mind tempering the dreaded Frederich with Ryland Lockbane." Kalliah arched an eyebrow and made a low humming noise. "I witnessed him duel in the King's Challenge swordfight a few years ago," she said. "He was delicious then and seems to be even more so now."

I snorted. I'd overlooked Ryland while overwhelmed with some of the other things happening around me at the ball. However, I certainly did remember those piercing blue eyes now. "I didn't believe you thought *anyone* was delicious," I teased. "He is exceptionally beautiful to look at, I guess. He doesn't seem too bad."

"See," she said, squeezing my shoulder.

I swallowed a lump forming in my throat. "This is what my life is boiling down to? A battle of arrogant and boring bastards, a horrific mustache, and the boy I made out with randomly at balls to pass the time?"

"You have forgotten one in particular, haven't you?" Kalliah picked up the ribbon off the floor, and slowly lowered her head next to my own. "Kade?"

"What about Kade?" I tried to say as nonchalantly as possible.

"What do you mean 'what about Kade'?" she said mockingly. "That dance, wow." She shook her head, staring at me, wide-eyed. "I have never seen two people move together like that. You could practically feel the room buzzing with energy. He's already aware of your extracurricular activities and likely wouldn't stop you in the future. Clearly, he is the front-runner, right?"

"Oh, you would have the winner be a man who has no care for me at all? Because it's what he told me. He is here for his 'own reasons' and said he would look good in a crown," I said. "Besides, we don't know if he'd let my extracurricular activities continue. We don't know anything about him."

Kalliah glared at me even harder.

"What do you want me to say? Is he handsome? Yes. Is he cocky as hell? Yes. Did some sort of crazy sensation overtake me and make lust rule over logic and reason for a moment? Also, yes."

Kalliah finally finished lacing the ribbon around my hair. "He may be a contender if you get to know him beyond what you have witnessed from the Hidden Henchman."

"Kade didn't mince his words. He is only here for the crown. Seems as if he would be the last person to be a real contender. A man who already has so much power, only seeking more, is a danger to me and our kingdom."

She pursed her lips. "Well, don't forget Ian is with you. He wouldn't be the worst choice."

"I will *not* subject him to this nonsense," I snapped.

Kalliah held her hands up and backed away. It seemed as if she wanted to say more but refrained.

I picked up a light lip balm and rubbed it on. "All I envision is a life doomed for misery. These marriage trials are proving to be as horrible as I imagined, and they have only just begun."

With my mind made up, the trials were proving to be a waste. There would be no contender good enough for Brookmere. Not one.

You're a disgrace. The kingdom deserves better.

A tightening sensation gripped my chest as my cheeks flushed. The air grew hotter and stickier, weighing me down as I struggled to get a real breath in.

I pressed a hand to my cheek. Those weren't my words, they were his. The last thing I needed right now was to succumb to this belief clawing at me. A belief that I would never be good enough for Brookmere.

I am better than this.

I am Illiana Dresden. I am stronger than the darkness within me.

The first trial began in an hour, but I needed time to compose myself.

"I'm going outside for a few moments. I will meet you at the stadium."

I knew Kalliah noticed the panicked look in my eye, but she knew me well enough to give me space for a moment while I gathered myself.

The small balcony just past the window sitting area beckoned me, providing the perfect escape, if only for a moment. I let the cool crisp air fill my lungs. While freedom didn't exist for me, even outside the walls of the palace, at least I could view the natural beauty surrounding me.

I closed my eyes and basked in the blazing warmth of the sun on this spring day. A whisper of a breeze played in the soft tendrils of my hair. The roses in my garden were in full bloom and their sweet scent filled the air, mixing with all the other light floral notes blossoming around me.

Soon, soaring in the cloudless sky, a familiar hawk circled above, gliding through the air in an effortless beauty. How I wished I could be free from the confines of gravity and soar through the sky like Ian.

He materialized next to me on the balcony, landing and shifting smoothly. "I just wanted to check on you before the beginning of the trials."

"You know me too well. Anxious. Nervous. Enraged." I choked, holding onto the edge of the balcony for strength.

"Everything will be okay, Lan. You know I will not let you down."

We stared at each other in silence for a moment, an uncertain feeling passing between us.

A small smile graced Ian's face. "I'll see you soon," he said and moved to shift.

"Ian, wait!" I fidgeted with layers of my dress, covering my dagger, before looking him in the eyes. "Please be careful today. You're not Brookmere's Captain of the Royal Guard right now, you are one of my best friends... one of my only friends. Even if we are fighting." A tear threatened to escape.

"I'll be fine. Careful as ever." Ian offered me a quick hug, kissing the top of my head before he backed up, running toward the edge of the balcony and shifting once more to prepare for his role in the marriage trials.

A contender.

In a competition with only the Fates knowing what's in store.

The garden was quiet, no strange sounds or stirrings. I was alone, a rarity. Not followed by guards, Ian, Kalliah, or anyone. I breathed in deeply.

My mind allowed only a second of peace before my thoughts shifted back to the marriage trials and that damn prophecy.

A prophecy I didn't even believe in. Straight from a woman more befuddled than the village drunks. How could what she said hold so much influence over my father? Her words were revered as if they were law.

The sound of my father's voice played in my head. He'd repeated the prophecy a thousand times in my life. On occasion, I crept to his private dining room and overheard him talking it over with my mother. Over and over, they thought about it, using it to define my entire life.

Void of magic, a heroine born,
Destiny calls, though faint and torn.
Many will come from across the land,
Yet only the strongest will win her hand.
With lover's touch, she shall ignite,
Without it, perish from the kingdom's blight.

I refused to believe the only pathway to the prophecy coming to fruition meant I had to endure such ridiculousness as the marriage trials. There had to be another solution.

It doesn't matter.

What's done is done.

Right or wrong, the Fates had spoken. I resigned myself to gathering my wits about me and setting my mind right for the afternoon to come.

I adjusted the dagger on my thigh. It brought a small comfort, knowing I could protect myself should something, or someone, get too close. Marriage trials be damned, I wouldn't be defenseless.

I exited the balcony and returned to my room, glancing in the mirror to ensure nothing had fallen out of place. I gave the mirror my practiced, fake smile as I gathered my confidence.

My father waited for me in the king's study. Per his

request, I had to meet him there so we could enter the trial arena together.

A trial arena which hadn't existed a few days prior.

"Lana, my dear," he said. "You're a vision before me."

I dipped into a curtsy and crossed the room, allowing him to wrap me in a hug. A hug I so desperately needed from my father. A hug of love, because even though he condemned me to this marriage, I knew he had done so from the goodness of his heart, for his kingdom. Our people.

He'd done all of this for me, too. The last line of the prophecy caused him pain the few times I'd caught him discussing it.

Without it perish from kingdom's blight.

In that regard, since he believed the prophecy, it made sense he kept me from the darkness, and why he wanted the trials. Although my irritation remained constant, with the prophecy promising something to ignite inside of me if I had love, I couldn't blame him for interpreting things how he did.

Despite my reservations, he and my mother had always been overprotective, ensuring my safety.

The only time they hadn't…

No. Not today.

I wouldn't think about my past today. What powers kept the truth from their minds for all these years? I had left the torture behind me, even if the monster who'd inflicted it still roamed the castle halls.

"Are you ready? he asked gently, pulling back and taking my hands in his.

"Will you be upset with me if I say no?" I said softly.

He cupped my cheek. "Being a father and a king is something I never thought I'd have," he said, his kind eyes tearing, and I softened toward him, meeting his gaze.

"None of them will be good enough for you, my heart, but perhaps at least one will prove themselves worthy of ruling this kingdom at your side."

His skin appeared dull, and I cursed the Fates for his sickness. This thing, this disease, unnaturally aging him, despite the best healers working on him.

Even with whatever ravaged his body, he looked at me as if I made it all worth it. In this moment, as he opened up to me, it was enough to give me the strength I needed to walk out to the arena with my chin held high.

"I'll make you proud, Father," I said, the picture of confidence, despite the acid rising up my throat.

He moved to my side. "You always have. I know you think this is the end, but please try to keep an open mind to the possibilities which await you. May nature guide you through these trials and bless your heart for future prosperity."

I laughed. "You are starting to sound like Vivienne, you old Fae."

He wasn't laughing. "Vivienne may seem strange. I know I would be, with words from the Fates constantly spouting in my head. But never forget, without her, the prophecy and perhaps your fate, will never come to be."

"Apologies, Father," I said. I would never need the reminder of who bore the responsibility of bringing this prophecy to life.

"Now," He patted his purple velvet robes to smooth everything down and settle his garment into place, "let's go meet our loyal subjects and begin." Despite his illness over the past few months, he had an unmistakable gleam in his eye as he led me by the hand, exiting his study.

Hand in hand, we walked down the halls and out toward the trials, his guards five paces behind us at all times.

We used one of the royal exits to the large backyard gardens before ascending a set of stairs to the back of the royal pavilion. We arrived with moments to spare.

"Darling, you almost missed the starting bells," my mother said, greeting us.

"As King, am I ever late, dearest?"

She laughed, swatting at his arm before she kissed my cheek.

The large royal pavilion allowed twenty people to mingle and sit comfortably. White-and black-streaked marble covered the floors and pillars. Sweeping curtains of vines and wildflowers formed a canopy above, while additional flowers and vines cascaded downward from the circular ceiling. With a flick of my father's wrist, the vines parted before us.

I gasped, observing the newly crafted arena. Earth Fae had worked for several days to create a colosseum made entirely of hedges instead of stone. Behind the circular-lined field, rows and rows of seats stacked high, accommodated the hundreds of Fae attending these events.

It was breathtaking. A marvel to have been magically constructed in such a brief time.

The king moved to the front of the pavilion, my mother entering from the side, taking a seat upon her throne. Vivienne stood at the foot of the queen's throne. The crowd bowed and curtsied as one, a hush falling over them as they witnessed me emerge with the king.

His smile grew as he gazed upon our people. All our kingdom adored the king. The reverence freely given to him was from love, not fear.

My gaze shifted toward the center of the arena where the contenders lined up before the pavilion, each on bended knee. They were dressed to impress, with their finest attire from each of their villages. Colorful robes, suits, and leathers adorned their bodies. None of them knew what adventures lay ahead. Neither did I, actually.

"Rise, my loyal subjects." My father commanded the air to amplify his voice throughout the massive arena for all to hear. As one, they all rose. "Welcome to this blessed day. The Fates have allowed us to come and begin the marriage trials for my daughter, the Crown Princess, Illiana Dresden."

There would be no turning back now. My marriage trials had officially begun.

CHAPTER 13

Despite the uncomfortable pit growing in my stomach, I moved to stand at my father's side. I offered a small wave of my hand, with a perfectly practiced smile upon my face to all those in the stands.

"Princess Illiana, before you are a group of eight contenders. Eight Fae, who believe they are up for the challenge to be the future King of Brookmere, and more importantly, your husband." His voice boomed across the vast arena, echoing even beyond the spectator stands and into the distance. The eye of every subject present homed in on my father, and myself.

"Contenders, you are here to prove yourself worthy of my daughter's hand in marriage, and with that, worthy to hold the title of 'King.' You will be required to complete three tasks over the next few weeks. You will not only have to prove the strength and agility of your body, but also the power of your mind, the fierceness of your heart, and the fortitude of your compassion for this land and its people.

"If you should fail any challenge, you will be eliminated from the competition. In each trial, the contender who comes last will also be eliminated. In the third and final trial." He paused, a smile blooming upon his face. "Princess Illiana will select her future husband from the top three contenders."

The king cleared his throat, pausing and shifting his head slightly as he stared each competitor in the eye. The silence was deafening as everyone waited for him to continue. Although as Fae we had immensely long lives, there weren't many remaining in the kingdom who witnessed the last marriage trials.

"The rules of the marriage trials are simple. Complete the tasks at hand and move forward through each level. Outside of the trials in the down time, you will behave like gentlemen and not attempt to thwart any other contender. Should I learn of such behavior, you will be immediately removed from the competition. Additionally, you will make no attempts to woo or detain Princess Illiana against her will. Predetermined times and places will be provided for conversations with the princess. Again, should I find you have sought her out against her wishes—" He stopped, his lip twitching. "Well, you wouldn't want to know what will happen." The king's jovial tone had turned to ice, allowing all of those present to grasp the seriousness of his command before continuing.

"Today's trial is all about the mind. You will have to complete three tasks to pass this first challenge. The first will test your ability for strategy. The second task will test your knowledge and fortitude. The final task will test your deductive and strategic reasoning. The top three contenders after today's competition will be given a reward."

Murmurs sounded throughout the crowd, anticipation and excitement growing with the start of the trials so close. "The reward will be drinks with Princess Illiana this evening, following dinner."

A cheer rang out through the stands, our people roaring their approval.

At his final comment, my gaze darted in my father's direction. He had not prepared me for this. I had convinced myself I only needed to be present for the trials themselves. However, after his heartfelt speech, I realized the trials would be ongoing, not just contained to the challenges themselves.

"Contenders, are you ready?" my father shouted.

The men on the field varied their return acknowledgments. Ian bowed his head, the Lords shouted with fists in the air. Kade caught me peering in his direction, and a devious-looking smirk formed on his face as he ran his hand through his black hair.

I wonder if his arrogance keeps his hair perfectly coiffed, or if it takes time to pretend he's naturally flawless.

Because he was, unfortunately, flawless.

"To your positions, please," the king shouted, moving from the dais.

"You enjoyed yourself far too much, my dear," the queen said behind her gloved hand.

My father winked at her, taking his place in front of his throne.

The eight contenders walked toward the center of the massive circular arena, where eight tables were lined in a long row, one for each contestant. Even from our vantage point, I couldn't be certain what the first task would be.

As the king spoke again, Vivienne appeared at his side. She placed her hand gently upon his arm, nodding toward the crowd in a silent request. Her wiry hair lay tamer today than when I encountered her in the hallway at the opening ball.

Today, she wore robes of this century as well, and her eyes were sharper than they usually appeared.

Vivienne, unable to command her voice like the king, spoke as loudly as she could. My father directed the winds to carry her voice to the uppermost areas of the arena stands. "Strength of men are mighty and bold, but what's in is out and out is in, for only one can sweep a fair maiden under her chin. Be bold you men of here and there, minds can trick, and

135

flop, and flee, steady now for the kingdom's heart takes more than one victory."

Vivienne cackled as she raised her arms above her head, aiming them high into the sky. A wide grin blossomed across her face as she basked in the sunlight above. The only sound at the end of her rambling was the rustling of the wind.

My parents respected the Seer, and all of the people throughout Brookmere had learned to heed what Seers heard from the Fates. Right now, though? Right now, every gaze focused on Vivienne, unsettled. Everyone stared blankly, clearly unaware how to respond.

My father bowed his head to her, and then started clapping, the audience quickly followed suit. Vivienne returned the gesture and went back to my mother's side, silent once more.

"Thank you, Vivienne, for those profound words," the king said. "May nature guide you and bless these lands."

Nervously, I balled my hands into fists, clenching my skirt. It was time.

"Dearest, you'll announce 'Begin' when you're ready," he whispered to me.

Would I ever be ready? Never.

I refused to expose my insecurities here, though. I strode to the front of the thrones, staring down at the field. There was nothing to do but watch the trials unfold. Before I could second-guess myself, I inhaled sharply.

"Begin!"

A less-ornate, gold-trimmed chair sat adjacent to my father's throne. My chair.

From it, I had a perfect view of the arena below. The contenders had a scroll before them, with instructions they were furiously reviewing. Although untimed, the last to finish would be declared the loser and be ejected from the trials.

All at once, ten dice appeared on each contender's table, along with five cards. Ian grasped the dice, giving them a quick roll immediately, all with a widening smile on his face. He *would* be smiling. He may have recognized the task before I had, but only moments sooner. How could I not recognize it when Ian spent our entire childhood constantly beating me at the game?

I turned to my father, eyes blazing. "You are having these men fight for my hand, to be my husband, and the King of Brookmere with a game I played as a child?"

Blinking slowly, I caught the disrespect flying from my tongue, seconds too late, especially in such a public place. Closing my lids momentarily, I tried to school my features, aware our world studied our every move.

The king reached for my hand, a performance for those whose eyes were still upon us. He kept his gaze straight ahead as he held my hand. His voice amplified once more, ringing through the arena.

"The first task is a game of Chance & Destiny." He sat back, leaning toward me, still clasping my hand in his. "How many times did you play Chance & Destiny and not end up in tears?"

My mouth shut instantly. As a child, I *always* ended up in tears after the game, easily frustrated with losing.

"How many times did you want to stop and never pick up those dice again?"

Too many to count.

"You see, Illiana, Chance & Destiny, is not just a children's game. It is a game of strategy, yes, but it reveals much more. It is the long game one must play in order to win. Someone who can win Chance & Destiny has the strength and fortitude to know when to take and when to give. For you cannot win without making sacrifices. Some work out, some don't." My father looked me in the eye, waiting patiently for my understanding.

"When they do not work out, how will the player react? When they are not beating the others, will they give up? Will they stay strong and try again? Our future King, your husband, cannot win without making sacrifices, regardless of where those sacrifices may lead. Hopefully, their choices will lead to the greater good. Ideally, the sacrifices and strategy will lead to the prosperity of our people. If not, they must continue to rise. So, while you may see this as petty and insignificant, please have faith in me that I have chosen tasks to find you a worthy husband and ruler of our lands."

I slipped my hand from his and placed it on my lap, nestled amongst the soft velvet fabric of my dress. Shame washed over me as it had when I was a little girl. No one wished to be scolded by their parents, but even less when your parent was a king. A king who had the foresight you could only dream of most days, even when infuriating.

"Pay attention and see what the contenders reveal about themselves as they play," he said with a knowing grin.

My gaze shifted back to the field below me. I needed to pay attention to see what they were doing, the strategies they were choosing, but, more importantly, who came out winning.

I snorted the moment I scanned the tables. Ian held the lead. He had secured two out of the five necessary trade cards, and seven of the nine necessary dice rolls. He only needed a few rolls to win and move onto the next task. He couldn't keep the grin from his face, and neither could I. His damn victory smile had been thrown my way more times than I cared to count.

Frederich and Hale were not too far behind Ian. They had four of their dice secured, and two of the trade cards. If they played their hands right, they could catch up quickly.

Kade seemed to be struggling with the dice, but instead, had secured all of the trade cards. Lord Thatcher appeared to be lost, while Lord West growled and muttered to himself, clearly having trouble with both dice and cards. Neither were handling this well. Every so often, the contenders would survey each other's progress in an attempt to catch up.

Ryland had secured one trade card and one dice but didn't seem deterred or frustrated in the least. In fact, I caught quite a few spectators cheering for him while he waved a hand, smiling, but remained focused.

The last contender, Edmund Fairweather, seemed to be less pleased with his struggle, even though he held the same number of dice and cards as Ryland. His features contorted with apparent frustration.

Clearly not everyone played Chance & Destiny as much as I had as a child.

The minutes dragged on as the stadium cheered occasionally, waiting for the first task to be completed. The sun crested to a peak in the sky. My father maintained a slight breeze moving through the pavilion to cool the air around us, as the warmth from the sun heated the nature-made arena.

Beads of sweat glistened from the poorer folks in the stands who stood in the back, not wealthy or connected enough to have garnered a seat and whose magic had to be reserved for every task. The division of magic had become more and more obvious the older I became. At first, I hadn't noticed much, content in my childhood bubble inside the castle.

It would be impossible to remain ignorant of the struggles of Fae with lesser magic, especially after noticing the hesitation women in court had accepting Kalliah, when I named her my head lady-in-waiting. Guilt lashed through me like a whip. I didn't have magic, and I knew I would be treated even worse than the lesser Fae if I'd have been born anywhere other than the royal house. There were even noble houses who had banished children who couldn't produce enough magic. Yet, here I sat, raised above those with more magic in their little finger than I possessed in my entire body.

My attention returned to the stands. While those with lesser magic were sweating, the stronger Fae manipulated the air and temperature around them. Several in the stands created their own shade by growing vines to block the sun's unrelenting glare in the cloudless sky above.

A slap of wood jolted me back into the present moment. My lip curled in disgust. Somehow Frederich had won the game. He quickly ran across the arena toward the second task.

Another slap of wood sounded before Frederich reached the next table. Ian had finished as well, sprinting forward and starting right behind Frederich as they began the next task.

The second task took place in a shadier part of the arena, the height of the stands blocking the sun from the field below. A small wooden table for each contender held four chalices of varying shapes and sizes, with eight archways just beyond the row of tables. The archways were each surrounded by flowers and beautiful twined vines outlining a door within. A thick bush spanning across the arena, going through each of their personal doors, provided the only option for each contender to pass to the third task.

"The second task has begun for some," the king announced. "Contender's Choice will have each of them selecting a cup to drink from. However, not all are safe, and only one will get them through the door ahead."

Cheering erupted from the crowd, along with a few shouts of surprise.

We were all learning about the trials in real time. I sat straighter in my seat, watching Ian study each chalice. Surely it couldn't be anything dangerous.

"Father?" I probed.

He volunteered a small smile. "One cup will let them pass through the door. One is poisoned with a itch-inducing potion that will render them incapable of continuing. One does nothing. And one..." He cleared his throat. "One is dangerously poisoned, paralyzing the body completely."

I gulped.

"With their Fae abilities, they should be able to heal with the help of Elisabeth by the end of the day."

He seemed completely unaffected by the prospect of serious injury, in what I thought were mere trials for entertainment.

A shiver raced along my arms.

Additional slaps of wood made me jump, looking back to the arena and to the contenders still on task one. Lord Casimir, Kade, Hale, and Ryland had all managed to pass and were quickly racing to their potion stations.

Edmund and Lord Thatcher were still sorting through their dice and cards, frustration evident in their expressions. Their brows were furrowed in apparent discontent at being bested by a game of Chance & Destiny. A few more moments, and Edmund slapped the wood beside him and proceeded to his potions table.

The anger boiling over from Lord Thatcher was palpable, even from afar, as he finished the game last.

Back at the potion's tables, my gaze furiously darted between the contenders, studying the various chalices of liquids. Keeping up with the contenders, and where they were in their tasks, proved difficult.

My father coughed a few times, attempting to hide the noise since we were in public.

Before I could reach him, Andras's grating, nasally voice sounded from behind my father's throne. "Your Majesty."

I peered over my shoulder to find Andras hunched close to my father's ear, and he discreetly handed him a small vial. He whispered quietly enough so I couldn't hear anything he said. My father dumped the vial into his mouth. His composed face darkened, and he stilled, turning to face Andras.

"It is happening again?" the king asked a little too loudly.

Though my gaze remained on the field, I desperately tried to eavesdrop on what had caused my father obvious fear. The second either of the two men knew I attempted to listen in on them, the conversation would cease.

"Yes, my King," Andras said quietly. "The village of

Demarva has been overrun again. We must send more troops now in order to quell the unrest."

Normally, I never heard these kinds of conversations. My father and his advisers were so careful when they spoke of the darkness, ensuring I remained far enough away so I couldn't overhear them. Whatever happened rattled the king to the point where he forgot I sat a few feet away. I had to take advantage of the opportunity when it presented itself.

"More troops at this rate could leave us vulnerable to—"

I leaned sideways, as their voices lowered to an almost undetectable volume.

My father rotated to look at me, so I quickly scanned the stands, giving the onlookers a loving smile and waved at a few, only to prove my thoughts preoccupied. They didn't start speaking again and I continued my crowd gazing.

Wait. What?

As my eyes passed over the men and women on the east side of the arena, I paused, narrowing them. A Fae, largely resembling Storm, sat in the front row of the stands. His gaze stood fixed on the contenders in the arena below. Apparently, Storm and Kade appeared as inseparable as me and Ian.

"No more than twenty, my King," Andras muttered.

Straining, I shifted toward them, stretching, trying to be inconspicuous with my eavesdropping. Suddenly, a howl of pain startled me, echoing from the field.

I fell off my chair, sideways.

"Lana!" my father called.

But my head jerked toward the arena, where the scream had sounded, as I quickly picked myself up and sat back on my chair. "No," I whispered, dread clawing through my body while trying to discern what had occurred below us.

Then, another scream sounded from the crowd, followed by shouts of fear.

Our entire pavilion's undivided attention had shifted to the arena.

CHAPTER 14

All discussions of troops and unrest paused as the king and Andras witnessed the commotion in the arena.

Lord Levi Thatcher lay on the ground, foam bubbling from the corner of his lips as his body convulsed on the ground. The veins in his face turned red as he gasped, desperate for air.

Lord Thatcher hailed from one of the stronger magical lines in Brookmere. I wondered how long it would take for his powerful magic to heal him. Would he be able to finish in time? Elisabeth should be nearby if he couldn't heal himself. I didn't care too much if he didn't finish the first trial. He had been uptight, slimy, and I could still feel his overly wet lips upon my hand before our dance.

But his actions did *not* warrant my wanting him poisoned. Or worse, dead.

The other contenders hesitated, frozen in place until the crowd's fright quieted. Though Lord Thatcher hadn't recovered, the others seemed to understand the contest continued despite the downed man.

Ian had pushed two of the four chalices to the side, removing them as options. Kade had done the same, catching up quickly to surpass some of the others who had edged him out in the strategy game.

Frederich's gaze darted toward Ian's table, then Kade's, as if he were trying to decipher what moves they were making. Almost too quickly, he appeared triumphant and made his final decision, tipping the chalice back, consuming the liquid in one gulp.

A few droplets caught on his massive mustache, which he wiped away with the back of his hand, as if he sat in a tavern instead of competing to be King. Victory was his for this round, and as he stood before the wooden door, it swung open for him.

Ian and Kade made their final decisions within breaths of each other and locked eyes as they, too, drank their chosen liquids. Both of their doors opened simultaneously.

Edmund fell to the ground, but not paralyzed like Lord Thatcher. Instead, he scratched his body as though bugs crawled atop his skin. I shivered, watching him flip over, rubbing his back along the grass.

Elisabeth finally darted onto the field, hovering over Lord Thatcher.

Ryland passed through his door, and Hale followed.

Andras resumed his conversation with my father. "What are your orders, my King?"

"Send the fifth Calvary to Demarva with instructions to return in a fortnight. I'm tired of so few of our soldiers returning."

"As you wish it, my King." Andras's oversized cloaks rustled around him as he bowed. His footsteps were hurried as they echoed from the pavilion.

Why weren't our soldiers returning from their missions? Did he ever plan on telling me about the anguish of our people? In some ways, I may be grateful for the trials as they allowed me to be present when he received troubling news. News he'd done his best to keep from me.

Down on the field, the only contenders remaining in Round Two were Edmund and Lord Thatcher. Edmund had a healer by his side, and he rose on unsteady legs. The crowd cheered, and he grabbed a chalice, tossing it back with more confidence than I could have mustered after having just been poisoned.

He staggered through his door, leaving Lord Thatcher behind as additional healers continued to treat him.

After a few more moments, they dragged him from the arena. The crowd's gaze was split between watching Lord Thatcher being taken to healing quarters, and the rest of the trial.

The remaining contenders were standing in front of more tables beyond the nature-made fence line, which held their doors. Each had a scroll laid out before them, as well as a quill next to it. Whatever they had come to, required them to give some sort of answer in order to complete the trial.

The king cleared his throat to get my attention and nonchalantly held up his own scroll as I furiously tried to keep up with the activities below.

"Can you figure it out? As our future Queen, you, too, will need to possess these same powers of deduction," he explained. "While you will become Queen without passing the trials, what kind of Queen shall you be?"

The king had a copy of the contenders' scroll. He cocked an eyebrow at me, ready to play another one of our games.

I gently lifted the scroll from his hand, unrolling it slowly. My heart pounded. I did not realize I would need to pass my own trial as well. Although maybe not as serious as my future husbands in the arena, this still meant something to me as my father wanted to see what I would do with this challenge.

I stared at the text.

I am your greatest friend and worst enemy,
Causing growth and destruction intertwined in every moment.

You are my greatest worshipper, and I am your greatest curse.
Fear some, fear naught, fear all,
For my beginning has no end and my end has no beginning.
In the darkest of moments, I consume you.
In the lightest of moments, I shine around you.
Amongst the greatest of warriors and poorest of paupers,
I treat all the same.
What am I?

Well, Fates above.

I hated riddles. Almost as much as I hated prophecies.

I read the scroll again, pausing after every line, determined not to disappoint my father. I wanted to be a queen he would be proud of.

Sweat formed on my back, my dress growing damp, as I continued to decipher the riddle, my heart beating harder and faster. I wanted to defeat the contenders on the field. If only I could compete and win my own hand.

I glanced down at the arena as the contenders hunched over the tables, attempting to figure out the riddle. My gaze shifted to the loyal subjects of Brookmere, waiting in anticipation of so much more than just a few trials. The air hung around us, heavy with suspense. The kingdom held their breath, watching and waiting, as we went through steps to learn what kind of king would lead them at their Queen's side. A breeze rustled through the arena, and the swaying wildflower fields surrounding the outskirts of the stadium caught my attention.

I closed my eyes and breathed in the sweet floral scent the wind carried. I let the air envelope my body as I searched within for the answer. Allowing myself to become one with the beauty surrounding me, I recited the phrase of our people—*May nature guide you.*

My eyes bolted open, the answer as clear as the sky above.

Triumphantly, I turned to the king, as I rolled up the scroll and handed it to him. My mother practically buzzed with excitement. Her fingers clasped together tightly on her lap. I allowed my eyes to lock with my father's. They blazed with excitement, a smile forming as he grasped the end of the scroll. I didn't let go.

"You may best me more than I best you, Father, but you'll have to try harder." I smirked. "A mighty Queen I shall be when the time comes, but until then, may *nature* guide you, my King."

Our eyes stayed connected as his smile widened. A slight nod of his head. "A mighty Queen you shall be my daughter."

Father -65, Lana -4.

Swiveling on my seat, quite pleased with myself, my attention returned to the trials below. Ian scribbled his answer on the scroll, and as he set down the quill, it floated upon a gust of wind to my father's hand.

A small nod is all he gave before one of the aides whisked Ian away. They strode toward an empty holding area on the outer curve of the arena.

Edmund rubbed his neck, putting his head in his hands for a moment, and I wondered if he still worked on overcoming the potion he'd consumed.

Frederich wrote his answer next, and similarly to Ian, took his place in a holding area after an acknowledgment from my father.

How could that man have finished second? I shivered.

Another movement of my father's head, and I noticed Kade on the receiving end. My pulse quickened, surprised at the flutter of knowing he came in third. I quashed it as quickly as I could and forced myself to not even pay attention to his entry to the holding area.

While the top three were now accounted for, the remaining five contenders were still furiously working to not come in last place. Nobody wanted to be eliminated during the first trial.

Lord West, Hale, and Ryland all completed the final task and were led to the same holding area with the others.

Edmund stumbled toward the holding area last, not led by anyone after getting the nod he answered correctly.

The first trial was complete.

"Lord Levi Thatcher is recuperating in the hospital wing from the poison ingested. While his efforts were valiant, it is not enough to secure my daughter's hand in marriage and be the future king of these lands. He will return to his town with honor and the kingdom's thanks for his loyalty and devotion to the crown." The king touched his heart as he bowed his head. "May nature guide him and bless his lands in his future endeavors."

The seven remaining contenders filed back into the main area and stood proudly before the pavilion. Edmund swayed, still sweating slightly, but at least he remained on his feet.

The king held his arms out wide. "Gentlemen! Congratulations on completing the first of three contests. You have proven your mind and fortitude are strong. Tonight, we shall celebrate your victories and movement forward in the marriage trials."

Addressing the crowd below us, the king grinned. "We thank all of you for supporting these victorious contenders. We look forward to seeing everyone again in a fortnight for trial number two."

Clapping and cheering sounded in a wave across the arena. The people of this kingdom were excited for more. The king raised his hand, and his loyal subjects began exiting their seats and the stands.

The king, queen, and I walked to the edge of the pavilion. The king now spoke solely for the contenders to hear.

"Tonight, each of you shall dine in my private dining room, with some of my most loyal advisers," he said. "After our dinner together, our top three, Captain Ian Stronholm, Frederich Hanslet, and Kade Blackthorn, will have dessert and drinks with Princess Illiana on the royal garden terrace. We shall see you at seven."

I caught Ian's eye before I left the pavilion and flashed him a smile. I still hated that he had entered, but I could be proud of him, nevertheless.

Frederich's eyes narrowed on me, but I refused to give him a lingering moment.

After all, now came the part where I actually had to interact with each of these men instead of watching from afar.

This dinner wouldn't be over soon enough. Unless, of course, I had the opportunity to hear more of what mysteries were evolving within the kingdom.

Suddenly, it seemed as though life breathed into me again. If I were to be forced into these trials, at least I could use them to my advantage. Learning the truth about the kingdom I thought I knew would be worth sitting through a few uncomfortable dinners.

And more.

CHAPTER 15

Outside my open window, the loud screech of a hawk cried in three short clips.

I dropped the brush in my hand, rushing onto the balcony, my hair flying behind me, since I hadn't yet had a chance to braid it into a crown atop my head for this evening's festivities.

Down the stone steps, I kept my feet light so as to not make any noise and draw unnecessary attention from passing guards. Once my path was clear, I disappeared behind the hedges of safety in my private garden for the second time today.

With Kalliah, and many other staff pulling double duties, my afternoon became overtaken with getting myself ready for dinner alone. Unfortunately, I'd lost track of time. Meaning I wasn't certain where the guards were in rotation and how much time I had before their next round around the garden.

This meeting would have to be quick, but I knew something must be urgent for Ian to come here instead of just talking to me at dinner. Besides, after today's events, I needed to stop fighting with him. Differences of opinions aside, the knowledge that he could get hurt in the trials outweighed my anger.

Ian waited amongst the hedges. "Are you all right?" I asked.

"Yes, I'm fine. The trials are harder than I expected. I did have to laugh at the game of Chance & Destiny, though. Your father knows you too well." He chuckled.

"I didn't realize the risk involved." I wanted to remind him he shouldn't be taking on the trials, but after observing Lord Thatcher poisoned today, I refused to continue pointing out my thoughts of his competing for my hand.

"Ian," I began again. "I'll never agree you should have entered the trials, but I understand it. I don't want to fight. I don't want the strain between us anymore." I launched at him, throwing my arms around him in a hug before he could respond.

"Agreed, no more fighting." Removing himself from my grasp, he met my gaze. "Now, what are we going to do about Kade being in the trials *and* being in the top three? How do you feel about it?"

I bit my lip. I hadn't told Ian about my run-in with Kade after the opening ball.

"Honestly?" I huffed. "I don't know. But..." I hesitated, knowing Ian well enough that he would lose it when he found out the one thing the hallway conversation with Kade did reveal.

"Lan?" Ian frowned.

Kade, now aware of our secret, made him a liability. Big time.

"Kade knows I'm the Hidden Henchman," I admitted.

Ian's gaze darkened. "What?"

"He recognized me somehow—well, recognized my unique style of cursing."

It was a good thing Ian and I were best friends because the

hardened stare he leveled me with intimidated the hell out of me.

"I saw Storm at the trials today, too, so they're sticking close to each other," I continued. "In the few days since the ball, he hasn't said a word. Nor has he asked anything of us. For now, he's keeping the secret to himself."

"Until he wants something like, oh, I don't know, the damn crown." Ian seethed. He rubbed his forehead, then ran a hand through his shoulder-length blond hair, still loose from the trials earlier today. "At least I'll be able to keep an eye on him," Ian muttered. "He doesn't know me."

"Actually," I said, "he picked up on it pretty quickly."

Ian pursed his lips. "Anything else you wish to tell me?"

I shook my head frantically. "I think that about covers it." I offered a smile, hopefully to placate the rage I sensed bubbling beneath Ian's skin.

"I am moving into the contenders' suites as soon as we're done here. I'm to remain there for the duration of the trials. As soon as I left the arena, Andras cornered me to inform me of the decision. They want all of the contenders in one spot."

I nodded as he continued. Ian rarely stayed in his bedroom, so I didn't think it mattered where he actually slept, or he would have put up a bigger fight.

"As far as we know, he doesn't know I can shift, I can follow him in the air if need be." Ian's sly grin spread across his face. "We haven't lost all the elements of surprise yet."

"If anyone can get to the bottom of who they are, it's you." I bit my lip in a nervous habit. "You think you'll still be able to get away to do the drops? We need to figure out the one we didn't get to earlier with Leif and Corbin."

Ian nodded. "Shouldn't be an issue. I'm still your guard with plenty of reasons to come here. We're good."

"Good" might be a stretch, but I didn't push.

"I should go before I'm missed," he said.

Nodding in agreement, I backed away, letting him shift and fly off before taking the stairs back to my chambers. Getting ready alone meant I'd need every last available minute to prepare for tonight's ball. My skill with a sword far exceeded my skill in styling my hair or applying makeup. With Kade and his friend suddenly far too engrossed in our lives, I'd need to be even more vigilant than before. Both my Hidden Henchman mask, and the mask of a perfect princess would need to be flawless to keep up with whatever Fate decided to allow next.

I shivered once, fidgeting with the bracelet around my wrist as I stood in front of the dining hall doors. The silky golden dress I chose for tonight's dinner caressed my skin reassuringly, akin to an old friend, I couldn't delay the inevitable any longer. I, Illiana Dresden, could survive a simple dinner.

Smoothing my hands over my dress, I steadied my nerves and pulled the door open. Those inside rose to their feet as I passed.

"Princess Illiana," my father said from his head table. He rose with everyone else, arms opened wide. "Welcome."

I walked down the length of the long, classically draped table, filled with contenders, and made my way toward my father. Candles flickered amongst the vases of wildflowers lining the center of the table. He stood at the end of a slightly raised platform holding the king's head table, consisting of my mother, Andras, Vivienne, and a few other trusted royal advisers.

Normally, I stood alongside them, which made me uncomfortable on the best of days. The elevated head table gave the perception that those on the dais watched a show, or on some of the worst days, it seemed as if the crowds were observing us as if we were fancy animals on display. It put my honed acting skills of being a powerful princess to good use, I supposed.

Regardless, a part of me burst with happiness to sit amongst the crowd itself tonight. A small reprieve from the necessities of royal advisers and protocol, even if it meant being surrounded by contenders for the crown.

The king made his way around the table and met me at the edge, leaning down to press a kiss to my cheek. Standing straight once more, he returned to his throne behind the table. I shifted on my feet, standing idly before the group of contenders, Lord Thatcher noticeably missing from the table.

Hopefully, he recovered quickly.

A loud cough drew my attention to the king. "Tonight, we dine and celebrate the completion of the first trial." His gaze shifted to me. "My dear, this is a chance for you to interact with these fine contenders. Please move between the open seats at the table throughout the meal to meet once more with those vying for your hand."

I inclined my head and immediately proceeded to the open seat next to Ian, near the end of the table. My father let out an amused hum, as if he knew where I would sit first.

Staff were already assembled around the table, ready to place our first course the moment I sat. Aware the room's eyes were still on me, I bowed my head. "Captain Stronholm, gentlemen, congratulations on your advancement to the second task," I said genuinely.

Hale sat to my right with Ryland across from me. Both immediately began to eat their vegetable soup, a personal favorite of mine, the moment their food lay before them. I nodded to my father once in appreciation for including my comfort food, which he returned with a quick wink.

I politely took small bites and engaged in conversation with Ryland. He asked me about my hobbies, and I explained how Ian taught me how to spar. Future husband or not, I would continue my training in the future. I refused to let these trials, or any of these men dictate all aspects of my life. Marriage would not take away my autonomy. However, not to seem overeager, I quickly changed the topic and asked him about his family origins. He didn't have any trouble rattling on about his sisters and family back home in Broham, and their annual trips to the cliffs amongst the islands. I took note of it positively as I sipped the rich broth. The carrots were still slightly crunchy, just how I liked it.

Ian despised vegetable soup. He took a few bites before setting his spoon on the soup saucer, indicating his completion.

"Princess Illiana, how is your soup tonight? I know how much you enjoy this rabbit food," Ian joked.

"Perfect as always. If you were smarter, you would eat your daily allotment of vegetables like the rest of us," I quipped in retort.

"I seem to recall you eating all the vegetable soup before one of the adviser appointment balls," Hale chimed in with a small laugh.

My anxiety soothed slightly at the ease in which he joined the conversation. It reminded me why he'd been a comfortable companion all the years I needed a friend amongst the nobility.

"I regret nothing. My actions merely taught everyone to double the order from then on. I did the kingdom a favor." I grinned at Hale.

Gratefulness settled over my heart at the easy conversation. I'd have to carry it with me as a way to ease into the dreaded interactions coming sooner than I'd hope. It wouldn't be long before I would have to move.

"Your Majesty," a deep, furious-sounding voice down the table startled me and I dropped my spoon into the bowl of soup. Broth splashed on my hands. Hale grabbed his napkin instantly and passed it to me.

Frederich had risen from his place beside Lord West, in

the middle of the long table. His face beet red and though he'd called for the king's attention, his ire remained aimed at our end of the table.

I frowned.

"Frederich?" my father asked, raising an eyebrow.

"I find the current situation before me highly inappropriate," he said.

He still glared our way despite addressing the king. Inappropriate? This Fae had lost his mind.

"You will have to elaborate on the concern you're bringing forth," the king said.

Frederich lifted his chin. "Captain Stronholm is the princess's personal guard and close *personal* friend. Come to think of it, Hale Bardot is as well. They have known each other for years."

The way he sneered the words "personal friend" made Ian's entire body stiffen, and Hale's face dropped. Seemed as if the court rumors flew far and wide over the years.

The king raised his hand, his eyes flaring, and jaw clenched. "If you wish to continue your point, I'd remind you whatever you choose to bring up has to do with my *daughter*. Choose your words wisely if you wish to be heard at all."

Frederich seemed to get the hint. "I mean no disrespect, Your Majesty. My point is merely that both men are already so close to the princess. She is more acquainted with Captain Stronholm particularly than any of us. What chance do we have of winning her hand against those whom she has known for years?"

The king arched an eyebrow.

Ian hadn't relaxed next to me. Hale's dark skin flushed as he clenched his jaw. I hated Frederich even more now. I would never choose him, regardless of who remained at the end of the trials.

"If I may, Your Majesty." Lord West rose to stand beside Frederich. "He speaks the truth. It hardly seems a fair contest at this point. Especially with the captain being one of the top three today and getting the opportunity for private time with the princess when he has had this opportunity for years."

A dry chuckle accompanied Lord West's declaration. My gaze darted around the room to learn who it had come from.

Kade.

"Perhaps Lord West should have tried harder in the trial if he wished to have been in the top three," Kade said, glancing my way with a grin.

His comment would not win me over, but I stifled my own smile at the sentiment and the fact he spoke up on my behalf.

Lord West snarled, clearly unamused. "Be that as it may, it still stands Captain Stronholm, in particular, has an unfair advantage. Should he be declared the winner, there will be an inquiry into the legitimacy of his kingship from my city."

"And mine," Frederich added, his pudgy finger pointed into the air dramatically.

Staring down the two contenders, I rose from my seat. "If it is my good graces you wish to be in, you will find bickering like children is hardly the way to win my affection. Least of all make me want to give you any of my time and attention, winner or not."

The king gave me a sharp look, and I immediately shrank into myself internally. I never snapped in public. I had lived my life poised and emotionless on purpose in these settings, and I allowed two Fae to cause a change in my public persona.

However, I was done letting men make decisions for me and my "well-being," and I would not allow my thoughts to go unknown any longer. Certainly not with insinuations to my private life laid bare, as if I wasn't there.

I curled my right hand into a fist, my fingernails digging into the skin in an effort to ground myself and return to my expected demeanor.

My father puffed out his chest, waving a hand. "Your

concerns have been noted. And I can't argue with the validity."

My jaw dropped. The absolute ridiculousness of this. Ian and I couldn't help we were close before these damn trials. Even Hale. How could I know this would have been my life all those years ago?

The king flicked his wrist to magnify his voice, ensuring everyone in the dining hall would hear his next decree. "Preparations have already been made for Captain Stronholm to be moved from the guard house to the contender's wing. Additionally, we are bringing in Princess Illiana's former guard to resume his role as her personal guard for the remainder of the trials."

My hand unconsciously flew toward Ian. *No.* I'd grown too used to Ian's presence. I didn't know if I could handle Ruppert again. His dreadful demeanor, eyeing me with disdain, his retirement brought me such relief. Besides, his absolute refusal to bend any rule dampened my hopes of continuing Hidden Henchman runs undeterred.

I needed Ian as my guard so we could have a reason to be together outside of the trials to discuss and carry out the Hidden Henchman requests. I trusted no one else. Not even to rely on to merely pass a message for me to Ian.

"Please know we appreciate the attention brought to this matter," the king said. "We are accustomed to Captain Stronholm's presence here. I didn't think of how it may appear to others from the outside, wishing to make a good impression on our kingdom, and its future Queen. However, should he win, after we have made such accommodations, I expect for the decision to be respected."

I hated my father's compromise to pacify the whining nobles. Even if a part of me understood he had to play their game. We were *always* playing the game. An inquiry would lessen the credibility of the throne. I knew we couldn't have the turmoil, considering my lack of magical abilities. Civil unrest, in a time of so much uncertainty, would make things ten times worse.

"Would these accommodations satisfy you?" the king questioned, arching an eyebrow.

Frederich directed his gaze back to me, a sly, wicked sort of grin forming, his mustache twitching. I refused to smile in return. Instead, I stared him down, wanting him to lose the next trial so we could be rid of him once and for all.

He would be king over my dead body.

"It is, Your Majesty." Frederich beamed. "We simply wish to have equal opportunities with the princess so she may get to know us as well." With a quick bow, he returned to his seat.

"The princess is still within her rights to accept or decline time with you outside of the trials. May I take this time to remind everyone, she is not to be forced into anything." The king's stony tone had Frederich and Lord West exchanging glances I could not yet decipher.

Andras's smug expression etched into my brain as I processed everything my father said. He relished every chance he had to put me in my place. That increased tenfold with Ian, since there were no limits as Ian didn't have his king's blood.

Instantly, I lost my appetite, pushing the bowl of soup toward the middle of the table. I didn't dare sit next to Ian any longer. I would have to find another empty chair to occupy. I refused to have it be near Frederich or Lord West, even though they both eyed the empty seat between them.

The only other open seat remained next to Edmund and across from the third to last person I wanted to sit with right now. I clenched my teeth, forcing myself to walk toward the open chair with some sort of dignity. "Option" being a strong word at the moment.

"Princess, you honor us," Kade drawled as I approached.

Pursing my lips, I replied, "There wasn't much of a choice."

I sat on the chair as the staff pushed me closer to the table. The moment I settled onto my seat a small strawberry salad appeared in front of me.

Conversation buzzed around me, and I closed my eyes, aware if I didn't participate in any way, it would reflect poorly on not only me but my father as well. Besides, after my outburst, I needed to don my princess mask and exude my normal behavior as much as possible. After all, we'd already had two men dare to threaten the legitimacy of the throne tonight.

I offered Edmund an attempt at a more genuine smile, however, I couldn't be certain if it appeared as forced as it felt. "How are you enjoying your meal thus far?" I asked him.

"Very satisfactory, Your Grace," Edmund said, lowering his head slightly at his response.

My gaze shifted to Kade, who stared at his plate, smiling. Part of me worried about dining with him, aware of his identity as the cloaked man I had met just a week before. Perhaps, there was more than meets the eye to this asshole, who now knew one of my deepest held secrets.

More to the Fae who saved my life twice now during battle. The drop played in my mind and the callous way he'd spoken of us, the accusations of not caring about our people. It had burned me then and infuriated me now even more as I thought of it. Yet, he had chosen to enter a trial and attempt to marry into the lives of the very people he thought didn't care.

I needed to use our history to my advantage. I may be able to get information from him. Information like, what the hell he needed aid for in the first place, only to turn up for the marriage trials.

"And you?"

He gestured to himself, lifting his eyebrows as if he were shocked I addressed him at all. "Not as good as back home, but certainly better than average."

161

"Where is home again?" I asked as sweetly as I could manage.

He chuckled. The sound, deep and stupidly irresistible, had me yearning to hear it again. My body could not continue reacting to this damn man over and over.

Something deep within me hummed in satisfaction yet left me wanting whenever he was near. A feeling I had not felt, perhaps, ever. However, this feeling may betray my better senses if I could not alleviate the growing need from lack of physical connection. I wondered if I should grab Hale for old times' sake only to bring myself much-needed relief.

"Brookmere, Princess," he said. "Brookmere is my home."

I scoffed, settling my attention back on Edmund before I engaged Kade any further and caused a scene. I shoved a bit of bitter greens and sweet strawberries into my mouth to buy a little time before needing to speak again. The acidic dressing tied it all together into a symphony of flavors on my tongue.

All too soon, Perdot, one of my favorite senior staff members, gently touched my back. He nodded toward an empty chair, signaling this course, and my attempt to avoid Frederich and Lord West had come to an end. I realized too late my decision to avoid the two men backfired, since the main course had arrived.

The longest one. *Fates.* I had not played my cards right.

I shuddered as subtly as I could after noticing a spinach leaf in Frederich's mustache, unbeknownst to the oversized man, but I obeyed the request from Perdot and moved down the table to the last seat I had yet to occupy.

"Gentlemen," I said tersely.

The word was a reach for describing Frederich, and I had yet to observe anything in Lord West's actions suggesting he respected women. Especially after he eyed my chest and called me his future wife during our first conversation. Their behavior here tonight only provided me with another reason to find a way to rid them from these trials as soon as possible.

Slices of herb roasted chicken, thyme and rosemary seasoned potatoes, and spears of asparagus rounded out the evening. The scent wafting toward me had my stomach grumbling. I dosed my meal with a luxurious pan gravy before even offering the men a glance again.

"Oh, I do enjoy a woman with a hearty appetite," Frederich pronounced as he leaned into me. "In all aspects of life." His eyes unnervingly fixated upon me.

It took all I had to swallow the potato I'd gingerly placed into my mouth without vomiting.

"Frederich, do cease your insufferable innuendos," Lord West began. "No one has an appetite when it comes to *you*. I will not have you defiling my time with Princess Illiana with your ludicrous behavior." Lord West snickered.

Frederich's face reddened with anger. "I've had less complaints from women than you over the years. Many more willing, too."

The food in my mouth turned to ash, inedible at the audacity of these men and their presumptuous attitude toward me. Neither of them were proper enough to be considered worthy of the crown. If only my father could hear this conversation. Perhaps he would be so offended he would dismiss them from the trials from disgust alone.

I should have guessed they were conspiring after teaming up with their accusations about Ian, but perhaps both men were only out for blood in the competition. Suddenly, however, observing them bicker instead of falling all over me seemed like a good distraction.

Before either could fling another insult, the doors to the dining hall slammed open, and one of the palace's healers ran toward the king's table, tripping once over the gold runner lining the floor. He ignored the stares and required protocols completely, quickly bowing, but not waiting for permission to approach the king. He reached the throne and bent forward, whispering quietly in his ear.

All eyes were on my father and the healer, watching the king's face fall. He glanced toward Andras but continued listening to the healer.

Finally, when the man drew away from the king's ear, he bowed again. His entire body trembled as he took a slow step back. Then, with the king's dismissive wave, he ran right back out of the hall. My mother reached for my father's hand, providing whatever emotional support she could as she, too, waited to hear the news.

My head whipped from one end of the room back to the other. My father signaled Andras to his side, whose eyes flared wide before returning to his normal snakelike glare. He bowed his head and left the king, stepping off the dais and hastily rushing out of the room as well.

Now I knew something wasn't just wrong, but *really* wrong. Andras would never leave my father in a room full of powerful Fae aiming to take his seat upon the throne.

I gripped the arms of my velvet-tufted chair. There weren't many times when I'd observed his face fall as it just had. In fact, I couldn't remember the last time.

The king rose slowly, hoisting himself into a tall stance, his face grave as he spoke.

"Lord Levi Thatcher is dead."

CHAPTER 16

D*ead.*

A contender. Dead, because of the trials.

I searched for Ian's face, but he focused somberly on the king, like most everyone else.

"Lord Thatcher should have recovered easily from the poison, with help from the healers. It appears, for some reason, his magic failed to fight off the poison's toxin."

A death of a noble at the palace would cause an uproar from Lord Thatcher's city. I wondered if anyone had thought the trials would turn deadly.

"While we are heartbroken to hear the news of such a fine Fae being taken too soon, I must use this time to reiterate these trials are meant to test you all. Death is an unfortunate possibility, so I urge you to tread wisely. These are not just silly games to be my daughter's husband. These trials determine your ability to be a king. A king who will rule these lands alongside its Queen."

I swallowed the lump forming in my throat. Did any of them know this when they entered? Did Ian know a result of entering the trials could be death?

"We will conclude dinner slightly early so we may get the

princess to her drinks and off to bed," he said. "With such harrowing news, we imagine some may want to rest this evening in private."

Frederich released a seething breath through his nose. "And now our time is once more cut short. Tonight, at drinks, Princess, I'll have your full attention."

As I stood, I wanted to tell him I'd rather die, but held my tongue. Maneuvering from the long dining table, I made my way toward the double doors, leading to the royal terrace and gardens.

My father left the room with his advisers, shuffling out collectively and leaving my mother behind. She gracefully glided toward me, reaching out her hands.

"Is Father okay?" I asked.

"The death of a noble is a precarious situation. However, it's a part of the terms of the trials. Each of the contenders were made aware of this danger beforehand," she said, squeezing my hand gently. "It will be all right."

The winds caressed my face, almost encouragingly, as we walked onto the terrace. A small table had a vase of flowers perched on its center, with a few drinks and small chocolate desserts.

A familiar friction rubbed at my calves, tickling my legs. "Lucien." I laughed, bending and scratching the pugron's ears.

"Illiana," my mother said, a scolding on the tip of her tongue.

"I didn't bring him with me," I murmured. "Besides, your dislike of my stray ended when I caught you reading with him curled up on your lap."

She tried and failed to hide her smile before looking at Lucien. "She'll be back this evening, go on now."

He obeyed instantly and disappeared into the gardens while his wagging tail ripped into the shrubbery as he passed.

"See anyone worthy of King yet?" I asked my mother as

we waited for the three contenders to join us from the dining hall.

She raised her eyebrows. "It *is* a bit soon to make a judgment. You never know how someone may surprise you."

I tensed, attempting to not be too flippant in front of her. "You can't convince Father to end this ridiculous trial?"

She faced me, lifting one of my hands to her mouth and pressing a kiss to my knuckles before enveloping them again. "Are you as presumptuous as his pompous advisers when it comes to knowing how this kingdom runs, my dear?" she asked, her eyes soft and curious.

I frowned, not understanding her meaning.

"Just because I stand quietly at his side, doesn't mean every decision isn't made equally," she said.

"But you never offer your opinions."

"That, you see," she said, nodding. "But make no mistake, I am as vocal as he is away from the public eye. Our guards can attest to it."

I shook my head. "Why wouldn't you show your strength to others then? So many believe a king rules alone."

"We are nothing without each other, and the beliefs you have are because of my own shortcomings, I'm afraid." She patted my hand. "The very first outing as King and Queen consisted of commissioning a new batch of royal guards. The king insisted I lead the proceedings."

I'd yet to hear this story. Her eyes shifted as though she replayed the memory instead of being here with me. A smile spread across her lips. "Andras made the mistake of insinuating a queen couldn't perform the task, and your father went feral. Raging over how Brookmere had always been ruled by its King and Queen, and anyone who believed otherwise didn't belong in his Court."

"I'm surprised Andras lasted then." I grimaced, wishing my father had removed him then and there.

"Hmm," she said before returning to her story. "Anyway,

167

I got up and froze in front of everyone. My stomach suddenly queasy, tossing and turning about. I stretched my hand behind me, hoping your father noticed my terror, and after he took over, I ran and vomited where no one could see."

"You threw up? Why?"

"I hate speaking in public. It terrifies me." She shook her head. "From then on, he has allowed me to have my quiet, supporting role in public, while giving him a piece of my mind in private. I make as many decisions as he does, and we never make an announcement without coming to an agreement together first."

Realization dawned. Tugging my hand away, I took a few steps back. My chest tightened, but my mother stood her ground. "You support the trials?"

She nodded. "You may not put stock in what Vivienne says, but we do. We know what she claims is true." She moved forward, leaning toward my ear. "He is sick, darling. He refuses to leave anything up to chance if he were to be taken from us suddenly."

Bile rose in my throat, making it hard to swallow. The terrace doors opened and Ian, Kade, and Frederich entered.

Kade shot me a devilish grin and made his way toward the drinks instead of me. Frederich's lips curled in a sickening smile, at least I thought it appeared like a smile from what I could view beneath all his hair. He moved toward me speedily.

Perdot blocked him, holding a tray of drinks, and I thought of kissing him for his interference. His slight step in front gave Ian time to reach us first.

"Your Majesty." Ian bowed his head before my mother leaned in and accepted a kiss on the cheek from him.

"Sweet Ian." She cupped his face with one hand and then removed it. "Oh, I better not play favorites."

"You flatter me, my Queen." He grinned back at her.

Flicking her hand daintily, she shooed us away. "I'm the

chaperone this evening, so leave the elderly Queen to her desserts. Have fun."

"Not likely," I hissed through clenched teeth.

Ian and I walked to the edge of the balcony, and he leaned against the marble railing. "Well, things are less than ideal now."

"Less than ideal?" I scoffed. "You mean impossible. Ruppert is a stickler. I have no idea how we'll continue—" I stopped, holding a hand to my chest.

My father's announcement removing Ian as my personal guard remained difficult to fathom in more ways than one. Most especially, because the well-executed patterns we'd developed in our Hidden Henchman activities would be disrupted.

My emotions got the better of me, considering the short-term nature of this arrangement. A small part of me knew it was irrational to be this worked up, but the Hidden Henchman had become the one thing giving me freedom to be who I wanted to be, despite the mask. The Hidden Henchman persona made me feel enough, more than enough.

Leaning onto the marble railing, I let the cool stone calm the fire burning within me. Gripping onto it tightly, I grounded myself in the here and now.

Ian rested one of his gloved hands over mine. "We'll figure it out."

He exuded confidence, both in himself and in our team. He would make it work somehow, regardless of the extra weight it put on his shoulders.

"I noticed Andras's favorite guard Warrick with a broken nose this afternoon." I glanced at my best friend, trying to gauge his reaction. It was well known that Warrick and Ian had sparred on more than a few occasions, both in and out of the ring.

"Well, it's what happens when you call your Princess a common whore." Ian clenched his fists at his side.

"What?" My smile fell instantly, the teasing nature of my comment sucked away.

Ian ran a hand over his face. "I'm used to the rumors I slept my way to the role of Captain. I can handle them. However, I refuse to listen to my troops trash the Crown. Even if you weren't the future of this kingdom, you're my best friend, Lan." He shrugged. "If he weren't being sent to the border in a few days, he'd be released from duty. The nose was a kind punishment from me compared to what he deserved."

I pinched the bridge of my nose. "So, it has gotten worse since you entered the trials."

"I can handle it," he said bluntly, his tone signaling the end of this conversation. Ian never liked discussing rumors. Kalliah could make light of things enough to tease occasionally, but overall, I knew this bothered him. His anger was geared toward the way it made me appear, more so than him.

"More people are going to the borders?" I asked. Although based on my father and Andras's conversation, I knew the answer.

Ian pursed his lips. "Another twenty men are being sent."

"And none are returning," I whispered. I shifted so even if Frederich or Kade were listening, they wouldn't be able to hear. "Andras approached my father at the trials saying as much. They're concerned about not having many more men left to blindly send."

Ian frowned. "The general is the only person above me, and even I don't have all of the information. Whatever is going on, they're keeping it tight-lipped. Rumors are spreading faster about whatever evil magic is running rampant at the borders. It may not be so far off, given what we have faced."

"Can we stop it if it comes here?" I asked.

"We don't know anything about it. No one has been able to talk to those at the border with enough frequency to determine what's happening, or how to make it stop. Kade and Storm might know more, but we would need to talk to them to learn what they know."

"Come, come, now Captain Stronholm. I believe I made my point earlier. You've had enough time with the princess," Frederich said, lumbering in our direction with his too-loud voice.

Ian squeezed my arm. "Apologies, Frederich. You are correct, I know Princess Illiana is looking forward to getting to know you. Please, enjoy your evening." He opened his mouth when he stood behind Frederich, taunting me as he backed away near my mother. I didn't miss how she swatted his arm as soon as he reached her side.

Kade stood back, watching me suffer with Frederich, swirling the sweet red wine in his glass. A glimmer in his eye told me he was simply biding his time without a care in the world.

He stood a few feet away, staring out into the garden, seemingly unbothered by having none of my attention yet.

Frederich, though, remained adamant and waiting. Unfortunately.

He put his arm around me, and I couldn't help myself. I grabbed his wrist, struggling not to yank it away like I wanted, and instead, demurely removed it from my shoulder. "Although your enthusiasm is noted, I'd appreciate it if you kindly kept your hands to yourself for now."

Even a few feet away, I noticed Kade's jaw ticked as he stretched his neck.

"My, you are a feisty one." He snorted, and his belly shook with the movement. "I do like a woman who knows what she likes. It's why I think we'd be perfect as King and Queen."

"Oh?" I asked, attempting to appear engaged enough so he wouldn't complain about me to my father. "What qualifications do you have to make you a good king?"

He tapped his fingers on the yellow vest covering his

protruding stomach. "Well, despite trade being down in the kingdom overall, my affairs are blossoming continuously. I manage to continue our fruit exports, despite some of the harsher issues amongst the border towns. My town, however, has not been as affected as the others, due to my incredible shielding magic. Starhaven may have been under threat the longest, but we certainly haven't needed help from vigilantes in masks, as I've heard some other towns have resorted to. Nobody crosses my borders and stays without my permission."

My ears perked. Men who bragged certainly did give away more than they realized, it would seem.

"Starhaven has been under threat the longest?" I asked.

He ran his thumb and forefinger over his mustache. "Oh, yes, just over two decades now. But no evil can thwart powerful Fae for long." He rubbed his stomach, complimenting himself. "The Hidden Henchman, or whatever they call the man delivering goods these days, hasn't had a single drop in Starhaven and never will. Any evil which comes our way doesn't seem to last long."

Maybe you've absorbed it all yourself with how condescending you are, I thought.

"In fact," he continued, unprompted this time, "Lord West even requested a private discussion with me later this evening about something he claims will push both of us up in Brookmere."

"Ah." I nodded.

"Besides, if I become King"—He took my hand, blatantly ignoring my request to keep his *own* to himself—"I would have my duties to you be my primary focus."

Yanking from his grasp, I subtly wiped my palms on my dress. "Running a business is a valuable endeavor. It's wonderful you're thriving despite others' misfortunes." I disguised my distaste enough, so he didn't seem to notice, however, a garbled choke from my left signaled I hadn't completely succeeded.

Stupid Fae hearing. Kade pretended he'd choked on his drink, not even bothering to look at us, when I knew very well, he heard every word.

"Tell me—have you taken any of those border towns under your care?" I asked.

"What do you mean, Your Highness?" Frederich asked, staring at me as if I'd spoken in an olden Fae language.

I elevated my chin, our eyes level due to his shorter stature. "I mean, since there are so many in Brookmere suffering, and you are not, have you offered goods at lower rates to those in need? Do you donate any of your blossoming fruit exports, or even travel services if the Fae in your employ are still capable of traveling so freely without fear?"

He shook his head. "Ah, an idealistic woman is our future Queen. Beautiful child, you will soon learn one does not succeed by giving things away for free."

"Well, this has been a fascinating discussion, Frederich. Congratulations on doing so well. I believe the final contender is ready for his time, and then I'll be retiring."

Again, the smarmy man took my hand in his, and placed a kiss upon it, squeezing it in a way that left the skin he touched crawling.

As he walked away, I grabbed a drink from Perdot, who had never been too far from my side, and downed it. "Tits and daggers, he's a prick," I mumbled.

Kade hadn't moved from the far side of the balcony. He turned as I approached, and I hesitated as his eyes darkened, like I'd seen before at the drop. They were more black than grey, the storms normally swirling turned to darkened skies. His jaw clenched.

"That's quite a unique mouth you've got for a princess." His gaze held me like tethers to him.

I glared, not breaking eye contact. "I'm told it's my best quality."

The darkness faded from his eyes almost instantly when a

half-smile formed on his face, as though it had never been there at all.

As his smile lingered, a current ran through me. "It's an awfully forward thing to say to a stranger. Is this what you plan on discussing with me during my esteemed private courting time?"

"Trust me, if I didn't have to give everyone at this gathering a fair amount of time, you'd have none of my attention." Even as I said the words, I knew they weren't true. He commanded my attention for some stupid reason.

He chuckled like he knew it. "Right, because your other company was so delightful." Kade tipped back his honey sweet wine, staring at the empty glass before setting it down on the railing beside us.

"I have been with plenty of men who are, in fact, delightful company—" I paused, realizing how what I'd said could be construed and clamped my mouth shut.

Kade raised his eyebrows and leaned his arm against the balcony railing. "Please, do tell me more. I didn't realize you were so accustomed to us men." The way he leaned in brought him closer to me than normal conversation. My heartbeat quickened, and I hoped the sound of his own voice distracted him enough so he wouldn't notice the effect his presence had on me.

"Have you ever been with a man before, Little Rebel?"

My jaw dropped at his forwardness, my breath hitching at the nickname, which so clearly got under my skin.

Kade's eyes danced at my immediate reaction.

"How dare you?" I snapped.

He shrugged, flicking a petal from the marble railing. "You started this conversation."

I narrowed my eyes, ignoring the sensation stirring in my gut. "Worried the goods you're vying for are sullied? Perhaps you should back out of the trials."

Kade grinned at my indignant retort, or maybe he just

enjoyed the fight. Either way, he held my stare as, I swear, a fire lit behind his damned eyes. "The goods look flawless. I couldn't care less if they're sullied as you say." He cocked an eyebrow, almost daring me to respond.

I hated the heat rising in my face, aware it colored my cheeks. I stepped toward him, my chest practically touching his. "Good. Because you certainly wouldn't be my first."

Kade reached for me, and I froze in place. Gently, so much so his fingertips whispered across my skin, he tucked a strand of hair behind my ear.

Closing the barely-there gap between us, he leaned forward, his breath warm against my cheek as he spoke. "But, I'd certainly be the best."

He took a step back from me, bowed his head, then retreated, although he still held my gaze.

"Sweet dreams, Little Rebel."

CHAPTER 17

Walking through the corridors to my room, my mind couldn't help but replay today's events. It rapidly jumped between the trials, further attacks upon our lands, a contender dead, and Ian no longer being my personal guard.

Then of course Kade's insufferable knowledge of my activities, complete with a stupid little moniker of his own. However, the latter was truly the least of my worries. His nonchalant and flirtatious attitude didn't escape my thoughts, though, as I wandered through the hallways.

As I took the south passageway through the castle, I couldn't help but stop and stare out of the massive windows to the moonlight gardens, spread across the palace grounds.

I leaned my head against the windowpane as the heaviness of today's events threatened to consume me. I needed a long sleep, and hopefully one without nightmares.

Fates, please let me survive these trials and be left with a partner and not another burden to bear.

A simple prayer to nature. One I had a feeling I would be repeating many more times over the coming weeks.

Winding my way through the corridor, I approached one

of the main hallway intersections, where one could access the stairs to my chambers, when I heard whispers.

I paused before slowly creeping to the corner of the corridor, peeking around to find who stood in the way of me and my bed.

Lord West and Ryland were standing at the bottom of the stairs. Too close to both my current location, and my private chambers for my liking.

How did they know where to find my room?

"All I'm saying is, if you want to be on the right side of this, you'll align with me," Lord West said aggressively, his finger pointed at Ryland's chest.

The pompous bastard.

First, the objection to Ian being my personal guard, and now trying to form alliances with other contenders? What was this man's problem? I leaned closer to the corner to try and hear more.

Ryland stood there, haphazardly running his hands through his already-ruffled hair. "I mean, I'm just not sure what you're saying makes sense."

"I'll give you all the information you want if you agree." Lord West sneered, stepped closer to Ryland.

Why did that sound like a threat?

Ryland snorted. "You think I trust you? A stranger with questionable manners, to what? Agree blindly to following some crusade you're on without knowing any further—"

Lord West whipped out a dagger and slammed Ryland into the stone wall behind him.

I gasped, a small shriek escaping my lips. My hands flew to my mouth as I pressed my back firmly against the wall.

"Who's out there?" Lord West demanded. "Show yourselves!"

He strode toward the edge of the hallway where I so desperately tried to stay hidden. The wild expression on his face as he held the dagger in his hand screamed danger.

The way he moved, his footsteps thudded against the lightly carpeted hallway. Tits and daggers, this couldn't happen right now. *Not right now.*

Fates, help me!

A cool breeze swept over my body, but instead of moving past, it lingered, swirling around me, similar to being in a cloud. I cracked my right eye open and discovered I now stood enveloped in shadows.

"Little Rebel, are you in need of saving, again?" The sultry voice in my ear sent tingles sweeping down my spine as Kade materialized before me. His body covered mine, but it wasn't danger his proximity had me feeling. No, it was safety.

Too afraid to make any further noise, I nodded slightly, barely noticeable except for the wisps of my loosened hair brushing against his chiseled chin. I couldn't breathe.

The *thud* of boots sounded deeply on the carpet.

Closer.

"Hiding will not save you, whomever you are," Lord West growled.

I trembled. I'd been here before. In this same damn hallway. As a child.

I squeezed my eyes shut so hard my face hurt.

I didn't want to get lost in this memory now.

"Come out, come out wherever you are Princess." His voice echoed in the hallway.

I needed to get to my chambers. I didn't want to go with him again. He was mean. He hurt me. I didn't want to hurt.

"We have work to do, and it'll only make it harder if you continue to resist."

"Breathe." A voice so unlike my nightmares brushed my skin, softer than a whisper in my ear, pulling me from my flashback.

I didn't open my eyes, but Kade took one of my hands gripping the wall and placed it on the hard muscle of his

179

chest. I didn't fight him as he rested my palm there, his heartbeat dancing beneath my fingertips.

"Breathe with me, Illiana." He said my name like he cared about my well-being.

My hand shook once, but I drummed my fingers to stop them. His chest rose and fell slowly, each breath obviously deliberate. Kade inhaled, held the breath in his lungs for a moment, and exhaled evenly.

Though shaky at first, I mimicked him, matching each breath, until eventually, my trembling ceased.

"I'll say it one more time," Lord West hissed with venom in his tone. "Who's there?" I opened my eyes, staring directly into the storms swirling in Kade's steady gaze. He leaned closer, and the way his right arm hovered above my head caged me and settled my sense of safety even more.

A movement to my right caught my attention. Lord West's boots were a foot away from us. If he peered farther around the corner, we'd be impossible to miss.

Fates above, please don't let him hear my frantically beating heart or notice Kade hovering over my body as though I were ripe for the taking.

Kade's shadows swirled around us, mesmerizing me almost as much as the fact we had yet to be caught by Casimir. A subtle flick of his wrist and the already-dim light grew darker as his shadows thickened. I couldn't even see Kade in front of my face, despite us touching.

"Why so paranoid, Casimir?" Ryland asked.

Casimir's boots retreated, the thudding now indicating distance between us. I couldn't seem to care if the two of them picked up their argument or not.

My body suddenly felt hot in ways it hadn't in years. Despite Kade's arrogance and wish for a crown, this was now the third time he had stepped in to help me from near certain peril.

Kade's head shifted back slightly so our noses were touching.

"This is becoming a habit, Little Rebel. How many more times will I have to save you?" he murmured, his breath hot on my face, the scent of the honey sweet wine we'd drank drifting into my senses. It mixed with the fresh smell of the earth after a storm as Kade's entire being enveloped me against the wall.

"I'm sure I could have saved myself," I whispered, gaining a bit of my inner strength back in our taunting.

I felt his smile, his lips so close to mine.

He'd saved me not just with whatever these shadows were, but, from my spiral into a nightmare. My spiral into a panic would have surely outed my position. Without even realizing it, he'd done what no one, save Ian, had ever been able to accomplish.

My breathing escaped unevenly as he moved slightly, bringing his left hand up to cup my chin, tilting my face toward his.

The darkness dissipated, and for the first time, I noticed Kade's sleeves were rolled up on his forearms. On his right arm, propped next to my head, a design of black ink swirled like the shadows he wielded, tattooed up his forearm before disappearing beneath the rest of his shirt.

It called attention to the way his muscles shifted. I glanced from his arm back to his eyes.

I'd lost my mind, but the adrenaline coursing through me moments before hadn't fully subsided. The wine I'd consumed encouraged me as much as the scent of this infuriating man did, daring me to make a move.

I licked my bottom lip, and he inhaled sharply.

There was no way he couldn't feel how my body melted into his. No way my intention and need weren't written all over my face. Still, he allowed me to make this choice, careful not to bring me any closer.

All it would take was one small movement and our lips would touch.

I lifted my lips to his. A whisper of a kiss in this shadowy retreat. My heart nearly beat out of my chest in anticipation.

Fuck it. Why the hell not, I thought.

My fingers curled into his chest, and I pressed my mouth harder against his. My core ignited in flames, a blazing heat with a never-ending burn as he matched my movements.

The other voices faded into the background, speaking again, but I didn't care.

How could I care when this man's lips claimed mine like he'd been desperate for me?

I wanted to moan into his mouth as his tongue claimed mine. The ever-present tingling sensations raged over me, pooling low in my belly.

Kade's hand slid to the back of my neck, as he pressed his body into mine, his hips pinning me to the wall.

"Lord Casimir? What are you doing? Ryland, why are you in this hall?" Andras shouted angrily.

I jumped at the sound of Andras's voice—the very *last* thing I wanted to hear.

Kade froze at my reaction, the shadows around us retreating slightly, so I could see him better.

Our heavy breathing mingled, both of us attempting to remain quiet. His gaze moved from my lips to my eyes, and the tug my body felt toward him painfully begged me to kiss him again.

"Sir, we were merely hoping to give the princess our best wishes this evening," Ryland stammered.

"Get back to your suite immediately. You heard the king. Don't let him catch you trying to favor his daughter without her approval. My silence cannot be bought, but I will forgive this one transgression if you leave at once." The asshole adviser sneered.

I heard footsteps fleeing down the hall.

"Lord Casimir, with me."

"As you command it, Andras."

182

Two more sets of footsteps left down the hallway.

I scarcely had the wherewithal to think of the strange interaction between Andras and Lord West.

Kade's forehead rested upon mine until the sound of footsteps could no longer be heard.

I closed my eyes again, waiting, panting.

Kiss me again, my treacherous body silently begged.

Kade's thumb traced along my jaw. "'Til next time, Little Rebel," he murmured.

Before I could even open my eyes, I sensed the shadowy tendrils disappear completely, the cloudlike sensation instantly gone.

A chill now whispered over my skin where his body left mine.

I knew Kade had left as my eyes fluttered open. The shadows of my savior disappeared before I could even speak.

"Thank you," I whispered into the emptiness.

Unsure how to quench the ache of the heat building inside of me, I remained with my back against the wall until my heart returned to a stable pace. I hadn't been this close to a man in a long time. His unmistakable good looks and arrogant charm were starting to wear on me.

A faint glimmer of light hummed in the darkened space around me and caught my eye.

It disappeared before my very next breath.

I blinked, wondering what it could have been before settling on the idea nature itself had granted me this gift.

A gift granting me a small reprieve from the darkness shadowing this day. A wish my soul would reach for to remember for whatever may be in store for me in the coming days.

A gift to remember Kade Blackthorn's lips against mine, as if they'd been created just for me.

CHAPTER 18

*D*rip.

> *Water leaked through two stones in the upper right-hand corner of the dark dungeon, deep below the palace floors.*

I noticed it after a year of coming here. It never changed.

Drip.

Slow. Steady. The water continued, constant. Sometimes, if I could remember to look for it, I'd know if the visions in the room were real or simply images I was made to believe.

Only sometimes, though.

Drip.

"Illiana." His voice cooed in a mocking, taunting sort of way.

He knelt in front of me, tugging my head back by my hair so I was forced to stare into his eyes, lip twitching, hate spewing from his every pore.

I wanted to be brave. I wanted it to stop. I would be seventeen tomorrow. My "sessions" hadn't stopped for five years.

Five long years.

The joy and exhilaration he achieved from what he did to me, how he tortured me, never faded, never faltered.

His eyes haunted my dreams. The way they seemed black, as if there was nothing inside of him but empty, cruel nothingness.

This man, who somehow hid his darkness around all others, even my mother and father.

Trusted. Honored. Revered by the Court.

Andras Braumlyn.

Royal Adviser.

I hated him.

Betrayer. Liar.

"Illiana, you must understand a queen with no magic is worthless. Give in to me. I am the only one who can help make you strong."

He tugged harder when I didn't respond. Our faces were so close, the stench of his breath inescapable.

"Your father is counting on me to fix you. He's too disgusted to do it himself." *He threw me down. My body lay prone on the dirt-covered stone floor of this torture chamber. Pushing myself up on my elbows, I turned.*

"That's a lie!"

No, no. Ian was here. No.

"You'll speak when I want you to," *Andras shouted, and a* thud *sounded like he'd kicked at something.*

"Ian," *I whimpered.*

"It's okay, Lan. You're okay."

I heard his voice, but when I looked up, he was too far away. Andras could do anything to him, and I'd never reach him in time.

Although he'd tormented me with visions of hurting Ian, my body trembled uncontrollably. Something had snapped and Andras had him here. Really here this time, not the illusion which he normally subjected me to.

"Is it real?" *I whispered.*

I waited for the code phrase we kept secret. The phrase we came up with when I couldn't overcome the fear and panic.

"Real as roses," *Ian whispered softly as tears fell down my face.*

I didn't want it to be real.

"Quiet, both of you," *Andras snapped.* "Illiana."

A ring of blue fire quickly formed a circle around Ian.

"Stop it!" *I shouted.*

"Use your magic to snuff out the flames, or Ian will burn, badly."

Perhaps even die." Andras *chuckled. "It would be tragic, but he's just a guard's offspring. He's replaceable."*

"Ian!" I screamed, tears streaming down my face as I crawled toward the growing flames. "I don't have magic. I don't have magic. I can't make it stop."

"It's okay, Lan."

Even staring death in the face, Ian didn't seem afraid. He never looked away while I sobbed. I held my hands to the fire, screaming, pleading with nature desperately, turning vile as help remained elusive.

Ian didn't even hiss when the fire started climbing higher and began moving inward and reached his legs.

"Weak. Pathetic."

Ian sucked in a breath as the fire rose so high it formed a wall between us.

"If you will not do what you're told, then I will force you to take magic from elsewhere."

My head snapped to Andras. A dagger rested in his hand, a black substance coating the tip, dripping once onto the floor.

Andras lunged for me, grabbing my neck and straddling my legs as he choked me on the ground.

Ian yelled my name, but it seemed far away. Too far away. He was trapped and so was I.

Andras twisted the blade across my chest slowly. Pure, unadulterated hate radiated from his body, his eyes gleaming in anticipation. "I cannot wait to see the fun we'll have pulling out your magic when you're older. Just a few more years."

I struggled against him harder, but I'd been down here for so long already, my body and mind faltered. Too exhausted to fight like I needed to.

"Ah, ah, ah. This will only hurt for a moment."

His sneer turned into something so much deadlier. A smile, a wide grin, filled with malicious glee spread across his face. He sliced my lilac nightgown open, across my ribcage and dug deep with the blade against my skin.

The knife bumped over the ridges of three ribs as I screamed, feeling the skin break.

"Tsk." He made a noise with his tongue. "Deeper."

He thrust the dagger inside of me. A surge of something attacked me, flowing toward me, but I wouldn't give in. I couldn't.

Ian was here with me. I was not alone. Andras Braumlyn wouldn't defeat me.

"I am Illiana Dresden, and I am stronger than the darkness within me."

I screamed again as he put more weight against the blade.

Screaming, I shot up from the bed.

My body shook as hard as it had that night. Trembling, terror coursed through me.

Sweat drenched my bed linens, dripping down my arms, my forehead. I was alone.

My head snapped back and forth, scanning my room, grasping the sheets in my hands, to ensure it truly had been a nightmare.

I wasn't there.

Ian was safe.

I wasn't in that room with Andras.

Tremors overtook my fingers as I pulled my nightgown up and brushed the tips along the jagged, angry-looking scar, which never fully healed, across my ribs.

Never again.

The scar throbbed. Years later, I continued to use a salve on it from Elisabeth, but the pain seemed stronger today.

I rose from the bed, wincing as the pain threatened to bring me to my knees.

Elisabeth would help. She'd have something.

Stumbling, I shielded my eyes from the brightness in the room as the sun streamed through my light-emerald curtains.

Suddenly, my door flew open.

Ian ran in with Kalliah on his heels.

I tripped moving toward him, and he wrapped me in his arms.

"I'm so sorry it took me so long, Lana," Kalliah said. "You wouldn't wake, and I had to find Ian's new chambers."

I nodded, holding out my hand and she took it. I squeezed hard in thanks, not trusting my voice would work properly now.

"You're safe, Lan. You're safe. It was a dream." Ian held me, brushing my hair away from my face.

We stood there, together, like we had many times before. When the last remnants of horror shook from my body, I looked up.

"My scar hurts. I need to see Elisabeth," I said, my throat raw from screaming. "Is it too early?"

Ian shook his head. "No, no, it's before breakfast, but you know she'll always see you."

Kalliah walked away, only to return with a thick, velvet, rose-colored robe, one I could move about on the top levels of the palace freely and not be deemed inappropriate.

I slipped into it, clutching it around me. The sweat had stopped, and my body shivered as it returned to a stable state.

"I'll take her," Ian said. "Thank you."

Kalliah hugged me. "I'll be here to get you ready for the day when you return. I'll make sure I get some dandelion tea from Perdot, too."

I smiled at her as we exited my chambers.

Elisabeth's room wasn't too far, thankfully. It had made it easy all the years she healed me from my Hidden Henchman work.

"What was it this time?" Ian whispered.

"The last time."

Ian stiffened, gently leading me down the hall. When the nightmares escalated to such a degree, he knew relief wouldn't come easy.

189

We moved in silence, Ian rubbing my arms every few minutes until we were in front of Elisabeth's door.

I grabbed his forearm, remembering I hadn't updated him on Frederich's comments from the previous night. "Before I forget, we need to look into Frederich's town, Starhaven. He claims they're unaffected by things happening at the border for some reason, even though they've been battling it the longest."

"What?" Ian seemed surprised by the statement.

"I think if we were to get answers it might be a place to start."

"I need you to think about *you* right now, Lan." He knocked on Elisabeth's door. "Save the rest for when you're feeling better."

"Too much is happening too quickly."

"I know. Still, try to feel better before planning out more missions, yes?" He poked at my side as Elisabeth opened the door.

She took one look at me and dragged me into her room.

"See you after teatime," Ian said.

Elisabeth didn't ask a single question. She hurried around her room, pulling out one of the tattered chairs for me at the small table near the fireplace. I'd spent so much of my life at this table talking to her, the familiarity had me settled before I even had to explain why I was here.

"I'm sorry to bother you so early," I said.

"Hush now this instant. What happened, sweet girl? What is it?" She sat beside me, taking my hands in hers.

"My scar is hurting despite the salve. I was hoping I could ask for more, and perhaps something stronger for the pain today." I rubbed my hands together anxiously. I hated admitting I couldn't handle the pain.

Elisabeth's eyes hardened. "Of course. Of course, I have just the thing."

She rose, moving to the cupboards stacked upon cupboards, filled with all of her supplies. She pulled out a few items and a mixing bowl, and I immediately recognized the salve ingredients. Once combined, she let it sit and reached up toward the middle of the cupboards, removing a small vial. Its brown container held a black stopper on top, which she removed, then tapped twice before dipping into its contents.

She walked back to me. "Head back, tongue out."

I obeyed and she released three droplets of the liquid on my tongue. It had a tart flavor and I reacted as I would if I'd sucked on a lemon.

"That's for the pain."

Absentmindedly, I massaged my ribs through my robe.

Elisabeth busied herself, putting the ingredients away and warming her black kettle over the small fire blazing in her hearth. Elisabeth had a fire burning every morning, even deep in the summer months. It was another constant in my life that soothed my soul.

She let me sit, observing in silence. Inside the walls of Elisabeth's room seemed more like home than almost any other place inside the massive palace.

I smiled watching her work, remembering sitting in the chair as a child doing the exact same thing.

"Did you think when I pestered you as a young Fae, with a million questions about healing, you'd be watching the marriage trials play out years later?" I asked.

She snorted. "I didn't think you'd ever get married. At least not until some ruggedly handsome man came riding through the gates on a white steed, claiming to be your mate."

I laughed at the thought. If only love were so easy. Ian had been right about one thing—mates were myths, legends, and wishing my life away for mine was pointless. As sacred as the blessing would be.

"I suppose I always did hold onto silly notions of love."

Elisabeth stood before me, brushing back my wild, morning hair. "I never said that, child." She frowned, jumping when the kettle whistled.

Fussing with teacups and sugar, she finally returned and sat down across from me. "Love is a gift, whether it's a true love match, or a love grown from respect. Love blossoming from friendship is written of nearly as much as the romantic notion of true love, or even the myth of mates."

"I'm guessing it means you're rooting for Ian in the trials." I eyed her over the gold rim of my rose teacup.

Elisabeth chuckled. "I haven't seen enough of the rest of them to make any sort of informed decision. But." She paused slightly. "You and Ian have loved each other through circumstances no children should have faced. There is nothing stronger than the kind of bond you share. Whether he wins and your friendship develops into romantic love or not, you know no matter what, he will always be by your side. His winning wouldn't be the most devastating outcome."

"You sound just like him, you know. But what of his sacrifice? What of him finding his own love?"

"If he's decided this is what he wants, let him do it. It's not your choice, it's his. Who are you to say how or whom someone shall love?"

I fidgeted in my chair. I'd never even considered him entering. He'd made his decision on his own. His choice. "I don't like how logical you two are."

She laughed again. "You never did. Now, onto more serious matters. You're not sleeping well."

I could hide what happened from her, but it wouldn't help in the long run. "The draught isn't working as well. For some reason, the nightmares have been worse and more frequent these past few weeks."

She pursed her lips. "I can increase the dose of some of the ingredients, but it would leave you vulnerable in your sleep. Meaning, it would be harder to wake you should something happen. With Ian not by your side, I'm not sure now is the time to take the chance. Especially with so many rakes running about."

I spat out my tea, laughing. "Rakes."

She made a humming sound. "I've seen how some of them eye you."

"I'll be sure to keep them in line," I said.

We were interrupted by a knock at her door. Elisabeth answered and spoke in hushed tones.

"I hate to cut this short, my sweet, but your father is asking for me."

My expression grew somber. I nodded once. "Go, I'll clean up here."

She took my teacup from my hands. "I have to warm some herbs. I have time." She grabbed my arm, and tugged me down toward her, placing a kiss on my cheek. "Everything that's meant to be, will be. Trust in your fate, my sweet child."

Telling her it was the absolute last thing I trusted wouldn't do anyone any good, so I simply nodded.

"I'll bring the salve, and some pain drops to Kalliah later."

"Thank you," I said before I walked out, feeling better than I had this morning by far.

I retied my robe and ran my fingers through my unkempt hair. Kalliah would have a huge task, transforming this mangled mess into some kind of decency for the day.

I smiled, rounding the corner of the hallway before the royal library, and stopped.

Toward the end, on one of the alcove benches lining the windows, sat Kade.

His hair fell forward into his face, but he hadn't removed it. Instead, he sat perched, unmoving, except for his gaze, which shifted back and forth, scanning a book resting on his lap.

Of course he sat perched there, flawless as a statue, while I looked like I'd lost three rounds against a razorven.

Swallowing down the obnoxious amount of desire growing in my gut at the sight of a sexy man reading, I cleared my throat to announce myself.

"I wouldn't have guessed you were a reader," I said.

He didn't even bother looking up from his book. "How else does one learn all there is to know?"

The last time I saw Kade, his tongue was down my throat, and now he couldn't be bothered to look up and acknowledge my presence.

I moved closer and tilted my head to the side, taking in the title. "The Forgotten Kingdom?" I asked before releasing a laugh.

That seemed to get his attention. His gaze scanned over me, the heat of it caressing my skin like he could see beneath my robe and straight through my nightgown. "You know it?"

"I read it as a teen," I answered, my voice thicker than it had been a moment ago. Books were what I'd used to escape from everything, especially from what happened with Andras. They'd saved me almost as much as Ian had. "It's not a bad fairytale."

"Mmm," Kade said. "They say all fairytales and folklore are based on a bit of fact."

"Oh? So, you believe there's an evil sorcerer trapped between this world and a forgotten kingdom, not a soul can see, or remember, do you?" I teased, daring to take another step toward him.

Kade flicked the book closed, tossing it on the seat cushions in front of him before rising from the alcove. He closed the distance between us as his shadows pooled at our feet, slinking their way up my body. "You look like you want something from me, Little Rebel. Another kiss perhaps?"

"You wish. I was merely on a walk."

"In your robe. Rebel suits you in more ways than one if this is the case," he said. He raised his hand, running a finger quickly over the knot I'd tied in the belt before dropping it back down to his side.

"You need to be careful with your 'little' play on words. I know I haven't said it yet, but I'm hoping you can keep certain things to yourself. My extracurricular activities are no one's business but my own."

"Which ones?" he whispered, his shadows jumped excitedly, quickening my heartbeat, as one stretched up and played with the bottom of my mangled hair. "The ones involving supplies, or my lips on yours?"

I shoved at his chest and waved his shadows away. "You know what I mean."

His lips curved upward in a devilishly handsome grin. "What if I need a bargaining chip? I could use the Hidden——"

I covered his mouth. "Not here."

Startling myself, I jumped back slightly, desire shooting through every part of my body the moment my hands pressed to his lips. The cool spring morning couldn't compare with him so near, warming me from the inside out, his shadows moving closer once more.

"Seems like it's good information to have. I could call in a favor, say winning one of the trials. Preferably the last one." He winked.

I wanted to enjoy the light tone he used, but something slithered beneath my skin— dread. He'd been clear he wanted the crown. What if getting close to me was the way he planned to get it and then use my secrets as leverage on top of my lust.

"Blackmailing me?" I asked, livid. "You're despicable."

"I never claimed to be anything but." He left his book behind as if it didn't even matter and shifted around me, sidestepping my body. "See you soon, I'm sure."

I watched him retreat, his shadows trailing behind him. I pushed the chasm of hurt and swirl of emotions back into the box hiding all my unwanted emotions. I didn't have time to feel hurt by a man I couldn't figure out.

It had only been a kiss. *Thankfully*.

But now? I refused to let it be anything more. Kade Blackthorn might be utterly irresistible, but danger oozed from his very being. With my secrets in his back pocket, I'd do well to not give him anything else to use to his advantage.

Like my damned heart.

CHAPTER 19

"How'd I do?" I asked Kalliah, tilting my head to the side so she could see my feeble attempt at a coronet braid. Braiding had never been something I mastered, regardless of how many times Kalliah tried to teach me. Slowly, but surely, I noticed improvement, though.

She shrugged. "Obviously it's not up to my superior level of styling, but it'll do I suppose."

Teasingly, I grimaced at the dig.

After announcing loudly, and only slightly dramatically to Ruppert and a few other nearby aides about how utterly exhausted I had become, I schemed to have lunch privately in my room today. With my two favorite people. Ian arrived late, and Kalliah turned up even later. Although I couldn't be too upset, because she'd stopped and grabbed extra lemon bars for dessert, one of my favorites.

"Leif mentioned your skills with your fingers, Kalliah," Ian said from where he sat in the sitting area of my chambers.

I spat out the dry red wine, which had just touched my lips. A sacrilege to waste such a delicious liquid, but I couldn't suppress my laughter. I patted the drops of wine off my dress before it could stain and put me in even more trouble with the laundress than usual.

Lucinda had been around for three centuries, so one would think she'd have seen it all. However, she constantly cursed at the dirt-stained clothes I sent down. *A princess should be proper, not rolling around in the muck with those heathen guards.* The constant muttering when she came to collect my laundry for the week usually consisted of unimpressed remarks about the state of my training attire.

Kalliah stared at Ian, crossing her arms. "Don't get me started on how much I've had to hear about *your* fingers, Captain."

"To be fair, there don't seem to be many complaints, and I don't mind hearing how I've been complimented. Gives me ideas for what to do next time," he said, stabbing the last bread roll with his knife and winking.

"Should we take the fact you're teasing Kalliah to mean Leif fancies her?"

I flinched as Kalliah walked up and pinched the back of my neck before she sat on the unoccupied chair.

She couldn't stop me now, though. "Or have you just noticed our dear Kalliah blushes any time his name comes up."

"I despise both of you, and don't know why I continue to be either of your friends," Kalliah grumbled.

Ian threw his head back, laughing. "I could see where his affections lie. Though, he stares at you enough, I'm surprised I didn't notice before training the other day."

"It's hard to notice anyone when your own fan club is continuously circling, waiting for a taste," Kalliah bit back.

"You say it like it's an insult, when instead, I find it flattering," Ian teased, winking again. "Besides, it's a pleasurable taste."

"Okay, you two—"

A firm knock sounded at my chamber doors. Kalliah

198

made a move to rise, and I waved her off. "I can answer my own door while you finish eating. Although if it's Ruppert, checking on me, *again*, I'm pretending I have suddenly come down with a highly contagious disease of some sort. Be warned." I sighed loudly. "I do not recall him being this insufferable."

I flung the door open, expecting to lock eyes with the stickler of a guard, and instead observed only a black tunic. Lifting my eyes, I found Kade.

And Storm.

My mood turned icy, and I growled. "What the hell are you doing here? Figure out more ways to blackmail a princess, have you?"

Kade cocked an eyebrow. "I must admit I was rather intrigued to find an invitation to your bedroom. Especially one that told me to bring Storm as well."

"You're insufferable."

"I invited them," Ian said, jumping up quickly from his chair, while giving me a not-so-subtle eye roll and waving the two men in. "They shouldn't be seen coming in, Lana. Use your brilliant brain for a moment."

"They shouldn't be here at all," I hissed back.

Kade brushed past me, inciting a spark spreading from where he touched me all the way to my toes. He paused, almost as if he felt it as well.

Arrogant. I shoved my shoulder into his chest. "Might want to move faster so I can close the door."

He flashed me a grin, bowing his head and walking inside toward the center of the room, close to Ian, who awkwardly stood next to the sitting area. Kalliah hadn't budged from her perch on the chaise next to him.

Storm's exasperated sigh as he passed revealed his own impatience with Kade. It gave me more satisfaction than it should, knowing he annoyed everyone, not just me.

"Well, apparently you called this meeting," I said, striding toward Ian while I tried and failed to keep the annoyance from my voice. "What was *so* important that it must be done without my knowledge and in the sanctuary of my chambers."

Ian cleared his throat, fidgeting on his feet slightly. "If you want to continue being the Hidden Henchman, then we need more help. Specifically, more men who can fight. The increase in attacks is bad enough, but there are too many dark ones ambushing the drops at once for our group to successfully operate alone anymore." He didn't even look at Kade or Storm.

Just me.

My shoulders slumped, but only because I knew he spoke the truth. I loathed asking for help, but the thought of asking Kade Blackthorn seemed even worse.

"As honored as I am at your *enthusiasm* of recruiting my friend and I," Kade said, tapping his chin and arrogantly cocking his brow, "we never agreed to join your gang of bandits."

Damn it. I was not prepared to have a mental image of Kade in my chambers. Why did he have to look so good? Even if he ruined it by running his mouth.

"Oh, no, whatever shall we do?" I mocked, feigning shock and sadness, my hand clutching my chest. "Well, we tried. Looks like we'll keep things status quo for now."

"Lan," Ian said. "They already know who you are, which makes them our only choice. Right now, it's this, or we have to stop until we learn more about what the dark ones are, and why they are getting closer to Ellevail."

Kade strolled forward, propping himself against my inner bedroom door. "Perhaps if Princess Illiana asked nicely, I'd be more inclined to offer my services."

"Fucking hell, here we go," Storm muttered. He hung his head in a clear sign of defeat, shaking it slightly.

"You prick." I planted my feet firmly in place, crossing my arms. "You're not the only skilled warrior in this realm.

We don't need you. I could find someone else I trusted. Besides, shouldn't you be off thinking of all the ways you can win this fates-forsaken trial so you can get your precious crown?"

"You saying you trust me is already an incredible start, Little Rebel." Kade's smile grew wider by the second. My dagger lay hidden on my thigh, as always. I wondered what would happen if I threw it at his muscular arm.

It wouldn't be too bad of an injury for him to heal quickly. He certainly had enough power. One little stab couldn't hurt.

I reached forward, my fingers curling around the fabric of my dress.

"Don't even think about it," Ian warned.

I frowned at him. "You ruin all my fun."

His gaze wandered down to exactly where my dagger hid, so I added another dig, despite the pettiness. "You're becoming more like Ruppert every day."

"I don't think tossing daggers at him will get him to agree to anything." Ian glared at me, unfazed by my attempt to rattle him.

"Oh, you don't know me very well then, my friend." Kade chuckled.

"You know, I've been wondering, how did you know how to contact us at the palace?" I asked. Pivoting, I glared at Ian. "I would have thought *you'd* ask that, actually."

Ian cracked his fingers, tapping his foot in frustration. "I did ask that."

"And?" I cocked an eyebrow.

"We took turns following the kitchen kid for over a week when we noticed he left town more often than other staff," Kade said.

"He's a grown man," I snapped.

Kade opened his mouth to continue, but Storm slammed a hand to his chest.

"Enough," Storm said. "Princess, if you tell us exactly

what it is you and Ian are asking, we'll be able to make a decision if we'll help."

"There was one more thing I wanted to know from you beyond how you knew the way to contact us. Why were you asking for supplies from the Hidden Henchman in the first place?" Ian asked. "And why track the dark ones after?"

"We have people we care for, like everyone, who has requested aid," Kade said.

Storm ran a hand over the side of his face. "We may have seen more of the dark ones than you have, but that hasn't given us much to go on," he said. "We wanted to get in touch with the Hidden Henchman, knowing the rumors of the aid you offered. We thought you'd have more information, but apparently, we were wrong."

I shook my head. "I've tried listening in during meetings, or gatherings to what the advisers tell my father, but even then, everything is done in hushed tones, or I'm rushed out so I cannot overhear."

"You must have something more," Ian said. "Even the smallest details could help. Do you know where they seem to gather?"

Kade shifted against the doorframe. Storm simply looked at Kade, waiting for his response, instead of offering one up of his own. "Starhaven and Valeford have always seemed to have activity, with Demarva a close third."

I tensed, glancing in Ian's direction.

"What?" Kade asked, sensing there was something we weren't telling him.

"Demarva is where we're sending more soldiers. Apparently, it's been overrun again," Ian answered, a grim expression on his face.

"Are the soldiers not questioned upon their return? It seems the men on the front lines would have even greater insights." Kade paused as no one spoke. "Captain?"

Ian stretched his neck. "Even being Captain of the Guard

does not afford me the knowledge of all the world's affairs it seems." He flexed his hand, barely able to contain his frustration. I already knew he felt like the general and the king were keeping important information from him. Every time we talked through the darkness, it became more and more evident just how much.

Ian questioned if it meant he wasn't good enough. Whereas I knew it had nothing to do with his ability. A dark part in the corner of my mind told me Ian remained uninformed because of our friendship. He could slip and share his knowledge with me at any time.

What could possibly be so horrible it had to be kept under lock and key? Other than our people not being safe, which had become more and more obvious. My destiny led to the throne, which meant I would have to know eventually.

"Besides," Ian added, "the soldiers aren't returning."

Kade and Storm were stunned into silence, evident by the way Kade's mouth opened and closed twice before slamming shut into a thin line. Storm leaned his head against the wall and sighed once more.

"We're sending twenty more men to Demarva sometime in the next few days," I added, jumping in to make it seem like I knew *something*. "I overheard Andras and my father talking at the first trial."

"So," Kade said, "no one knows anything, and whatever it is, is slowly eliminating the entire guard you have."

"That about sums it up," Ian responded, glancing toward the balcony doors. "Our associates are waiting for us, but I leave it up to you two," He gestured to me and Kade, "if we continue talking or not."

I studied Ian carefully, attempting to gauge what he really thought. He'd invited Kade and Storm here and must have trusted them thus far. As for me, Kade *had* kept me safe, saving me in more ways than one now.

At the rate things were changing, if the darkness grew

stronger, there wouldn't be much of a choice. We needed more fighters, and the pair of them were damn good.

I walked up to Kade, standing so close I had to tilt my head to meet his gaze. "If I let you in, if we take you to meet the others, you're in. You keep our secrets safe. You play by our rules. Do you agree?"

He cocked an eyebrow. "And what do we get in return for our assistance with your little project?"

I moved even closer, the cool scent of fresh rain and sweet summer air swirling around. "You get to live and continue on in these ridiculous trials. *Your* treasonous thoughts and activities are also safe with me."

"I've never been good at playing by the rules, Little Rebel."

"Kade!" Storm grunted, exasperated. "Yes, we want to figure out the darkness, too. Yes, you can trust us. Yes, we will help."

I waited for Kade to acknowledge his friend's response. Electricity seemed to dance between us. He brought his hand up, gently knocking underneath my chin. "Your secret is safe with me."

He stared into my eyes a few moments longer. Regardless of how hard I tried, I could not break away from the storms filling his gaze. He released my chin, and I finally freed myself from this trance.

Nodding toward Ian to lead the way, I followed, touching Kalliah's arm as we passed, steadying myself for a moment.

"Great, leave me here to explain why five men's voices are coming from inside your private garden," Kalliah grumbled. "Can't wait."

"We haven't been caught before, we will *not* be caught now." I touched her shoulder in quiet thanks.

"You mean before the hulking, broody contender for the crown lazily stood outside your door."

I snorted but kept walking out to my balcony.

"She forgot handsome, sexy, alluring—"

"I'm not sure I've ever met anyone who enjoys the sound of their own voice as much as you do, Kade," I said.

Storm coughed, but it sounded more like he tried to cover a laugh.

"Now, shall we discuss the details of our next drop, or would you like to continue this tirade?" I asked, my eyebrow arched.

We descended into my garden. My sanctuary now held more people than it ever had before.

As the men behind me left the staircase and fully stepped onto the lush floral masterpiece, I stretched my arm out. "Welcome to my private escape."

Storm gave a slight nod and kept moving forward, following Ian.

Kade had stopped, his fingers gently touching a beautiful dark-blue hydrangea bush blooming amongst storm-grey roses. I loved this spot.

"Some of the Earth Fae enjoy experimenting with combinations of floral colors," I said. "Corbin, he's one of the men who accompanied us on the last drop, and who you will meet in a moment, has an incredible knack for creating colors. He's mastered every combination I've asked for." I didn't know why I felt the need to explain this to Kade, but for a second, it seemed as though he cared. Besides, I couldn't help but love sharing the beauty which could be created here.

I knelt next to the roses, inhaling deeply.

Suddenly the color seemed too familiar. I'd asked for these a few weeks ago after returning from meeting Kade and Storm, and damn it all, this grey practically matched his eyes.

Clearing my throat, I rose, but Kade still stood, studying me. "I think finding the right colors to complement and work together can be just as magical as growing larger trees or

205

crops. Status amongst society be damned, I'm grateful for the talent of those around me." I fidgeted, my fingers twitching as I rambled.

I turned quickly, brushing past Kade and toward the others, slightly embarrassed at sharing so much of my inner thoughts. Especially sharing them aloud whether Kade had been interested in them or not.

Leif and Corbin were speaking to Ian and Storm when we approached.

"The roses turned out perfectly," I said to Corbin, gently bumping into his shoulder. "Thank you."

"I had fun."

I laughed at the straight face in which he replied. Corbin was the most stoic of our group. His recalling something as fun was rare and made me love the work he put into helping me even more.

I'd caught him smiling alongside Ian and Leif more than once, but he didn't express joy easily. Still, his steady presence could not be ignored. He told things like they were, which most people strayed from when speaking with royalty. He never balked when I asked for help in my garden, but he never shied away from telling me when my ideas weren't going to work, either.

For a second, my chest tightened. I'd spent so long believing Ian and Kalliah were the only friends who saw and understood me. Yet Leif and Corbin were two more Fae, risking their lives for a notion I'd come up with. Simply because I'd asked. They'd been loyal, and never demanded elevation of their status, or asked for anything in return.

A part of me wondered if I'd been too callous assuming I didn't have more Fae I could count amongst my friends. If I considered all of which Leif, Corbin, and Elisabeth had done for me, there were three more people right there I depended on fully.

Now Kade and Storm joined our mix. I highly doubted I would trust them nearly as much as Ian or Kalliah, but the promise of a new kind of bond tethering between us seemed right. It softened the jagged edges of a part of me I didn't realize needed acceptance.

"This spot is secure, as there is no access save for the one we created ourselves, or up the stairs and through Lana's room," Ian said since we were all gathered in the safety of the garden. "All conversations about the Hidden Henchman should happen here, or out on the road if necessary."

"Noted," Storm said, nodding.

Kade shook his head once, too.

"Leif Ivans, he works in the kitchens and handles securing most of the food requests." Ian turned and then pointed at Corbin. "Corbin Jansen. He works in the stables, securing transport, and serves as the point person receiving all requests and letters for aid through a network I'm not sure even I've deciphered yet."

Corbin's lip twitched as he shook Storm and Kade's hands.

"Technically, you met at the last drop, sort of," I said. "Informally."

Leif and Corbin readily accepted Kade and Storm, making me wonder if Ian had already let them know we needed more muscle. Which meant my buy-in was the only hurdle left to conquer.

"Lan?" Ian asked.

"Right, well, thanks to Fredrich's blabbering during his time with me, Starhaven seems to be the place where the darkness has lingered the longest," I said. "However, it's also the place with the least issues. There are no Hidden Henchman requests, something he quickly pointed out, and his business is thriving."

"How does that make sense? Others are falling easily, and

they withstand it the longest with no dip in his coffers?" Storm asked, frowning.

"Exactly," I said. "I think it's a fairly good place to start looking for answers."

"It's only a day's ride from the drop site at Logan Lake," Corbin said. "You could go straight to Starhaven and return from there. One and a half days out, one day back. It'd be a hard ride, but doable."

"Leaving us more vulnerable if we're attacked, given the exhaustion of the horses," Ian added. "Though, there may not be a choice."

I swiveled my gaze between my companions to gauge their responses.

"How soon until the goods are prepared?" Ian asked.

Leif shrugged. "We're all set. Just need to get the carriage out the day before and we'll be ready from there."

"How do you do all of this with no one noticing?" Kade asked suddenly. "Is there so much surplus missing items don't matter?"

"We're strategic with when and how much we take. We store extra items in various places until we are able to meet letter requests," I said. "We've been doing it for so long, it's second nature."

"And if you're caught?"

"Technically, we're stealing from the Crown," Leif chimed in. "For Corbin and I, we'd be executed."

He said it so casually. As if it weren't an issue at all.

I gaped at Leif. For the first time, I realized just how loyal these men really were. They risked their lives on a plan I'd come up with haphazardly, perfected by Ian. He'd done it alongside them, with their input and help, but the risk to me was a scolding. The risk to them? I'd selfishly never considered it.

Neither Leif nor Corbin had asked for protection if anything were to go awry.

"I'd never let it happen," I said, suddenly needing them to know I valued their trust.

"You do this, anyway?" Kade asked.

Leif's gaze shifted to me as he spoke. "I believe in the future of Brookmere and the queen who I bow to even as a princess."

A lump formed in my throat, listening to Leif proclaim his devotion in a way no one outside of Ian and Kalliah ever had. In a way which sparked that deep-rooted fire inside of me. The one I felt when I knew people were suffering. The reason I wanted to be the Hidden Henchman.

That same spark had driven me to strengthen myself, to train and break from the shell I'd become after enduring years of torture with Andras.

Kade's eyes locked on mine. The way he watched, Fates, it rattled me. My chest tightened, waiting to hear his response. Finally, he grinned, clearly making a decision. "Then I suppose I'll bow as well."

He took a step toward me, undeterred by the others observing. "I gave you my word to keep your secret, but I give you my sword for whatever else you need, Little Rebel."

"Thank you." My heart skipped a beat.

Ian studied Kade through his theatrics, undoubtedly picking apart anything he could to give him a sense of their honesty.

"Well, then." Corbin cleared his throat. "I must return."

"I'll give you the date of the next drop by sunset tomorrow," Ian said. He clasped his hand against Leif's arm, who followed after Corbin, leaving Ian and I with Kade and Storm.

"Not to state the obvious problem, but how are we going to get nearly three days away with the princess and two contenders?" Storm questioned.

"That's where Kalliah will come in. We need to work out a few final details. All you need to do is wait for the sign we're leaving." I waved my hand in front of me, a silent gesture indicating the men should use the staircase to move along.

Shockingly, Kade obeyed without any snide remarks.

Once we ascended the balcony stairs, silence fell over the group. Ian ushered Kade and Storm out, leaving behind only myself and Kalliah, who had been patiently waiting for us to return.

We gathered back in the sitting area, when Lucien bounded in, breathing into the fireplace, and lighting a fire.

"No," I groaned. "It's too hot for fire."

His eyes fell at my rejection. "Elisabeth will want one, though, she always needs your help." With a scratch under his chin, he ran from our meeting, undoubtedly off to sneak to Elisabeth's chambers. How the animal came and went in the palace without needing us to let him into rooms was beyond me, but I'd stopped questioning the animals of Brookmere long ago.

I refocused on Kalliah and filled her in on our plans. The tension in her face grew more taught as I finished. "Wonderful, so now we trick an entire castle about where three of the most important Fae in these trials are for two and a half days."

"Oh, come on now." I grinned. "What's life without a little adventure?"

"Not a life with you, I can promise you that." She massaged her temples. "Leave it to me."

"I love you," I whispered as she flung her hand over her shoulder at me and exited my chambers.

That night alone in my room, I replayed the afternoon, the words Leif had said, and the camaraderie we'd suddenly found ourselves building with others outside of our small world.

The spark inside of me flared again, but this time, I could name it.

Hope.

For the first time since things spiraled out of control with the Hidden Henchman, the dark ones, and the marriage trials starting, I felt hope again. I slept soundly for the first time in weeks. A sleep free from the nightmares so desperately trying to plague me.

CHAPTER 20

Hunched over with my warm, purple and gold quilt around me, I made a scene, clutching a teacup from Elisabeth as she escorted me back to the main hallway of the palace.

"Call me immediately if you begin to develop a fever," Elisabeth said, loudly enough for all to hear. Adjusting my quilt, she patted my arm and gazed lovingly into my eyes. A moment later, she turned and disappeared down the hall.

Coughing and sniffling, I shuffled my feet slowly.

"Princess." Fredrich's boisterous voice echoed down the hallway, already grating on my nerves.

It took all my willpower not to flinch, but this had to be done. I knew he'd be the nosiest and would spread the word of my "sickness" the fastest.

I timed this orchestrated fake parade perfectly, with his daily walk amongst the castle halls after breakfast. A walk most other contenders tried to avoid, as they found him as insufferable as I did.

"You're ill?" he questioned, trying to establish where Elisabeth had disappeared down the hallway. "How is your healer unable to assist you?"

I wiped an imaginary bead of sweat from my brow. "I would never waste our healer's time with something as insignificant as a few aches and a cough. She has far more important things to tend to than a simple cold. It's nothing a few days in bed can't fix."

"How noble of you, Princess," Kade said, sauntering over from his perch atop the stairs. If I so much as glanced at him, I'd likely ruin the ruse. "May I help you back to your room?"

"There's no need to make a fuss." I shifted, standing taller and grasping my quilt in one hand while I balanced the tea in another. "Don't you gentlemen have things you could attend to while waiting for the next trial? It seems like the perfect opportunity to get to know others from around Brookmere and improve our overall relations. Trade agreements would be most logical while in person, if I do say so myself."

"Of course, Princess. What a fine idea. Even if you did get the idea from me." Fredrich touched the tip of my nose with a finger. "I see my words have value to you."

I may *actually* be sick if he continued babbling on.

"Well, if you'll excuse me, I'm just going to lie down and rest for the remainder of the day. I look forward to seeing you both once I am well. Good day." With a quick bow of my head, I slowly hobbled down the remainder of the corridor, pausing to clutch my quilt tighter as I climbed the stairs to my chamber.

The act was complete. I made it to my chambers, closed the door, and laughed to myself at how easily Frederich had bought our tale. With a sense of purpose, I quickly changed into my Hidden Henchman ensemble, clasping the cloak around my shoulders. I kept my mask tucked away in the inner pocket of my cloak. I wouldn't need the cloak or the mask for the entirety of our journey, but until we snuck out of Ellevail and were on the open road, I needed to be unrecognizable.

For a moment, I took in the roses left on the mantel above

my hearth. The range of colors were so exquisite. It reminded me how grateful I should be to live in a world where such elegance existed. While I couldn't contribute to the prosperity of our kingdom in any magical sort of way, I knew discovering information about the darkness was something I *could* do. Something I didn't need magic in order to accomplish.

The chime of the clock struck nine a.m. Where were they?

Anxiously, I peeked around the curtain, through the window, into my private garden. Empty.

Trying to keep myself occupied, I fluffed the pillows on my bed to make it appear like I was lying there, asleep. I adjusted the sleeve of the nightgown, filled with towels, draped across my sheet. My "hand" landed underneath the mountain of pillows, invisible to anyone from afar. Kalliah would be at my bedside to ward off any unwanted intruders who made it through Elisabeth's warnings to let me rest.

Kalliah whispered "Hello" as she opened and closed the main doors, before she entered the room. Slowly, she exhaled a breath the way she always did to calm her nerves and nodded. "Good luck."

"Thank you, my friend," I said sincerely, holding my hand to my heart. "I owe you."

A caw sounded from the garden.

The time had come.

Kalliah and I stared at each other a moment longer, before running toward each other, our embrace saying all the words which would go unsaid. I hadn't been away from the palace overnight since childhood. Which meant, I hadn't been away from her, either.

Pausing at the balcony doors, I glanced back into Kalliah's eyes once more, giving her a reassuring smile as I readied myself for the journey ahead.

"Be careful," Kalliah whispered as I quietly slipped through the doors, quickly leaping down the steps to my hidden alcove. I could not be seen by any of the passing guards, or the ruse would be for naught.

Ian's hawk form landed in the garden and his Fae form appeared before me, his eyes the last part to shift. While I had witnessed his transformation a thousand times, it still fascinated me. When his eyes were in the form of his hawk, it seemed as if he could see into the depths of my soul, reaching parts of me I didn't even know existed.

"Is Kalliah in place?" he asked.

"Yes, she's in the room, the bed is made up," I replied. "Elisabeth is going to be around in about an hour to declare my fever has spiked and I am to be left alone until it is broken."

"Are you sure you want to go through with this? Sneaking away at night is one thing, but leaving for two and a half days? What if your parents come looking for you? The likelihood this will work is slim." Ian's voice rose slightly higher with each question. He seemed more anxious than usual.

"It has to work. We have to find out what is going on with the darkness." I made sure to steady myself before we left. This was the right thing to do. I could feel it. "I can no longer wait for my father to provide me with information. It's clear he is not going to tell me anything, and the longer we let this go, the worse it might get. No more doubting, Ian. Let's go!"

I grabbed him by the hand and dragged him through the hedgerow toward the concealed exit beyond.

Hunched behind gloriously large hydrangea bushes, I murmured, "Where is everyone else?"

"Kade and Storm are meeting us at the edge of Eomer Forest. I didn't want them to know about our getaway tunnels. Leif and Corbin are staged on the main street, per their usual route. We will meet them at the edge of the forest once they're through."

"Smart. While they have earned some of our trust, they don't need to know all of our secrets just yet."

Ian snorted. "Right, and it would only be an additional nuance for you and Kade to argue about."

I pinched Ian's arm, but he didn't react.

Know-it-all.

A few beats more, and the Royal Guard on duty rounded the corner, signaling our window to escape had begun.

Quickly, we ran the route we knew so well. The route which led to the reason I persevered without magic. The route which helped so many people of Brookmere. The route which led to freedom.

While I'd been to the forest for Hidden Henchman duties plenty of times, something about this journey made freedom seem so different. As soon as the grate opened and we made it past the wall, I ran, allowing the wind to sail over me, kissing my skin and encouraging a smile.

In fact, I didn't stop running until I jumped over a fallen tree into the woods of the forest. Ian kept pace but gave me space to enjoy myself.

He didn't say a word. I flung my arms out, basking in the morning scent of fresh air that filled my soul with determination.

When I opened my eyes again, Ian watched, a faint smile on his face. "Ready?"

I nodded, excitedly following behind as he led the way toward Kade and Storm.

As Ian and I broke through the clearing where we'd first met, a slow clap reverberated throughout the space.

"Bravo on the sick performance," Kade praised. "Fredrich told everyone who would listen, that once again, there'd be no time with the princess."

I bowed at the waist, obnoxiously low.

Ian rolled his eyes, nudging me toward the horse Storm held by the reins, as he approached Kade. "Any problems?"

Kade shook his head. "Apparently, your guards couldn't have cared less about our leaving with two horses in tow. They seemingly forgot we failed to return our two other horses from our early morning jaunt in town."

The waiting horses grazed on a patch of grass as they waited patiently for our upcoming adventure.

"Contenders are free to come and go as they please," Ian said gruffly, mounting his black stallion with ease. Adjusting himself on the saddle, I could practically see the wheels turning in his mind about the conversation. He took the comment as an insult about his ability to keep his kingdom safe.

"The others?" Storm asked, stroking the neck of his bridled mare. Her tail whipped in annoyance, ready to go. She had been prancing in place, eager to move.

"Meeting us closer to the drop and sticking to the main roads." Ian clicked his tongue as he led his horse to the front of our group, driving us deeper into the forest.

The sweet notes of birds singing, calling back and forth to one another, a beautiful polyphony of melodies nestled amongst the leaves. The breeze felt warm, and the sun shone bright, peaking through the top of the tall trees in full bloom.

Perhaps nature would guide us on our journey these next few days, protecting us from whatever lurked in the darkness —in the corners we had yet to discover. Just to be safe, I said a quick prayer that we wouldn't be disturbed by any dark ones this time around.

Kade steered his horse behind Ian's left side, while Storm hung back with me as we rode quietly through the forest.

We rode in companionable silence, quiet for the first hour of our journey.

I glanced at the warrior to my right. His brown hair shifted as his body kept time with his steed. He had it pulled back like normal, half of it swept into a bun. The waviness to it made me jealous and I couldn't help but grin. I could only achieve such a look after sitting for hours with Kalliah, wrapping my hair in long pieces of fabric. An agonizing process I avoided at all costs.

Storm's eyes were serious, shifting around before us and taking everything in. His beard, though subtle, highlighted his sharp jaw—further complementing his bulking muscles, proudly protruding from his short-sleeved tunic. An inky black band wound around his bicep, curling down his forearm. It appeared to be a beautiful composition of flames and ribbons.

He cocked an eyebrow and glanced my way.

"What does that mark mean?" I asked, gesturing to his arm.

Storm stared forward, taking a deep breath. "It is tradition for warriors to receive them after their first kill. It reminds us even when justified, taking a life leaves a mark."

I hadn't been aware of any such customs in Brookmere, but I didn't want to presume I knew each one of our village's cultures intimately.

"It's beautiful." I didn't know if it was the right thing to say, but Storm offered me a soft smile and nodded in thanks.

"What about the ones on your arm?" I directed my question at Kade, already knowing he listened in, regardless of whether I addressed him or not. His damn Fae hearing would have picked it up, anyway.

He peered over his shoulder. "If you want me shirtless, you need only ask, Your Highness."

"Tits and daggers. You shirtless seems about as appealing as listening to Lord West talk about how great he is," I bit back.

"There's the foul-mouthed tavern princess I know and love," Ian teased.

Kade stared, open mouthed at me. "Tavern princess? Well, a tavern princess would certainly enjoy me shirtless."

My face heated. "You arrogant, conceited—"

Storm huffed. "You two were made for each other."

Ian attempted to cover his laughter with a mock-coughing fit that had me wishing I had something to throw at him. My stare would just have to bore holes into the back of his head instead.

"Something to say, Captain?" I added.

"There's something in the air, I think," Ian said as he wiped away a tear leaking from his eye.

Storm coughed next, waving his hand around. "Oh, yes, I feel it, too."

Kade laughed so deeply, I stared, wide-eyed, as he threw his head back, his Adam's apple bobbing.

I shifted my gaze forward, focusing on Ian's back instead of the man beside me.

"I've never had Storm help me with my jokes, Captain," Kade remarked. "Not in the fifteen years I've known him."

Storm leaned toward me. "It's because he's the only one who finds his jokes humorous."

The path we took through the forest was used frequently enough that the horses could easily navigate by themselves, with little direction. Without having to pay such close attention to what lay before me, my mind wandered into curious territories.

"How did you become friends with this one, Storm?" I asked. "He seems far more arrogant than you."

Kade rotated his entire body, so he rode his horse backward. My mouth dropped as he called, "It's only arrogance if the things I boast of are untrue."

"This may shock you, Princess," Storm chuckled, "he's usually quieter. More docile." He remained unbothered by the murderous glare Kade shot him as he righted himself on his saddle, huffing with disapproval.

"Far less social," Storm continued. "Honestly he's a bit of a grump when we're home."

"Are we talking about the same man?" I asked, jaw

hanging open slightly once more. "The one who tried to flirt with me while pressing his sword to my throat during battle?"

"I merely matched the violent energy you were throwing my way, Little Rebel." Kade's voice was indignant, but if he turned around, I had a feeling there would be a playfulness to his gaze.

Storm shook his head as we rode. "Ellevail seems to have changed him in new ways. Including his idea of flirting. Though, he hasn't done much of that since I've known him, either."

I couldn't help joining in on the laughter this time.

Kade turned his horse around, trotting in a semicircle. "I haven't needed to resort to flirting. Especially not to show off in front of other Fae before." Kade winked at me as he fell in step with his steed beside me. I closed my eyes at the intensity of the way the simple contact of his leg brushing mine caressed the inner parts of me.

"Perhaps Ian could give him some lessons," I told Storm. "He has always managed to woo the eligible women of Brookmere. However, I wouldn't expect such behavior amongst contenders for my hand," I quipped. My mouth ran away on its own, from my proper princess demeanor, choosing to let out my inner lustful barmaid. She threatened to take over more times than I cared to admit. Usually, my non-proper side only appeared in the presence of Ian and Kalliah.

Something made me feel at ease now, and I realized I had to be careful. The walls I'd spent carefully constructing couldn't disappear just because Kade Blackthorn had a sexy smile I couldn't get out of my head.

Kade's eyes widened in Ian's direction, who had remained relatively quiet this trip, observing everyone interact and taking it all in. I knew Ian well. He analyzed every move and each step we took on the journey, always prepared for what may lie in wait.

He shrugged nonchalantly at the new attention and offered a sly smile in Kade's direction. "Magic and swords may hurt like hell, but the company of a woman at night should always leave with a satisfying ending."

"It appears I have underestimated you, Captain," Kade said.

A branch snapped and our heads swiveled to the right. An orangish-red fox trotted along, unbothered by our intrusion into his home. The animal, normally protective, was usually content to ignore Fae. It sniffed the air in our direction before it turned, disappearing farther into the woods.

A few minutes went by before a calm returned to the forest once more.

"So, do you think this new version of Kade should get a chance at being King?" I asked Storm as he continued to meticulously survey our surroundings.

"Despite the fact that he's behaving like an absolute prick at the moment, he doesn't need to do anything to earn the title of 'King' in my eyes. He's loyal and usually a damn good friend." Storm's voice seemed nonchalant, but the weight of his words wasn't missed. I watched as he trained his gaze forward, not looking to gauge my reaction, or Kade's for that matter.

"I pay him to sing my praises," Kade whispered. "Don't get any ideas, I'm not some knight in shining armor, ready to sweep you off your feet."

Ian held up his hand. "If you all are done chattering, we're two miles out from the drop site. I'd like to proceed without the extra banter."

Storm trotted his horse up to Ian and gave him a curt nod.

I pursed my lips, obeying, and felt Kade's presence lessen beside me as he dropped back. My palms were slick as I re-gripped the reins in my hand.

We'd yet to come out of a drop with no attacks, and we were almost to our destination.

In the distance a call sounded in the sky, one which mimicked Ian's hawk.

My heart stuttered in my chest.

It was Leif. Or Corbin.

I just didn't know what it meant yet.

CHAPTER 21

No one spoke a word as an additional call sounded.

Ian raised his voice. "We're clear."

The three of us followed his lead, racing toward the drop point, ducking under the branches, and jumping over the thicker brush, which crept into our path. As we cleared Eomer Forest, the lakeside sparkled in the sun before us. The sky reflected onto the water, a vision of the sunset lay upon its turquoise surface. The carriage of goods Leif and Corbin packed came into view.

We waited approximately an hour by the side of Logan Lake for the Fae in need. While we were focused on remaining safe as we waited, the raw magnificence of nature filled me with awe. I had never traveled this far out of Ellevail before, and it took my breath away. I knew I would never be able to memorize every color of the blazing sunset before me.

Without any interruptions or ambushes, the Fae retrieved their request and left. Unharmed. It was a simple drop. Simple like it used to be. My shoulders sagged with relief. I lifted my head toward the sky, whispering my thanks to nature for its protection on this day.

With the first part of our mission complete, we set up

camp for the night. While we could likely make it to Starhaven before morning, traveling at night could lead to disaster, especially with everything that had happened recently, and the creatures who liked to lurk in the dark.

"Perhaps, it's a sign—the luck we've had thus far," Ian said as he began gathering wood to make a fire. We'd left Storm and Kade at the campsite to set up our bedrolls and prepare the area.

I found a blueberry bush nearby and collected a plethora of berries in an extra bag for us to eat, popping a few in my mouth for good measure along the way. The sweet juice slicked my tongue.

"I'm not sure, but I am grateful it went as smoothly as it did."

Ian's hands were filled, ready to return. I hadn't had as much success as I wanted to yet, so when he turned to head back to the campsite, I waved him on. "I think that's a raspberry bush just around the corner. I'm going to pick those and be right back."

Ian hesitated a moment, an internal struggle within to give me space in this unknown area and to fulfill his duty as my personal guard. But a moment later, he relinquished the reins and allowed me to continue down the path to the raspberry bush alone.

One day, I'd return Brookmere to safety. Enjoying various trips, and the lushness of the land outside Ellevail wouldn't be a rarity anymore. I'd make sure of it. Somehow.

Exactly as I thought, near the edge of the woods, bloomed a raspberry bush. Its plump ripe red berries were bursting to be picked. I followed the trail of bushes, grabbing the reddest of the bunch.

Once my bag couldn't hold any more berries, I followed the windy path to exit the woods. The trail led to a small, secluded part of the lake to my left. A runoff perhaps, since I hadn't noticed any additional water source earlier while we waited to complete the drop.

I savored the silence and the moment alone. The trickling water hummed, resembling a gentle lullaby in the night air. I turned to head back to camp when I noticed a pile of clothes on the ground next to the edge of the lake.

I frowned, reaching down to pick up the garments when Kade's head surfaced to the top of the lake, his black hair slicked back as he stared out into the calm waters beyond.

Slowly he emerged, and the thick muscles, upon muscles, rippling along his back stole all my focus—and my rationality.

Fates above. The man was utterly intoxicating. Water beaded on his skin as he stood higher, eventually stopping when the water hit his hips.

He ran his hands over his hair, his muscles tightening as he did. The swirling black marks I'd only seen peeking from his shirt before, continued up his arm and around his right shoulder. Gorgeous. A deadly-looking twining of inky shadows crawled over his skin.

I wanted to run my fingers over them, tracing the lines slowly.

Get it together.

I clenched my teeth, somehow believing the move could subdue the need coursing through my body.

I am a grown woman. I've seen plenty of shirtless men.

Even if I couldn't put my finger on it, something about *this* shirtless man put all others to shame.

My heart quickened at the sight, palms sweating as I couldn't take my eyes off his incredible physique. I refused to even breathe, too afraid of being caught.

He twisted slightly, and I froze. He moved, only to dunk back under the water. I took the opportunity while he remained submerged to run back toward camp, losing a few raspberries along the way. Better to lose a few berries than be caught staring at a shirtless Kade.

Less than an hour later, I'd reined in my uncontrollable lust from seeing Kade's body in the water. It helped that he took his time returning. I remained quieter than usual, observing, instead of interacting, in hopes I didn't do or say something idiotic.

Working to control my thoughts allowed me to instead think about where I stood. Away from the palace. Away from the gilded cage, which locked me up for so long. The thought of spending the night beneath the stars was more than I could ever wish for. Like so many times before, peace settled over my body when I lay beneath them. A feeling of home, like the night sky called to my soul.

As a child, I would sneak into my gardens at night and fall asleep next to the statue of my father. Ruppert would begrudgingly bring me back to my room once the hourly guard went by for his normal rounds and found me. He never asked me to stop, though, likely a request from my father.

Storm easily ignited the fire for us with his magic as Kade brought out the venison stew and crusty bread Leif had so kindly left with us before he and Corbin returned to Ellevail.

We were all quiet as we completed our respective tasks. Despite the fact we hadn't known Storm and Kade for very long, and had decided to trust them for even less, we worked together as if we had been companions for years.

I glanced at Kade while I finished organizing the berries I'd gathered, and he appeared strained, his body tense, as though he fought an internal battle of some sort. I tried to not be so obvious, but I couldn't look away. The normally composed Fae tried to hide his pain under the surface. However, if anyone bothered to look closely enough, it would be clear.

The dark expression on his face disappeared, and he returned to his normal demeanor before I had a chance to check on him. He wasn't the only one who tried to hide from his demons, because I did the same thing. I'd been doing it my whole life. Hiding truths one couldn't outwardly share, pushing down those lingering emotions into a sacred box of untold truths.

Storm whispered in his ear. Kade nodded once, but Storm remained by his side. Something was wrong with him, or perhaps memories haunted him like they did me. Either way, the exchange served as a stark reminder that I didn't know him very well. He had secrets. Just like I did.

The fire blazed, warming the small campsite by the time we finally sat around it. Despite it being summer, the nights were cool. A three-stick crane held our stew over the fire, and it gave off a hearty aroma. Stirring the meal, Ian said, "A few more minutes and this should be ready."

My stomach grumbled, betraying my hunger. The grumbling of my companions' bellies also seemed to reverberate in our small camp.

Ian served the portions of venison stew to the three of us before taking a bowl for himself. We eagerly inhaled the hearty dinner. Chunks of meat, carrots, and potatoes filled our empty bellies.

"How do you two know each other so well?" Storm asked, finally speaking. "You seem to have a relationship much closer than just being the princess's personal guard."

Kade barely moved, except for a wisp of his hair fluttering in the breeze, but I noticed his gaze flick between Ian and me.

Ian and I stared at each other for a moment, and I waved at Ian to answer the question. How much of his story he wished to share was up to him.

"My father was the king's personal guard," Ian answered. "We grew up together."

I smiled softly at him, but his face remained tight. Ian didn't speak of his past often, so his response remained vague, whether it be from the question itself or our company. Perhaps even both. Ian couldn't relax and likely wouldn't until we

229

returned to the palace, even if he attempted to appear settled beside the fire.

"It's hard to not be close when we have spent almost every day together since we were so little. A friendship I truly cherish," I replied, hoping Ian understood I appreciated him and everything he had done for me.

"That friendship is not enough to earn the princess's hand without the show of a trial?" Kade asked bluntly, his eyebrow cocked.

Storm rolled his eyes dramatically and barely contained his sigh of indignation.

A flash of irritation hit me as I stared at him. "Ian has nothing to prove to my father, or anyone in this kingdom, and especially not to me. He's one of the best captains Brookmere has ever seen."

I didn't take my eyes off Kade, waiting for the next snarky comment he planned to offer.

"My job is to protect Lana in all things. Even the marriage trials." Ian stared at the flames, not bothering to glance up, clearly troubled by the direction of this conversation. If I had to be honest with myself, I didn't quite know how to respond, either.

Kade raised his hands up defensively. "I don't mean to pry."

"Yes, you do," I said.

He rubbed his hands together, lowering the tone of his voice to be as seductive as possible. "I'm merely curious if I'm the only one the princess is kissing in palace corridors. One can never be too sure of the competition."

I let out a dry laugh. "If you think for one moment you can act like a mongrel, pissing on your territory to claim it, think again, Kade Blackthorn."

"Why the trials at all if your childhood friend is willing to be King beside you?"

My jaw clenched. No one knew of the prophecy, and it

wasn't as if I'd tell him, of all people. "There's much you don't understand, which makes sense, given you can hardly comprehend palace life and the duties we have. You have no real home, just traipsing across Brookmere, right?"

"Right. Traipsing across Brookmere." Kade chuckled dryly. "Well, with all my travels, I have seen what is threatening your kingdom and the suffering of *your* people. Knowledge is power, and I choose to barter with a currency that is priceless."

I stared at Kade, refusing to speak, the heat of the fire stoking the flame of anger within me. This man had some nerve.

"I wonder why you possess such loyalty to a father who wouldn't allow you the courtesy of choosing your King, or preparing you for what lies ahead. If Storm and I can see what's happening, be sure he knows as well." He shifted his gaze to Ian. "How does the same King retain the loyalty and devotion of a Captain of the Guard, who he keeps leashed and uninformed?"

The crackle of the fire served as the only sound interrupting the awkward silence between us. My right eye twitched. I had to compose myself before responding. I needed Kade and Storm on this journey right now, and leaping across this campfire and beating the hell out of him would be an unacceptable response.

"My father is a good and just ruler. I don't need to defend him to you. If you'd prefer to spend your time in the dungeons for your treasonous tongue, it can be arranged." I curled my hands into fists on my lap as tears rose to my eyes.

I hated that my body's response to anger was crying. I had never been able to overcome this reaction. How *dare* this man speak such words against my father.

Yet, I hated myself even more in the moment. I hated how I had thoughts similar to Kade's. Hated the way they made sense because I, too, questioned so much as of late. However, I refused to let it be known to others.

"Enough," Ian whispered threateningly. "We offered you an opportunity to find information with us, but do *not* mistake our kindness for weakness."

Kade stared at Ian and eventually inclined his head. "How do you feel about the other contenders?"

Storm cleared his throat, likely to silence Kade from another series of questions, which were certain to get him in trouble.

"It's not for me to have an opinion about them," Ian said curtly.

I rose from my seat, grabbing my blanket from the pile as I turned to my bedroll, located just behind me. "I think I've had all the fun I can handle for one evening. Goodnight, gentlemen."

I couldn't hide or find a place to collect my thoughts without being watched. Straying from the fire would only cause me to be cold. I shuffled into the bedroll, my back toward the fire, and closed my eyes tightly.

The men didn't chatter, but they moved around me. Ian leaned down and squeezed my hand, keeping the silence between us, but providing his comfort. Storm grumbled he would take the first watch as we all finally settled.

Ian laid his own roll out farther than mine, and I didn't bother rolling over to note where Storm and Kade set themselves up for the evening.

The warmth of the fire had not yet reached my toes, but a gift from the Fates, or more likely one of the men across the way, cascaded along my body. A gentle heat enveloped each part of me as I snuggled further into my bedroll.

The sky above me sparkled, clearer than I'd ever seen. There were so many stars to behold in the void of blackness above.

I wanted nothing more than to stare at them all night and

imagine what life could be outside the confines of the palace walls. A life with no prophecies or marriage trials. No incurable illnesses for my father, and definitely no crazed Fae trying to attack my people. I didn't want there to be secrets my father kept from me, and I didn't want to hold on to the dark secrets of my past, which I had yet to share with him, either.

Then, despite the thousand more important things to focus on, my mind wandered to the man sitting a few feet away from me at the campfire.

Why did he rile me up so much?

I feared the answer was clear. The stirring in my gut had been enough to realize my attraction to Kade couldn't be ignored.

And then the damned kiss had to happen.

I curled even further into my bedroll, determined to stop thinking of Kade, his treasonous thoughts, his lips, and everything else I had yet to experience with the egotistical man.

CHAPTER 22

The warmth against my back made my toes curl in delight.

I'd fully expected to wake up shivering from the cool morning air, so the pleasant surprise of heat cocooning me encouraged me to linger a moment longer before waking entirely.

The dying embers in the fire cast a gentle orange glow in the pile of wood. I arched my back to stretch out and immediately froze.

Slowly turning my head to the side, I took in the sight of the solid body behind me. It took everything within me to stifle the groan working its way up my throat.

The damn bedroll had nothing to do with keeping me warm, but Kade certainly did.

Ian hadn't moved all night, still in the same place from when I fell asleep.

How on earth had I ended up pressed against this insufferable man?

And why did it feel so damn good?

Getting caught like this, though, would be beyond embarrassing.

I moved slowly, attempting to pull away from him, but he twitched, flinging his arm over me. He tugged on me tightly, pulling me in close to his warm, hard body.

"Looking for another kiss, Little Rebel?" he whispered in my ear. His deep voice was huskier in the morning and sent a delicious shiver coursing down the length of my spine and straight to my core. *Damn it.*

"Absolutely not," I hissed in return. "You're the one wrapped around me." I lifted his arm and rolled out of his reach.

Kade's eyes were still closed. "I'm just as surprised as you are, Princess."

"The sun is barely up," Storm grumbled, raising his head before he paused, giving Kade a glare which could kill. "Aren't you supposed to be on watch right now?"

"The shadows are keeping watch, don't you worry."

Storm continued to mutter to himself as he rose from his own bedroll, marching off in the direction of the river. I scurried farther away from Kade as Ian rolled over, cocking an eyebrow suspiciously between the two of us.

"It's a three-hour ride to Starhaven," Ian said. "If we hurry, we can make it there, investigate, and still be back on the road by this evening."

His lack of comment about learning how I kissed Kade, and whatever happened last night unnerved me. At some point I was certain I'd hear his point of view on Kade, and this "thing" between us.

No.

There is nothing between us.

This silly attraction needed to be quashed before I did something stupid. Right?

Giving into my lustful desires, or even worse, developing feelings for him in the middle of the marriage trials could only lead to disaster.

With the early hour, we packed and mounted the horses in

relative silence. I wished someone would say something. Riding in the quiet gave me too much time to think about the tension pulling taught between Kade and I, and all the questions left unanswered.

Two hours in, and my thighs were screaming. Aching. Despite my riding skills, it had been years since I'd been allowed to venture away from Ellevail enough to amass more than an hour riding at a time. Day two of this had me dreading how sore I'd be once we returned to the palace tomorrow evening, cursing myself for forgetting Elisabeth's salve. The first thing I would be doing would be taking a long, hot bath and having that blessed concoction soothe my aching muscles.

I only lasted a few more minutes before I needed a distraction from the pain radiating through my body. Ian and Storm were in front of me while Kade rode beside me. His face seemed serious, deep in concentration. His brows were furrowed, and even with the breeze and cooler morning temperatures, sweat beaded across his forehead.

"A little horseback riding has you all hot and bothered, Kade?" I teased.

He didn't say anything, didn't even acknowledge I had spoken. I hated the way my heart sank. Perhaps he wasn't in the mood for joking around. I kept my gaze trained forward so he couldn't see the pain in my eyes. Silence continued until Kade abruptly stopped his horse in the middle of the path. I tugged on the reins of my own horse to halt as well.

"Today is a special day for some of my friends," he said quietly. "A sort of anniversary of when we all realized we weren't so alone. I haven't seen them in a long time and was merely thinking about how I miss them."

My chest expanded as he shared this piece of his soul with me. I knew he wouldn't have shared it with just anyone. He looked down at his horse, patting the mare's neck before our eyes locked once more.

The deviation to something more serious than the bickering between us surprised me. "I'm sorry you are away from your friends and helping me instead." My heart jolted, suddenly heavy, thinking of what I would do if I were ever away from Ian and Kalliah for any length of time. I couldn't be sure if I would survive without them. "Some people make friendship look so easy, but it's something else entirely when you find people who understand you. Truly understand you."

He mirrored my small smile and neither of us looked away until Kade's eyes darkened, and he stiffened. He closed his eyes, shaking his head and allowing whatever shadow passed through him to clear. Gone almost as quickly as it had come, he shifted on his saddle, urging his horse forward once more.

"Why are you helping us?" I asked. "You have no reason to. You offer your aid and skill to towns where you have no allegiance. I haven't promised you favor in the trials. So, what's in it for you?"

"Well, Little Rebe—" Kade stopped, tensing.

Ian came to a halt, his right fist quickly rising in the air. A signal for all of us to be silent and stop moving.

Even the breeze stilled around us. Ian swiveled his head, as Storm and Kade matched his movements. They searched the trees and skies for any indication of danger, any indication to explain whatever they all sensed.

Suddenly, it encompassed me, too. Even without magic, something stroked my skin. Something ominous, heavy, and wrong. A hum of dark energy lay just out of reach.

A whistle sounded throughout the air seconds before an arrow struck the ground in front of my horse's hooves. The beast reared. "Easy, girl, easy," I said, trying to soothe her angst.

My eyes widened, and moved slowly from the arrow to Kade, then to the trees beyond.

We were under attack.

I quickly pulled the dagger from its sheath at my side.

Ian turned his horse, facing me and Kade. "Go, as fast as you can. We have a better chance of making it if we can get to the next field where they will not be able to hide in the trees."

"What about you?" I asked, but as I spoke, Ian jumped from his horse and leapt into the air, shifting into his hawk form.

"Damn, I've never seen a shifter transform so quick," Storm said. "Come on."

Without missing a beat, Storm grabbed onto the reins of Ian's horse, and the three of us galloped as fast as we could through the remaining parts of the forest. We would have to ride close to the tree line and through one more patch, before entering the open field. We had no other option.

Storm pushed his horse harder, begging her to gallop faster as we followed.

As we fled through the forest, arrows soared above our heads the entire journey. Only they weren't even close to hitting us. They volleyed over and over, always landing near our horses' hooves, or behind us.

Thump. Thump. Thump.

They whizzed but remained *just* off by a few inches. Almost as if they were trying to miss us.

A screech from the air stopped my heart. I knew that cry, Fates help us.

We cleared the forest and into the open field before we immediately came to a halt.

No.

An audible gasp escaped my lips at the sight before me. At least thirty dark ones rushed toward us. We'd ridden straight into a trap.

There were too many. Re-gripping my dagger, I knew there would be no time to hesitate. No time to panic.

The dark ones descended upon Storm first, and he

239

jumped from his horse. He hadn't even reached for his sword this time, like he had done previously.

"What are you doing?" I cried, scared for him as he held his hands out to his side.

Fire ignited in each palm, winding up his arm. "Come and get me," he snarled.

Ian landed in hawk form, shifting quickly as he grabbed his sword from his horse's pack. He turned, barely removing it in time to get to the attackers.

Kade swung off his own steed, blade in hand. He appeared to float as his shadows unfurled from his limbs and reached out, grabbing the first three attackers near him and snapping their necks.

I stared in absolute awe at the magic I witnessed. Storm and Kade were stronger than any Fae I knew except for my father. They were honed like they'd been fighting their entire lives.

Honed just like Ian, if not better, given the magic they possessed.

Where had they been hiding such magic? Why had they been hiding it?

I'd seen those shadows, though. They'd protected me from Lord West *and* Andras in the hallway. They'd curled around me playfully tugging at my hair when I found Kade reading. Fates, I didn't realize how powerful they were at the time.

I didn't have long to stare before two dark ones reached me. They stalked toward me, assuming I was weaker, and they could take their time. Snickering as if I were a toy to play with, not a woman who could actually fight.

"I'd grab a weapon if I were you." I grimaced before darting forward, using the techniques Ian and I perfected in the pit.

One thing I learned to love most about a battle was the moment of shock on a person's face when they realized they'd underestimated me. With a smile, I knew I had the dark ones caught off guard and had sliced through one of their necks before he had time to grab a blade.

I wasn't as lucky with his friend. More prepared, he hissed at me over the death of his comrade.

He attacked violently and without any structure, swinging with a strength much stronger than mine.

An arrow flew toward me, and I veered as the dark one lunged with his sword, a move which likely saved my life. The arrow grazed my thigh, leaving a cut, but landing directly where I had been standing.

As I blocked the sword of the Fae I battled, something pierced my side.

I didn't make a sound as I hit the ground. Nothing came out, no cry for help, even though my mouth opened wide.

Ian screamed at me. The dark one circled me with glee. I tried to stand up and immediately wavered, my knee buckling and giving out as an agonizing pain consumed me. The dark one had stabbed me, with a small dagger, through to the hilt.

I heard a shout, angry and violent. Then nothing. Blood pooled quickly onto my shirt at the wound.

The dark one before me froze, a blade thrusting through his chest, and then suddenly, vanished from my line of sight.

Ian's face paled as he hovered over me.

I couldn't even hear what he said. My eyes were off in the field, astounded at the way Kade wielded his magic. His power called to me in a way I had never experienced before. It promised vengeance. Shadows seeped through his fingers, wrapping around the necks of the attackers, cracking them in one swift blow.

How was it even possible?

"Breathe, Lan. Breathe." Ian's fingers prodded the area near the wound.

My stomach knotted. I may be sick.

Ian's furrowed brow and twisted features betrayed his anguish as he struggled to decide how he should pull the dagger out. Or if he should at all. With no healers, I didn't know if I'd survive it.

"It would be a really good time to have magic, huh?" I tried to joke, coughing. A ring of fire sprouted up, circling around Ian and myself.

Storm had found us. "It's mine," he shouted, before hurling another fireball toward one of the attackers.

The flaming circle didn't stop two dark ones from jumping in and rushing toward me and Ian. He cursed under his breath as he left my side to enter the battle and keep them away. "Kade!" Ian shouted. "Help me!"

I noticed Kade's body through the flames as he spun in my direction, slicing the throat of another assailant aiming to end our lives. The moment he locked eyes with me on the ground, he ran. His shadows surrounded us, smothering Storm's fire, and casting a blanket of darkness around us.

Taking down two more dark ones on the way, he fell by my side. "This is going to hurt," he said, yanking the dagger from my side.

"No—" My words were too late. Blood gushed from the wound too quickly.

The dagger should have stayed, without it, I'd bleed out. A hazy blackness swarmed the edges of my vision.

"Lana, what are you waiting for?" Kade yelled. "Heal yourself!"

"I... I... get Ian..." I barely mustered. My fingers shook as I clutched my side, the warm stickiness of blood coating them in rivets.

"Why aren't you healing?" Kade's panicked tone soaked into me. I wanted to soothe his fear, but at this rate, perhaps he had reason to panic.

"Ian, I need you. *Now*," Kade shouted, his shadows crawling over me, shifting my fingers away as they pressed against the wound. I hissed. He tried to cover my injury and stop the bleeding himself. "Something doesn't feel right. Why isn't this working?"

Ian rushed to my side, shoving Kade out of the way. "You took the blade out?"

"She wouldn't have healed around it," Kade growled.

Kade and Ian stared at each other for a moment, and Kade's shadows glowed with an orange light. Storm had created a second ring of fire around us, trying to buy us whatever time he could.

"I don't have time to explain," Ian said to Kade. "Fuck!" Ian ran his blood-soaked hands through his hair. "She's not going to heal, and I don't have strong enough abilities to even attempt to heal this kind of injury."

I watched Kade's face fall as he stared back at me. "Neither do we," he murmured, his voice barely a whisper.

Inhaling sharply, I winced as pain lanced from my side through my body.

"You're going to be okay. Lan, we're going to make sure you're all right," Ian reassured, stroking my head.

Storm bellowed from beyond our shadows and fire. There were still dark ones attacking and no one to help him.

"Help him," I managed to hiss.

The heat from Storm's flames were unbearable and there wasn't much time. They needed to be safe, too. I needed to know they would all be safe.

"Go. Take her now and get back to the damned palace. Storm and I will stall for you," Kade said, as his shadows continued to flow from his body, unending, growing darker by the second. A scowl covered his face as rage radiated from him.

"There's so many—" Ian started, but then he glanced at me again and nodded. "We will meet you there. Get back as soon as you can. Stay with her while I grab a horse."

Ian left and Kade turned back to me. "No," I whimpered.

"No, too many. You can't." Suddenly, an all-consuming fear forced me to fight harder.

Not for myself. Not because of this wound, which would surely kill me.

But for him.

"You can't fight them all," I said, a tear falling down my cheek.

"Are you worried for me?" Kade's calloused hand cupped my cheek, and his thumb brushed away the stray tear.

A horse neighed.

Kade leaned down, kissing my forehead before pressing his own to mine. "Don't you dare die on me yet, Little Rebel. We're not nearly finished with this thing between us."

He disappeared from my vision as Ian grabbed me, jostling the wound as I cried in his arms at the shot of pain, despite attempting to fight it. He threw me onto the horse, and Storm's flames receded as we left its enclosure. It hurt so much, and my vision filled with black spots. I couldn't be certain how much longer I would stay conscious, the dark spots growing larger. As though Kade's shadows were entering my very mind.

I watched Kade and Storm battling the remaining Fae, outnumbered and alone. My tears fell freely now. I couldn't stop them.

"They're going to be okay, Lan. You need to focus on staying awake. I can't lose you. Do you hear me?" Ian spoke reassurances and curses at me as he galloped harder than ever from the battle toward home.

I jostled again, my head too heavy to hold up on my own. Ian held me firmly in place.

The next time my body shifted, I didn't think I felt as much blood coming from my wound. Did I have any left? Perhaps it slowed somehow?

Those were my last thoughts before I lost consciousness

completely, surrendering to the shadows and pretending like we were all still together, and safe.

CHAPTER 23

I couldn't control my own body.

An endless cycle of chills and sweat coursed through me. Stopping wasn't an option.

Ian's voice was hoarse the few times I regained consciousness. He spoke to me, desperate for me to hear him.

"This is why I didn't want you coming. I can't lose you. Lana, I can't. We've been through too much to let one of those fucking animals be what takes you."

I desperately wanted to reassure him, but my mouth had dried hours ago. At least I imagined it had been hours. I couldn't talk. My fingers twitched, touching his skin. I faded again, but hopefully he felt me squeeze his hand before I slipped into unconsciousness once more.

If anyone could get me to Elisabeth in time, Ian could.

The oblivion offered a reprieve from the anxiety, the fear this would be the end.

It reminded me of shadows. Night. I breathed in and out. I was safe here.

"She lost too much blood."

Kalliah's voice filled my ears. Were we home?

"I've never failed her before, and I'll die before I fail her now. Bring me the blue bottle on my middle shelf, the brown one, bottom right, and the black dropper immediately next to it. Go." Elisabeth quickly barked out orders.

I couldn't open my eyes, but hearing her voice soothed my soul. She would fix me.

Ian had done it. Now, the Fates would decide if they wanted to keep me around.

The silence and blackness surrounding me stretched on. Unending.

"Andras is suspicious. Which means so is the king," Ian said. "They can't find her like this."

"I can only heal her as fast as I can, child. You know better than to rush me," Elisabeth scolded.

I coughed, smiling.

"Lan?" Ian's strong hands wrapped around mine. "Come back to us, Lan. You can do this."

I forced my eyes open, blinking. It hurt. It hurt so much, but everyone fought for me, so I could fight, too.

"I'm—" Oh, bleeding fates I couldn't talk.

"Get her water," Elisabeth said.

Kalliah stood next to Ian, pouring me a glass, and raising it to my lips.

"Slowly," Elisabeth instructed.

I gulped the cool liquid. "I'm okay," I whispered.

"Barely," Kalliah choked out, stroking my hair.

Ian still held my hand.

"Give her space," Elisabeth spoke softly, and as Ian and Kalliah stepped back, she came into view. Tears were in her eyes. "If you ever scare me like that again, I will kill you myself." She cupped my cheek, and I pressed my head into her touch.

"The king is demanding to see you," Ian said, "but we don't know if you'll stay awake long enough."

He was unable to hide the deep notch of worry in his furrowed brow. His face scanning my own, searching for answers to questions yet to be asked.

I hated this. Denial, anger, rage—it all swirled in my gut, thinking of how everyone had to lie for me. How Ian had to race home because I couldn't heal myself.

Weak. Magicless. Unworthy.

All the words flung so callously at me for years were true.

"Kade and Storm?" I asked.

Ian shook his head. "It took us a full day riding. You were out most of the time, and you've been out for a day and a half here." He'd answered my next question, already knowing my thoughts.

My lip quivered, but I forced the fear of not knowing what happened to Kade and Storm aside. Not now. Not when I needed to sell our story of my recovery, since we were home.

"She looks like she's been on death's door. We will not fool him," Kalliah said, her comment directed toward Ian and Elisabeth, rather than me.

"I can hear you." I glowered. "I can do this." I shifted to the side of the bed, the healing site of my wound aching.

"It was deep, and you suffered significant damage to some of your organs. It's going to be sore, even with my magic," Elisabeth said. "We'll have to watch for any permanent damage. I'm not as strong right now as I normally am."

I nodded. I could handle recovery. The last thing I wanted to do was take from Elisabeth when she already drained so much of herself for my father. He needed it more than I did, and I refused to be the reason he didn't get the healing he required.

I stood from the bed. "I have to help and do something. You all have taken care of everything you can."

"You can't do anything if you're dead," Ian said harshly, but firm. Logically I knew he was right, and he'd only snapped at me out of fear. The nonlogical part of me, though, balked. I doubted myself enough as it was.

I took a step toward my friends. "See, I'm fine." As soon as I said it, I stumbled forward, Ian having to reach out and catch me.

He snorted. "Back in bed. We'll figure it out. He can see her sleeping, at least he'll be able to put eyes on her."

"It can work. I'll make sure I'm here," Elisabeth said with a nod.

I groaned. Ian held me, grasping my arms and helping me in bed. Lucien paced atop the comforter, agitated, but no one shooed him away.

I caught a flash of my bloodied tunic.

I should have been dead.

"I'm sorry," I whispered, and once more, pain and exhaustion took me away from them.

Ian.

Ian was bleeding out.

"Healing is a basic Fae ability. The mongrels on the streets can heal cuts, Princess. Please tell me you're not so pathetic you can't even do that."

"Ian," I cried.

His body lay unmoving, and blood pooled around him. A still, crimson pool.

I couldn't heal him. I couldn't heal myself.

I sobbed as Andras's dry, humorless laugh echoed throughout the dungeon.

I took a deep breath. No, that scent. It didn't belong here.

The frigid air inside the dungeon accosted me greedily while grime and mold crept over the corners where the water endlessly dripped. Ian's coppery scent of blood normally filled my senses.

But that smell.

I moaned as something stroked my hair, and a voice broke through my memories, calling to me. No, comfort didn't belong here. Not in this nightmare.

Comfort never appeared in the dungeons with Andras.

Not ever.

I pulled my body from my normal nightmares and returned to the real world. Squeezing my eyes shut, I stayed frozen in place until I felt the soft bed plush around me.

The familiar smell, lingering in the darkness remained, despite the nightmare ending.

The scent of fresh rain, of the storms dancing through Ellevail during growing season, swept over me as I inhaled. I couldn't stop myself from latching onto the feeling. Safe. The feeling of comfort remained, too.

As my eyes fluttered open, I cried out at the man in front of me.

Both had come from him.

Kade wore an unreadable expression, but if I knew him better, I might say I caught him by surprise, opening my eyes. His hand had been raised, but he brought it down to his lap.

"Were you stroking my hair?" I asked.

I raised myself up onto my elbow, wincing, but wanting to look at him. He was wet, hair dripping onto my floor as he sat on a chair, which hadn't been bedside before.

He cleared his throat. "That doesn't sound like me at all, Princess."

I swallowed, realizing we were alone in my room for the first time. I hadn't seen him since Starhaven. Days ago.

"Are you all right? Are you hurt? Where is Storm?" Something about the way he sat with his forearms leaning on his knees, completely wet and quiet, made me nervous. The cocky man, poking jabs seemed to be in total opposition to the man here now. He looked beaten down. Tired and alone.

Scared.

"He's back as well, unharmed. The dark ones are gone. Mostly dead." He sighed, running his hand through his damp

251

black hair. "After everything that happened, I just——" He stared at me for a moment before bringing his hand down and brushing back my hair with his fingers. "I needed to make sure you were alive with my own eyes."

My chest tightened. I didn't move away from his touch, instead, I fully embraced it. I inhaled the scent of him as it continued to wrap around me, cocooning me in a damn blanket. The familiar caresses of shadows on my arms and my legs were heavenly, bringing me the serenity only they managed to provide. I stifled a moan at how much better I felt for the first time these past few days.

When my eyes opened, Kade hesitated, not bringing his hand down to touch me again. His eyes were dark, everything about this man was dark, and yet the way he studied me made my entire body feel light. Feel alive.

I couldn't help but stare at his beautiful face. Almost flawless, save for a tiny scar above his lip. A scar unnoticeable unless you were up close, just as I was now.

Raising my hand, possessing no self-control, I touched his cheek. His face, hell, his entire body, appeared as though it belonged to the sculptures in the royal gardens. A masterpiece to be worshipped.

His lips parted. "I thought you weren't going to make it, Little Rebel."

"Careful, Kade. You're acting like you might actually care whether I live or die," I teased. The crack in my voice gave away my confidence.

He didn't say a word. Not a damn word, but he lifted his hand, this time brushing his thumb against my cheek before he let his fingers sweep deeper into my hair. "That would be ridiculous. I only came here for the crown."

"Well, get in line." I smiled at him, but he didn't return the gesture. A sharp ache in my chest pinched, wondering if perhaps the comment hadn't simply been a joke. Maybe this feeling was exactly what he wanted me to have. All part of his plan for winning the trials.

Kade stared at me, my lips, my hair, everywhere, except my eyes.

"You should go," I whispered as I realized I didn't want to know if it was real or not.

He nodded but didn't move. His fingers were still in my hair, and he leaned in closer.

Resolve snapping, his lips met mine, hurriedly, frantically.

I whimpered as his tongue skimmed over mine, possessively. I leaned forward, matching his urgency. His hand stayed in my hair, my whimper escalating to a moan.

His breathing grew ragged as we ravaged each other's mouths.

I tugged on his tunic. "Why are you soaking wet?" I asked in between breaths.

His thumb ran over the front of my throat. "It rained as we rode through the night. I left my horse at the stables and came straight here through the garden so no one would see."

Damn this Fae. He came to me first. Exhausted, battle-worn, and he came for me. Before anything else.

I tugged harder. "I need more," I whispered against his lips.

He devoured me, stoking the fire lit inside me, which hadn't fully dissipated since we met in the woods a few weeks ago. It may have been a while since I'd had a man in my bed, but none before him had come close to feeling like this.

And we were merely kissing. What would happen if he gave me more, gave me all of him?

"You're still hurt." He stopped kissing me, panting, but he didn't move away. He hovered over my body, his weight fully held up by his left arm, while his right remained on my neck.

His heavy breath ghosted across my skin, mixing with my own.

"Please," I begged.

He remained still, until I lightly brushed my fingers along his jaw, where stubble had begun to grow.

He groaned and then pulled my blanket off of me, lifting me so gently, trying not to hurt me. As if I were important.

"Can you sit?" he asked tenderly.

I nodded, and reclaimed his mouth, needing it back on mine. I bit his lower lip as he sank onto his chair, wrapping my legs around him, my hips shifting to relieve the pressure building between my legs.

With a little movement forward, I connected to the hard length of him, and despite both of us being fully clothed, I broke the kiss, shivering with a cry as I rubbed against him.

He hissed. "You have to be careful—careful you can't—fuck, Illiana, you can't move so much with your wound."

"I don't care. Kiss me," I demanded.

He obeyed, and this time, he tilted my chin with his thumb and kissed down my jaw, licking and nipping at my neck.

I arched back, wanting to feel his chest against mine even through clothes. Pain shot through my side at the movement, and I sucked in a breath, wincing.

Kade froze. "This—we shouldn't—"

He stood, lifting me back to the bed and setting me down, immediately backing up to put distance between us.

My brain was scrambled. His kiss had consumed every rational part of my soul.

Fates, the last thing I should be doing is making out with Kade on my bed, wounded at that. Especially moments after he reminded me he came here for a crown and my kingdom, not for me and my love.

His eyes flashed, almost as if my acceptance of the distance caused him physical pain. A wicked grin quickly replaced the fleeting expression instead. The man who had been worried about my life and owned me with his lips, faded as the arrogant Kade appeared once more. And damn if he

254

wasn't just as sexy this way. "I knew the benefits of gaining a crown would be exceptional."

His teasing tone didn't help soothe the sudden sinking of my heart. Without realizing it, his words confirmed my uncontrollable fears. "You're abhorrent," I said, crossing my arms. "Last I checked, you kissed me. Not the other way around."

"I believe you begged me." He licked his bottom lip, and I wondered if he even realized he'd done it. "Besides, I thought I should accept your request in case you decided to go and get wounded and die on me again."

Before I could protest and insult him further, he frowned, then lunged. Kade reached around me, pulling the book from atop a pillow on my bed. "I wondered where my book had gone to." He smirked.

I made a move to snatch it back. "My castle. My book. I didn't see a problem taking what's mine."

He chuckled and handed the book back to me. "I'd like it back when you're done. To know how the story ends for the fate-blessed lovers."

"Get out," I huffed, rising, and making my way across the room to my door. "I don't need rumors going around I'm fucking two contenders."

Kade bristled at my comment but didn't say anything. His smile disappeared. He came to stand in front of me, his hand hovering above my neck. As he'd done on the battlefield he brought his forehead to mine. "I'm glad you're alive, even if I am abhorrent to you." He pressed his fingers to my skin and then kissed my forehead. "Goodnight, Princess Illiana."

He bowed before leaving my bedroom. As soon as I heard my chamber door shut, I slammed my head back, bringing my hand to rest where his had been on my neck. This ridiculous mix of emotions overwhelmed me, especially when it came to hearing my name on his lips. I barely knew the man. He had secrets. A power which could kill with a flick of his wrist. He had made it all too clear that the crown served as his sole purpose here.

The last thing I needed when taking on my kingdom with no magic, was someone like him ruling my land.

I needed to shake Kade from my thoughts, and my body. *Quickly*.

Or we'd all be in trouble.

CHAPTER 24

My room had turned into a revolving door.

Visits from Elisabeth, Kalliah, and Ian were continuous, and beyond them, my father finally had his way and came to see me. When he entered, I instantly became more concerned about his appearance than my own.

"Are you okay?" I asked, failing to hide the worry in my voice. His beard was scruffy, not trimmed to perfection like normal, and he'd lost weight. A significant amount. His robes hung off his body, two sizes too big now. His face appeared gaunt, and the dark circles beneath his eyes made it seem like he had been in a fight.

Despite his appearance, he still smiled at me like I provided his endless source of happiness. "Are you saying I look poorly, my heart?"

I chuckled, shaking my head.

"I'm more concerned with you. You've been in bed for days."

"I'm much better. I promise. Thank you for allowing me some time to rest." Guilt clawed at my gut for lying so blatantly to his face, but I'd get over it. I had to.

"The second trial is set for this afternoon. You'll be okay, yes?" he asked.

His eyes were trained on me, looking for something. Hesitation, perhaps. However, the manner in which he asked made me think it wasn't necessarily a question and more of a notice to be prepared.

"I'll be ready."

A knock sounded on my door. "Oh, for fate's sake," I muttered under my breath.

My father chuckled, rising and moving to the head of my bed. I had propped myself up to read so he didn't have far to lean down to offer me a kiss on the cheek. "I'll see you in a few hours."

Ian walked in as the king was leaving. He bowed, as he always did. Ruppert grumbled loudly in the hall about the number of visitors.

"There is no need to bow and treat me as King in these chambers, Ian my boy." The King clasped my friend's shoulders. "You look more like your father every day."

Ian's back straightened, his posture impeccable, despite the king's insistence at casualty. "Thank you, Your Majesty."

The king tsked. His face fell, and he had yet to remove his hand from Ian. "I miss him. Especially during tedious Court gatherings. He made things far more bearable." His eyes teared before he quickly blinked them away. "Much like I've seen you do for Lana."

I knew my father had plenty of private conversations with Ian, and I wasn't privy to knowing how many had been about his own father. Witnessing the exchange firsthand, though, twisted something in my stomach. The concern from earlier ate at me even further. My father addressed Ian as though he wanted to ensure he told him his feelings, before he no longer had time.

Which meant whatever plagued him wasn't getting better.

Ian watched him go with longing in his gaze, as though he wanted to know more.

"That was sweet," I said.

Ian smiled. "He talked about my father more when I was a child, but it's been a while. Hearing that from him meant so much." He sighed.

Holding out my hand, I motioned Ian to move close to me. Leaning on him for support, I rose from bed.

Kalliah's scoff sounded from the doorway. "You've barely left your bed since your return. How are we going to pull off sitting through a trial?"

"I'm much better, I swear. I woke up this morning feeling nearly back to normal. Stop fussing."

Ian let go of me, as if he wanted to test what I said, and I surprised them both by not only remaining standing, but also tilting my hip, pressing a hand on it, and sticking my tongue out at both of them. "Overbearing friends. Both of you."

"Don't you have a trial to prepare for?" I asked Ian.

He nodded, running his fingers along the side of his cheek. "Yes, I don't have long, and there are two things we need to talk about."

"Go on." I waited for his big revelation.

"First. No more Hidden Henchman activities. After what happened to you, and everything going on with the trials, it's too much. Once this is over, we will figure out how to start again. It's not worth the risk over the next few weeks."

As much as I hated to admit it, he was right. The risks were too great at this point. Especially since he, Leif, and Corbin would be in danger continuing Hidden Henchman activities, too.

I conceded. "I have to agree with you, for now. But the moment these trials are over, we return to our plans to help our people."

Kalliah clapped her hands in agreement, giving me an

incredulous glare while Ian took a moment and assessed my seriousness. "We'll discuss it again after the trials. Now, more importantly, I have news to report."

"News?" I frowned, unsure what information we had been expecting and didn't have.

"I did some additional digging into Kade and Storm. After Leif and Corbin came up short, I used some of my contacts as Captain of the Royal Guard to inquire further."

A deep crease between his eyebrows told me something hadn't panned out.

My eyes widened in expectation. "And?"

"Nothing." His face was expressionless.

I stiffened. "What do you mean nothing? There has to be *something*."

"I mean, there is no record of a Kade Blackthorn or 'Storm' anywhere in our lands," Ian said. "Nobody knows who they are or where they came from. It's like they appeared out of nowhere."

I threw my hands up in the air. "So now what do we do? They know too much about us, about me. Do we just throw all of it away because our shoddy records aren't up to date?"

"They have given us no real reason not to trust them. Storm especially feels genuine with his intentions, but I think we need to proceed with caution. You, especially." He gave me his "judgmental Captain" look, pursed lips, with a cocked eyebrow, as if he dared me to argue. "I see how you and Kade look at each other."

"Wha—"

Ian threw up his hand toward me. "Stop, don't even try to deny it. Or deny it all you want, but I know what I've seen. We've been friends far too long and I know all of your tells."

Kalliah chimed in from the back of the room, "It's true, Lana. There is clearly something going on between the two of you, whether you want to believe it or not."

I eased myself into the nearest armchair. "I don't know

what you are talking about." I couldn't prevent my foot from tapping nervously on the floor.

Ian and Kalliah exchanged an exasperated glance, and they shook their heads in defeat.

"I need to go get ready for the trials, Lan. Please be careful, and please don't push yourself. This is all for nothing if you aren't here with us, in one piece." He walked over and pressed a kiss to my cheek before leaving my chambers for good.

An hour later, I finished dressing, ready for the second trial. My skin had been scrubbed raw, removing the distinct odor of bed rot I developed over the last few days fighting for my life. My hair had been brushed and curled into soft waves. A small, jewel-encrusted pin held back one side of it. It glittered in the sun, beaming through the pavilion of the arena.

I wore a satin, aquamarine A-line dress, equipped with hidden pockets and a slit up the leg. Just how I liked it. It made it easy to move at a moment's notice and concealed my dagger. Considering everything that happened recently, I refused to take any chances and be unarmed.

In the pavilion sat Andras, Vivienne, and Elisabeth, along with the other royal advisers, and Ruppert. After speaking with my father briefly, Elisabeth approached and gave me a quick hug and a once-over before exiting out the back to prepare her workstation should anything happen to one of the contenders. The small satchel around her hips made a clinking noise, and I smiled at the idea of the mini arsenal of magical medicine she carried with her. She saved me more times than I could count, and after this had passed, and my father recovered, I would find a way to repay her for her years of generosity and friendship.

I wrung my hands together as I sat in my seat, the last to

arrive. My nerves were shot to hell between what happened on the road and worrying about what to expect in the second trial. We'd already lost one contender, what could possibly be in store today?

As if sensing my anxiety, Lucien jumped onto my lap. Although it made me smile, I knew he couldn't stay. "Don't you get too comfortable. You'll singe my dress, or worse, rip it to shreds if you get excited."

He opened his mouth, tongue hanging out, panting in the summer heat.

Andras said something to one of the advisers, and Lucien's head whipped around. Growling, he jumped from my lap and disappeared behind me. He hated that man as much as I did.

My gaze swept across the field. Shock didn't begin to cover the sight before me. What had been a basic setup of tables and archways in the first trials, now seemed to be an entirely different stadium.

The arena had been transformed into an obstacle course, which included a forest, ponds, and brush. The entrance tunnel opened to a sandpit, with a variety of sharp- and dangerous-looking items spread throughout. They were scattered both on top of the sand, making it appear impossible to cross in some places, and above the sand, making it worse to stand all the way up. Past the sand traps sat a tiered smattering of wood, which rose higher until leading to the platform of a long bridge. The bridge consisted of two narrow walkways, only big enough for one contender at a time, leading to a forest area with plenty of open space for quick, short fights. Beyond the forest were a few ropes suspended in the air with magic, leading the contenders to a small, revolving platform, until finally another smaller bridge led over a small reservoir of water to a grassy area with a wall to climb right before the finish line.

Somehow the Earth Fae had outdone themselves even more and managed to lower the arena into the ground, so the audience had a relatively unobstructed view into the entire trial field below.

I'd never seen anything like it before. What they had been able to accomplish in the last two weeks between trials was nothing short of amazing.

It may be a death trap of an obstacle course, but one of remarkable ingenuity when thinking about the magic it took to create.

The king raised his hand, signaling two guards inside the arena. They parted to either side of the entryway tunnel into the stadium, and the contenders filed into the arena, all donning battle armor. Sweat beaded on my neck as the sun shone directly onto my back. The breeze my father would have normally conjured was noticeably absent. Before I had time to worry about why he wasn't using magic, which should have come as second nature to him, he spoke.

"Welcome, friends, to the second marriage trial." His voice, while amplified, didn't seem nearly as loud as before.

The crowd in the arena burst into applause and whooped out a loud chorus of welcoming roars.

My father put up his hands and the crowd quieted once more. "I am pleased to see so many loyal subjects here to witness today's events. Today our contenders will demonstrate their physical agility and bravery, along with their magical abilities, as they make their way through the obstacle course set up before you in the arena.

"Contenders! Be prepared, for only the most agile of you and skilled with your magical abilities, will be able to complete the course behind you. The top three contenders will take Princess Illiana on a one-hour date at a place of your choosing."

The crowd erupted into more cheers, excited at the notion of the contenders courting me.

My father had to stop and regain his balance. His subtle grip on the arm of his throne would only be noticed by those of us here in the pavilion. My heart broke. Had he become so weak, even speaking for this short amount of time caused him to stumble?

Vivienne stood and joined my father at the front of the dais and requested to speak.

"Some fates know what others do not. May speed and magic guide you home." She smiled down at the contenders.

Her words were short for a change, and somewhat more understandable than usual. If home meant the finish line at least.

The audience clapped along with my father, everyone ready for the second trial to begin. Anticipation hung in the air, identical to a thick humidity on the late days of summer.

"Contenders, take your places on the starting line," the king exclaimed as the contenders moved from the tunnel's exit to the marked white line on the arena floor. "You have one hour to complete the course. Fail to complete the course within the allotted time, and you will be eliminated."

With a wave of his hand, an hourglass appeared, hovering above the arena for all to see. Roses and blooms coiled along the handles in a spectacular display of elegance.

"Unlike in the first trial, you may use whatever special abilities or magic you possess. Show us your magical strength! Be strong, be brave, and be smart. Prove to me you are worthy of sitting in this chair! May nature guide you!"

A loud clang of bells behind me caught me off guard as I jumped out of my chair. The second trial officially began.

From behind, Andras curled his hands around my shoulders, knowing he scared me, enjoying every moment of it. "Apologies, Princess."

I jerked forward, out of his grasp, not caring how others could perceive it. The slimy man usually refrained from touching me at all, and I refused to let him think it acceptable to do so now.

I focused my gaze on the arena as the contenders ran onto

the course. Kade's eyes met my own, and he winked before running off after the others. This time my heart was torn with annoyance at his arrogance, and the sexiness of his confidence.

I heard my mother's voice. "Are you all right, my King?" She rubbed his arm.

"Yes, yes, just tired, that's all," he replied sweetly to her worry. "Come, let's see what our exceptional Earth Fae have concocted for our contenders today."

Ian shifted and flew over and under the sand pit traps with such ease that when he shifted back into his Fae form on the other side, he gave a shrug toward me like he had nothing to worry about. He could fly over the entire course, but it wouldn't have been his style. He'd like to show off his agility too much. Women in the crowd cheered his name, practically falling over themselves in some areas of the stands.

My deep belly laugh earned a sharp glare from a few guards around us. At least I knew if he didn't win this, he'd have the undying devotion of his fan club to fall back on.

A loud bang sounded, and I watched in awe as Ryland flicked his hand forward toward a large, sharp wheel-shaped object in the sandpit, and it exploded. Shock rippled through the stadium as he did the same with two other pieces in front of him, blasting his way through the pit's obstacles while also clearing a path for those behind him.

Blast magic.

Hale bounded across the mismatched wood pillars, and I gasped as he moved discarded debris to form a pathway for himself to get to the narrow bridges, making it seem like nothing at all. He had simply created a bridge for himself.

Summoner magic.

I had known what his abilities were, of course, but observing him construct a bridge mid-jump proved more exciting than lifting his fork without holding it at the dinners we'd attended together.

The crowd's entertainment was obvious as laughter and cheering echoed throughout the arena. I had to admit, seeing everyone make the course look simple slightly eased my worries and concerns.

Ian approached the wooded area when he froze, his head whipping around as if he'd heard something. Lord West came up behind him, lunging forward, but Ian shifted and avoided him, flying sideways.

A flash of white darted from somewhere within the forest, knocking into Ian's hawk form, sending him flying into a tree and shifting back.

I screamed, standing from my seat as the white blur solidified.

A razorven.

Jerking my head toward my father, I asked, "What are you thinking?"

The king's frown turned grave. My mother reached for his arm, and they whispered amongst one another.

Ian kicked the beast off of him, unsheathing his sword. Before he could move again, Lord West approached next to him. Thankfully, two of them could likely fight off the razorven with no issue. But Lord West grabbed Ian, taking him completely by surprise and spinning him, pressing him to the ground.

"Ian!" I shouted, leaning over the dais.

They were arguing while the razorven stalked closer, its slit tongue licking over its rounded snout. Lord West shoved Ian down again and then jumped up, shifting into Ian's hawk.

My mouth hung open, and when Ian rose, he shook his head in a daze.

Lord West was a siphon and he'd just drained Ian's magic. For how long, I didn't know.

"Ian, *run*," I tried shouting again, not knowing if he could hear my voice over the crowds.

The razorven approached him now, head lowered,

prepared to pounce. Ian swayed, still regaining his composure, but he gripped his sword, holding it tightly.

Black, inky shadows crept near Ian's feet as the beast leapt in the air toward my best friend.

Ian's body jerked to the side, blackness surrounding him, before he reappeared next to Kade.

I sighed with relief. This time Ian held his sword steady as he and Kade faced off against the razorven.

Fates, how had a creature so dangerous gotten in?

Hale sprinted up to the pair, having been only shortly behind them, but when he slowed, appearing conflicted about helping Ian and Kade, Ian made the choice for him.

"Go," Ian directed him. "Keep going."

His head swiveled between the men and the razorven. Ultimately, he listened to Ian and continued running.

A pit formed in my stomach, growing stronger with each passing moment as I watched Kade and Ian's battle against the wild creature with no business being on palace grounds.

A prickle on the back of my neck added to the rising unease.

Kade's shadows rose, wrapping around the beast and finally holding him in place, while Ian plunged his sword into the razorven's chest.

A monstrous howl came from the animal before it crashed to the ground with a mighty *thud*.

Relief should have been the only emotion coursing through me, and yet the pit growing in my gut didn't dissipate, even though their fight had ended in triumph.

Andras shifted in his seat on the other side of my mother, leaning forward and watching the arena with rapt attention. Too much attention. In fact, he seemed to be teeming with excitement, a rarity if someone wasn't being tortured. Perhaps he delighted in setting my nerves on fire. Nothing good could happen when Andras felt happy.

When my father and my mother's eyes widened, I jerked

my attention back to the field. A skirmish had broken out between two more contenders. Edmund and Frederich were locked in a one-on-one battle.

Frederich angered many, but Edmund had been so reserved, I couldn't imagine what would have set him off. Or what could have happened to make those two feel the need to fight in the middle of the trials? Edmund's movements were rigid yet wild, and stronger than they should be. In fact, I would have sworn he had mid-level magic at most with how he acted and carried himself. Yet, he wielded some sort of power that frightened Frederich immensely. A prickling sensation crawled up my skin. The magic here didn't feel right.

In fact, the longer I sat and observed, the more I realized this entire thing didn't feel right.

The two of them had made it up the wooden platforms and onto the narrow bridge. Frederich stepped out backward onto it, and Edmund pursued.

My heart beat erratically. The only time I had sensed this hum of energy before, occurred when we'd been around the dark ones.

But we weren't at the borders. We were safe inside the walls of Ellevail, and Edmund had previously been fine.

Now, the mediocre contestant had overpowered Frederich, moving him backward across the narrow bridge at a harrowing pace.

I thought the obstacle course may have some fighting involved, but this far exceeded my expectations. If someone didn't stop this battle, one of them would be seriously hurt. Frederich backed himself down the path and tripped at the platform, falling onto his back as he inched toward the forested part of the course.

The crowds' cheers had quieted, an eerie silence descending as we all watched the duel unfold.

"What are you doing? Stop *attacking* me," Frederich

screamed at Edmund, desperation in his tone. His pudgy body scooted backward, unable to gather himself. He rolled forward into a sitting position, flinging his hand out toward Edmund. The gust of wind ruffled Edmund's hair, but it didn't deter him.

In fact, the entire time Frederich continued flinging his hands outward, Edmund dodged the attacks with apparent ease. It was as though he could detect what was coming, or perhaps Frederich no longer possessed the strength to put up any sort of fight.

This felt wrong.

"Father," I said, fear clouding my voice. My eyes widened, before I could say another word, as Fredrich screamed.

Blood flowed profusely from his nose, and he frantically tried to wipe it away, soaking the sleeve of his tunic.

Frederich rolled over, facing us and reaching toward the dais. Blood dripped from his ears. His panicked expression frightened me.

"*Help*," he screamed toward us. "Help me!"

With glazed eyes, Edmund stared at Frederich, waving his arms wildly, as more and more blood flowed from every part of Frederich's face.

Ian stopped running and his gaze flicked toward me. I stared at him in horror, gesturing behind him, shaking my head, not knowing how to communicate something was very wrong. He stopped and turned to see what everyone was looking at.

Another scream sounded.

With a few motions of his arms, Edmund appeared to be sucking the very life out of Frederich. The portly man clutched his neck, gasping for air. "*Help*," he tried to scream again, but it came out garbled.

Frederich had backed himself into a tree, stopping any further retreat. He clawed at his throat as Edmund continued toward him.

"We need to stop him," I whispered, so stunned by what happened in the arena, I had trouble steadying my breath.

With one last gasp of air, Frederich's eyes bulged even further from their sockets, his head fell to the side. Edmund drew a sword and sliced forward, stabbing the already-dead Frederich.

Blood. So much blood. I clutched my stomach, wrapping my arms around me to steady my shaking. Although Frederich's lifeless body slumped over, his blood continued to trickle around the tree he was propped against.

Screams echoed amongst the audience, some Fae standing, searching for an escape route.

Before I could even comprehend the catastrophe, Ian screamed, "Kade!"

No, not him, too.

Kade stopped just prior to the final climbing wall and turned to find Ian frantically waving at him to come back.

What were they doing?

As they ran in the opposite direction of the finish line, I knew. They were too damned honorable. We all had come to the same conclusion.

Edmund had been overtaken by the darkness.

Now every contender was in danger. And so was everyone else if he escaped the arena. Ian wouldn't let it stand, and I knew Kade wouldn't, either.

They'd put themselves in harm's way to protect the people of Brookmere, instead of finishing the trial. Which meant this couldn't go on.

I turned to my parents. "Stop the trials! Another contender is dead, you have to stop this!"

Andras answered as the color drained from my father's face. "The trials stop for nothing. Not even death." A sly smile formed across his face as my breathing stopped.

A dark thought clicked inside of me. The excitement on

his face, the joy. He knew. Somehow, he *knew* this was going to happen. Or at the very least, he didn't care.

Just as the childhood version of me knew this man was evil then, I wondered how much more evil he had become since those years in the dungeons. I wondered if Edmund wasn't the only person who had darkness inside of him.

CHAPTER 25

I turned to my father and mother again, begging them to see reason. "Please, this has to stop. We are condemning these contenders to death!"

"Oh, Lana, my heart." My father coughed so much he stopped talking for a moment. Andras rested a hand on my father's shoulder. "Every once in a while, there is a rogue contender, who takes things just a little too far. All will be fine."

"Rogue contender? Father, it seems like far more than a rogue contender. He *killed* Frederich in cold blood!"

The king's eyes narrowed. "The trial continues, Illiana, now sit down."

I looked at my mother for some sort of validation, but clearly, she sided with my father, regardless of how she truly felt. Her face, cold and neutral, as her rigid fingers grasped the edge of her throne, whitening the longer they held on. The other royal advisers were all whispering about the disaster on the field.

Kade caught up to Ian as they raced toward Edmund and the now-deceased Frederich.

Lord West glided across the finish line, still in Ian's hawk form and shifted back.

Fucking coward. Stealing magic so callously and not doing a single part of the obstacle. He cheered, acting as though nothing was amiss with the others, and standing, waving at the crowd. His brow furrowed at the lack of attention he received. I grinned smugly, glad he had been forgotten about. The guards on the field quickly corralled him into the winner's area. He'd taken first but lost what little respect I may have had for him.

Ryland sprinted past both Ian and Kade as they ran in the opposite direction, not even bothering to stop and ask what they were doing. Clearly most of the contenders would have no distractions when it came to winning this trial.

Ian and Kade continued to run toward Edmund, who became more and more erratic, his sights set on the crowd fleeing directly above him. They stopped in front of the devastation of Frederich's body. Edmund basked in the path of Frederich's blood, letting it coat his shoes.

"Be careful," I shouted down to the pair. My palms were sweating as I watched them approach Edmund.

The once-reserved- and quiet Fae now knelt in a pool of blood. Nausea overpowered me as he dipped his hands into the stream of crimson, wiping it down his face before he shifted to face Ian and Kade.

He had turned Frederich's blood into war paint.

Pure horror rattled my body. Fae in the stands were exiting swiftly, shouting, and crying as nobody understood what was happening.

The Royal Guard didn't know what to do, either. Everyone stood lost in a state of confusion, no one daring to interfere with the trials.

"Father!" I grasped his arm. "This is madness."

The king sat stoically, as glued to the scene before him as

the rest of us. One crazed Fae wasn't enough to warrant stopping the trials apparently.

Ryland crossed the finish line, hands on his knees as he tried to catch his breath. For someone so athletic, cardio was not his forte.

Ian, sword drawn, lured Edmund from Frederich's limp, bloodless body. Edmund made the same arm movements he'd done before Frederich, and Ian's step faltered, blood appearing on his face.

No!

But Ian was the decoy and served enough of a distraction to allow Kade to tackle Edmund to the ground.

Kade punched Edmund in the face, and even without any magical abilities, I could hear the crack of his nose as it thundered throughout the arena.

Edmund merely laughed.

The blood flowing from his nose grew darker, thicker than the blood already on his face.

I was going to be sick.

Edmund tried to sit up, but Kade repositioned himself on top of him, pinning his legs to the ground with his hips and punching him in the face once more.

What was he waiting for? Just end this already!

His shadows could have taken care of this easily from what I'd observed a few days ago.

"Do you have him?" Ian shouted.

Kade's growling response was so powerful it reverberated in my chest. "Yes, make sure he's alone."

"It'll be by foot," Ian shouted.

He moved away from Kade and Edmund, looping back toward the earlier obstacles, surveying his surroundings. I knew he searched to find if anyone else lurked in the area as Kade continued to work with Edmund on the ground.

If I hadn't witnessed Kade fight before, and if I hadn't been so focused on him, I would have missed the whisper of shadows leaving his fingertips and weaving around Edmund's neck.

Edmund jerked, just once, and then his head fell back, limp.

Finally done. Gone.

Kade ran in Ian's direction, and when he caught up to him, he clasped his shoulder. My useless ears could not hear the conversation that passed between the two of them.

Checking the timer, it neared the one-hour mark. Ian and Kade would have to hurry to finish the trial to keep from being eliminated.

"The time," I screamed from the stands, reminding them not finishing would mean elimination since these fates-forsaken trials weren't ending despite the horrors experienced here today.

They took off toward the end of the obstacle course, Kade's shadows behind them, pushing them faster. They cleared the forest, climbed the wall, and bolted to the finish line with mere seconds to spare.

Both were covered in blood, furious, and panting, trying to catch their breath as soon as they crossed.

Lord West, Ryland, and Hale stood off to the side in their pristine clothes. Shame and guilt riddled Hale's face as he took in the sight of Ian and Kade covered in blood.

My father stood before the remaining crowd, amplifying his voice once more. "The second trial has ended. Please, everything is all right. My people, there is no threat."

Some of those retreating paused, wary of the words which didn't match the atrocity that had played out before them. Others continued to flee.

"This happens sometimes, as evident in recorded history of the trials. Contenders use advantages to try to win, and Edmund fell prey to the thrall of the trials. No matter. Congratulations are in order for our top three contenders, Lord Casimir West, Ryland Lockbane, and Hale Bardot. The trials and contenders' date will continue over the next two days, as will the Festival of Blessings! May nature guide you and be safe on your travels home this evening."

Shifting to face my father, once more, my disgust morphed to outrage, bubbling inside of me, ready to explode. "What *was* that?"

The king turned to me slowly and sighed deeply. "It appears Edmund had been cursed with the darkness. The very same darkness has been taking over some of our lands."

"You lied to them," I spat. "And what the hell was a razorven doing here?"

The king's expression hardened. "The razorven I do not know about and will assume Edmund had something to do with letting a beast like that in, given his predicament. And of course I lied. What would have been better, Illiana? Allowing mass panic to take over? Having people believe it might be unsafe here in Ellevail? Inside the palace grounds of all places."

Andras stepped forward and stood beside the king, like an equal, grinning. "Fear not, Princess, it appears the captain and Kade were able to take care of the erm, *issue,* for us today."

The king's eyes narrowed, and he called Ruppert to come forward. "Send for Ian, now. Both of you will accompany Princess Illiana back to her rooms."

Ruppert started to protest, but my father silenced him. "I don't care if Ian is a contender or that he is currently covered in blood. He will accompany you both, ensuring Princess Illiana goes *directly* back to her rooms. I want the palace secured, and I want to figure out how this came to be. You will provide updates on the hour."

Ruppert bowed his head and waved me forward. The other royal guards had already begun to move my father and mother out of the pavilion and back inside the palace.

Ian was already waiting at the bottom of the pavilion stairs by the time Ruppert let me move.

277

Ian grasped my hand, and though I wanted to ensure he was truly safe, he kept me at arm's length, whispering in my ear, "We'll talk in your room. Not here, not now."

I nodded, and the three of us moved quickly through the open grassy area, into the gardens, and then entered the palace through a staff door instead of the usual main entrance.

The different entry point didn't help. The palace was in utter chaos. The staff were running about, whispering to each other as we tried to move through the halls, to my room. Nobody knew what to do, or where to be, between ensuring the stadium cleared, and securing the halls.

There had never been a time in recorded history where the palace had been attacked. We had not reviewed such protocols in so long. Well, if ever, but we especially hadn't reviewed protocols for what to do when we had so many additional guests roaming the corridors.

We rounded the corner before the central staircase and Kade appeared, armed to the teeth with daggers and swords. Clearly, he had stopped by the armory after leaving the arena. How did he even know how to find it? Unless he had his own personal armory with him.

A question I would have to ask when our lives were not upended, and additional killer Fae weren't potentially waltzing around the palace.

He tossed me a sword, and Ruppert's jaw dropped as I caught it with ease. He didn't let his surprise distract him for long and moved to contain Kade, but I grabbed his arm. "He's okay. Let him be."

"The king said Ian—"

"I trust him," I said, shocking myself with how adamantly I meant those words. "I said to let him be, Ruppert." I didn't give my guard a chance to utter any further protests.

We dodged Fae running wild throughout the passageways, guards joining in, trying to escort groups of them out through the corridors, sectioned off for the public. Most of the entrance and exit plans were going to shit.

At the next flight of stairs, Hale joined us, running forward with two swords in hand. "Thought you might like additional eyes on the princess," he said.

I offered him a smile, grateful he thought of me, even if I could handle myself. Well, mostly. The thought of the magic the Fae used on Frederich and then Ian made me shudder, but we pressed on. Only two more flights to go before we reached the royal wing of the palace.

The closer we got to my rooms, the fewer people we encountered, reassuring us the chaos might be over soon. Finally, reaching the last staircase, we made one last push toward the safety of my chambers. Cresting the landing, Ruppert took the lead, with Ian and I next, and Kade and Hale close behind.

Ruppert abruptly stopped in the hallway, and I ran into his back. Shoving him forward, I asked, "What are you doing? Don't stop."

I stepped around him, surprised he didn't respond at all as he stood, unmoving. Insufferable man.

But when I finally looked up, I, too, stopped moving.

Stopped breathing.

Ian and the others hadn't noticed the body on the floor yet. It was dark, as some of the lamps had gone out. The clothes on the woman blended into the rug lining the hallway.

Cautiously, I stepped forward. I knew that apron. I knew that greying hair.

"Elisabeth?" I whispered.

A faint moan was all I heard in reply.

"Elisabeth!" I screamed as I dropped my weapons where I stood, the clang of metal on the corner of the tile peeking beyond the carpeted floor, reverberated throughout the hallway, as I raced to her side.

Whatever happened behind me, I knew nothing of it. My

world stopped. My eyes, my mind, all of it focused only on Elisabeth. I collapsed next to her, instantly feeling my dress dampen in the pool of blood forming beneath her body.

"No, no, no, no. Elisabeth." I choked on a sob as it bellowed out of me. "You have to heal yourself. Ian," I cried. "Ian, do something. Call another healer!"

I peered behind me, wondering why no one moved. Ian just stood there, his hand over his mouth, completely pale. He shook his head. Ruppert, Hale, and Kade all stood beside Ian in silence.

"Don't just stand there," I bellowed.

"My sweet, sweet girl." My head whipped back to the woman who had practically raised me alongside my parents. "I love you with all of my heart."

"No, no. This can't be happening!" My hands shook and I moved her clothing around, trying to locate where the blood originated in order to stop the bleeding on her side. Regardless of how close I inspected her, I couldn't find a lone source. The bleeding stemmed from too many wounds. Wounds which covered her entire chest. There were too many.

I frantically searched for her satchel. Noticing it off to the side, I quickly rummaged through the bag. "What can I give you? Elisabeth, what would work?" When she said nothing, I whimpered. "Please, please talk to me. Help me."

Elisabeth placed her hand upon my own, and I dropped the bag next to me.

Useless.

Magicless.

Useless when it mattered most.

"Hush now, child. There's no coming back from wounds like this. I have mere moments more. Let me look into your eyes one last time."

Tears streamed down my face as I stared into Elisabeth's eyes. Her beautiful brown eyes dulled as the life drained from her body. "I can't lose you."

"I have loved you from the moment you were born. Never underestimate yourself, my child. Trust in the king and queen and trust in the prophecy. Find yourself a good healer, you're going to need it." She tried to laugh, but it came out as a choke.

"I don't accept this." I held my hands over her chest. "Give me something, now!" I argued with nature, pleaded, and begged in a way I never had before, not even for my own life in those damned dungeons. "I will honor you. I will make sure Brookmere adores you. I'll give you anything. You can't take her."

I couldn't see, the world blurred around me as my tears blocked everything. My body convulsed from sobbing so hard. I sat there, shaking, and repeating my oaths to nature over and over, until my hand dropped. Elisabeth's chest slowed to an almost unmoving stop.

I rested my head on her chest, and she used energy she didn't have to stroke my hair for the last time. With her dying breath, she said, "Love is the most powerful magic there is. Don't let the darkness rule this land, or your heart. You are the light, my love. You are the light. And I will—I will always love you."

Her body released one last, small breath, barely noticeable to anyone else. But I saw it. I felt it reverberate through every part of my soul as she left this world.

I heard screaming. Screams reminding me of torment and agony. I clung to her, not realizing they were coming from me until they muffled when I lowered my head into Elisabeth's side, curling up.

I clung to her. The woman who knew me better than my own mother. Who had healed me time and time again, without question. She knew more about me than most, and I could not live my life without her.

She never failed. I could not fail her now.

I lifted my bloodied face to meet Ian's gaze. "Where is the healer?"

Hale ran down the hall, to where I cared not, except if it were to find someone to fix Elisabeth.

"Lan." Ian approached me as if I were a wounded animal, and I hated it. I hated the look in his eyes. "She's gone. There's nothing more we can do. I am so sorry."

Ruppert put his hand underneath my arm to pick me up, and I shoved him away. "Don't touch me. I will not leave her!"

"Give her a moment," Ian scolded.

"My job is not to coddle her, boy, know your place," Ruppert said with authority, as if his opinion mattered.

"This is why you are a terrible guard. And lest I remind you, I *outrank* you. You will listen to *my* command like the soldier you are."

"How *dare* you speak to me that way?" Ruppert seethed as he tried to pick me up once more.

I shoved him away, harder this time, as sparks flew from my fingers. Ruppert jumped back in shock as I clung once more to Elisabeth's body. "You're going to be okay. You're going to be okay, Elisabeth. I love you."

"Lan." Ian's voice broke as he knelt beside me. When I looked at him, the sadness on his face made it harder for me to pretend this would be okay. That somehow, she would return to us if a healer arrived.

"She's gone," he said.

Ruppert bellowed at Ian, and he left my side, the two arguing in hushed voices.

Let them argue. Nothing mattered.

I stroked Elisabeth's hair, closing my eyes to pretend she just slept. This couldn't be real.

I felt a whisper of heat down my arm as a warm hand rested on my shoulder. "It's time to get you to safety now, Little Rebel."

The smell of a summer's rain, and the cool breeze of a familiar shadow enveloped my body.

"I will not leave you here. I will *not* leave," I whispered as I rocked back and forth beside Elisabeth's body. The shadows were alluring, enticing even. Perhaps they would make it all better. But I couldn't leave her.

Something sickly sweet accosted my senses, and a vial appeared under my nose. "I'm so sorry, Lan," Ian whispered in my ear.

Kade's shadows wrapped tighter around me.

"I have to get you to safety now," Ian said.

My body swayed once, and the last memory before my world faded to black was of stormy eyes watching me as though they could take my grief far away from here. Forever.

CHAPTER 26

*D*rip.

Drip.

Without magic, you'll ruin this kingdom. You're nothing. Soon everyone around you will be nothing. Pathetic and worthless.

Drip.

The luxurious gold bath handles were dripping like that damned spot in the dungeon. Fitting, I supposed, since I felt like I was back there.

I didn't move.

The water in the tub had long lost its warmth, and goose bumps prickled my flesh. All of the remaining bubbles, which once covered my body, now clumped into a few spots at the foot of the tub. I couldn't move, though, so I gripped my arms around my knees tighter.

Andras had been right.

All those years Elisabeth and Ian tried to help me fight off the nightmares, tried to convince me that being magicless didn't make me weak. But at the end of the day, Andras had been right.

If I'd had the magic I should have, I would have been able

to help Elisabeth. I would have been able to do something until a healer arrived.

Instead of just sitting by her side and *letting* her die like the pathetic princess I was.

The tears streamed freely down my face, even after Ian had sedated me long enough to carry me back to my bedroom. There was nothing left inside of me to muster the strength to stop them.

Elisabeth's death left an empty hole in my soul, which would be there forever. A hole that not only ached at her absence, but one that reminded me I hadn't been enough to save her like she deserved.

I blinked slowly, my eyelids heavy and swollen.

My legs bore cuts and scrapes on them from when we'd been fighting and out on the road. Elisabeth's healing magic had concentrated so much on my side, the lingering minor scrapes remained. Another stark reminder of everything I couldn't do.

What if Elisabeth had been so drained from healing me, she couldn't heal herself? Another thought which would stay with me forever.

I sobbed, a guttural sound, exploding from my chest. My face warmed beneath fresh tears. Apparently, I still had something left inside of me after all.

The handle to my washroom clicked behind me, but I didn't care who entered.

I closed my eyes as the door opened, sensing who it was before seeing him.

Kade.

He could stay. He had helped me. Whether it was him or his shadows, I didn't have the energy to care. As long as he didn't antagonize me, he could stay. I didn't even bother raising my head to give him a smart remark about seeing me naked or being in my private bathing chambers.

His footsteps clunked softly in a slow beat, and then

stopped, a sad sigh escaping his lips. "I learned long ago there are no words that can be said to lessen the pain of losing someone you love. Anything I'd offer would be nothing which could ease your grief, even at my best."

I rested my head on my arms, breathing in a shaky inhale. I noticed him from my periphery, sitting propped on the marble bench connecting to the back of my tub.

The words did help, though. Or perhaps it was his voice that helped. I didn't have the energy to care yet.

He rose, walked to the front of the tub, and drained it.

I groaned. "I'm not ready."

"I know." He turned the golden handles, and warm water replaced the frigid as he ran his hand under the spout. He reached beneath the tepid surface, re-plugging it and letting his shadows turn the once-clear water into a storm-filled sky.

When the tub had filled, he twisted the handle hard enough so the damned dripping ceased.

"Let me help you, Illiana," Kade said, walking behind me again.

I finally lifted my head, meeting his gaze, aware my tear-streaked face must look pathetic to a warrior who had undoubtedly lost plenty of people in his life. "With what?"

Kade smiled at me. A real, soft, fucking heart-wrenching smile. He reached over the tub and picked up one of my bathing oils, lathering the rose-scented concoction in his hands.

"Turn around," he whispered, and without argument, I obeyed.

I leaned into his steady hands as he worked the shampoo over my scalp, slowly circling his fingers until he reached my neck and rubbed at tense muscles, which I knew would never ease.

"Tell me about her?" he asked.

He didn't stop lathering, and rubbing circles over my head

287

and neck, and I had yet to loosen my grip on my legs as I sat curled in a ball, even if I had shifted my head back for him.

"I have nightmares often. The first person I braved speaking to about them, besides Ian, was Elisabeth. I turned up at her door with horrendous dark circles under my eyes and burst into tears," I recalled. "She took my hands—I loved the way hers always enveloped mine. She sat me at her table and brought out dandelion tea. I remember turning my nose up, but she told me to trust her. She brought out this tin, which had the word 'Linen' on it, and inside, there were these tiny little lemon cookies."

My arms relaxed as I spoke.

"They were the best cookies I've ever had. And that damn dandelion tea." I chuckled, although it came out strained and wet with fresh tears. "It became an instant favorite. Every week since then, we met for tea and secret cookies. Some days, I sat quietly and watched her work. Other days she sat and listened to my mindless prattle." I smiled, pulling away from Kade's fingers when I pressed my forehead to my arms, closing my eyes and picturing her small workroom and the smell of lemon and tea.

"Every time I left, I felt like there would be nothing too hard to handle. That everything would be okay," I whispered.

Kade poured water over my back to clean the shampoo off without moving me.

Inky dark shadows curled over the sides of the tub, caressing the water, and breaking the surface until they rested on my shins and calves. Just like before, they comforted me, surrounding and pressing on me just enough to make me feel, safe.

Ridiculous for inanimate objects.

But true.

I relaxed for the first time since last night, tilting my head back as Kade rinsed the rest of my hair. I let my body relax and stretched my legs out for the first time in hours.

It sounded like he rummaged around behind me. "What comes next?" he asked.

I sniffled and twisted to the side, pointing toward a smaller bottle. "That one," I said. "It goes over the top of my hair smoothly. Not scrubbed in."

He grabbed the bottle and turned back to me, suddenly stiffening. He released a low, menacing growl, curling his lip. His eyes were low on my body, and I looked down, suddenly aware of what he'd see.

My scar.

"Who did that to you?"

I cleared my throat, turning around to face the front of the tub, letting his shadows cover my side once more. "No one. It's just a mark."

"I know what a fucking stab wound looks like, and this one is worse than most," he said, his voice ragged, dry, and filled with fury. "Who. Did. It?"

The shadows in the tub had stilled, but I wasn't afraid, despite my tremor.

I tapped my head, hopefully signaling to him to keep going while he stewed. I couldn't face talking about Andras tonight. Not after losing Elisabeth.

Not after truly believing the words he'd tormented me with for the first time in my adult life.

Kade's hands in my hair were gentle, despite the anger radiating from him.

"I'm not ready to talk about it," I said finally.

He paused. "Is the person who marked you dead?"

The silence between us lingered, and Kade resumed running his hands through my hair steadily.

The silence strained further. But I gave him the answer. "No."

He didn't pause or hesitate this time. He merely continued stroking my hair. Fates, how was he so good at this? "They will be. When you're ready."

His words, the tone he took, the rigidity the shadows now possessed, everything about him was menacing. Threatening. Yet, I wasn't afraid. I didn't doubt his words, nor feel pressured to tell him more. The way he spoke was like a vow.

I closed my eyes, letting go of everything as he rinsed my hair. His hands, unfailingly steady, stroked at the strands until he finished.

"Done," he said, letting go of me. "Now we should get you into bed."

I hesitated before I rose from the water, more aware than ever the second I stood up, he'd see me completely naked. Before I could voice my concern, Kade sent his shadows to cover me, forming a dark curtain around my body. He grabbed my nightgown, which had been strewn across the sink.

I lifted my hands above my head as he slipped it down my body, the shadows flowing out beneath it, keeping close to me until my nightgown covered me. The absence of them once they withdrew left an additional strange loneliness.

He took my hand, patiently walking me back into my room. Leading me to the edge of my bed, he pulled my covers back. I couldn't help but stare at him as he moved with such confidence, knowing exactly what to do without overstepping. He ran his thumb across my knuckles before bringing my hand to his lips. "Try to get some sleep."

He started to walk away, but I refused to let go of him. "Please don't go."

Kade stared at me, for once, unsure of what to say.

Before he could come up with some sort of snarky response, I tugged his hand, jerking him toward me. He stumbled on the edge of the bed as I pulled him into my arms. Our eyes met, and warmth finally returned to my darkened, worthless-feeling soul.

With one hand still clasped in mine, he raised his other around the back of my neck and into my wet hair, our lips grazing lightly. He didn't give in like I wanted. Like I needed. Instead, he drew away.

"I don't want to be alone," I whispered, staring into his eyes.

He shook his head, battling something inside of himself as his gaze darted from my lips to my eyes. "You're grieving." He kissed my forehead. "If you still want more when you've had time to process what's happened, I will not deny you again."

I brought my hands to his unbuttoned tunic collar. "You're hardly a hero, you don't need to act like one now."

His lips quirked into a half-smile as he ran his fingertips along the side of my face. "I'm sure I'll be back to my normal asshole-ish self tomorrow. For now, try to sleep, Little Rebel."

I wrinkled my nose, but very subtly jerked his collar. He leaned forward, pressing his lips to mine, in a more chaste kiss than before, but one I felt everywhere, nonetheless. He removed my hands from his tunic, kissing my knuckles before gazing upon my face again and rising, leaving my bedside.

He didn't glance back, but his shadows lingered a moment longer than he did before following, reluctantly trailing him.

Who would have thought Kade Blackthorn knew care and compassion?

My lids were heavy before the luxurious bath, and now were almost unbearable to keep open. I needed to sleep.

He'd kept the demons at bay once again, without even knowing it. With Elisabeth gone, there was a small part of me grateful I had another person to feel safe with.

I sat on the edge of the bed, fighting sleep. The nightmares would surely come for me tonight. A small pot of salve sat on my bedside table, which Elisabeth had prepared. Fresh tears threatened to fall as I held the canister of sweet floral-smelling salve to my chest. Inhaling the aroma that would forever remind me of her, I rubbed some on my hands and legs.

I paused. My legs were clear, perfectly healed, unlike prior to my bath.

The way Kade's shadows had moved up and down my legs, they must have been healing them. Perhaps it explained why they were so comforting.

That night, instead of the nightmares I feared, my dreams were filled with tea and secret cookies. Except joining me with Elisabeth, in what I knew would never happen now, was Kade, smiling at the woman I would love until my dying breath.

CHAPTER 27

"Please, please, promise me you will not kill Lord West on your date."

Kalliah's warm green eyes stared me down, and I believed each of us knew she pretended to be only *half*-joking.

In the mirror, I gave her my best attempt at a smile as she stepped away after completing a sweeping up-do of curls atop my head.

I clutched onto Lucien, who'd been resting on my lap. He'd barely left my side, sleeping near me and constantly on guard. I set him down, aware he'd be close.

I'd been allowed one day to grieve.

A small reprieve my father had granted before reminding me I had a duty to fulfill, even during heartbreak. My role in the trials continued.

The upcoming Festival of Blessings would kick off the third and final trial. Meaning now, I only had a few days until this would all be over.

I gripped my chair as I rose, realization hitting me. This would soon be *over*.

All of it.

I had no idea what it would look like, or who might come out victorious on the other side.

"You haven't promised yet." Kalliah bumped into me as she teased, trying desperately to break through the wall surrounding myself after Elisabeth's death.

I snorted. "I'm unsure I should promise such things."

"At least it's a walk through the city. Why he thinks it's a worthy date when he's trying to win your affections is beyond me," she said, "but I guess we can't expect a Lord who is responsible for nothing but himself to actually plan a date with you."

She pulled out a pair of shoes I normally wore for more casual outings around the city, and I practically kissed her. While others may expect me to dress in the latest finery for this date, I had no intention of greeting the city like a visiting dignitary in shoes, which would have me falling all over myself and twisting an ankle.

A small pit grew in my stomach, for I knew if I hurt myself now, I couldn't run to Elisabeth any longer.

Slipping them on quickly, I gave her a brief hug. "I promise. But only because I don't want you having a mess on your hands."

Her laughter remained with me as I closed the door behind me and walked into the hallway.

I turned, staring at the patch of carpet, which no longer bore the stain of Elisabeth's blood. The patch no one would know she died on in a few centuries time.

The pit in my stomach grew larger, the longer I stared at the carpet. Swallowing down the pain still swirling inside of me, I walked down the steps, slowly, dragging out the little bit of time I had alone before being stuck with Lord West.

I hadn't forgotten his strange interaction with Andras after the first winner's dinner.

But rules were rules, apparently, and this charade of granting him an hour of my time as the winner was mandatory. Given that I had been playing charades my whole life, hiding who I truly was, and what I truly thought, an hour was inconsequential in the grand scheme of it all.

My father, mother, and Andras stood alongside Lord Casimir West at the entrance to the palace. The four of them were huddled together, engaged in a whispered conversation I could not hear. My father held onto my mother's arm for support, his weakness becoming more evident with every passing day. Andras grinned slyly as he noticed my approach. I would never be able to shake the feeling of unease when I saw him, regardless of how many years it had been since I last left that dungeon.

Casimir stood tall, waiting for me at the entrance to the palace, his copper-red hair slicked back, despite its short length. He donned some of his finest attire, it appeared. The seams of his dark-grey pants and emerald tunic embroidered with a golden thread so thick, it reminded me of the upholstery on one of my least favorite chairs in our library. A golden swirling broach was pinned on the upper right section of his chest.

"My dear, we were just here to wish you both a wonderful hour together. Ruppert will accompany you across the city," my father said, hugging me quickly before they all turned to leave.

"The princess is safe with me, my King." Casimir's expression displayed utter confidence as he nodded toward my father.

"Princess Illiana." He bowed before me, grabbing my hand and kissing it lightly. "You are a vision. No one would know you were in mourning. Well done."

I tried not to shudder at the lack of empathy in his words, and his tone. I only had to smile and tolerate this man for one hour. *One hour.*

"Lord West, a pleasure to see you. I hear we are going for

a walk around the city. A fine choice," I responded, attempting to smile genuinely. I likely failed.

"Yes, it seemed right to greet our people together."

I clenched my teeth tightly at the comment. *My* people would *never* be his.

He opened the door, oblivious of how his words angered me, and led me down the path toward the city, holding his arm out for me to take, which I did reluctantly. Little did he know, in three swift moves, I could have him down to the ground, with a knife to his throat, a knife still conveniently sheathed on my thigh.

The thought brought a genuine smile to my lips this time.

Ruppert followed diligently, ten paces behind us. Too bad I couldn't feign some sort of illness to get out of this date, but Ruppert believed in rules. In fact, he *lived* for rules. If the king ordered me to be out with Lord West for an hour, Ruppert would ensure I stayed for the full hour.

Lord West spoke of himself and his many accomplishments so much so, I didn't even have to pretend to interject my thoughts and comments. He wasn't paying attention to my responses, anyway, instead walking through the streets of Ellevail as though he owned them and all of its people.

In fact, he didn't ask me a single question about myself. Not as if I cared. I would never choose him to win this competition. He served as another reminder that most of the men were here for the title and a Queen, not a wife or a friend.

The happiness I'd grown accustomed to enjoying as I walked this path through the city seemed stifled, suffocated by the man next to me. It must be the hot air he spewed. He certainly enjoyed hearing himself speak.

As we left the more affluent area on Duke Street, we approached my favorite part of the city. One I'd gladly flaunt to any visitors.

Although I was certain the wealthy would object, to me, this was the main street of the city of Ellevail. A street lined with shops, butchers, and florists. Anything one needed could be found on this street. Filled with a community, a sense of belonging, a place where our people looked out for one another, even with their limited magical abilities.

"I love this place." I sighed, interrupting the lord. I didn't care if he answered or not, I simply wanted it to be known.

He straightened, looking farther down his nose around us, if it were possible, and assessed each passing Fae with an air of disdain. He looked down upon my subjects, as if he held the position of King already. As if his gracing these villagers with his presence should be applauded. It repulsed me.

Who did this man think he was?

A group of tattered children from an alleyway bounded toward us. Ruppert didn't flinch, as he was accustomed to my walks around the city and interacting with all of its citizens. I also had it on good authority he pined after a woman who lived in this part of town.

The thought of Ruppert being attracted to anything but work made me smile and peer at him over my shoulder. Proving my point, his expression remained as stiff as stone, observing the incoming children as though they could possibly be a threat.

"Princess Lana!" a young boy leading the pack shouted. "Princess!"

They joined in unison, shouting my name. The young boy skidded to a stop in front of us and gave me a quick bow, the others in the group following his lead.

Lord West stepped back and snickered in disgust.

Each of the children, five in total, held out handfuls of dirt, and Lord West's eyes widened. "Be gone, children," he snarled. "This is the princess, she has no time for your antics, or piles of rubbish and dirt."

I grabbed at his arm, failing to hide my disgust. "They're children, my Lord. They enjoy showing off their magic."

He snorted. "From the looks of them, it can't be that impressive." He ignored me completely, turning back to the children. "Run along. I only get one hour with Her Highness, and I will not have it wasted watching magic tricks from children."

A little girl with bright-red hair tied into pigtails stuck her tongue out at him as she shoved her hands forward, revealing a beautiful purple carnation, sprouting from the dirt in her hand. She offered me the flower earnestly, beaming with pride at her creation.

I clapped. "It's beautiful."

I knelt, ignoring the indignation and grumbling from Lord West behind me. Each of the other children followed and handed me their flowers, creating a small bouquet for me to take back to the palace.

I studied their faces, the excitement they had at creating life. Each of them were blessed with earth magic, and the way they gingerly handled their dirt and sprouted flowers seemed so innocent. So beautiful.

"Thank you so much for this incredible gift," I said. They launched forward, hugging me, until we were all laughing.

As quickly as they'd come, they ran away again, returning to play. Only once they disappeared did the moment of joy turn to a sharp sting in my chest. A painful reminder, for even these children, so young and small, who clearly worked in the fields maintaining our crops, had more magic than I could summon.

I wiped the dirt off the skirt of my dress watching the last of the children run off.

"Shall we keep going?" I asked before resuming our walk down the street, choosing to ignore his spiteful comments from earlier. The man behaved like a weasel, and I would stop at nothing to ensure he didn't ascend the throne.

His lip hadn't relaxed from the snarled curl before he could answer me, when an older woman approached, bowing low.

"My condolences on Elisabeth, Your Highness."

I reached for her hands, recognizing her immediately. "Thank you, Thea." I blinked away tears threatening to spill and not stop. Clearing my throat, I quickly changed the subject. "How are the young newlyweds holding up?"

The woman's voice transformed from one of empathy to one of pure joy. "To be young and in love." She chuckled and bowed her head again. "I can't thank you enough for your generous food and gifts. It was too much."

I shushed her. "A wedding deserves to be celebrated fully." I grinned. "Besides, if I recall, there wasn't a single time I ran through Ellevail as a child which didn't end with a chocolate milkshake in my hand."

"Well, the milkshake kept you and Ian distracted from purchasing my entire stock of pastries every week." The woman chuckled, patting my hands before releasing me. "I will let you be on your way." She bowed her head and backed up before heading back toward her shop.

Thea and her husband ran a small bakery in the lower levels of town. They made enough to make a living, and their baked goods rivaled even the best bakers the richer nobility used. Ian and I stopped in frequently, and even though I could have paid for it, Thea and her husband never allowed me. Ian made sure payment showed up anytime they were in need though, which made me feel better accepting their generosity.

Lord West coughed into his hand before holding a finger under his nose. "We should return to Duke Street."

"I enjoy being with all of my people, Lord West."

He looked me up and down. "It sounds as though your handouts may cost your kingdom. Does your father know of these activities?"

I clenched my hands into fists at my sides, and my lip

twitched. The implication that I provided goods without my father's consent wasn't the problem. Fates, I was the Hidden Henchman and *had* been doing such things for over a year now. No, it was the audacity to imply I needed approval to assist my people. "They are citizens of Ellevail. I'm allowed to give gifts and assistance to whomever I wish."

He snorted. "You'll have to obtain a savvier business acumen when you take the throne."

"Well, it's a good thing this is a city of Fae I love and care for as if they were each a member of our palace, who will repay those acts of kindness tenfold when asked and able. Sounds like the only person in need of savvy business acumen is you, Lord West." I took a step away from him, veering back to the castle, noticing it far in the distance. I longed for it to be closer, or to run through the hidden tunnels to take me straight to my room. I'd been out here with this man long enough. "We should head back. By the time we return, the hour will be complete, and I have another date to prepare for."

I didn't wait to hear his response before I walked back toward the palace. All I had to do was change into my training leathers for a date with Ryland and then endure whatever he had planned.

After that, my day would be complete. I could see Hale tomorrow and then get back to ensuring contenders like Lord West would never have a chance at becoming King.

CHAPTER 28

I stumbled to the side, sword in hand, tripping on a small root that suddenly sprouted from the ground.

"Good, Leif!" Ian's praise echoed through the training pit, and I spun abruptly to observe my friend.

"Magic *and* swords, watch out world." I laughed.

His smile grew wide with my praise.

My training hadn't involved weaving magic into attacks, since I clearly lacked any. I encouraged Ian to do so with Kalliah and Leif, even if their abilities weren't powerful, they were there, and those skills could be honed if trained.

I'd been right.

My date with Ryland yesterday afternoon had been sparring together. He'd remembered it was one of my hobbies I briefly mentioned during our first dinner together. I was taken aback he recalled such a minute detail of my life, but I appreciated the date had a purpose, instead of just being seen in public on the princess's arm. He taught me some of his own specialty maneuvers he had been perfecting for years. The movements were fluid yet stealthy enough that I wanted Ian to incorporate them into our training. I was concerned when the date began that Ryland would want to use magic in our session, but he seemed content to keep it physical.

I'd been surprised at how easy I envisioned a friendship forming with him. Our conversation flowed freely and easily, but it lacked any sort of spark. Besides, I was still concerned about his conversation with Casimir. Although it sounded like he turned Lord West down, my trust wouldn't extend *that* far to others yet. Or perhaps ever.

I'd even tried to sneak in a question about how he felt about the other contenders to see if he would bite, but he failed to take the bait.

While it had been fun, Ryland lacked some of the characteristics I hoped for in a husband. I didn't feel as if he could succeed on the throne, without exceptional handholding, which I had no intention of providing.

He would, however, make an excellent addition to Ian's guard if he ever wanted a place here in Ellevail. I'd have to mention it to Ian when all of this finally passed.

"Okay, rest," Ian said, bringing me back to reality. "Lan, come here."

I bounced on my toes, shaking out my shoulders and stretching my neck before standing in front of Ian.

Leif jogged to the outskirts of the training ring to retrieve two glasses of water for us. In the distance behind him, I noticed Kalliah practically skipping along the path from the palace to the ring.

Leif handed me a glass as Kalliah approached our group, her eyes gleaming.

"Well, do tell. What has you all giddy?" I asked her as I downed the cool water. Sweat seeped through my shirt since I finally stopped moving.

"I was asked to the Festival of Blessings!" She clasped her hands together.

Leif immediately spat the water out of his mouth, spraying it across my face.

"Leif!" I shouted as I turned and stared with indignation, wiping the spray from my cheek.

He ignored me completely and immediately questioned Kalliah. "And you said yes?"

Kalliah paused, and shifted to face Leif, glaring at him with utter indignation. One I would not want to experience. "Yes, I did. I believe one should take advantage of the opportunities which are afforded to them, instead of waiting around for something which may never happen."

Leif opened and closed his mouth before clenching it shut.

"That's what I thought," she said. "Lana, we must be off to prepare you for your next date. Good day, gentlemen."

Kalliah grabbed my hand and pulled me quicker than I anticipated. I barely had time to shove the now-empty glass into Leif's hand before stumbling after Kalliah. She gripped my hand like a vice. I didn't even get a chance to glance at Ian to see his reaction to the news and Leif's stammering.

Finally, when we were far enough away and she had slowed down, I said, "Cruel, Kalliah. Cruel. I didn't know you had it in you."

"What was cruel?" She cocked an eyebrow at me.

"Oh, no, don't you play coy now. Leif will likely cry himself to sleep tonight," I said. "Hand me your handkerchief to get his spit off my face please. Fates, did no one see how hard his water left his mouth?"

Kalliah's eyes narrowed. "Leif is only concerned with baking and his Hidden Henchman duties and has yet to pursue me at all after our talk at the ball. I refuse to wait around for him to ask me for more of my time. So of course, when Dimitri asked, I agreed to go with him," she said, clearly trying to convince herself she made the right choice.

I knew something had happened at the contender's ball. "You are trying to make him jealous," I countered, grabbing her arm to stop her focused walk toward my chambers.

Kalliah bit her lip, her darker cheeks blushing. "I'm not

303

trying to be cruel. I just, well, if there's a chance at love, I want it. And Dimitri is handsome and kind," she said, shrugging.

"And?" I pressed, tilting my head, not at all buying my savvy and fierce friend didn't have an ulterior motive.

"*And* I've watched my best friend hold a competition for her hand, so why not create some competition for myself." She grinned, almost evilly while tossing me a wink.

I looped my arm through hers, laughing all the way back to my chambers.

A quick thirty minutes later, I finished bathing and Kalliah swiftly braided my hair for my date with Hale. A knock on the door was the only warning before Ian entered, barely able to contain his laughter.

"What's gotten into you?" I asked.

"Oh, Kalliah, you have done it now." Ian collapsed onto a chair in the sitting area, leaning over the arm with a devious smile on his face. "Leif was beside himself when you left. I walked back with him to the kitchen to grab an apple, and he was muttering to himself. I didn't even have time to tease him about anything before he picked up a sack of flour to bring inside."

Ian snorted, unable to control himself. "Who should come around the corner at that exact moment with a stack of the cleanest pile of our Queen's laundered gowns?"

My jaw dropped, eyes alight from the story. "Please tell me it was Lucinda." The royal laundress was notorious for wreaking havoc on everyone in the palace at the slightest inconvenience.

Ian inclined his head. "As you can imagine, Lucinda was none too pleased when Leif collided into her with the sack of flour. I'm not sure who had it worse! Lucinda covered in flour along with her laundry, or Leif fumbling over the old Fae's clothes, trying to brush it off of her." Tears were streaming down his face from laughing so much.

I tried so hard to keep my giggling to a minimum, but I couldn't help myself. Kalliah quickly pulled my head back into position as she finished the braid, rather roughly.

"Serves him right. Maybe if he got his head out of the clouds, he would see what is in front of him!"

"Oh, Kalliah," I started to say when she gave me *that* look through the mirror. "His head wasn't in the clouds, it was wrapped around *you*."

She glared at Ian next, scolding us. "Neither of you will ruin this for me. I will be with Dimitri for the Festival of Blessings whether you like it or not. I expect these wishes to be honored!"

Ian and I shared a glance, and in unison replied, "As you wish." Ian even rose and bowed.

Kalliah couldn't contain her own giggle any longer. It felt so *normal* to be with them, laughing. To have this moment of levity with my best friends at a time where there was so much unknown.

"I would have paid to see Lucinda's face, covered in flour." Kalliah snickered as we settled. "Since we've had plenty of fun at my expense, how about you, Captain? Do you have your date, or shall I say 'dates,' for this year's Festival?"

"Yes, Ian. What fair maiden do you have in your grasp this year? Hopefully not that dreadful barmaid from two Festivals ago." I snorted.

"Or two dates like last year," Kalliah chimed in. "The drama of trying to keep them from knowing about the other was exhausting."

His face turned serious. "I'm a contender, Lana, need I remind you. I have no date for this year's Festival because you are my date."

"Oh," I replied solemnly, "I assumed with all the gaggles of women who were falling at your feet, you would have asked one of them by now."

"You're unbelievable." His movements were rigid as he stood again, the joy draining from the room.

"I'm just saying, Ian. Don't let these silly marriage trials stop you from having a good time. You aren't technically my personal guard this year, and since the general is being light with your Captain duties while you are in the marriage trials, it seems like an opportunity for you to be free. An opportunity to not be wasted on saving yourself for something we know would just be an arrangement of convenience."

"How many times do I have to tell you? This is not just some temporary arrangement for me. I am taking this competition seriously. I can't have you ending up with the likes of Casimir."

I studied him for a moment, desperate to bring back the normalcy of our friendship. This was too much. The strain of everything demanded too much of him, of me, of our relationship. I hated the trials all over again.

"Next year, my friend, I hope you have the most joyous Festival, filled with all of the eligible maidens across the land."

Assuming he wasn't King. Did I want Ian to win? The thought of Kade immediately popped into my mind, and I swallowed the lump in my throat as I realized my feelings for him were growing. If they continued, perhaps Ian wouldn't need to keep up his absurd charade to win. Especially if Kade became a contender who could win and not be a miserable bastard.

The thought terrified me.

We all stared at each other a moment longer in awkward silence, before Ian coughed and headed back toward the door. "Hale and Ruppert will be by the front entrance in twenty minutes. I already scouted out the location earlier today, but Ruppert will be there just in case."

"Thank you, Ian," I said. Regardless of being stripped from the role of my personal guard for the trials, he hadn't let it deter him from maintaining those duties throughout the entirety of the competition.

What Hale had planned, I did not know, but with only a few minutes to spare, I had to shake any sense of unease and pull myself together. Out of all the dates I had to endure this round, I was the least worried about my time with Hale.

When I walked through the open palace doors, only my mother appeared beside Hale at the entrance. My father's absence felt disheartening. I arched an eyebrow, but she shook her head slightly as I approached, already guessing what I'd ask. It would seem a conversation for another, more private time.

"My dearest," she said, grabbing both my hand and Hale's, "please do enjoy your time together. We look forward to seeing you soon."

Just outside the door, Ruppert waited in position as Hale and I began our descent into the city. Ruppert may have been a terrible guard before, but he knew I liked to enjoy the lands around me and allowed me to travel in peace.

"I thought we could have a late lunch and enjoy a few minutes away from the heaviness of the last few days," Hale said as we made our way down the path. He offered his arm, and I gladly accepted. "I'm sorry about Elisabeth. She'll be missed."

I grasped his arm, squeezing it once. "Thank you, Hale."

We wandered down the path and into the city, and while I had just been here with Lord West yesterday, it seemed entirely different with company who appreciated *all* of Ellevail. Hale and I stopped to talk to a few Fae along the way before we ended at Millie's Café.

"You remembered." I laughed.

"There's only one place to get your favorite meal." He shook his head. "You brought it up at least once a week when we were younger. I'd be dimwitted indeed if I couldn't remember such a piece of information."

Ruppert nodded and indicated he would be outside should anything arise. For once, he actually allowed me the privacy I wanted and needed. Something he failed to do previously as my guard.

The café was empty, which surprised me, considering the hour. I surveyed our surroundings, now understanding why Ruppert had been fine to leave me alone.

"Where is everyone?"

Millie bustled from the kitchen, wiping her hands on her faded red apron. "Oh, come now, child. An hour-long date with the princess can certainly be accommodated to give you some peace and quiet." She winked at me before patting Hale on the cheek. The short, brilliant cook had to reach up, practically extending her arm to do so.

She shuffled back to me, grabbing my shoulders and pulling me toward her. "I heard about Elisabeth, my sweet child. She loved you more than life, I hope you know that." Millie pulled back and cupped my cheeks, patting them once before she drew away.

"Sit, sit. I'll be out in a moment," she instructed.

I realized right then that perhaps the reason I loved being around the lesser Fae so much, why Ian and I had loved it our whole lives, was because they treated us like family. I wasn't Princess Illiana when something was wrong. I was one of them. Their own. Just as they were mine.

None of the nobles expressed their condolences, but every single lesser Fae made their sorrow known. My heart cracked.

Millie walked toward the front, yanking her blue polka-dotted curtains closed, shutting off the view from the crowd gathering outside, hoping to see more.

Hale held his arm out for me, revealing a small table at the back of the café already set for the occasion. A delicate bouquet of hydrangeas was displayed in a crystal vase at the center. He pulled out my chair for me as we took our seats.

"I already took the liberty of ordering our lunch, I hope that's okay," Hale stammered.

I reached across the table and took his hand. "It's more than okay, Hale. Thank you for planning such a thoughtful date."

He smiled and seemed to relax a bit more. The conversation ebbed and flowed, just as it always had. Millie returned, laying out two bowls of vegetable soup, and I couldn't help but feel grateful. I knew he'd remembered from the joke he made at dinner the first night of the trials, but to see it here again warmed my heart.

I genuinely smiled and breathed in the rich beefy broth. "This might be the best date I've ever been on," I admitted.

We took a few bites, and I paused, looking up at him. "I owe you another round of thanks for the first dinner. I was rather nervous, and you made me feel more at ease. Thank you for your kindness."

Hale blushed, a small smile gracing his lips. He hesitated, trying to find the right thing to say and dropped his spoon on the floor. I bent to pick it up for him, where it had landed by my feet, but he flicked his wrist, and it flew back onto the table. Millie ran over and replaced it with a clean one instantly.

"Thank you, Millie," he said, his cheeks flushing further. He waited to continue until she disappeared into the kitchen, leaving us alone in the empty café.

He coughed and sat up straighter this time. "Princess Illiana, I know you have much to consider during these trials, but I'm grateful to have been given this time so I could tell you how I feel."

I sat up straighter, too, placing my hands on my lap as he took a drink of water before continuing.

"For the last several years, you got me through so many of our Court gatherings and balls. Being with you made me feel alive and provided an escape from the boring life I know we both live. Especially with the pressure of constantly being under the watchful eye of our parents and advisers. Our time together has been a blessing."

"Oh, Hale," I started, but he cut me off.

"No, please let me finish, or I may not find the courage to say this to you again."

I nodded and let him proceed, taking a drink of water myself, just for something to do with my hands, before placing them on the table.

"I know I may have been inexperienced before, and perhaps I was young and naïve, but I have grown over these last few years. I know you have, too. If I were given the honor of your companionship, I would make every minute count."

He reached for my hand, bringing it to his lips, and kissed it softly.

I had never had anyone speak to me the way Hale had. I should have been flattered by someone regarding me so highly and wanting to be with me so much. Even with the warm, and generous words, something didn't feel right, which would make it hard to choose Hale for myself.

"I'm not expecting you to feel the same way or answer me with any sort of returned affection. I merely wanted to ensure you knew, should I win the trials and be a contender for you to select, I would honor you. I would honor the role of your husband, just as much as I would honor the role of being the king."

It was a beautiful sentiment, and I stood to give Hale a hug. I looked back on the evenings we'd spent together with fondness. He had gotten me through so many nights of drudgery and boring Court gatherings in the same exact way he claimed I had for him. I owed the man before me for maintaining my sanity during those times.

"Thank you, Hale. I appreciate it more than you know," I whispered in his ear before letting go. "You have to know you made it easy to be your friend. Regardless of what happens in the trials, I'd be honored if I could continue to call you my friend."

He nodded. "Always, Princess."

We finished our lunch, reminiscing a few more times, and then Hale filled me in on some of the latest gossip I'd missed regarding recent engagements.

Our laughter continued until Ruppert poked his head through the doors. "Your Highness, it's almost time to return to the palace."

After thanking Millie, and Hale again, I linked my arm through his, walking Ellevail's streets side by side.

The closer the palace came into view, though, the heavier my heart grew.

There was one day left before the final trials. The decision to select a husband and future king crept closer, and a final choice would have to be made.

Through it all, one man kept entering my mind. Not Hale, who I knew I wouldn't find love with, but would have a loyal companion.

Not Ian, who would die for me, and who I'd do the same.

It was Kade.

Kade who invaded my thoughts in a way that terrified me. I knew nothing of him, and yet, I couldn't shake the feeling he had become the front-runner, and I hadn't even noticed it happening.

CHAPTER 29

The explosion ricocheted into the night, echoed with "oohs" and "ahhs" from nearly the entire city of Ellevail as it burst open in the sky, revealing the purple and gold colors of the kingdom.

The fireworks went off for hours during the festival. The colorful display served as one of the many attractions bringing Fae from all over Brookmere into Ellevail for the celebration. Although we weren't the only city celebrating the Festival of Blessings, ours certainly boasted the largest event.

My skin warmed as I moved closer to one of the many bonfires, waiting for our King to officially begin the celebration, since the first firework had been spent. The clear crystals woven into the bodice of my silver taffeta gown, sparkled with the colors illuminating the sky. A large diamond necklace hung around my neck, making my entire ensemble glisten with my every move.

"My people," he said, his voice gravelly but amplified enough for all to hear. "Tonight, we welcome you to the annual Festival of Blessings, for tomorrow, the growing season shall begin."

A roar sounded in the sky, as everyone clapped and cheered. "As we do each year, we take tonight to revel in all nature has granted us. Brookmere is what we are because of the first queen, Queen Evelyn Everhart.

"Queen Evelyn rose to her power, growing in might, and though she married, the king at her side abandoned her when war arrived, his name unworthy of being recorded in our history. She bore the weight of Brookmere alone, surviving wars, and heralding in the centuries of peace we have long enjoyed through her sacrifice, and her bravery."

Cheers rang out in the streets again at the mention of the beloved queen's dedication.

"Tonight, we offer our sacrifice to nature, so it continues to find us as worthy as Queen Evelyn." He brought out a small amethyst-encrusted ceremonial dagger, slicing his hand and dripping his blood into the fire as our custom required. My mother followed.

Then, she handed the dagger to me. I took it, slicing a small cut along my palm, too afraid to do anything more with Elisabeth gone should anyone see my unhealed hand. A single drop of blood fell into the fire. It sparked, soaring higher.

My eyes widened in surprise, as I looked up and into the crowd. Storm stood a few rows back and winked, before disappearing with a grin behind the heightened blaze.

"Our sacrifice is accepted as worthy." My father beamed at me.

I returned the loving expression, listening to him continue. "We honor nature's blessings." He bowed his head, silence rippling through the crowd for a moment. "Now, let us enjoy each other, our friendships, our love, nature, and the magical Festival of Blessings. May nature guide you!"

He threw his hands into the air as a barrage of fireworks launched into the sky.

Music from a large band set up to the right of the bonfire

drifted around us, and soon, Fae danced merrily, swinging between partners as the celebration truly kicked off. Smaller fires appeared up and down the streets, and I knew many would soon venture to their own cliques. For now, we were one country, one people, and it was beautiful.

I remained in my place, where all could see me, as well as the king and queen, as I did every year. A tingle on the back of my neck made me smile, and I searched the crowd for Kade. I didn't even need to see him, but somehow, I could *feel* him there. With a quick wave, Kalliah ran toward a drink stand to get some wine for her and Dimitri. I lost sight of them soon after, while I continued to search for Kade amongst the revelry.

"Your Highness."

I froze. Andras stood in front of me, bowing, before reaching for my hand. I gritted my teeth.

"May I have the honor, as Royal Adviser, of the first dance." The fire reflecting in his eyes made him appear as evil as I knew him to be.

I glanced at my father, who frowned at us. Andras had never been so bold as to make such an inappropriate request. Not in recent memory at least. He'd spoken loudly enough for those around to hear, ensuring his request could not be ignored.

It would be more of a headache to deny him, but it did nothing to soothe my racing pulse. Fear of touching him, of being close to him in any way, had my heart beating wildly. I nodded, moving rigidly toward the center of the dancing circle.

His hand curled along my back as he tried to pull me closer, and I bit my tongue, tasting blood, as I forced my body to keep from trembling under his touch. Closing my eyes, I attempted not to let my nausea take over as he moved us to the beat. Eventually, I failed, needing to open my eyes before I retched from the blind movements, and a tear leaked from the corner of my eye.

"Still unable to control your emotions, I see." His eyes flashed with glee as a cruel smile overtook his face.

I held my chin higher. "I can control myself more than you realize."

I may be afraid, but I'd look him in the eye as he taunted me. He couldn't force my submission. I grimaced, as a clawlike sensation scratched at my brain.

He chuckled mirthlessly as we spun in time with the ever-changing beat. "You forget I've seen you weeping and begging for mercy on the floor of my dungeons, Princess. Hard to be intimidated by someone so easily broken."

A surge of anger coursed through me, heating my body more than the fire ever could. How *dare* he? I tried to pull a step back, to put distance between us, but his hold was relentless.

We twirled by Ian, whose expression turned cold, unblinking, as he stared at Andras. I shook my head as subtly as I could to tell him not to make a scene.

Thankfully, he didn't make a move. Andras wasn't crazy enough to try anything, at least I didn't believe so. The fact that he spoke to me so callously *and* in public about his "training" sessions made me believe he'd grown more arrogant, but too bold. Or perhaps even crazy himself.

He hummed as we danced, behaving as though we did this all the time. As if it were something we enjoyed. Ian lingered, farther from us now, as Andras continued moving both of us in time to the song. "Are you rooting for any of the contenders in particular? Besides the captain of course." He snickered. "He always butts in where he doesn't belong."

"He belongs here with me," I said.

Andras smiled. "He belongs in the ground like his father. Peasants like him have no business running around palaces like they matter. Like they have a place at the king's table."

My teeth ached as I clenched my jaw. "I swear if you harm him—"

"You'll what?" Pulling me tight to his body, he whispered in my ear, "A magicless princess and her band of misfits are no match for me."

The brazen way in which he acted shocked me to my core. He'd implied things in the dungeons, whispered things in passing, had gotten Ian and I into trouble where he could. But he'd never been this open and disgusting in such a public place.

I started to pull away again, not caring what others might think. Immediately, I searched for Ian, and this time when our eyes met, he moved instantly, trying to get through the crowd to my side.

But Andras had purposefully moved us away from Ian. Away from help.

I stared at the man, as if somehow, I might be able to find the answer to his newfound confidence. The scratching sensation occurred again, and he eerily stared into my eyes.

My stomach churned, but I couldn't look away.

My shoulders sagged. Perhaps dancing with Andras wasn't so bad. He'd been in the family for years, he wouldn't actually hurt me, not too badly at least. My father trusted him. He was a Royal Adviser after all.

I pulled back immediately, shaking the thoughts from my head, knowing something was wrong. My eyes narrowed as the song came to a conclusion. "What did you just do to me?"

Andras leaned in, a sinister look flashing in his eyes.

But then, a pair of sturdy arms wrapped around my side. "Princess."

I stiffened, expecting Ian to have been my savior, but it wasn't him.

When I made eye contact with my savior, I found Hale.

Relief filled me but didn't give my body the permission to

relax yet. "May I have the next dance?" he asked, glaring at Andras openly.

Andras sneered, exposing his teeth before seeming to remember himself. "Until we meet again, Your Highness."

My body couldn't let go of the fear thrumming inside of me until he disappeared from sight.

"I apologize if I came across too forward. You seemed like you needed assistance," Hale said with a tight smile. "I've never seen you so panicked."

My body still trembled from the sensations of Andras's hands on me. Sensations that triggered hateful, horrifying thoughts that refused to leave, but I stared into Hale's eyes and breathed, finding it easier to feel safe again. "Thank you," I whispered. "You don't even know how much I appreciate what you just did for me. I can't begin to——"

"I don't need to know anything," he said. "Try to breathe and take a minute. I don't mind."

I let Hale hold me, leading me through the rest of the dance. Ian finally came into view, relief flooding his features. He hung back, now that I had escaped Andras's clutches.

As the song played on, melody building, Hale twirled me around the dance floor, the sense of panic and unease fleeing my body. I even managed a laugh as Hale flung me out and our hands slipped apart.

Catching my breath as the song ended, I gave Hale a quick curtsey before Ian approached and scooped me away for the next dance.

"I'm sorry I couldn't get to you in time." Ian gripped me tightly, rubbing a small circle on my back. "What did he say to you?"

"He was brazen. Referencing our time in the dungeon. Here in public. And then, Ian, I swear he got into my mind and made me think he wasn't so bad. I caught it, I stopped the thought, but what if he can control people? What if he is controlling my father?" I rested my head on Ian's shoulder, not wanting to reveal any further fears.

"No one knows his power *except* your father," Ian said, lifting my chin and holding my gaze. "Do not be alone with him again. If you are, scream, cause a scene, something."

I nodded, knowing I would never be put in that situation again. The absolute arrogance of speaking to me in such a manner, in public, made me wonder what else he'd have the audacity to do. I'd never risk the alternative of being taken somewhere by Andras again.

Ian held me tightly as we danced, adjusting our pace as this song slowed. "How are you holding up?"

I hugged Ian closer, enjoying a brief moment with my guard down now that it was just the two of us. "I'm terrified of what else the trials will take from me," I admitted. "Ian, I don't know how I'll get over Elisabeth's death, let alone if someone else—" I couldn't continue the train of thought. It took me to a dangerous territory. Territory that the dance with Andras had only exacerbated.

"You will not get over her death," he said, his hand drawing me closer as he squeezed me tightly. "None of us will. But we'll live a life that will make her proud." He spun me out, smiling at me freely, before twirling me back to him. "And as for losing anyone else. We'll be vigilant. All of us. I swear it."

I nodded, refusing to give into any thoughts other than belief in him. Belief that we'd make it through the trials. Alive.

"Leif is absolutely beside himself, you know," he said, lightening the subject. "Kalliah really has done a number on him by coming with Dimitri tonight."

As Ian spoke, I noticed Vivienne on the other side of the fire, her hair wildly arranged as usual. I blinked a few times, realizing she stood in front of Kade. The Seer lifted her hands to Kade's head before jumping back, his shadows dancing at his feet.

"Mmm, is that so?" I responded, hardly paying attention to what Ian said, doing everything I could to discern what happened between Kade and Vivienne.

Whipping my head around as Ian spun us, I took in the sight of the two of them again. She bowed low before him, a wide grin spread across her face, then she clapped her hands together and skipped away.

"Lan, are you even paying attention?" Ian scolded.

"What, no. Yes! I'm sorry. I got lost for a moment." I shook my head, refocusing on Ian.

The song slowed to an end, and as if sensing I stared at him, Kade's gaze met mine. He passed by groups of Fae milling about as he strode toward me, ignoring Ryland and Lord West as they huddled together arguing by a nearby fire.

"Mind if I cut in?" he asked Ian.

He rolled his eyes. "Ah, now it makes sense. Lost, were we? As long as I don't have to listen to the banter, or whatever it is you two do, be my guest." Ian bowed and left my side while Kade stepped in.

I hadn't seen him since he put me to bed after Elisabeth's death, but it didn't mean he hadn't been on my mind. He'd preoccupied almost all of my thoughts actually.

His shadows curled toward me, tingling as they caressed my skin. I realized I'd missed their touch as well as his, without even knowing. This was dangerous. A stranger on the throne would be unheard of.

A stranger who already carved a path to my heart.

Without a word, he grasped my hand and pulled me close as the sultry notes of a lone violin pierced the air.

We didn't speak, but Kade held my stare, like maybe, just maybe he'd been thinking about me, too. Everything around us melted away, my skin humming with excitement, electricity coursing through my soul. The song was a common one played at our events, a melody about a lover's quarrel, building deep, passionate notes, as their love faltered.

"How did you win over Vivienne?" I asked. "I noticed our Royal Seer bowing to you, and you're not even a Lord."

Kade shook his head as we glided across the makeshift dance floor. "She may be considered slightly crazy here, but she reminds me of someone from back at home." He smiled down at me.

Fates above, his gorgeous, sinful smile. His lips were right there, and I could claim them. It would be easy to get on my toes.

I blinked away the thought. If I could even consider being reckless and giving my heart to a stranger, I needed to know some truths. At least answers to some of the mystery surrounding this man.

I forced myself to swallow, attempting to break the spell he had me under. "Kade, I have questions." My voice was lost in the chaos of the festival, as a loud *bang* echoed through the air from another onslaught of fireworks.

"Well, don't keep me waiting, Little Rebel. Do continue." His voice hitched as shadows pooled from his palms in such light wisps, I wondered if they were truly there. They wrapped around our hands as we danced.

"Why don't you exist in Brookmere? Nobody knows who you are. You are not in any record book, on any ledger. It's as if you are a ghost. Yet you are helping the citizens of Brookmere as if they were your own. Someone with your power would have been known throughout the land. It's not making sense."

He dipped me low, before bringing me back up. "Looking into me, are you?"

"You can hardly think I wouldn't." I cocked an eyebrow.

His smirk this time held a note of pride. "Of course. You have your secrets, Princess, and I have mine."

"I need more than that to trust you with my—" I

321

swallowed to stop myself from saying what was desperately trying to come out of my mouth. *My heart.* I cleared my throat and tightened my hands in his, finishing the thought, "Kingdom." I wanted so badly for him to give me something. Anything.

The violin and cello answered each other with ravaged notes as his shadows coiled around my legs, spinning me around before the final verse began.

"What exactly is your power?" Perhaps he would answer something simpler.

He stared at me quizzically as his shadows played with the lining of my dress. "Isn't it obvious?"

"Shadow magic hasn't been seen in thousands of years."

His face tightened. "Add it to the growing list of secrets between us."

"Do your shadows always act like this around women then? Is it your magic which makes me feel that—" I frowned, trying to find the words. "That tingling sensation. Almost like electricity?"

He blinked, his jaw dropping slightly. I'd caught him off guard. "You feel it, too?"

I snorted. "It's coming from you, I assure you. I have no —" I immediately hesitated, surprise washing over me as I'd nearly just revealed my biggest secret. And to someone I knew nothing about. Someone who refused to answer a basic question of his origin.

The air heated around us. "Maybe try to keep your shadows to yourself, at least in public. We wouldn't want anyone thinking you were cheating in the trials because you had my favor," I said, spinning myself this time as the final notes were about to be struck.

"They're not the best listeners, but I can certainly try if it's what Her Highness wants. Although..." He yanked my hand, spinning me back in until my back slammed into his broad chest. He leaned down and whispered in my ear, his warm breath rushing over my skin as I shivered in anticipation. "I can feel all your coiled up tension. I know what you truly want. When you're ready to beg for it, I will not deny you again."

Dancing around the bonfire was far more intense than dancing in the throne room had been. The flames flickered over his shadows, and the way Kade watched me through the light of the fire, had darkness twisting my insides into knots. I had become exactly that coiled-up ball of tension he claimed.

"Will you tell me anything?" I asked as my gaze met his. "Anything at all about you?"

His perfectly stormy eyes took me in as if they'd lock me in place forever. He inhaled a sharp breath as his gaze flicked to my lips, then back to my eyes. "Storm told you I'm usually quieter."

I nodded.

He swallowed, drawing me closer until our bodies were pressed tightly against one another. It took every ounce of strength I had not to close my eyes and fall into him.

"I think meeting you, being around you, has made me feel more myself than I have in my entire life. Who I've been with you, Little Rebel, is who I've only ever hoped to be."

And as the band struck their final chord, he dipped me low, and we were left panting as the world came back into focus.

Pulling me upright, he kissed my hand before bowing and disappearing into the night.

My heart and head were fluttering too quickly as my rationality spun out of control. My body wanted so much more. It ached for his touch. My mind was at odds with my heart, a battle of logic and emotion.

Could I allow this mysterious man to take a place in my heart while keeping so much from me? Because right now, I was falling hard, and fast. Perhaps if I had a taste of Kade, I could reconcile the man before me with the one he portrayed to the world.

Perhaps he wasn't *just* here for a crown, despite the numerous times he had told me otherwise. Perhaps he was lying to himself. Everything I am screamed at me to be near him. Despite all logical reasoning. This electricity between us meant something. It had to.

And I needed to learn exactly what that something was.

If I didn't, I'd spend forever wondering "what if." And that would be a fate I could not accept.

I scanned the festival, unable to stop smiling at my people and the way they were consumed with their partners and celebrations. I could hear the rambunctious animals, pets, and beasts alike on the outskirts. The wind blew, nature reveling in our commemoration.

Across the square, Kalliah was dancing slowly with Dimitri, a soft smile gracing her face like I hadn't seen before. Ian had disappeared into the crowd, somewhere. Before Ryland or Casimir could corner me for dances of their own, I made the decision to leave.

I would end this evening before I was forced to dance again against my will.

One final pass across the crowd, and I noticed Kade with Storm, partially hidden amongst his shadows, leaning against the corner building.

A small tilt of my head toward the palace was all I gave him before heading in the direction of the palace grounds. Floating orbs of twinkling lights illuminated the path, guiding my way back home. Ruppert fell into place a few paces behind.

As we made it to the palace walls, I pivoted to Ruppert behind me. "Take the rest of the night off, Ruppert. It is the Festival of Blessings, and I am returning to my chambers for the evening."

His eyes narrowed, but before he could say anything, I

pointed behind him at a petite woman waiting by the gate. "Honestly. Go have fun. It's one night and it looks like someone is waiting for you."

He turned, and his breath caught for a moment, realizing who was waiting at the gate. I could sense the anguish radiating from his being, to go to the woman he so clearly adored or fulfill his duties as my personal guard. He held a finger up, signaling for a moment to her.

"I'll agree, only this once, if you allow me to escort you to the door and ensure you shut it behind you. The guards there should be sufficient enough after that."

I took him by surprise, touching his arm. "Lead on, Ruppert."

Sure enough, there were two guards posted outside of my door, and I offered them a nod. "Thank you for your watch," I said, quickly opening the doors to my suite. "Now, go, Ruppert," I said. "I'll see you in the morning." He bowed his head, and I quickly entered my room, not allowing him to second-guess his decision.

I closed the door, wondering if I'd second-guess my own decision to let Kade know of my location. After his comment about begging, it shouldn't have taken more than my nod to let him know I wanted him.

The festival would continue for hours, but I had no intention of being anywhere but the safety of my room as I replayed the night. I grasped the edges of my vanity and stared at myself in the mirror. The moonlight cascaded through the window, illuminating the rose-gold hues of my curled locks, which had fallen around my shoulders. Moments passed as I truly looked inside my very being, strength and determination filling my mind.

I unlatched my necklace, setting it on the vanity and moved to my bedroom. I would allow myself one night to let my heart win, for tomorrow, logic and reason would be my only option. For the good of the kingdom.

Leaning against the smooth wood of my bedroom doorframe, I paused, trying to calm my racing mind.

A cool wisp of a shadow circled my ankles as the balcony door swung open. I allowed myself one more moment before turning around to face the man who consumed my logical thoughts.

Gazing at me, with a dark and hopeful look in his eyes, was Kade.

CHAPTER 30

Using his shadows, Kade closed the balcony doors behind him, not breaking eye contact with me, as his presence filled the room.

His eyes followed me, like a predator tracking his prey, exuding an anticipation I knew matched my own.

"I was hoping you would come," I whispered.

He shook his head. "I'm not used to acting impulsively, but I had to see you. I took a chance that your nod was an invitation."

He strode toward me, and I clenched my eyes closed momentarily before looking back at him. "You confuse me and infuriate me. Yet you've cared for me in a way few have. You have forced yourself into my life. You say you are here for the crown, but could you also be here for more?"

A pregnant pause filled the air as tension expanded between us.

Kade closed the distance, placing one hand above my head and brushing a strand of hair behind my ear. "I'm not just here for the crown."

My breath quickened at the sight of storms of desire swirling in his eyes. "Kade," I whispered.

"I'm here for the queen. I came here for you."

He tilted my chin, staring at my lips, bringing his closer. His hot breath had me melting beneath him. "Please. Say yes."

I paused as his lips hovered above mine, waiting in anticipation. "I want to trust you."

One breath, then two.

"I don't know if I'd make a worthy King, Little Rebel, but I do know you were created to rule a kingdom. Fates, you could bring an army of Fae to their knees. Your role should never be to sit idly by anyone's side. Not even mine."

Oh, Fates. This. This was what I hoped for.

"Yes," I said, answering his earlier desire without any reservation.

The tension between us snapped. The unleashed aggression, and passion ignited into a flame. I wanted, no, *needed* it to consume me. My body finally crumbled beneath Kade's touch, giving into what it had been craving for weeks now. A warmth flooded me, so hot, I could barely contain myself as I pressed against Kade's muscular figure.

He grabbed my face with both hands as we furiously kissed, his body holding mine against the door. He had me pinned effortlessly as his tongue stroked mine, and with nowhere else for my hands to go, I placed them on his chest. How I longed to run my hands through his hair, if he would just move his damn body out of the way.

I could feel the length of him hardening against me as we unleashed ourselves upon each other.

Needier, my insides were molten now, while at the same time, feeling as though I would drown in the desire building and rising. I rubbed myself against him, desperate for friction, for him. I needed to move, and I needed him inside of me.

I nipped his bottom lip. He chuckled, and I finally gathered my strength and pushed him back a few steps, so I wasn't stuck against the door any longer.

One of his shadows curled against my back, stroking and pressing me toward him. I couldn't help but laugh. "Your shadows certainly are playful tonight."

"My shadows don't play, they destroy."

"I don't know about that." I snorted. "They make me feel safe." The word felt too powerful to be true, but I had no other way to describe it. More than once his shadows had protected me, caressed me, like they knew me inside and out and wanted me despite all I was, and all I lacked.

"It's like you're purposefully trying to tear down my ego, Little Rebel," he said. "Shadow magic is the most powerful and unique Fae magic, and it merely makes you feel *safe*. What am I going to do with you?"

I pushed away from him, running into my bedroom.

He caught me easily, turning my body and holding me up by my ass. My legs wrapped around his center. "The last time someone shoved me like that, they got a black eye," Kade murmured as he trailed kisses up my neck, stopping once he reached my ear. "But for you, the punishment shall be quite different." He backed us onto the edge of the bed before we fell upon it. My body on top of Kade's, hands on either side of his face now, my hair falling to create a cocoon around us.

"I am willing to accept whatever punishment you deem necessary," I proclaimed.

Kade moved my hair behind my ears. My heart beat harder and faster than it ever had before.

His throat bobbed. "How do you swear again? Tits and daggers?" He smiled. "You are stunning."

I laughed as I walked my hands back. "Get me out of this dress, now." I rose and turned for him to unlace the corset of my gown.

"Yes, Your Highness." Kade's fingers moved deftly as his lips and tongue brushed over my neck. He took a painstakingly slow time undressing me and I squirmed beneath him, pressing my legs together. "Patience," he whispered.

He let my dress fall. I turned my head, peering over my shoulder before spinning toward him.

He growled, pulling me in close again as he kissed me once more. I could not get enough of his touch. My skin burned everywhere his hands roamed.

I shrugged out of my lace garments as he paused, leaning back on my bed to stare at me. The way he watched me, with those hungry eyes, he made me feel beautiful. Desired.

He made me feel... *alive.*

I bit my bottom lip, stepping between his legs and reaching my hands under his tunic. My fingers caressed his hardened muscles, and Kade tilted his head back for a moment, groaning. "If your hands feel this good on my chest while I'm still dressed, I don't know what I'm going to do when you're writhing beneath me."

I shivered in anticipation, tugging off his tunic before reaching down to unbutton his trousers. His cock bulged underneath the pants, and I leaned my body forward, wanting all of it. All of him.

He lunged toward me, pulling his pants the rest of the way off before spinning us and adjusting me on the bed so I lay beneath him. His lips lingered on mine, claiming every inch of me until I writhed under his muscular form. Then, he held onto the back of my neck, trailing kisses along my jawline before working his way down.

I could feel his hardness on my legs and pressed wherever I could get into him.

"Kade, if you don't do something soon, I'm not the only one who's going to be punished." My breathy voice made me sound less serious than I intended.

"So impatient, Little Rebel." He licked at the side of my neck, drawing a moan from me. "The best part of pleasure is the anticipation. I'll have you begging before I'm done with you."

"I'll be begging someone else to handle—" I yelped as he reared back onto his knees and splayed my legs open to rest on either side of his hips. His hands ran up my body at the same time his shadows unfurled, inching their way up my legs. My words were lost to the haze of sensations.

Kade traced his hands around my breasts, watching them and his shadows, as his eyes darkened. "Fucking perfect."

He leaned forward, his lips moving torturously slow along my collarbone before lowering them and licking at my nipples, more gently than I expected. He took his time, methodically, as if he could be here forever.

"Kade," I whimpered, my hips moving with nothing resting between them to give me friction.

His smile against my skin sent me into a frenzy. He blew his hot breath over my left nipple. "These are absolutely flawless." He blew again, teasing, and ready to give me more. "They deserve hours of attention, and it still wouldn't be enough time to worship them like they deserve." He lowered his mouth and sucked, his right hand massaging my other breast. The opposing sensations sent a wave of mind-blowing desire traversing throughout my entire body.

My hands were possessed, running through his hair, wanting to touch any part of him I possibly could. His mouth alone worked me to a dangerous edge.

The heat building in my core seemed unfathomable. It felt unlike any other feeling I had ever experienced. No one had done this to me. It had never been like this. My center soaked wet with need, the anticipation of what was to come made me cry out before he even touched me where I craved him most. I felt a cool breeze around my entrance as he continued his trail of kisses down my body.

His shadows sensed my shiver and crept lower, gently

stroking along my stomach, then my thighs. His lips finally moved lower, tracing the same line as his shadows.

I arched my back. "Please, Kade. Please."

He stopped as he got to the top of my slick entrance. "I know. I know, Lana. Trust me."

He grabbed my ass to lift me closer to his mouth. That tongue so wicked in the trials, taunting and teasing me during battles, slid firmly, but slowly along my center and up to my clit.

I snapped. "Kade," I cried, gripping at his hair as he moaned into me.

"Fates above, you taste like sin." His voice was husky as he continued to lick and torture me in the most excruciatingly satisfying way. "For even the poorest of men, feast like the mightiest of kings when they devour the woman before them."

Another lick and I moaned louder. My hands firmly grasped the slight curl of his hair. More, I needed more.

He began a leisurely pace of stroking me with his tongue, taking his time to learn the dips and curves of my inner walls. Slowly, the heat built inside of me.

"Kade, oh, fates. Kade." I writhed beneath him, enveloped in pleasure as he claimed me like I was his.

He paused and ran a finger up my entrance, soaking it in my need before pressing it inside of me. Slowly he massaged the inside of me, adding another finger, while continuing his feast.

Moving faster, he lapped up my desire. The air swirled around us, playing with me as well. His shadows swept across my upper half, teasing at my chest, and caressing my skin everywhere. I lost track of everything, as the colliding sensation coiled up inside of me and rose to the surface.

This man, this arrogant, cunning, protective man undid me.

A crescendo of desire hit its peak, as I exploded around his fingers. I screamed his name, as waves of my orgasm were unrelenting. My body lightened. It was everything and yet not enough. My skin stretched, feeling the energy everywhere, glowing. Like I had damned well been reborn.

He kissed upward, crawling over me and I felt his smile on my skin. Everywhere his lips touched heated me further. I should be sated. It should be enough for at least one moment.

"I still, I'm——" *I'm what? Desperate?* Part of me wanted to be embarrassed at my utterly wanton needs, but the other part couldn't care less.

He lifted his head, running his thumb over my lower lip. He leaned forward, flicking his tongue inside my mouth. "See how divine you taste," he whispered against my mouth before kissing me.

I shuddered at the words only spoken to me in my fantasies. He lowered his body to mine as his hard length pressed against my stomach, making me want him even more.

I turned my head to meet his gaze, bringing my hands up on either side of his face.

There weren't words to explain the thunder ravaging through me. As I stared straight into the storms of his soul, I knew I wasn't alone in whatever this was between us. His grey eyes darkened.

Whatever darkness lay inside of him, I would bring the light.

This time when I kissed him, his cock sat at my entrance until I bit his bottom lip. As I did, I shifted, forcing him to take me. His moan filled the air as he thrust into me, pausing and shaking as he held back.

"I want everything," I said.

He chuckled. "Slower, Little Rebel. I don't want to hurt you."

I dug my nails into his back, trying to push him all the way inside of me. "I swear, Kade, if you don't——"

My words were cut off as he thrust the rest of the way inside of me and groaned.

So full. Fates, I didn't think it was possible to feel this full. He sheathed himself inside of me so perfectly I trembled around his cock and whimpered.

Our bodies moved as one as he thrust himself over and over again, relentless in his need for our joining.

"Come for me one more time, Princess," he said. His shadows slid perfectly between us, dancing over my clit as the rhythm brought me higher.

"So good. Kade, it's—ahh," I cried out, falling helplessly over the edge and into oblivion.

His shadows filled the room and practically sang in delight as the waves of contractions brought Kade to his own release. "Lana," he murmured as if he worshipped me, bringing his forehead to mine.

We lay there, forehead to forehead until our breathing slowed. He rolled off me, and I tensed, thinking he'd disappear now that he had his fill, my heart sinking.

He didn't leave, though, instead tugging my blanket out and sliding both of us underneath, dragging my body to his.

I rested my head upon his chest, my eyes heavy from being fully satiated.

More so, my soul sang. Filled with happiness I couldn't put into words.

I'd never been in love, even if I had begged nature for it. Although I didn't think this could possibly be love yet, especially not knowing enough about Kade Blackthorn, it was far more than anything I had felt before.

My soul didn't just feel happy.

It felt at home.

CHAPTER 31

"Go away," I mumbled into my pillow as a steady knocking at my chamber door became more insistent and demanding.

My body was loose, relaxed. I'd gone the entire night without a nightmare, wrapped in Kade's arms.

The knocking persisted. Instead of jumping from bed and discovering who disturbed our peace, Kade's arms tightened around me, pulling my back against his chest. He sighed, his breath tickling the nape of my neck.

It was tempting to be nervous, to pull away, to return to the logical side I promised I would after tasting Kade. But for once, I felt unfathomably content. Right now, I wanted to be closer to Kade, with nothing between us.

I, too, ignored whomever stood on the other side of the door and nuzzled into him, burying further into the heaven, which was waking up in this man's arms.

I was in so much trouble.

"Lana," Ian called out sternly. "I know you're in there."

My eyes shot open, and my body stiffened. Ian wouldn't give up. Others would have, but not him. He'd stop at nothing until I answered the door.

I threw my blanket back and frantically searched for my robe, strewn across the chaise by my vanity, throwing it on as I tripped over my chair.

"Stay here." I pointed at Kade as I tied the string of my robe closed.

He propped himself up on his elbow, staring at me, his hair splayed wildly from our activities the night before. But *tits and daggers*, he looked delicious.

What would it take to make him open up to me? To have him trust me implicitly. To make him mine because he wanted me. Craved me the way my body clearly craved him.

His lips raised slightly. "I don't take orders from anyone," He looked me up and down, "but I think I could get used to taking them from you."

"Flirt," I muttered, rolling my eyes and leaving my bedroom. I hurried to the larger chamber door, cracking it open before fluffing my hair out of the robe and taking a breath.

I yanked my chamber door open. "Sorry, I…" Pausing, my cheeks heated as I came face-to-face with Ian *and* Storm. "Overslept."

Ian pursed his lips as he tried desperately to hold back a smile. Storm had his arms crossed, eyeing me with the same playfulness he had last night at the festival.

"Can I help you?" I asked when they didn't say anything.

Storm cocked an eyebrow. "I think we both know the only reason I'm here."

"I don't know why you're here actually." I lifted my chin defiantly.

Ian snorted. "Even I'm not that dumb, Lan." He brushed past me, walking straight to my bedroom door, without taking his eyes off me once. He pushed it open, still staring at me. "Good morning, Kade."

Storm's laughter rippled through the air as I stammered and dropped my face into my hands.

"I will throw each and every one of you out." I shoved Storm and grabbed Ian's sleeve to drag them out. Kade moved to get out of bed, and I threw my hand out toward him. "Except you."

Storm howled louder with laughter.

Ian wasn't as entertained, but he wasn't angry, either. Although, he shook his head at me, clearing his throat. "I told Ruppert you wanted to speak with me this morning, so you're welcome. Can you imagine if it was him banging down your door instead of me?"

I crinkled my nose at the idea.

Kade shuffled in the bed into a sitting position as we all stood at the foot.

This was awkward.

"Whatever brought you here better be the most important things of your life," Kade grumbled to his friend.

"I do have news, I promise," Storm said, holding his hands up defensively.

We watched him expectantly as he leaned against the wall next to the door. "There's no way Edmund could have worked alone. Ian and I retraced the contenders' steps the entire morning. The razorven wasn't part of the obstacle course either, meaning we have to assume Edmund had a hand in that as well."

I frowned, trying to comprehend.

"He had help," I said.

Storm nodded along with Ian.

"From inside the palace?" I asked.

"It would have to be," Ian confirmed. "Because he was infected with the darkness, we're dealing with someone who knows enough about it to not only have somehow turned him, but who also knows the happenings inside these walls to have coordinated it."

"Fuck," Kade said, wrapping my sheet around his waist.

My mouth watered as he stood, taking in the way his

muscles shifted with each movement of his body. The blessings certainly had been bountiful at this year's Festival.

Heat pooled between my legs and the current I'd gotten so used to feeling from him swarmed over me, this time joined by desire.

Focus, Lana!

Shaking my head, I brought myself back to reality. "We need to tell the others. I want to make sure Kalliah knows to be vigilant." I wrung my hands together, this time looking at Ian. "I can't—I will not make it if I lose her like I lost Elisabeth, Ian. We need to figure out who our most trusted guards are and keep them close. To all of us."

I paced around my room as the others stood there staring at me. A thought stopped me in my tracks. Pivoting slowly, my heart hammered harder in my chest. I faced all three men, fear threatening to turn my stomach at what the answer to my next question might be.

"Does my father know?"

The three of them shared a glance, Ian stepping forward. "No, he doesn't. He's been with your mother and Maria, the new head healer, since the festival last night." Ian scrubbed a hand over his face. "He's getting worse, Lan."

The pit in my stomach churned. Elisabeth had been the most gifted healer in Ellevail, and I'd bet my life the entirety of Brookmere as well. If she hadn't been able to heal him, what hope would Maria have? I couldn't dwell on such thoughts right now, though. The next trial was coming up in a few days. If a traitor hid amongst us in the palace, we needed to do something.

"Do you think he will postpone the next trial?" I asked, knowing what the answer would be, especially with my father getting worse.

"No," they all said in unison.

Storm stepped forward and stood next to Ian. "There's three days until the final event. I'll take to the city streets and see what I can find. Someone may slip with the right encouragement and reveal some sort of information."

"Kade and I can work on ensuring the palace is as secure as possible. We'll keep an eye on Casimir, Ryland, and Hale. I'll also have Corbin and Leif see what they can find out, too. The staff might have noticed something in the contenders' suites."

I rubbed my forehead as my frustration grew. I'd been given nothing to do, a fact I knew Ian had done on purpose, by the way he avoided my gaze. "And what am I supposed to do? Sit around and twiddle my thumbs? Braid my hair and play with my pretty dresses?"

Kade snorted. "Careful, Little Rebel, you make it sound like you didn't have enough excitement last night."

Storm sighed while Ian slugged Kade in the arm. "Come on, not in front of us. She's the damned princess."

Kade didn't back down or pay either of the men any attention. His hungry stare focused on me, daring me to argue.

"You wouldn't be able to handle the amount of excitement I can take," I huffed.

"Fates, Lan. You two are unbelievable," Ian mumbled.

I opened my mouth to say more but Ian groaned. "Enough. Your parents are expecting you for breakfast, so any 'excitement' is going to have to wait."

I rolled my eyes. "Oh, please, we're tame compared to *your* stories, Ian Stronholm. Now out, all of you! I have to get ready."

Storm immediately headed for the door, while Kade leaned against my bedpost. "I'll just collect my things."

Ian grumbled, muttering under his breath. "I will be waiting outside to walk you to breakfast. Ruppert is attending a meeting at my request. Be quick." He closed my door a little harder than necessary, and I could hear him pacing outside, waiting for me.

Kade, somehow, was already halfway dressed by the time I turned around. After the evening that transpired between us, I didn't quite know what to say. Fortunately, his shadows had been pooling around my back and were already pulling me close, tilting my chin toward his. "Goodbye for now, Little Rebel." He leaned down, this time kissing me softly. "I'll see you soon." I shivered against his mouth, his lips claiming mine like some sort of promise.

But I knew that wasn't what this was.

I had only given into my desires to get Kade Blackthorn out of my system. The newly reformed Illiana would stand tall. That had been the point of last night. I had gotten what I wanted, what I needed from him, and now I could move on. I could make a safer choice for King. One without secrets.

Except, having Kade did only one thing—leave me craving more.

Craving. Wanting. There wasn't a strong enough word. My body hummed with energy, demanding it.

Kade peered over his shoulder once before he and his shadows disappeared off the balcony and into the gardens below.

I wrapped my arms around myself, my skin noticeably cooler now from the lack of shadowy touches caressing me.

My goodbye had to mean more. A true goodbye, not one laced with a promise of more when it couldn't be.

"Goodbye, Kade," I whispered.

Despite the coughing, and the hunched presence of my father, he still smiled at me as I entered the private dining room for breakfast.

My mother clung to his arm. Despite their arranged marriage, their love was agonizingly written into everything they did. I never understood how they weren't fated mates. I used to dream that even though mates only existed long ago, that they somehow broke a spell, and their love would allow for my mate to find me as well. Even if it was only a childish notion, if I couldn't have a mate, I'd want a love like theirs.

I smiled, remembering how often my father spoke of knowing my mother was his true love long before she did. They joked about how stubborn she had been, and how terrified she was to admit she loved the king.

I'd grown up envious of their connection. Their love so unyielding it could inspire poetry, songs, and more, and yet now she watched her husband, the man she loved, dying before her eyes. Even knowing her time with him was limited, she still smiled, staring at him as if she couldn't take her eyes off of him.

"Good morning, Mother." I kissed her head, rounding the table to my father. I enveloped him with my hug a little harder, a little longer than I normally would have.

"Come, my heart," my father said, gesturing to the chair beside him. When I sat, he took my hand in his. "Are you all right? I was deterred from being with you after Elisabeth's death."

His eyes held unshed tears, my mother not strong enough to hide her own.

"I don't know if it'll ever be all right," I whispered.

"So many times we speak of dying for those we love. We rarely acknowledge you can live for those you love as well," he said, gripping my hand tightly. "The greatest gift we could give her is to live."

I hung my head, staring at my lap as his words fell over me. Living for her. Living for her would mean grabbing life and running with it. Not being afraid.

But there was so much to be afraid of right now.

I had more responsibilities, more worries, and more to figure out about our lands and our kingdom, than just simply living a life I might love.

"We've dedicated a spot in the garden for her," my mother said. "The main one. There's a bench she loved, and we spent many hours sitting there talking throughout the years. We are having the plaque made now."

I nodded. "I'm sure she'd love that and fuss about it being too much."

We all laughed, remaining in silence once it died down.

My father coughed again, pulling his hand from mine and grabbing a napkin to bring to his mouth until the fit ended.

"Now," he said, "we live. Tell us who you may favor coming out of these trials?"

I popped some of the sweet fruit into my mouth. "You, as the king, have better insight than I do, Father. Has anyone stood out to you?"

"Nonsense. I mean the favor of your heart."

I didn't correct him. If the trials had been about my heart, we wouldn't have had them at all, but I didn't want to argue. Seeing how weak and fragile he appeared, now was not the time nor the place.

"Ian will always have my love," I said, smiling at him and my mother as they both nodded, as if it wasn't news. Well, it *wasn't* news.

I hesitated, debating if he asked because he wanted to check on my well-being, or if he was truly curious. What I'd said though rang true, both of my parents had sharp instincts and may help me.

"Casimir is vile," I said. "He looks down upon lesser Fae, and although I know he's always been a Lord and it's how things are, I don't think it would do anything good for our kingdom having him as King."

"I agree," my mother said sternly. "The way he stole Ian's powers in the obstacles and left everyone to fend for themselves when the razorven appeared. Well, it showed his true character."

My father shrugged. "That is how the trials go, my dears.

We cannot fault any of them for using the powers they were gifted from nature and the Fates themselves," he said, pausing to take a breath, "but, hearing him speak a few times, has me concerned. His character itself is indeed flawed."

"Hale isn't a bad choice," I said. "I think he'd be loyal and wouldn't be one to take the crown and rule without me. We have known each other for so long, so it would not be starting from scratch. I think he'd remain loyal, even once he learns I don't have magic."

They nodded.

I managed to take a drink of the sweet juice at my place before I continued. "Ryland is fine, but nothing more. I don't see him as a real contender. I do think he would make a great guard, though. I plan to talk to Ian about it once all of this is over."

"What about Kade?" my father asked.

I blinked a few times, staring blankly at him. "What about him?"

My mother wasn't subtle about the grin she poorly hid behind her teacup. I frowned. "Nothing in particular, dear."

"We don't know enough about him," I said, taking another bite of the fruit in front of me.

"Never trust something is as it appears at first glance." He smiled while he took a bite of his eggs. "Did you think our lessons were only for the creatures of Brookmere?"

I frowned but didn't respond. Choosing Kade held too many uncertainties. "I'll keep your wise counsel in mind. Now, enough of the trials. How are you feeling?" I asked to change the subject.

The king leaned back, eyeing me and then waved a hand in front of his face. "We don't need to discuss me." His eyes drooped, exhausted from something as simple as sitting and eating a meal.

He wouldn't last long if this was what he'd become.

"We should give your father a rest," my mother said.

"We need to focus on the mission for the future." He lifted his hand, head lolling to the side. "She has to be strong. To strive for truth and keep the history we've—"

My mother went to his side, kneeling next to him. "Rest now, my love. Rest." Patting his hand, she brushed a few strands of his hair from beneath his crown before rising and facing me.

She tilted her head to the side, wordlessly telling me to follow her out the door. "Tell me, sweetheart," she said as soon as the door closed behind her, "are you ready to make this decision?"

I shook my head no. "I will be, but right now, it's terrifying."

My mother brushed her thumb over my cheek. "Love always is."

"This isn't about love, that's the problem," I said quietly.

She sighed. "As the queen, a queen who preferred observing as your father took the spotlight, I've learned to read people. To notice things others think they are hiding. I believe you do know who you want to choose, but you're scared of who you are. Scared to find out how he might feel, or you're scared your feelings won't be returned. Whatever it is, darling, you can't be honest with anyone until you're honest with yourself."

"And what if in the end I've chosen wrong?"

She smiled her beautiful smile. One which had the entire Court loving her, even without knowing much about their Queen. She was radiant. The light of Brookmere, as my father called her in public. "Do you think Ian will let anything happen to you? Kalliah? There are staff I've seen come to your side, Corbin Jansen and Leif Ivans for two. Not to mention our dear Perdot, who would hold on hundreds of more years, only to continue to be by your side in the palace."

I shook my head, embarrassed by her assumptions that these people respected me beyond their duty.

"You've built your own Court around you, and you don't even know it, do you?" She studied me, her curious gaze searching over me. "They may not hold the formal title of a royal court, but they are yours, my love. Trust yourself to continue to surround yourself with people who are not only loyal, but who are friends. They wouldn't let you be steered wrong." She cupped my cheek. "Now go. I need to tend to your father."

"He's worse," I said. A statement. Not a question, even though I wanted her to refute it. I wanted her to say it was a bad day, or he showed more hope than what I'd seen.

Her face fell, and for the first time ever, my mother's shoulders crumpled. "He doesn't have long if I had to guess. A few weeks?"

"But Maria is trying, right? Trying to do something?" I shook out my hands and shifted my weight. "We can do something to give him more time, right?"

My mother shook her head. "He's in pain. He's holding on as long as he can, though. Trust in that. After the trials, we'll ensure we can all be together more."

She didn't say the words "until the end," but I felt them hanging in the air between us. Hanging like an axe.

She left, going back inside the doors and I didn't care who saw, I slumped to my knees. Tears poured down my face. How had so much changed so fast?

This was why he pushed the trials so hard. Because he may not be around and needed to know I'd secured the crown once he died.

Which meant whomever I chose would be King sooner than they likely suspected.

Elisabeth dying had broken me, but losing my father? Watching the strongest Fae in our lands, the strongest Fae I knew succumb to an unknown sickness? It would destroy me. I didn't know how much more of my heart remained to make it through his death.

But my mother spoke with certainty, even though it pained her. My father was dying. And he'd let go as soon as I married and had a King to rule beside me.

I had to choose the right man.

My brain told me Ian. I knew he'd be amongst the top finishers and would be an option.

But my heart? My heart didn't want to trap him and lead us both to lives of loneliness. My heart sang for Kade, even though it didn't make sense to me. Perhaps, this newfound Illiana needed to reconsider her logical position.

The last thing I wanted to do was choose him and start a lifetime together with a lie. If he were to win, he'd learn I had no magic, and whatever life he envisioned would be far different than I was certain he expected. Yes, he'd get the crown he wanted. But even strong and powerful in his own right, he wouldn't be getting a powerful queen. That truth would be enough to change anyone's mind.

Although I didn't believe Kade loved me, even if he merely wanted the title of King, telling him the truth was something I knew I had to do.

There were a lot of things I could live with if necessary.

Trapping Kade Blackthorn in a marriage wasn't one of them.

CHAPTER 32

Nature seemed to be extremely blessed from the festival since it rained for two days straight.

Not a light summer drizzle, but the kind of relentless rain, which made it impossible to do anything. The kind of rain, which was wonderful for the first day, to curl up and read, but by the second day, drained the happiness from you.

It didn't rain like this often in Ellevail, but when it did, all one could do was wait out the storm. The growing season had officially begun.

With all of the unknowns about who to trust in the palace, Ian had sequestered me to my room until the final trial began to keep me safe. The order drove us absolutely mad, and Kalliah and I were more than a little stir crazy.

Two days wasn't much in the long run, but it seemed like an eternity. Especially when the people you cared for were busy hunting down the evil infecting our land, while you were forced to sit idly by and do nothing.

One positive thing did come from being sequestered from everyone, and everything. It had given me some time away to work through the emotions overwhelming my mind. Soon I would have to make a decision, which would change the course of my life and all of Brookmere. Even being away from Ian had helped put things into perspective. While I missed him, after seeing him almost every day for years, I craved Kade more.

It didn't make sense, but I missed him, and his damned shadows.

However, there was still something I just quite didn't trust about him. There were so many unknowns about him, and I had a hard time reconciling how then my heart could be so attached.

Yet, my body longed for him in a way I couldn't understand. It felt almost torturous to be apart from him, anxious energy shifting inside of me in a way I couldn't comprehend.

But should I take such an enormous chance on a strange emotion? What would he say if he knew I didn't have magic? He came here for a crown. I believed that, and if I believed what he said the night of the festival, he came for a queen as well. But what would he think of a queen who couldn't be his equal, especially in power and magic? He may believe I was born to rule, but how would I keep this ruse up once I ascended the throne. It was all too much to think about.

These were the marriage trials. My choice had to be the best one for my people, since it was, well, forever. There would be no second chances.

Kalliah sighed loudly from the chaise in front of the window, reminding me of her presence. Flopping her arm from her chest to hang off the side, she groaned loudly. The rain had stopped, and a sliver of moonlight peaked through the clouds, illuminating her face as she sat up.

"All right. I'm going to call it for the night. I fear if I stare at the Forgotten Kingdom for one more moment, I am going to become forgotten myself. We have a big day tomorrow."

I swallowed. A big day was putting it mildly.

"I'll be by in the morning with breakfast. Hopefully tomorrow the sun will be shining, and we can at least go outside. Otherwise, I'm not sure where they'll hold the trial."

I quickly jumped up from my chair and gave her a long hug before she left. "Thank you for keeping me company these last few days. Fates know I would be lost without you."

Pulling away, she smiled at me. "And I would be lost without you, too, my friend. I'll see you in the morning."

"Good night, Kalliah."

She picked up our dirty dishes from dinner as she exited, securing my chamber door behind her.

I settled onto the chaise Kalliah had left and stared out of the window for a few moments more, knowing I needed to get ready for bed soon, too. These next few days were going to be long, and I needed to get some rest while I still could.

Rest seemed impossible, though, since my mind wouldn't cooperate and settle. Perhaps a bath would relax me before trying to sleep. I still had some of the calming salts Kalliah had gifted me on my last birthday. They always seemed to help.

I changed out of my clothes, pulling on my heavenly, silk-lined robe, not bothering to tie the sides as I moved toward my bathing chamber. A quick knock rattled my chamber doors, and I folded the sides of the robe to cover myself. Kalliah must have forgotten something. I sauntered over to the door to open it for her.

But it wasn't Kalliah waiting there.

It was Kade.

"May I come in?" he asked.

I blinked twice, shocked to find him at my chamber door instead of the balcony.

He glanced sideways at the empty post Ruppert should have been occupying and shifted on his feet. Was he nervous?

Nodding, I shooed him into the room and peeked down the hall. Ruppert appeared, and I jerked my head back. He must have been returning from his hourly rounds. I quickly shut the door behind Kade.

"What's wrong? Is everything okay?" I made sure my robe was tightly secured around me if we got interrupted. "Do you have news about the darkness?" I whispered, not wanting to be too loud.

Kade stared at me, his brow furrowed.

"Are you worried Ruppert will hear?" I asked. When he didn't answer, I grabbed his hand and led him to my bedroom, shutting the door to get more distance between us and the hallway.

He finally snapped out of his trance and grabbed my hand to pull me to the edge of my bed, while he sat, keeping me standing before him. We were fairly far away from the door, not as if it would have any effect on the Fae hearing Ruppert possessed. Perhaps Kade's shadows could cloak our voices as well as our bodies.

"I think I'm losing my mind," he whispered, pulling me close to his chest.

My body unconsciously relaxed, molding to his as best I could, even if my mind still panicked.

"I can't stop thinking about you. It's as if my shadows need you just as much as I—" He cleared his throat and then sighed, running a hand over the back of his neck. "As much as I need you."

He wrapped his hands around my waist, and I leaned back to stare into his grey eyes.

Kade needed me? Perhaps he did have stronger feelings for me than I thought. Maybe he initially came here for the crown, but perhaps he could be here for *me*, too. I didn't say anything, but I couldn't look away.

"With the final trial being tomorrow, I had to see you and know what you were thinking. I had to know if you felt what I do. These trials have been more deadly than I anticipated, and if something were to happen." He paused, his throat

350

bobbing as he collected his thoughts. "I-I wanted to spend one last night with you if this is all the time the Fates will allow."

He tucked a strand of hair behind my ear. "If I'm not what you want, right now, or tomorrow, then I accept that as well. I just needed to see you to know."

While I wasn't certain if I was ready to make a decision about my future, I was more than ready to have my fill of Kade Blackthorn again.

Fates knew I'd been consumed with thinking about him, too.

I smiled as I leaned in closer to whisper in his ear, "Take off your clothes."

His expression shifted into a sultry smile immediately upon hearing my words. "So bossy."

He slowly removed his black tunic, the muscles of his arms bulged as he threw it to the floor. I'd lick all over his beautiful tattoo tonight if I had my way.

Painstakingly slow, he began to remove his pants. I bit my lip, watching him watching me, his eyes darkening slightly. It was impossible to miss how hard his cock was as it sprung free.

Not wanting to wait a moment more, I relieved myself of my own clothes, throwing them haphazardly on the floor.

"On your back," I ordered.

Kade smirked. "As Your Highness commands it." He moved across my bed, obeying, and lying on his back.

His shadows seeped from his body, surrounding the bed. "We don't need ole stick in the pants out there knowing about your, how shall we say this? Nightly activities."

So, his shadows could block out sounds... interesting.

I couldn't take my eyes off of him, this man who had captured my attention from the first time I laid eyes on him. To appreciate how breathtaking he looked, waiting for me. Wanting me.

No fear. I'd have no fear. Not tonight.

He sucked in a sharp breath when I finally made my

move, crawling up the bed toward him. I reached out, running my palm over his rigid and incredible cock before I lowered my mouth onto him. Fates, he was so hard and wanting.

I allowed myself a few moments to pump him inside of my mouth, my hands cupping his balls gently, massaging. He moaned already, even though we'd only just gotten started.

For the first time in my life, I felt like an equal. It didn't matter if I had magic or not.

"Fates, your mouth is everything, Little Rebel." His groan, this time more drawn out, his hips moving as I worked him in and out of my mouth. He gripped my hair. "I will not last much longer if you keep this up, and my plans for you involved more than spilling down your throat during the first minute of our time together."

It was all he needed to say before I made my next move. I wanted to be bold, to try everything I'd always wanted and hadn't been able. I sat backward on his chest, peering over my shoulder once before I lowered myself on his length. I wanted to ride him, to take all of him, but he was so big. I slid down slowly. Painfully slow. Allowing myself to adjust to him as he slid inside of me.

His hands roamed over me and down to my ass, grabbing it as much as he could. "You are a perfect, stunning creation."

He finally slid all the way in, and I paused, feeling how full and perfect we fit together. Then, I rode him. I moved on top of him, hard, bringing my hands up to massage my breasts. I lost grip of reality, simply existing in a place of needing and wanting more. More of him. More of this. Harder and harder.

Kade shifted, propping himself up on a forearm, not letting me move all the way off of him as he pulled my hips down, my back toward his chest. I hadn't experienced this angle before. Tits and daggers, it was so damned good.

I'd rarely been vocal before, but with Kade, I couldn't stop the sounds spilling from my mouth.

He brought my hand to my core.

"Show me how you like it," he said into my ear. "I want to see you make yourself come with me inside you."

Oh, fates. If it wasn't the hottest thing anyone had ever said to me.

I obeyed him gladly, rubbing myself in time with his thrusts. Small, slow circles around my clit, as he continued to grind his cock inside of me. He grabbed my breasts and played with my nipples. Shadows swirled around us, gliding over me more urgently.

I moved faster. Faster. Kade met my every pace. My legs shook, trembling along with my body, aching for release.

Kade gave my ear a playful nip. "That's it, Lana. More."

I continued, moaning as the pressure built to a high I thought would destroy me.

"Harder," I commanded, unable to catch my breath.

"Let go for me. Show me you're mine and let go." Kade's words triggered my release. I exploded around him.

"Fates, yes," he moaned, holding me tightly while he let me ride out my pleasure. His cock pulsated inside of me as my own throbbing began to ease. He didn't chase his own release, though, not yet.

He pushed my body up once I caught my breath, leaning forward, and I gripped his thighs.

"Kade," I hissed as he ran a strong hand down my spine. I would finish what I started now and bring him his own explosion of pleasure. I needed it as much as I'd needed my own.

I rode this beautiful man for a few minutes more. My head tipped back in pleasure as the fullness inside overwhelmed me.

As Kade found his release, his hands tightened on my ass. "Lana," he cried my name like a prayer.

There would be a bruise. A bruise, for once, I would want to remember. A bruise I wouldn't want someone to heal.

As our breaths evened out, I slowly eased myself off of him, turning so I could see his face once more.

We laid together in silence for a long time, just basking in the sense of calm surrounding us. Some of his shadows rested on my body, while others whipped around us, cascading through the air.

He nuzzled his head into the crook of my neck, pulling me closer to him. He began pressing sweet kisses along my bare skin and gently caressing my ribs. He didn't stop when he reached my scar, instead, running his fingers along the raised flesh as if he could heal it somehow.

That damned scar left from Andras.

Suddenly, I knew it was now or never. I had to tell Kade everything. I needed to. Regardless of how much I didn't want to lose this moment.

"Kade," I whispered, steeling my nerves. "I have to tell you something." My heartbeat quickened and threatened to catapult from my chest. I was about to reveal more of myself than even my father knew. The only person who really knew everything was Ian. This man would hold the broken pieces of my life, and I hoped he didn't break them even more.

I sat up and took his hands, biting my lip, so nervous to say these next few words. I hadn't ever told another soul my secret. Ian had been there. It was how he knew. But to speak of what happened, it would take everything.

"Before tomorrow's trial, I need you to know something." I paused as he nodded for me to continue. With a deep breath, I let go, "I have no magic."

Kade's brow furrowed. When I didn't continue right away, his eyes widened, and he opened his mouth to speak. I held up my hand to stop him. If I didn't keep going, I might not be able to get through this conversation. I bit my lower lip, steeling my nerves to continue.

"And this scar?" I ran my fingers over my side. "It's from

Andras." My voice quivered, but I shook my head, squeezing my eyes shut. I refused to give him this power anymore. I wanted to let it go. "I was tortured for years by Andras under the guise of him trying to coax my magic out of me."

Kade's jaw clenched, his shadows rushing out of him and darkening the room. His eyes shifted from the alluring grey, to black, as I'd witnessed a handful of times before.

"He'd take me to the dungeons, this horrible corner dripping with water, as though no one cared that this part of our castle decayed beneath us. Sometimes he'd hit me. Leave me hungry for days. Sometimes…" I swallowed the lump in my throat. My eyes grew misty, but even if I spilled tears, I'd continue on. "Ian told his father, but before he could do anything, his father died suddenly. We both think it was Andras.

"Once his father passed, he'd bring Ian down and hurt him in front of me. Other times, he made me believe Ian was dead because of me. He sent me visions and made me believe what I was seeing was real when it wasn't. I lost myself so many times."

Kade reached for me, but I pulled away. His touch would stop me from talking. I needed to finish.

I'd never bared my soul like this. To tell of the torture Andras had inflicted upon me, and Ian. The years of pain and anguish we were forced to endure. I could feel the anger radiating from Kade's body as his shadows collided and smashed into each other around us. Tears began to drip down my face.

"One night, he made me believe Ian was burning alive. I could hear Ian shouting, trying to reach me to tell me it wasn't real, but I couldn't hold onto it. When I fought back, Andras took this dagger, which had something around it and stabbed into my side. He lost control of himself, and when he came to, he left us there, free to go. Ian carried me to Elisabeth, and she helped us. He never took me again. He's made my life a living hell but has not physically tortured me since that night."

My lip quivered but I finally let out a long breath. Kade held my gaze, blackness in his eyes and all. He shifted, moving slowly, stretching out his hand. This time, I let him touch me, and as soon as I didn't fight it, he grabbed me, pulling me toward him into a hug.

A long hug. I sobbed against his chest as he stroked my hair, not rushing me or asking anything while I mourned what happened all over again. His heartbeat steadied, and eventually, its rhythm allowed me to breathe again. It allowed me to compose myself once more, sitting up slightly and wiping away the last of my tears.

Kade's eyes had faded back to their beautiful grey as he stroked my cheek with the back of his knuckles. "How was he allowed to be near you?" he asked, now I had gathered my strength again. "How is he allowed to be a Royal Adviser?"

"Andras has some sort of influence over my parents that I don't understand," I answered, rubbing at the lessening ache in my chest, finally relieved of the pressure of carrying such secrets for so long.

"I swear, the next time I see him, he's dead."

I shook my head. "Kade, no. He can't know you know."

He frowned and stared at me, trying to make peace with the fact he couldn't just murder the Royal Adviser of Brookmere. "He needs to be punished, Little Rebel. Besides it being treason, he hurt you. He's tried to manipulate you, even though he's clearly failed, seeing the woman you've become."

"I worry about him doing something to Ian," I said. "I can't worry for you, too."

"As I promised you in the bath," He leaned forward and pressed a kiss to my forehead, "when you're ready, revenge will be yours."

He took my hands, and the weight of everything lessened.

He hadn't run out on me, and still sat here talking it over with me. Perhaps this would be okay.

"As for no magic? I've seen you—" He paused, realizing he had never seen me do anything. He shifted but didn't let go of me. "That's why you couldn't heal yourself when you got stabbed." He frowned, likely going through memories of our time together as if I may not be telling the truth.

Finally, he shook his head. "I've never heard of any Fae being born without some kind of magic, let alone the heir to the royal throne."

Tears pooled in my eyes. This time from fear. I didn't want to be wrong about trusting him. "You have to promise you will not tell anyone. No one can know. We have worked so hard and so long to keep this secret, and I can't have anyone finding out now. Not when my father is so sick. I know this might make you feel differently about me and what you thought you were getting yourself into. These marriage trials are for just that—marriage. Not a date or two with a princess. This is forever. These trials are for the crown, to be King of Brookmere. I didn't want to lie to you, in case you decided a magicless queen isn't what you were looking for."

My head hung low as I tried to control my breathing, growing more rapid by the moment. Panic at what he might say, what he might do, overtook my body.

Kade took my chin in his hand, tilting it up to face him. He leaned in and kissed me. Softly at first, but it grew into a fiery, breathy mess of want and need. Our tongues crashed together as my hands gripped the back of his hair.

Kade drew away and pressed his forehead against mine, pulling me onto his lap, as I wrapped my legs around him. Thankfully, we still had a sheet between us, or with one small motion, he would have been inside of me once more, and we wouldn't ever finish this conversation.

"So, all this time, all of those fights and battles, you do all of that without magic?"

"I'm not weak," I said sternly.

Kade chuckled at the audacity of my words. "Weak? Lana, you are a force. You are a damned brilliant fighter, a rebel with a heart of gold, who puts her kingdom before herself. You are filled with vengeance for those who have been wronged and are sexy as hell while doing it. Fates, Illiana." Pushing a fallen strand of hair behind my ear, he seemed like he wanted to say more, but stopped himself.

His gaze moved to my lips. "Whatever comes, you are the most unexpected and beautiful thing that has ever happened to me. I crave you constantly. I need you constantly. I want to be selfish with your time. I don't want you anywhere near the other contenders. Yes, it includes Ian, even if I know you are only friends."

He kissed my forehead and held me close. "I've never been selfish with anything in my life, and I find myself wanting to be with you."

It wasn't a promise of love, or devotion, or even an indication of what he would do tomorrow. If he'd fight to win. My heart tightened in anticipation.

What did that mean?

I crawled out of his lap and reached for my nightgown, which had been hidden under a pillow, pulling it over my head. We lay on my bed, and he rubbed my back, soothing the anxiety riddling my body, his shadows still swirling around us.

Those shadows and the warmth of his body provided the safety I had been wanting for so long. The safety I craved. The safety I had lost when Elisabeth was murdered. The safety that not even Ian could provide, even after all of our years of friendship.

A feeling given to me by someone who I barely knew. One I had known for mere weeks.

A stranger who now held my darkest secret and could destroy my life in a moment.

As he rubbed my back, pulling me into his body, I had the thought perhaps he wasn't such a stranger at all anymore.

Perhaps, he was the kind of man I could trust with my heart, and my kingdom.

CHAPTER 33

My nerves were shot.

I hadn't slept at all, even with Kade beside me. When he finally snuck out of my garden early this morning, I lay in bed, staring at the ceiling.

I'd been too scared to ask him if he wanted to win the trials. If he wanted to be chosen.

Part of me feared the answer would be no, which only made it worse.

At the same time, he hadn't run. He'd comforted me and stayed, even after finding out I lacked any sort of magic. It had to count for something.

Now, here I was, marching up the stairs toward the pavilion, where I'd watch the final trials and determine from the winners who would become Brookmere's King.

Kalliah walked beside me, step by step, giving me space while providing her unyielding, silent support.

I had barely touched my breakfast while Kalliah prepared me for today. Today, I wore structured armor. One which made me appear fierce, my hair braided tight into a coronet upon my head. While I knew wearing fitted dark pants and my finest purple and gold tunic would be frowned upon by my parents and Andras, too much had occurred, and I needed to be prepared if something happened again.

It wasn't only that, though. Whomever I chose today to be the future King of Brookmere needed to know they were going to be marrying a warrior. One who wouldn't be told to sit on the sidelines. Magic or not.

My appearance radiated strength, and I'd pull from it to force myself to feel it, too.

I couldn't be certain my father had the kingdom under control after the attack during the previous trials, but at least I could hide a dagger or two upon my person much easier this way if anything went wrong.

Kalliah, who was unreservedly disgusted by my choice of clothing before I explained my reasoning, had still opted to wear a fitted corseted dress, flowing with layers of blue tulle. She would have made a great princess.

I didn't let go of her hand as we reached the steps before the pavilion overlooking the arena. My breath faltered as I attempted to place my foot on the first step. Unable to move, my body froze in fear. The trials cost me Elisabeth.

I clutched my stomach as it churned, and my chest tightened. Losing her was too much. I couldn't make it up the stairs and face another trial. Not without her. What else would be taken? My heartbeat pounded in my ears, drowning out the world around me.

Kalliah shuffled around before reaching toward me, quickly adjusting my belts and buckles to provide me a moment to regain my composure. Despite some of her brashness, it was her empathy and kindness that allowed us to have such a close friendship. She made my hesitation seem to those passing as though she was adjusting my outfit, giving me the space to breathe when I needed it most.

"You are Illiana Dresden. You are strong. You are worthy. You are a damn princess, born to rule this land," she whispered while the guards looked on from the left suspiciously.

"I miss her." I shut my eyes, letting my grief roll over my shoulders and down my back.

Kalliah knelt, pretending to adjust my shoe. "Elisabeth may have been taken from this world, but she can never be taken from your heart. She will *always* be with you. With all of us who choose to remember."

Taking several deep breaths, I grounded myself, sinking my short heels deeper into the dirt below me. I let myself feel the soft ground, the floral scent sprinkled in the warm wind.

What do you see? Elisabeth's voice rang in my ears.

Kalliah's determination shone on her face, portraying how much she believed we'd be okay. My people's cheers in the arena may have been from excitement at the entertainment of today, but I knew they were worthy and honored the throne.

What do you feel?

Scared. Nervous.

But not alone. Kalliah was right. I was the damn crowned princess, and I would not falter now. I looked down at her as she worked the laces of my shoes. Exhaling slowly, she looked up, straight into my eyes.

"You are Princess Illiana Dresden, and you are stronger than the darkness within you."

I am Princess Illiana Dresden, and I am stronger than the darkness within me.

Steeling my nerves, I grasped Kalliah's hand, pulling her to stand beside me. Together, we made our way up the marble staircase to the pavilion of advisers waiting for us.

Waiting for me.

I refused to let go of Kalliah's hand in case Andras forced her to leave and sit in the stands or stay in the palace to prepare for tonight's celebration. Lucinda almost always managed to steal Kalliah away to assist with the laundry, or some other menial tasks. She hated someone who should be a mere servant, being seen as so much more. Kalliah had earned her place at my side, and I would be damned if I didn't prove to my kingdom her importance today. Things would change in Brookmere. They would change with me.

My parents were already seated in their respective places, and the curtain of roses hanging around the pavilion rustled in the wind. Andras whispered something into my father's ear as he frowned.

My throat tightened the second I rounded the thrones to face the king and queen. I froze. The dark circles beneath my parents' eyes were threatening to take over their entire faces. The pure exhaustion Fae so rarely displayed was more evident than ever. My father's shoulders were hunched, and the glow and joy once exuding from their souls seemed matte and tame. My mother's body now matched my father's, even though I knew she wasn't ill.

The worry consuming me earlier was nothing compared to the absolute terror I felt looking at the two of them. How could we be worried about a foolish marriage trial when the king looked like this? We needed to be scouring the kingdom far and wide to find a healer who could replace Elisabeth. Not that Maria wasn't great, she did her best. There just had to be someone else out there who could assist with my father's healing. He was the king!

I couldn't lose him, too, not so soon. Not ever if I had my way.

Kalliah squeezed my hand firmly as she brought me back to the present moment. She gave me a stern glare, seeming to say, "Get through today first."

Right. She was right.

Pushing my worry down to the darkest parts of my being, I rolled my shoulders and strode forward to the front of the dais to join my parents.

I am Illiana Dresden, and I am stronger than the darkness within me.

A podium had been placed at the front of the dais, for my father to stand behind. A subtle tool for him to be able to support himself without appearing weak in front of the kingdom and amplify his voice with help from magic already imbued into the stand. The small, glowing orb of power hidden from everyone in the crowd would give the illusion of the same amplification of his voice they were accustomed to. In reality, the assistance he required served as a stark reminder of his lessening powers. He managed a flick of his wrist to open the flower veil before him. A roar from the audience heralded our appearance.

"Welcome one and all to the final marriage trial! After today's trial, we will have the final three contenders from which Princess Illiana will select, not only as her husband, but as the future King of Brookmere!"

A roar from the crowd drowned out even the amplified nature of my father's words, their excitement building.

"Today, you will witness one of these contenders alongside your Princess and know who has been selected as worthy to become Brookmere's future successor." He raised his hands as the crowd somehow cried out even louder.

The five remaining contenders entered the arena in a single-file line from the holding area. Casimir and Ryland waved to the crowd in delight, Ryland with more of a smile than Casimir. Hale blushed with embarrassment, but tried to remain calm, waving here and there. Ian and Kade remained stoic, gazes trained forward, determined, even if the crowd chanted loudest for them. I swear I could hear both of their names rising from the spectators.

As the five men paused to stand in front of the king, he announced each of them to the crowd. When their name was called, they pivoted, taking a bow in front of the stands.

This part of the trial was a complete and total show. It was all for the Fae. As much as all of our lives were on the line to change, they needed to think we were just as excited as they were.

Hale smiled wildly in my direction, waving eagerly to the crowd and placing his hand upon his heart, bowing low to me before turning to the spectators.

When did Hale become such a good man after all?

Ryland gave a quick smirk, but quickly became preoccupied and stared off into the distance.

Ian shot me a small wink when his name was announced, and the crowd didn't even wait for the king to finish stating his name before they cheered.

Kade was announced last. While he gave the crowd the wave they were obviously yearning for, his body stiffened. When he turned to face me, I couldn't help but feel a shock of excitement run up and down the length of my spine. His shadows began pooling beneath him, and I longed to reach out and wrap myself around them. They were a magnet I could not ignore. The way they branched out from him only in my direction, I let myself believe they wanted me just as badly. The arena echoed with a deafening roar. Even I clapped a little louder for Kade as the king signaled he was ready to continue.

"Today our mighty contenders will test their strength and ability with a weapons test. They must show they are capable of protecting themselves, their kingdom, and the throne. There will be three tasks of sword fighting, archery, and hand-to-hand combat."

This week's arena had been marvelously recreated to a flat stadium. Divided into thirds, a cache of weapons stood to the right, a bow range in the middle, and an empty ring to the left.

"Be brave, my fellow Fae. Show the queen and myself, as well as Princess Illiana, how you are willing to fight for not only her hand, but the Kingdom of Brookmere!"

The crowd's unyielding excitement didn't falter. They'd have to grow weary at some point, wouldn't they?

A moment later, Vivienne appeared beside my father to offer her blessing for the trial.

He took her hand and let her stand next to him by the podium, his knuckles white from gripping the edge so hard.

Vivienne's unruly hair stood tall all around, framing her face. She looked like she had been struck by lightning.

She glanced warily at my father before speaking, "Times a foot, times a foot. Take heart contenders."

Her head jerked to the side strangely, eyes widening as she glanced at me, her body taught.

"Danger! Fights! A change of fate! Beware the tide that shifts too late."

Her eyes gleamed with worry. She turned to the king and grabbed his arm, attempting to tell him something, but with the podium already amplified, it echoed across the arena.

"King, King! Trials of fate, or not, it mustn't! Something dark and wicked tries and binds. Everywhere it runs."

He rubbed her arm. "We are almost done, Vivienne, please."

She shook her head erratically. "Fates be wary. Turn back before the darkness clings to life and hangs the future on a pin with a knife."

She rocked back and forth on her feet, her eyes darting around as the words flowed through her being.

My mother rose from her throne, standing at Vivienne's side to gently take her other arm and try to lead her away.

The king shook her hand off of his arm, turned back to the crowd and smiled. Carefully, raising his arms above his head, he took a breath to continue.

Vivienne panicked and appeared as though she were going to collapse. She turned to me, and the king laughed to try to calm the crowd.

The Seer knelt before me, hidden now by the podium as

my father attempted to play off her words of the danger we might behold today. She grasped my arms. Tears were brimming in her eyes. "Mustn't linger. Mustn't stay! You'll know when Fate has had its say."

I shook my head. I didn't understand what she was muttering. It was all nonsensical. Something seemed different about her, and as I stared at her, I gasped. Her eyes were completely white. What was going on?

I directed my attention to my mother, whose face turned ashen in shock. Whatever was happening, the queen believed every word our Seer spewed, and she was worried.

Shifting back to Vivienne, I tried to ease her hands from my arms, but she gripped me so tightly she left a mark. Elisabeth respected Vivienne. She'd been her friend. I couldn't ignore a small voice deep within me telling me to listen now. "Yes, Vivienne, I'm here. What are you trying to say? I'm listening. I'm listening."

She continued to mutter unintelligible words, completely panicked. I didn't know what else to do to calm her down, holding her hands, repeating I was here for her, was all I could think of doing. A loud *boom* sounded as the trial commenced.

As much as I wanted to help her, I didn't want to miss any of the trials. My fear for Ian and Kade was too great from what happened in the other two trials. I squeezed her hand. "Let's sit down." Nodding to a guard, they took our Seer's trembling body and walked her back to her seat. She relented, seemingly calmed from the vision supposedly blessed by nature.

Watching the chaos of her mind play out, it made sense why there weren't any other Seers. But for the first time, my heart ached for Vivienne. I didn't know what I believed, if her words rang true or not, but experiencing what she just did couldn't be easy. What a lonely, terrifying existence.

I twisted in my seat, facing the arena below. I'd make amends with the Seer when the people I loved were safe and done with these trials. I didn't have to believe her to treat her kindly.

The five contenders had moved to their respective positions in front of the archery course. Quivers were hung across the backs of all the contenders as they nocked their arrows, gathering their sights. Kade, Ian, and Ryland, were clearly apt at archery as the string of the bow sat tight against their lip faster than Casimir and Hale could move.

Ryland released his arrow as a tremor shook the arena, trailing up into the stands. The entire pavilion vibrated as well.

Hale, about to shoot his arrow, stumbled as a second, larger tremor ricocheted throughout the grounds.

The once-voracious crowd grew eerily silent. All we heard was the whistle of the arrows hitting their targets as the second quake ended. The shock and surprise of what had rippled twice through the arena fully captured all of our attention.

Vivienne fled the pavilion, panic-stricken. No one followed her. The guards were clearly too afraid of what the Fates might bestow upon them should they attempt to stop her.

Kade and Ian turned to each other on the field before both glancing up at me. I rose from my chair, moving to the front of the dais as the silence stretched on, my heart beating wildly. A familiar electric heat filled the air around us.

Silence broke as a lone shout echoed across the arena. A loud, wailing cry followed immediately after.

Not just any cry, though, a battle cry, and it roared across the palace lands.

Before I could gather my wits, or look at my father, the arena flooded with hundreds of Fae. But not just any Fae.

Fae clearly infected with the darkness. An army of dark ones. At their side, terrible creatures from Brookmere's forests joined them, flooding into the arena.

The Palace at Ellevail was under attack.

CHAPTER 34

The terror in the arena was palpable.

Screams of fright permeated the air as hordes of dark ones filled the stands and made their way toward the pavilion. Thorny vines shot through the arena floor as some of the more gifted Earth Fae tried to quell the onslaught of the attack.

This wasn't a horde of Fae. It was a battalion. This was going to be an all-out war.

The Royal Guards on the pavilion immediately sprang into action, taking their place in front of the king and queen, with Ruppert moving to stand in front of me.

"Get the king and queen to safety, now!" I ordered the guards next to me. "Ruppert, I need a sword!"

The last thing I wanted to do was use my daggers if I had other options.

"Princess Illiana, you will go to your room now, and I will take you there myself," Ruppert replied sternly, but I knew worry laced the bravado he tried to portray. He had never been to war before.

None of the guards had truly, except those who had been

371

sent away to monitor the spreading darkness. Most of them never returned to Ellevail.

Pushing past him, I reached for my mother, bringing her close. I would get to hug my mother one more time should anything happen to me today. "Get her to safety, *now*," I growled as the guards stood momentarily frozen, attempting to assess the situation unfolding before them.

A fireball streaked across the air, and I caught a glimpse of it from the corner of my eye. Storm was here, which provided some relief for Ian and Kade, who were in the thick of the dark ones in the arena below.

"Lana, my love, you have to get to safety, too. We need you to survive. To take the throne should something happen," my mother pleaded with me, grasping my arm.

I was no longer a young girl. I was an adult. Trained and capable of taking care of myself. With or without magic.

"I will not stand idly by and let our people be killed by this darkness alone." I reluctantly pulled the dagger hidden on my thigh since Ruppert had yet to relinquish a blade. "I will fight."

"You are all we have," my father tried to yell, but his voice faltered. He stumbled forward, trying to get to me. "You will stay with us, that's an order."

I cupped his face. "I will be with our people. I will protect Brookmere." I turned to the guards. "Stop lingering, go," I commanded.

"I will stand beside you, then," he said.

My heart cracked. I fell before him, taking his hands in mine. My warrior father was being sidelined. When it mattered most. I knew how it felt, deep in my soul.

"You know you are not strong enough right now," I whispered, tears forming in my eyes as I looked up at him. "Let me make you proud. Let me earn my place as Queen. Just as you earned yours all these years watching over us."

I nodded as two guards took him and my mother by the

arms more forcibly. I didn't know when they decided to listen to me, but given the king's weakness, perhaps they knew it was the only choice.

My parents and their guards moved toward the back of the pavilion and down the marble stairs.

Looking behind me, I searched for Kalliah. Our eyes locked, and she pulled her own dagger from the sheath hidden beneath her dress. "You and Ian taught me well." She smirked.

I couldn't help but grin, vastly inappropriate for the horrors currently unfolding before us, but I'd been faced with the dark ones before. And like each time I'd met them before, I'd do so fighting alongside the people I trusted.

"We stick together and fight before they force us back to our rooms. This is why we trained so hard. Swords *and* magic today."

Kalliah inclined her head, sending a rush of air up my back. "Give them hell, Lana. I'm right behind you."

A brief moment passed between us. The pang of potential heartbreak threatened to overtake our better senses, yet we bowed our heads in silent agreement. *Together. For Brookmere.*

"Take the side stairs," I said, running toward the edge of the pavilion where we could jump the railing and get to another set of stairs leading us down into the arena.

Before I descended, I took stock of the situation, no, the *chaos* before us. Spectators fled in every direction. Some trapped by the dark ones, some stood their ground, fighting alongside the guards. It was complete and utter madness.

The Royal Guards appeared from all pathways and assembled to form their battle lines. The general strode to the front and barked orders at his men while Ian shifted and flew high into the sky to assess the battle from above.

His pained cry reverberated through my heart. Something was wrong. With the sun blazing in the sky, it was hard to find him as I landed on the floor of the arena itself.

When I looked skyward again, I caught sight of him, locked into a battle with a Strox.

Oh, fates.

The ancient battle bird hadn't been seen in a thousand years, thought to be a mere memory from Queen Evelyn's reign. Its sharp pointy talons pierced the skin of many fallen soldiers centuries ago, while its razor-sharp teeth could easily clean a battlefield by devouring an entire carcass, bones and all. Those beasts were a thing of nightmares, glimmering feathers a hue of blue, as deep as the night sky, perfect for hunting its prey in the cover of darkness.

The shouting on the ground grew frantic, and I knew I would have to worry about whatever was happening in the sky later. There were too many innocent Fae frozen in shock, left in the stands and watching the onslaught, unprotected.

They needed to get out now.

Running toward the nearest stand, I almost lost my footing multiple times. Roots and rocks had sprung from the ground as those who were choosing to take part in this battle used their magic to create their own advantages.

Thankfully, the trial today involved so many weapons, there were plenty to pick up and arm my people with along the way. I managed to grab a sword, another dagger from a fallen soldier, a quiver full of arrows, and a bow.

Kalliah ran right behind me, also making her way to the cache of weapons.

Halfway across the arena, I was forced to battle a petite dark one, dizzy from being struck by a fallen tree previously conjured by some powerful earth magic. The dark one swayed, and I didn't hesitate, slitting his throat with my sword as I pushed him to the ground. A clang behind me stopped my forward movement, and I turned to see Kalliah engaged in her own fight.

Behind her, a dark one charged forward, and I dropped the sword, knocking an arrow in the bow. I paused, exhaling slowly as I released the arrow and struck the dark one in the chest.

A nearby guard finished him off as he fell to the ground.

I refocused on the stands in front of me. "Get out! Run!" I yelled to anyone and everyone who could hear me. The path to the exit remained mostly clear with Kalliah and I working the crowd.

Another tremor through the earth forced me to the ground as a heavy layer of darkness spread throughout the arena.

It wasn't the darkness we feared, though, at least I didn't. This darkness came from the shadows I trusted.

Kade's shadows had overtaken the entirety of the left side of the arena, farthest from the start of the attack. Where the poorest of Fae had been seated, their magic unable to keep up with the battle, he protected them by keeping them hidden. Forcing the dark ones to move onto more accessible targets.

"Kalliah, we have to move, now," I shouted behind me. "We have to help Kade."

We raced toward the closest entrance, Fae desperately trying to leave the stands around us.

"Keep going, get to safety." Kalliah ushered them along, helping those who had lost their balance where she could.

A dark one charged at us from the shadows, and I fired an arrow, then two. The Fae continued charging, undeterred by my strikes. I dropped the bow, out of arrows. Forcing myself to grab the extra dagger I'd stowed in my leathers, I fought hand-to-hand.

He shoved me to the ground without touching me, using his own magic blessed by nature, or whatever entity was fueling his craze. I screamed as a strange surge of power traced my skin. It was dark, cold.

If I didn't move, he'd have complete control of my body.

My legs surged forward, and I twisted, ramming the

dagger into his gut. He collapsed, twitching, arrows still protruding from his chest.

Kade's shadows began to recede around me, and the battlefield came into view once more. Ian, now in Fae form, ran toward me, as blood trickled down the side of his face.

"Behind you!" I screamed as a dark one wielded a hatchet, ready to swing at Ian's neck.

Ian ducked and engaged him, leaving me mesmerized with his swiftness and skill. Kade's shout broke me from my trance.

"Lana, get down," he bellowed as vines shot across the space above me.

Panting, I tried to collect my breath at the shock of nearly being taken out, when a tug at my foot knocked me to my side. I hadn't seen the second vine coiling around and up my leg, and it clung to me, yanking me back and away from the fray. It pulled me closer and closer, back to the arena exit. Another vine chased up my body, wrapping around my chest, despite my struggling.

Harder and faster, the vines dragged me across the entire arena. I didn't have my sword anymore, and the dagger I'd been using was lodged in the stomach of the Fae I'd just killed.

I twisted, reaching toward another dagger, hidden on my leg, but I couldn't move fast enough before it had been overtaken by the vine. All I could do was scream.

Debris dug into my skin, sharp and painful, as I bumped and slammed across the destroyed arena. My body marred with scrapes and scratches the more the vines tugged me away.

Desperately, I clawed at the vine, trying to rip it apart and break it with my hands and nails. "Help! Kade! Ian!"

My cries for help went unanswered as they were both locked in ferocious battles of their own.

I searched for Kalliah, only to find her slicing at a hedge of holly bushes blocking her path toward me. "Hold on," she shouted as she battled the thorny leaves to come to my aid.

The vines stopped. I jerked my head over my shoulder, and the smile which haunted my nightmares for years appeared before me.

"Playtime is over, Princess."

Andras.

Andras had me against my will. Something I vowed to never happen again. My screams became even more frantic, trying to get anyone's attention. I couldn't let him take me again. My attempts to get my dagger and free myself from these vines grew frenzied, more desperate.

Andras grabbed the trail of vines holding my legs and dragged me the rest of the distance toward him.

I struggled, clutching at the dirt of the arena floor, as if it could somehow give me purchase to free myself.

A small roar echoed behind me, and I watched in horror as Lucien flung himself at the vines held by Andras. He breathed fire onto the patch so fiercely, I felt a wave of heat on my ankle.

"Stupid beast." Andras grabbed Lucien by the tail and flung him backward.

"No!" I shouted as his body hit an outer wall of the arena before crashing onto the grass.

Boots *thudded*, storming forward on the ground.

Casimir walked toward me, inching closer.

Thank the Fates.

"Lord West, help!" I screamed. "Casimir, please!"

He stifled a laugh and stood by Andras's side. "This was easier than I thought."

My body went rigid. *What?*

Andras grinned at him, his eyes brimming with a bold, deceitful darkness. "Soon, Lord West, you will be the only contender left alive. We can put these ridiculous trials behind us and let the kingdom grieve for the loss of its Fates-forsaken

King and Queen." Andras's body hummed with excitement. "And then, perhaps in a week or so? We can let the kingdom rejoice with the marriage of Lord West to Princess Illiana, the new King and Queen of Brookmere." He practically hissed my name as he spoke.

"I will *never* marry him!" I spat at the ground.

This man, this traitor, had the audacity to laugh at me. "Oh, but, my dear, you will." He flicked his wrist, and one of the Royal Guard's walked forward, carrying Kalliah in his arms, passed out. "Or your precious lady's maid here will die."

I gasped. "Kalliah!"

Andras bent down, crouched before me as he savagely grabbed the back of my head. "Trust me when I say I'm not using my power of illusions to enter your mind. This is *real* and there is no one to save you."

Illusion magic.

Mind Magic.

My entire twisted childhood suddenly snapped into place. How the torture in the dungeons seemed so real. It was why I needed Ian to tell me if things had actually happened or I'd dreamt them. Almost all of it had been a figment of my imagination.

Put here by this man blessed with a magic unheard of due to its dangerous nature.

"My parents never knew what you were doing to me, did they?" I asked, as I continued to fight against the vines overtaking my body. I had been using my nail to cut through one of them while Andras had been speaking. I was nearly there.

Andras threw his head back and cackled. "Ignorant girl. No magic and no brain. The kingdom will not miss you. The darkness will thrive, and your kingdom will be lost, while Fae who deserve wealth and power will reign."

"I will never do what you want." I seethed. "Never."

Andras cackled again. "You will, or your time in the

dungeons will seem like child's play for what I have planned. All of your insolence throughout the years will not go unpunished."

A tingle down my spine, and the warmth of a familiar shadow cooled my panic, soothed it despite the impossible odds. I looked up to find Kade armed to the teeth, anger seeping from his very being.

His shadows pooled at his feet, agitated, and ready to fight.

"Remove those vines from her now, or death will seem like a mercy compared to what I have in store for you."

CHAPTER 35

Kade had come for me.

Even if we were still outnumbered, the thought alone gave me hope that nothing Andras said would ever come to fruition.

Kade's eyes were deep pits of ebony storms as his wrath consumed the space around him.

His deadly stare focused solely on Andras and the tether of vines he'd weaved around me.

Ian fell to the ground, shifting from his hawk form alongside Kade, followed by Storm, who took out a dark one approaching us, as if it were nothing.

They'd all come to help. To fight for me.

"The Royal Guard is rounding up the last of your dark ones now, Andras." Ian seethed. "It's over."

Andras tilted his head to the side, scoffing. The vine around my waist crawled up and over my breasts, inching toward my throat, my fingernail unable to reach the spot I'd been furiously cutting.

"Dark ones. What a precious nickname. But you have no idea what they're capable of, *Captain*," Andras spat. "In fact, right now, there are more tearing through the streets of

Ellevail. The cries of your people will echo here soon. You will not defeat us. Brookmere will be ripe for the taking."

Andras yanked me backward, tugging me out of the arena as dark ones rushed past him, toward my friends. A chasm of thorns erupted, blocking their path to me.

"No," I screamed, renewing my fight against him.

We reached the gardens, people running and screaming around us.

Someone bellowed in pain behind me. *No, please don't let them be hurt.*

With a fury inside I had felt more than I cared to admit lately, I ripped my hand from beneath one of the vines and latched onto it, screaming all of the hatred I had for Andras.

An unfamiliar light sparked under my hand as the vine beneath me shriveled. Whatever nature blessed me with in these dire moments, I prayed would continue.

I whirled on the man who'd tortured me all those years, and he snarled as the doors to the palace behind him flung open.

Andras smiled as if he knew the dark ones were with him. He raised his hands to his side, roots crawling toward the surface, morphing into another thorny vine, and he flung it in my direction.

Everything happened too fast to process. I couldn't move quickly enough, but someone else did.

Leif came out of nowhere, hurling his body in front of mine as the vine tore through his thigh, pushing out the other side.

"*Leif*," I cried, falling to my knees next to him. "Why, Leif? Leif!"

"I'm fine." He clenched his teeth. "Get out of here, somewhere safe, Lana. Go." He pressed his hand toward my shoulder.

"I can't leave you here. I won't leave you."

"I've got him." Corbin appeared a second later and smirked at his friend. "Had to be the hero."

"I told you, I'm fine. Go!" Leif shouted to me, before grasping Corbin's arm.

I nodded, standing, only to notice Andras's robes flowing behind him as he strode through the open doors and into the palace.

Someone shouted my name from behind, but I refused to stop.

Andras wouldn't walk away unscathed today. I couldn't watch him harm another person I cared for. Not if I could stop him.

And I would. I'd fight to the death if that's what it took to rid Brookmere of his evil.

I chased after him, thankful for all the running Ian made me do. Every time I thought I'd caught him, he turned down another hallway. Then another.

I shouted his name, "Andras!"

He moved too fast. I had to get him to stop somehow.

"Are you too scared to fight me? Even without my magic?" I screamed.

He stopped and turned.

My chest heaved, and not from the run, but from the adrenaline flowing through my veins as I stood face-to-face with my enemy. There was *no* mistake.

Andras was the enemy.

Of me.

Of Ian.

Of all of Brookmere.

"You have no idea what's coming," he said. The grin on his face worried me, but I refused to acknowledge the emotion long enough to give it merit. "You being magicless is the least of my worries. Brookmere is ours. The kingdom will belong to the darkness forever."

"Not if I have anything to say about it," I said, whipping a dagger from my boot.

He laughed at the sight. "There's nothing *you* can do. Casimir is hunting down the king now, and soon this will be an incredibly unfair fight when he has the king's magic."

"He will *not* get it from him," I said, gripping my dagger tightly.

Andras remained unarmed and undeterred. It would take one dive if I could get close enough to make him bleed. Although he may heal fast, he couldn't heal if I kept stabbing him.

"You worthless girl. Foolish and predictable," he said. "Do you think because you made some powerful friends you can do anything to stop what's been in motion for years?"

I kept my mouth shut, not understanding what he admitted.

"Your precious father is dying *thanks to me.*"

I stumbled back a step, but kept my dagger raised.

The candelabras in the hallway flickered as if reacting to the news as well.

"I've been poisoning him for years," Andras hissed. "I gave up on our little sessions and moved onto the better part of our plans."

Our? He hadn't done this alone.

"He's been fighting me so fiercely. But even he is no match for the power of the darkness." He tilted his head to the side, studying my surprise. "When Casimir finds him and drains his magic, there will be nothing anyone can do to prevent me from invading his mind. The darkness will win, and with the king's powerful magic under his control, there will be nothing anyone can do." He stalked forward, pointing at me. "Especially a weak child with no magic in her bones."

"You've been doing this to your King? You're a *traitor*," I shouted, slowly taking a few steps toward him. I couldn't startle him, or he'd run.

No, I wanted his blood dripping down my blade for what he'd done.

"I will be rewarded. Just like I have been given more power for eliminating Elisabeth."

I froze, every fiber of my being ignited by his words, alighting with a fire never to be quenched unless I stood over this Fae's dead body.

"Ah, surprised?" He sneered. "She got close to countering my poison, and I couldn't have that. So, in the chaos of the second trial, I killed her." He grinned gleefully. "Soon everyone will be bowing before me or will be destroyed, just like her."

"Bow to whom?" I bellowed. "You? In your dreams. You are nothing."

He moved faster than I was prepared for, wrapping one hand around my throat, and the other around the wrist of the hand holding the dagger.

No.

He raised me from the ground, squeezing harder. I was running out of air. "I'd kill you now, but I want to see your face when I drain the magic from your pathetic father. I'll watch your pain when he dies, when all those you love— Kalliah, Ian, all of them—die fighting to save your worthless life."

He nuzzled his nose against my face. "I'll take what I want from you, frame Casimir for what happened today, and ascend the throne beside your weak, compliant body. The hero who saved Illiana and Brookmere." He inhaled, and slowly licked his tongue from the corner of my mouth to my cheek. "I will be King and take all of what's mine."

Nausea churned inside my gut at the thought of his hands on me. The way he bent my body, even now, to his will, all because I didn't have the magic I needed to defend myself.

I am Illiana Dresden, and I am stronger than the darkness within me.

Energy danced inside of me, something growing—fury, rage, anger. I screamed, and that same precious light exploded from within me, sending Andras paces away.

I gasped, inhaling deep breaths as oxygen flowed into my lungs again.

"Has someone decided they're ready to play?" he asked, his lip curling as he stared at me.

I didn't care what had happened, it got him off of me. I lunged for the dagger, which had fallen from my hands, and ran toward him, ready to stab him.

I slashed downward, missing, and slicing through the forearm of his tunic as he barely avoided my attack.

He ripped at it, flinging it off with a fierce yell. "There are ways to get what I want with or without you cognizant, Illiana. But without you will mean pain for the ones you love."

He spread his arms out arrogantly, and I caught sight of a mark on the forearm I'd stripped bare.

A black circle, surrounding an eye. The same mark I'd seen on the dark one Storm had on his knees a few weeks before. *What the hell?*

I narrowed my gaze, wrath burning within me. I needed him alive to provide answers to all of this. I ran toward him, but Andras tossed his hands in the air, laughter echoing around us.

And disappeared.

"No," I yelled, frantically searching around the hallway.

He was gone. Running off again like a true coward.

With Andras out of sight, I knew I needed to go back. I needed to find Kade.

And more importantly, my father.

Whatever Andras had planned with Casimir wasn't over yet. My father needed to be protected at all costs.

Now more than ever.

CHAPTER 36
KADE

"This is not how this was supposed to go."

Storm's angry ranting flowed brashly as he beheaded another dark one. "Also, I've killed more than you," he added. "Do your part."

I grunted, snapping the neck of the dark one fighting me just as he brought his sword back to strike. "You have a way of exaggerating your numbers."

Storm chuckled at my taunt and spun to look at me. "Are you feeling all right?"

"I miss Jax and Raya. They would never ask me in the middle of a battle about this," I muttered, swinging my sword at the dark ones rushing toward me.

Storm slid his blade into the approaching attacker's chest.

"That counts as mine," I said.

"Your shadows are dimming," Storm countered, lunging to the right at a battle cry from one of the few remaining dark ones around us. "You're welcome for caring."

I chuckled as Storm battled the next victim he'd selected to be added as the next tally mark on his death scroll.

Just to prove him wrong, I commanded my shadows to the dark one he fought and choked him, eliminating air from his lungs as he collapsed. Storm distracted me, after I erupted when Andras took Lana. His hands on her, her screams, it had been more than I could handle. And now, I'd destroy every last Fae in my way of finding her.

Storm jerked his head toward me with a scowl. "She doesn't even have magic."

"I know this wasn't the plan," I bit back. "But we needed a queen, and I got us a queen, didn't I?"

A hot blaze of fire heated my right side, and my eyes widened at Storm. He shook his head, gesturing behind me.

Lana's pet stood atop a fallen dark one, its tail bloody, but the fire burning from him eliminated the Fae beneath his small body.

His gaze flicked to me, and I raised my hands in defense. "Good boy."

He sniffed, grey smoke emerging from his nose.

"She'll be happy to know you're alive and well," I added.

Storm grunted, and down the hallway, the double doors to the throne room flew open. The king ran forward, followed too closely by Casimir, the dark ones appearing from every damned corner.

"What the hell?" Storm started to ask before the king bellowed down the hall.

"Kade, with me," the king said. "You," He pointed to Storm, "Lord Casimir West must not be permitted past you. Do whatever you need to do to stop him."

A few guards fighting down the hallway finished slaying their own enemies. Storm whistled, garnering their attention as he called them over to help.

I obeyed the king, grabbing his arm as he directed me around the corner from Storm and the others.

He gestured to a door, opening it and standing just inside the threshold with me. The guards ran by but didn't stop.

Though vibrant would have been a stretch for how the king appeared when we first arrived here at Ellevail, he had definitely seen better days now. I knew he was sick, his long Fae life slipping away from him against all odds. The king had just given it his all, escaping from Casimir and a group of dark ones. Whatever sickness riddled his body, it hadn't fully taken him over yet.

"Listen to me, boy," he said after a short pause to catch his breath. "I am dying. A fact many are well aware of, given the proclivity for gossip in this Court."

I didn't bother arguing with him. His hand gripped my shoulder, the pressure stronger than I thought him capable of in his current state.

"Casimir is a siphon. He is working with Andras, and they are coming now to take my powers and destroy me. If he succeeds, they will be unstoppable in their coup."

I nodded. "Tell me where to take you, and I will. What do you need?"

I barely knew the king and didn't need him for my plans. He wasn't a part of the future that mattered. But I did know my Little Rebel adored her father. If I could spare her from seeing him die the way she had her healer, I would.

And fuck, I didn't want to know why.

The king glanced behind me, searching the hall. Briefly, I thought of taking him with me. If I could get him and Lana to come with Storm and I, he'd be safe.

Safer than he was here.

"I need you to kill me."

I stepped back from the king immediately. He was mad. Something in his sickness had seeped too far into his mind if he thought asking for death made sense as a solution.

"Your Majesty?" I asked cautiously.

"I am centuries your elder, Kade. I know right now my mind is my own. I need you to kill me, now, before Casimir has any chance of taking even a bit of my power. Before Andras can use me like a puppet to his whim." He focused his stern gaze on me, unyielding.

Unflinchingly firm in this request.

"I can't do it," I answered. "I'm sorry, Your Majesty."

He took a step toward me, and for once, I walked away from a fight. I wouldn't go through with his request.

"You must. I'm dying, anyway, and if they are anywhere near me when I do, they'll take my magic, and I will not be able to stop them. If we manage to hold the palace today, then they'll find another time. This is the best chance we've got at stopping them. No guards around. No one to know where I am. It must be now."

My lip curled in disgust. "You understand what you're asking of me? I don't kill for fun."

"You will do this." He raised his voice slightly. His piercing eyes revealed the knowledge that his impending death lay before him. "For Illiana, you'll do this. You think I don't know when someone is hopelessly in love?" He scoffed. "I'm married to my mate. Trust me when I say, I know true love."

"She's not my mate," I said, shutting down thoughts of how much my shadows reacted to her. The feel of her. This wasn't the time. Mates didn't exist anymore. I would know. My knowledge of what truly happened with the dark ones far exceeded what anyone here could possibly fathom.

It was how I knew what he said couldn't be true.

Mates were part of the original sacrifice.

So how was the king convinced his queen was his mate?

"There haven't been mates in millennia," I retorted.

The king smiled, holding a hand over his heart. "I would have shouted it from the rooftops of every city in Brookmere that my Queen was mine if I could have. There's Fate magic at work here, boy. Until this moment, I've never been able to speak the words out loud. There *are* still mates. The queen is mine. She is *my* mate." The king's eyes turned glassy with tears as he squeezed my arm.

Perhaps love would be enough to get this ridiculous notion

from his mind. He couldn't possibly have to die right now. Not by my hands.

"And you'd leave her?" It was low, but I grasped at whatever I could to change his mind. I couldn't kill him and think Lana would ever come with me.

And I needed her to come with me. It was the whole reason Storm and I were here.

For her. For a queen.

"I'd protect her with my life, gladly knowing that when her time comes, we'll be together with those who've gone before us," he said. "Time runs thin. You must do this, Kade Blackthorn, and you must do it now."

"No." I turned, heading toward the doors. "Find someone else. It will not be me. I will guard you here, but I will not kill you."

Swords and shouts drew closer.

"He will come for her." The king barely whispered, but it echoed through my body like an explosion. I looked over my shoulder at the man, at his lips pressed in a grim line.

"He will use my power to bend her to his will. He will not do so kindly. He will take her and try to break her."

"No," I growled. "He will not get anywhere near her. Not with any power. Never again. He. Will. *Not.*"

The king walked slowly now, moving just as I'd spotted him staggering across the pavilion. His hunched shoulders betrayed him as he shuffled forward, falling as I grabbed onto him. "I don't have long. There is a letter in my pocket. Give it to her once you ensure my life is gone. You must make sure I'm dead and gone, with no chance of being revived, before you leave."

I reached where he'd indicated and pulled out a parchment sealed with his golden royal crest.

"She loves you," I said. "She will not do well losing you."

But my words lacked conviction, even if they were true. He'd succeeded in hitting me where it counted. The thought

391

of Andras getting anywhere near Lana caused the battle inside of me against the king's wishes to falter.

If what the king said rang true, what lengths would I go to in order to protect her? To keep her from falling into Andras's hands ever again?

Could I murder the king of Brookmere to save her? To save the kingdom itself, if the king were right?

It was her right to rule this land as Queen. If I accomplished what I needed to, she may stand a chance, but if Andras and Casimir obtained the king's powers? There would be no stopping them. Even I knew the king held more magic than anyone here.

"She's my heart," the king answered, nodding like he knew I was right there, giving into him. "Let her in, and she'll be yours as well."

Little did he know just how deep Lana had buried into my heart already. Or perhaps his wisdom as a king, with the love of his mate by his side, allowed him to see what I was too stubborn to admit. Lana held more of my heart than anyone ever before.

The king handed me an amethyst-hilted dagger. "Quickly now, son."

I flinched at the words, unable to stand the caring nature with which he said them. He willingly gave his life not just for his family, but for his kingdom, going so far as convincing me to kill him.

"I'll help you. I just don't have the force to drive it in, in my state. Please." He brought the dagger to his chest and wrapped my hand around his, holding the dagger in place against the exact spot that would take his life.

I shook my head. "I'm sorry you feel it has to be this way."

"Protect her."

I made sure to look him in the eyes when I responded. "I vow it. As you've given your life, I shall give mine if that's what it takes."

I gripped the blade, hiding the tremor that shook my hand. With a final nod from the king, I plunged the dagger into his chest, and he sharply exhaled.

He staggered to his knees, an expression of relief calming his features, even though I knew the pain he must feel.

I held his body in my arms, careful to treat every second of his last moments with the dignity and respect he deserved. As he collapsed in my arms, I stared down at him. Stared down at this man who had given everything for his kingdom. I knelt, still holding his body and the dagger as blood soaked onto my hands.

The sounds of battle drew closer outside the doors, raging around us, only broken by a gut-wrenching, heartbreaking scream.

CHAPTER 37

LANA

My throat was on fire, pain clawing angrily through my body as I released my scream.

My father, my King, fell to the ground.

My knees shook, almost taking me down, too, before I stumbled forward into the room. Kade held the dagger in his hands, still plunged into my father's heart.

Kade. My Kade.

No. He wasn't my Kade. He'd *never* be mine. Not now.

"What did you do?" I crashed into him, shoving him backward away from my father. "What did you do?" I yelled louder, crawling toward the king's body.

"Wake up, Father. Wake up. Do you hear me?" I shook him before falling over his chest. "Wake up."

His chest barely rising and falling, his eyes remained closed. They *wouldn't* open.

This couldn't be happening. I couldn't do this again. I couldn't be here at the side of another person I loved being taken from me. "Please, you can't leave me."

"Lana, we have to go." Kade's voice thrummed, and I jerked my head in his direction.

"I'm not going anywhere with you. I trusted you."

Although Kade momentarily stole my attention, I refused to let go of my father.

I turned and forgot about the treasonous bastard in the room with me. His time would come. But right now, I needed my father.

The light nature had given me to push the vines off of me might still be inside of me. The light which pushed Andras. If I had light, it could help me bring him back. It had to.

Hovering my hands over my father's body, he coughed once. "You're okay. You're going to be all right," I chanted a few times, focusing everything I had into my hands and pleading with nature.

Light exploded out of me, and I was so overcome with joy, I laughed hysterically. This had to be magic. A temporary, insane level of magic nature had given for a falling kingdom. It had to be enough.

"Please be magic," I begged. "Please."

Nothing happened and I screamed, staring at the ceiling as if I could see out to the sky itself. "I've never demanded anything of you," I continued shouting. "Heal *him*. Heal him right *now*."

My gaze flitted back and forth over the king's fading body, and another burst of light poured from my hands. "I'm to be Queen. I've lived in hell and never demanded you give me magic when you cursed me to have none. I have sacrificed enough in the name of nature, so listen to me and heal him!"

The light pouring out of me flickered, then disappeared. When I looked down at my father's face, his eyes fluttered open.

"Lana." Kade's voice held a warning, but I refused to look at him.

My father looked at me with so much love. When he turned to face Kade, his head lolled like he nodded. "He will not hurt you again. I will not let him," I soothed.

My father shook his head. "You don't understand, my heart." His voice came out scratchy and not his own.

His eyes rolled back, and I gripped his shirt, pulling his head onto my lap. "No, No," I said. "Stay with me. Father, please," I begged. "Stay with me."

Blood trickled from the side of his mouth as his lips curved into a small smile. I held my hand to his face, giving him a tear-filled smile of my own.

"There's much I need to tell you—"

"Shhh," I cooed. "Save your energy for healing. I'll find someone. Someone more than me. Someone who can save you."

My father moved his head back and forth twice. "There is no one more than you, my heart. And I will love you into whatever beyond awaits. Always."

His hand loosened in my grip, but I held it to my face, refusing to let it fall.

"Please don't die," I whispered.

He exhaled, a slow torturous sound as the air rattled from his lungs.

Shouting approached closer now, but I didn't care. I didn't care if dark ones themselves took over the room, I didn't want to leave him.

"Be strong now, my child. It will hurt, but it's you—you who will save us." His breath rattled in a raspy whisper, and this time, when his chest exhaled, it didn't rise again.

I screamed.

Kade cursed under his breath and his shadows snaked toward my father. "What are you—" I started to ask.

The shadows snapped my father's neck.

An anguished sound I didn't even recognize as my own tore from my lungs.

Arms snaked around my center. "We have to go."

I twisted my body, pushing Kade away. "Get off of me. Don't touch me. I will kill you." I gripped onto my father's tunic, hoping he could somehow survive Kade's shadows, knowing deep down it was useless. Still, I silently pleaded with anyone listening for this to be a dream. His blood pooled beneath him, forming a puddle around his too-still body.

I cried, letting everything out of me I'd tried to hold back. I wasn't enough to save him.

Someone else ran into the room, and Kade's shadows moved away from my father.

"What did you do?" Ian cried, stumbling toward the king just like I had. His knees hit the floor, not caring that he fell into blood as he checked my father's pulse and looked up at me, sorrow etched across his bloody face.

With no warning, I was forcefully yanked from my father's dead body. I banged my fists on Kade's arms as they wrapped tightly around me. "Let go of me."

He didn't say a word as he fought to contain me, whipping his shadows out.

"Ian," I sobbed and struggled to get out of Kade's grip so I could run to him.

But Kade was stronger, and his shadows snatched me to his chest, holding me there despite my fighting. "Get your hands, shadows, and everything off of me."

Kade ignored me, instead focusing all of his attention on Ian. "I don't want to hurt you."

Ian drew his sword from his side, his face a mask of rage. "Then get your hands off of her."

Storm bolted into the room next. "We need to go."

"I know," Kade shouted. "Having a bit of trouble."

Storm glanced at the king, then back to Kade. "What the fucking hell?"

"I'll explain lat—Behind you!" Kade shouted.

Storm spun on his heels, knocking the dark one behind him off balance. He lit him on fire and shoved him from the room. In seconds, the Fae turned to ash.

My eyes widened in fear. Storm and Kade were so much

more powerful than they ever let on. We'd stupidly trusted them, bringing them into our inner circle.

I seethed, taking Kade by surprise as I turned into his arms instead of trying to get away. "Murderer. Is it why you fucked me?" I shoved at his chest, reaching down into my boot for my last dagger. "You wanted to get close to the royal family you've been criticizing since we met?"

"This isn't what it seems, Illiana. Stop!" His voice was firmer now, but nothing he said would make me listen to him.

Nothing.

"We will not hurt you," Storm said behind me, moving toward Ian, who turned his sword from Kade immediately on Storm.

Ian snorted. "Right, but you murder our king?"

Kade lunged, wrapping his arms around me again, shadows tighter than before.

I renewed my vigor in struggling, stomping my foot on Kade's. He grimaced, but didn't budge, or even flinch in his hold on me. "I hate you," I wheezed out, my strength fading.

What was happening? My body weakened, and even though it slackened, Kade still held me.

Storm started talking in low, hushed breaths to Ian, his hands in front of him. The second Ian let his guard down, Storm wrapped his arms around Ian's neck.

"No," I shouted.

Storm's lips were moving next to Ian's ear, and then, his eyes rolled back.

"Ian!" I cried, something irrevocably breaking inside of me. I was trapped. Trapped in a hold like I was trapped in a cell all those years ago. Trapped while I watched Ian die. With nothing to do to save him.

"Shhh, it's all right. He's not dead. I swear it. We would never." Kade's shadows stroked my hair, and I could hear his voice, trying to reassure me in my ear. But I didn't trust anything he'd tell me.

Not ever again.

"I don't believe you." I kicked my leg out and fell, Kade picked me up, while his shadows kept my arms tightened to my body.

"I'm so sorry," he whispered. "Please forgive me and know all of this is for your own good."

One of his shadows danced closer to my face and shoved a vial of liquid into my mouth. I knew this bitter taste. A sleeping draught.

"I'll hate you for the rest of my life," I managed to whisper.

My body sagged into the solid muscles of the man I thought I was falling in love with, and the pain and torture my heart had just gone through faded into oblivion.

CHAPTER 38

KADE

My shadows whipped around us as we rode at breakneck pace across the Kingdom of Brookmere, closer to safety.

Lana's body remained limp against my own and I tightened my arms around her, to keep her from jostling too much.

I worried about the bruises covering her body when she awoke, but I knew in the end, a few bruises paled in comparison to the death and torture had we stayed.

She is strong. She will survive, physically.

Emotionally, I couldn't be so sure.

Killing her father in her arms felt like the worst kind of pain. I'd been used for years by my own father, his shadow-wielding weapon. Death wasn't new.

But knowing what I did would cause her pain punched me in the gut. The hatred in her eyes as we left broke me in ways I hadn't been prepared for. Losing her father so close to Elisabeth would likely take her to the edge of her sanity.

Hopefully when she woke, I could explain what actually happened compared to what she believed she saw. I had to trust she would listen enough to know it wasn't my choice.

I did it at *his* request. I tried to say no.

I would do everything I could to help make her whole, while completing our plan. A small voice inside of me, tucked so far in my shadows, told me I may do everything I could to make her whole, even at the risk of *not* fulfilling my mission. Fates be damned.

I reached into my horse's satchel, putting my hands on the letter her father insisted I give to her, reassuring myself it hadn't fallen out. Hopefully, it would provide some answers for her.

The horses in the stables had been running wild during the chaos of the palace attack. Storm and I were lucky to have found the two we had to make this journey, but it meant Lana was stuck with me. If she woke and wanted to be with Storm instead, I'd oblige.

I think.

You will not, my shadows seemed to say as they flared at the thought of her riding alongside anyone but me. Even if it was Storm.

I brought the reins up to rub my face. Fates, this was not supposed to happen. When had my focus shifted from my mission to this beautifully infuriating Fae princess?

Storm kept by my side, riding silently beside me for two hours. I knew he was just as upset over what happened. He didn't like many people in this world, but he liked Ian. He respected Ian. Hell, I respected Ian, too.

This had all gone to shit.

Knocking him out in the palace after he witnessed the king's shadowy death, would only add to the seeming betrayal of whatever friendship we had formed over the last few weeks. With him *and* her other friends.

Leaving him unconscious by the king's dead body was not at all what either of us wanted. Especially when we had no idea of knowing how much longer the battle would rage inside the palace, and out. But we had to get out of there.

I had to get Lana out, and to safety.

But Ian had to survive in order to protect the current queen. To help Brookmere survive so there would be something for Lana to return to when she did ascend the throne.

It would be safer for all of them if the queen survived and stayed in power, but with the magic Andras had been collecting, it seemed unlikely she'd remain on the throne. And losing her mate? It would be a miracle if she could take over with a sound state of mind.

Her mate. I still hadn't worked out how it was possible the king thought he'd been with his mate.

The horses were tiring, as was I.

Storm finally spoke, "Brookmere will be in ruins."

"It wasn't the plan," I grunted. "None of this was part of the plan."

"You don't say. I didn't think killing the king was even an option," Storm grumbled.

"I told you what happened. I told you why—"

Storm's fire lit, a sign of his distress and anger, which rarely presented itself. "I know. I know. But we need her. We planned this for three years, Kade. Three. Years."

"You think I don't know that? You think I wanted to change our plan?"

Storm finally looked at me, his fire died down around him, but his eyes were ablaze as if the fire magic now burned within him. "*Our* plan? You mean the prophecy," he spat. "Fuck, Kade. It's a prophecy, not some random idea we made up underneath the stars one night."

"Ugh," Lana groaned as her head rolled to the side. She had started to wake.

I wrapped my arms around her, preparing myself for her anger.

She lifted her head, her body going rigid until she realized where she was. Or at least that she wasn't inside the palace anymore.

As expected, she immediately went into fight mode. She beat at my arm, scratching at my side, anything she could do to release my grip.

"Get off of me, you monster," she said. "Where are you taking me?"

"I will tell you everything when we stop for the night," I said, trying my best to keep my voice calm and reassuring, despite her panic.

"And what the hell do you know about the prophecy?" she asked.

I stilled on the saddle, although the horse pressed on. I frowned, trying to catch a glimpse at the woman in my arms. "What do *you* know about the prophecy?" I retorted.

Wiggling herself forward, she tried to break my grip as the space between us grew, but I stiffened my arms and brought her back to me so she wouldn't fall. We were still galloping across open fields. I wasn't willing to slow down. Not until we had more distance between us and the siege happening in Ellevail.

"Why have you kidnapped me?"

"We aren't kidnapping you," I grumbled.

"Technically, we did knock her out and are taking her against her will, so…" Storm chimed in.

"Not helping," I gritted out through clenched teeth.

"You killed my father! You hurt Ian! Why would I go anywhere with you *willingly*?" Her voice rose in panic.

I sent a tendril of a shadow down her back, attempting to calm her as they'd always been able to do in the past. "Please. You don't understand, there's more than what you saw."

"I know what I saw. There is nothing you could say to explain killing the king." Lana seethed.

"Stop fighting me or you will fall," I said, trying to regain control.

404

She gripped the saddle tightly, hissing, "I don't want to touch you."

Finally, we were able to slow as we approached a small village close to Demarva. It was on the outskirts and not frequented by many. They didn't even have their own town name. But it was perfect for us, especially since we wished to come and go unseen.

Slowing the horses to a walk, allowed the animals to catch their breath as we approached a small inn.

The centuries-old inn, *The Knotted Willow*, stood before us, and despite its tattered windows and thatching, the flowers surrounding the knotted wooden door were beautiful. Pinks and purples wove in and out of an ivy vine. This inn had been home too many times to count over the last few years, and the loyalty of the innkeeper had been bought with coin time and time again. This time would be no different.

"Go secure the rooms, Storm," I instructed. "We're right behind you."

Lana, who had refused to look at me until now, turned and glared. "They will know who I am. I am a princess after all. I will scream the entire time we're here."

"Please don't make me knock you out again." I was exhausted.

Her eyes narrowed even further. "You really are a monster."

"You have no idea, Little Rebel."

Storm returned quicker than expected. "Last one on the second floor. The one on the left."

"One room?" Lana snarled. "I am *not* sharing a room with you two heathens. Let alone the man who snapped my father's neck like it was nothing," Lana proclaimed.

"Nervous to have both of us so close? The ideas are exciting." I knew it was the wrong thing to say, but I couldn't help myself, trying to relieve the tension.

I could practically see the smoke coming from her ears. "*Never. Again.*"

I dismounted from the stallion and left him with the stable boy to be fed and watered, while Storm did the same. I offered Lana my hand to help her down, but she jumped off by herself. She appeared wary as she surveyed her surroundings. Ian had taught her well.

Storm entered the rundown inn first, and we followed, my shadows leading Lana, since I knew if I touched her, she'd just struggle further. William, the old innkeeper, sat watch from his normal spot behind the bar, empty, save for one lone traveler passed out on a table.

We were halfway across the room, when she turned toward William and started yelling, "Please, help me! My name is Princess Illiana Dresden. I've been kidnapped by these men! They killed the King of Brookmere!"

The old Fae was unfazed, his lips drawn in a tight line, and he bowed his head once as we passed him.

"Food in our rooms, William. When you can."

A grunt was all I got in reply.

I had to force Lana up the stairs, but eventually, we made it to the top.

She whirled on me. "This is treason, and I'll never forgive you for this."

"Yes, you keep reminding me, Little Rebel," I grumbled before pressing a hand to her back and shoving her up the last few stairs and into our room.

CHAPTER 39

LANA

The beef stew tasted surprisingly good, even if I could only stomach a few meager bites before laying back down.

I curled up in a ball on the bed, listening to soft snores coming from the couch where Storm managed to fall asleep almost immediately after downing his dinner. Kade sat on the floor in front of the fire, staring at its crackling embers, his back facing me.

It was a good thing he wasn't looking at me, although I knew he felt the daggers boring into the back of his head.

I had trusted this man with everything.

How could I have been so wrong?

The man I had trusted with my body, and nearly with my heart, killed my father. Tears silently fell as I thought of the life fading from his eyes. The way he'd smiled at me even as he lay dying, trying to convince me I was something worthy.

"Was any of it real?" I whispered, wiping the tears away. "Or was this all a plot to kill my father and ascend the throne?"

Kade glanced over his shoulder. "You seem to have your

mind made up already, Little Rebel. I'm not sure there's anything I can say with the grief so fresh that will change it."

"Stop calling me that," I hissed. I hated that name now. I hated how much my heart broke hearing it fall from his lips.

"I would have chosen you, you know. If you had won. You didn't need to kill him." A small sob escaped into the pillow. The last thing I wanted to do was wake up Storm and have another arrogant man to deal with. One who would surely back Kade in whatever excuses he gave me for his actions. If he even bothered to give any at all.

Kade sighed and slowly stood up, stretching his back. A crack of his bones cut the silence. He reached into his pocket and handed me a piece of parchment. "Your father asked me to give you this."

I snatched the paper from him. The parchment shook in my hand as I examined it. The envelope remained sealed with my father's crest, unbroken.

"I don't know what it says, and despite what you may be thinking, I didn't magic it open and read its contents. Whatever is in it is meant solely for you. We will be leaving just after first light tomorrow morning. I suggest you sleep." Looking me over once more, Kade retreated and lay down by the fire.

Carefully, I lifted the seal, preserving the wax, now one of the only things I had left of my father.

My Dearest Illiana,

If you are reading this, then things have gone terribly wrong. There is much I need to tell you. Please believe everything your mother and I have done has been for you, to protect you, and to raise you to be the Queen of Brookmere.

When you came to us as such a small child, we knew we would love you with our entire heart and treat you like you were our very own. But we didn't have the honor of birthing you.

Your birth mother, Princess Fallon Dresden, was my sister. I loved her, and her husband, your father, Sebastian Rykes, was one of my closest friends. When you were born, Vivienne felt you held no power. We all feared what that would mean, and to keep any of the Court from learning you may not be able to protect yourself, we sent you away. We sent you away to Valeford for your protection, to be out of the public eye as we tried to figure out what to do.

The night of your parents' death, Vivienne had a vision. A vision so strong that it had her riding fast and hard to Valeford herself. There has been an evil infecting our land, infecting our people. It makes sensible, strong Fae, ravenous for power and unable to contain a darker nature. They burn, and destroy, and battle our forces, and although we've tried to contain them, we haven't eliminated them.

That night, it was this kind of infected Fae who had overtaken the village, and Vivienne arrived too late. Your birth mother and father, Fallon and Seb, perished in the gruesome attack when you were only six months old.

Vivienne found Elisabeth holding you to her chest in the small cottage they lived in. They saved you, and as you know, they have been watching over you your entire life.

When Vivienne put you into my arms that night, she had the vision of the prophecy.

Your mother, our beautiful Queen Roxana, could not have any children. She had lost so many babes over the years. When your parents died, we decided we'd raise and love you like our own. Hopefully, honoring Fallon and Seb in the process.

I choked on my sobs, clutching the paper to my chest. What was I reading? What had my entire life been?

I used the cheaply made blanket on the bed to wipe my face and try to finish the letter.

Illiana, you are the key to Brookmere's survival.

409

Your mother asked she be buried with a journal she kept, passed down from each generation in the royal family. She needed it secret. Safe. You must go to your parents' home and find it. I ensured her request was met. In it, she always believed you'd have everything you needed to save our lands.

Be strong, my heart. You are brave and worthy and everything Brookmere needs in a Queen. You will rule this kingdom with fairness and grace. You will make all of us proud.

Trust the prophecy and remember to never trust something is as it appears at first glance.

I will miss you with all of my heart. I loved you with even more.

May nature guide you.

Love,

Your grateful father

Tears flooded my eyes. Betrayal, anger, and grief, all swirled into an emotional cyclone racking my body. Why did they hide this from me? Did they think I would love them any less, knowing they weren't my birth parents?

A long painful sob escaped as I shoved my head into the pillow to muffle the sound.

Kade stirred. "Lana?"

I cried even harder, clutching the letter to my chest, curled into a ball beneath the thin blanket. A Fae could only handle so much, and I was nearly at the end of my limit.

I must have misread the letter, throwing my feet over the edge of the bed, I sat up in a flash, determined to read it again, to reveal its true contents.

Kneeling before me, Kade grasped my shaking hand as my tears stained the parchment wet. "I know I am the last person you want near you right now, but what do you need? Tell me how I can help you."

Ripping my hand from his, I tried to regain some control. "I *need* my father back." I stared directly into his eyes, my voice rising. I didn't care if Storm woke up at this point. "You took him from me. You took him from me before he had a chance to tell me any of this!"

Kade stiffened but remained unwavering in his presence. He allowed some shadows to swirl around me.

My body reacted to his nearness, the hum of energy between us never ending. It wasn't just desire. It was the undeniable need for someone to tell me everything would be okay. I didn't want him to read the letter. This man would gain no more of my secrets, no more of me. He could sit there and wonder about the pain and anguish I endured.

I needed my parents.

I needed Elisabeth.

I needed Ian and Kalliah. *Fates*, I hoped they had survived the attacks.

An unwavering resolve, deep from the recesses of my being, forged after facing Andras, surfaced. A sense of purpose renewed within me.

I would get to Demarva. It was only a short distance from where we were right now. I would escape these two asshole Fae and head west to Valeford to find whatever it was my birth mother had left me. I didn't know what good it would do, or why my father needed me to retrieve whatever was hidden, but I would do it.

Alone.

I would find a way to rid myself of this murderer and his sidekick and gain my throne. Without a king, I'd be the queen Brookmere deserved. A queen *all* of my parents knew I could be.

The sound of birds chirping a joyful tune seemed wrong as I opened my eyes in the bright sunlight, streaming through the cracks of the worn-down window.

411

Perhaps it had all been a dream. A terrible, horrible nightmare.

I felt warm, and…safe?

The comfort I'd been so desperately seeking yesterday was with me now, although that had to be impossible. Because there was no comfort to be found with everything I'd lost.

I peered over the bed, finding Kade on the floor beside me, but all around me were his shadows, like an extension of his arms, holding me. They wrapped around me like a blanket.

It was a good thing I'd always thought of them as separate from him, because they'd somehow kept me safe, even from my own thoughts so I could sleep.

A nightmare-free sleep, too.

Now I would be rested enough to escape from Kade and Storm and return to Ian and the others.

Kade rolled to the side, stretching as he immediately directed his gaze to the bed. His eyebrows shot up, as if he were surprised to find me covered in *his* shadows. He pulled them back into himself without a word.

The moment they were gone, I missed how they felt, but I kept my mouth shut. I'd never ask Kade Blackthorn for anything, ever again.

"We only have an hour's ride ahead of us," Kade said. "We should go." Although he didn't even look at me as he spoke, I knew it was for my benefit. Storm would know where we were, and where it was we were going.

"Demarva is only a few miles, it shouldn't take an hour," I argued.

"We're not going to Demarva."

Before I could ask anything further, Kade rose from his uncomfortable-looking spot on the floor and walked out of the room.

I glanced over at Storm, half-expecting the man, who I'd thought was becoming a friend, to offer me words of wisdom. Something to tell me they weren't the villains of my story.

But he said nothing, giving me a sad sort of smile as he followed Kade.

The innkeeper handed me a basket of bread and cheese before I walked out the door. I managed a "Thank you," even though I was furious, they seemed to know who I was and had done nothing to help me.

Kade and Storm were already mounted when I exited. I stalked toward Storm, but he trotted away, leaving me no choice but to get on the horse with Kade.

He held his hand out to me, but I refused. After three attempts of not being able to get on myself without knocking him off, his shadows lifted me, depositing me in front of him.

"Hold on," he said as he wrapped his arms around me.

Fates, I wanted to kill him.

No, it wasn't true. I wanted him to hurt, though, the way he'd so easily hurt me.

The ride was hard, especially in silence, but as we approached the edge of Brookmere's landscape, Kade reined in the horse. Storm dismounted, taking the steed by the bridle, and walked.

Kade easily slid off the mount and held his arms out to me. This time, I used him for what I needed before stumbling away a few steps.

"What are we doing?" I demanded. "What's the point of standing by the ocean?"

I needed them to tell me something of whatever their plan was so I would know when I'd be able to escape. Aware it would be two against one would make escape near impossible due to their unnatural strength. But if they'd be going to get supplies, or setting up camp, it would be a perfect opportunity to run.

"It's not an ocean," Kade said.

He and Storm were both quiet as Kade swirled his hands

around and in front of him, in some sort of a wave, as though he could see something I couldn't.

The view of the ocean rippled.

Wait, how could that be? How could my view be rippled?

Kade took a step forward, and suddenly, the ocean disappeared altogether.

Instead, we stood before a thick, dark mist, spanning outward.

My breathing picked up. The mist, it was darkness personified. Like a poisoned-looking place, dreary and deadly. I stared forward, fear filling me to the point where I felt suffocated.

"What is that?" I whispered.

Kade looked back at me. "Part of the darkness."

"You." My voice cracked. As if killing my father hadn't been enough. Betraying me hadn't been enough. Now this? "You brought the darkness here?"

Storm turned around, brows furrowed at me, and Kade sighed. "No, I did not. Believe I'm a monster, or evil, or whatever all you want, but this"—He waved his hands behind him—"isn't because of me."

He grabbed my hand, then tugged me toward Storm, taking his hand as well.

"Let go of me," I said. "No, I will not go in there with you. I don't even know what it is."

"Stop," he said, his voice rising. He yanked me closer to him, pulling me to his side. He was stronger than me. I couldn't fight him.

I didn't scream, but clenched my eyes closed as Kade escorted Storm and I into the damn mist itself.

A tugging sensation pulled across my body, as though I were being squeezed into a space entirely too small.

And then, suddenly, a soft *pop* sounded in my ears.

Kade let go of our hands and I scanned our surroundings,

taking in the hazy-covered land. We stood in a trench, dug out from the Earth itself, a sense of decay encompassing us.

It was hard to see beyond a few feet in front of us. Squinting, I noted upturned trees, appearing like roots, growing into the sky.

"Where are we?" I demanded, my voice trembling. "What is this place?"

"Welcome to Mysthaven, Little Rebel," Kade said, his face stoic. He didn't seem happy to be here. In fact, suddenly he appeared much more like the man I met the first time at our initial meeting in the woods—masked and unemotional.

"There's nowhere in Brookmere named Mysthaven," I said.

He scanned the area around us before looking at me once more, cocking an eyebrow. "That's because we're no longer in Brookmere."

"Where are we?" I asked warily.

His gaze softened the longer he stared at me. He inhaled deeply, and the expression on his face seemed hopeful, but for what, I couldn't yet be certain.

"You may know it better as the Forgotten Kingdom."

Continue the Broken Prophecy Series in
Shadows of Ruin, Book 2.
Available Now!

WHERE TO FIND ANNA & HELEN

We're most active on Instagram & in our Facebook Reader Group! We'd love to hear from you there!

Facebook Reader Group:
Anna & Helen's Enchanted Society

Anna's Instagram:
https://www.instagram.com/authorannaapplegate/

Helen's Instagram:
https://www.instagram.com/authorhelendomico/

ACKNOWLEDGMENTS

A few months ago, a spark of an idea hit when talking to our besties ... a spark we started running with until the idea for *The Broken Prophecy Series* poured out of us, like it had been there all along, just waiting for the right time to come...

Maria, thank you for being a constant cheerleader, incredible friend, and all-around light. Clare, thank you for pushing us to be better and not letting us settle for anything less than our best. Megan (Megara/Magiggles) thank you for diving into our Marco Polos and rounding us out with your laughter, humor, and support.

To our Beta Readers *Danielle, Katie, Missy, Clare, & Maria* – Thank you for raw-dogging this first book and getting through the unedited mess we gave you. Blooms of Darkness would never be what it is today without your feedback and encouragement.

To the Bookstagrammers/Booktokers who have become friends, thank you for supporting us, even before reading a single page. Thank you for your enthusiasm and for your time! We are SO grateful!!

To Jessica Allain at Enchanting Covers for the insanely perfect cover and character art, your talent immediately captured our vision and allowed us to build our excitement before we'd even finished our story!

From Anna:
Thank you to the Book Nerds. I've said it before, but I'll

write it so it's immortalized—I wouldn't be here today without you. At my lowest, at my darkest, God led me to you ... first by laying the groundwork to have us all in the same dorm at JMU, then back together again through a shared love of Rhysand and ACOTAR. I'm so grateful.

Thank you to my daughters, who put up with a book obsessed mother. Thank you for pushing me to strive to be better. And thank you for the excitement asking how my book is going, without knowing anything about it, but just because you believe in me unconditionally.

The biggest, loudest, inspired thank you to my amazing co-author Helen. I am so freaking proud of you for plunging into writing a book without a second thought. THIS IS HER DEBUT NOVEL, PEOPLE! Insane! You've done more for my confidence in the past few months than I was able to do in the previous ten years. I'd all but given up on writing and being an author, and then this book changed everything ... you made it possible and gave me the confidence to try again and reignited my passion for doing this. Thank you for pushing me to get out of my own way, for believing so fiercely in us, and for encouraging me with your constant "why not" attitude that has changed *everything*. I can't wait to continue writing this series, and hopefully many more together! Thank you for being my friend, and my co-author.

From Helen:

First and foremost, I would like to thank Anna for encouraging me to write this book with her. I had never thought about writing a book before, but it is always one of those "bucket list" items you never thought you could achieve, and yet, here we are! Without you, your wisdom, and encouragement I would never have been able to check this box. Thank you for answering my thousands of questions and always pushing me to do more! Thank you for not thinking I had absolutely lost my mind every time I said "So, hear me out..." I am so thankful for our friendship, which started 18 years ago (!!!!) and am so excited for everything yet to come. Here's to many more books together!

To my husband and my two kids. Thank you for giving me the space, time, and understanding to allow me to write this book. I know there were many late nights, weekends, and naptimes I was occupied, but I couldn't have done this without your love and encouragement. Your never-ending support has meant the world to me. I love you all so much!

Finally, I wanted to give a big shoutout to all my friends and family who had to hear me talk about Blooms of Darkness incessantly over the last nine months. Thank you for always being a listening ear and a sounding board for all of our infinite ideas and ramblings. Without your support, we wouldn't be where we are today!

We are so excited to be on this journey together and we can't wait to share more of Kade and Lana's story with you!

ABOUT THE AUTHORS

Anna Applegate is a USA Today Bestselling Author. She writes fantasy romance and lives tucked away in rural Maryland surviving on coffee, champagne, and an unchecked book addiction.

Anna is an avid reader, especially if it involves morally grey love interests. She enjoys escaping into the fictional worlds she creates - filled with strong heroines, surprise twists and turns, and "destroy the world for her" leading men.

She loves hearing from her readers and interacting with them on Social Media.

Instagram: https://www.instagram.com/
authorannaapplegate/
Facebook: https://www.facebook.com/
annaapplegateauthor/

Helen Domico published her first romantasy in 2024 and has no plans on stopping. Writing a book was always a bucket-list item, but when the opportunity knocked on her door to do so with one of her best friends, she couldn't say no!

When not writing, you can find Helen reading, spending time with her family, and sneaking in a glass of cabernet. Helen resides in central Maryland with her husband and two children.

Helen would love to connect with her readers and interact with them on social media. She can't wait to get to know you!

Instagram: https://www.instagram.com/ authorhelendomico
Facebook: https://www.facebook.com/profile.php?id= 61560814239670

Find Anna & Helen on their website at:
www.annaapplegateandhelendomico.com